Praise for *The World of Suzie Wong*

"Reminiscent of Somerset Maugham at his storytelling best . . . Suzie Wong is enchanting." —*New York Herald Tribune*

"One of the most tender and enchanting heroines to find her way into print in a long time." —*Saturday Review*

"A thrilling, imaginative experience." —*The Washington Post and Times Herald*

"Refreshingly different . . . excitingly real and vivid." —*The Boston Globe*

"One of the tenderest, most beautiful, agonizing and interesting love stories of the year . . . magnificently effective." —*San Francisco Examiner*

"The reader falls in love with Suzie as Mason weaves his magic spell." —*The Detroit News*

PENGUIN BOOKS

The World of Suzie Wong

RICHARD MASON was born in Manchester, England, in 1919. He joined the Royal Air Force, where he learned Japanese, in 1939. After the war, he lived in Hong Kong, where the intersection of East and West inspired him to write *The World of Suzie Wong,* his third novel, which was published in 1957. He traveled widely throughout his life, touring Africa and Europe in the 1950s with his first wife, Felicity Ann Cumming, restoring an apartment in Rome in the 1960s, and raising sheep on an estate in Wales with his second wife, Sarette. He remained close friends with both of his ex-wives. In the early 1970s, Mason returned to Rome, where he met his third wife, Maggie Wolf. They had two children together and were popular hosts in Rome. In addition to his novels, Mason also wrote screenplays and sculpted. He died in Rome in 1997.

The World of Suzie Wong

Richard Mason

PENGUIN BOOKS

PENGUIN BOOKS

Published by the Penguin Group
Penguin Group (USA) Inc.,
375 Hudson Street, New York, New York 10014, U.S.A.
Penguin Group (Canada), 90 Eglinton Avenue East, Suite 700,
Toronto, Ontario, Canada M4P 2Y3 (a division of Pearson Penguin Canada Inc.)
Penguin Books Ltd, 80 Strand, London WC2R 0RL, England
Penguin Ireland, 25 St Stephen's Green, Dublin 2,
Ireland (a division of Penguin Books Ltd)
Penguin Group (Australia), 250 Camberwell Road, Camberwell,
Victoria 3124, Australia (a division of Pearson Australia Group Pty Ltd)
Penguin Books India Pvt Ltd, 11 Community Centre,
Panchsheel Park, New Delhi—110 017, India
Penguin Group (NZ), 67 Apollo Drive, Rosedale, Auckland 0632,
New Zealand (a division of Pearson New Zealand Ltd)
Penguin Books (South Africa) (Pty) Ltd, 24 Sturdee Avenue,
Rosebank, Johannesburg 2196, South Africa

Penguin Books Ltd, Registered Offices:
80 Strand, London WC2R 0RL, England

First published in the United States of America by World Publishing Company 1957
Published by Signet Books 1958
Published in Penguin Books 2011

1 3 5 7 9 10 8 6 4 2

Library of Congress Cataloging-in-Publication Data

Mason, Richard, 1919–1997.
The world of Suzie Wong / Richard Mason.
p. cm.
ISBN 978-0-14-312042-1
1. British—China—Fiction. 2. Painters—Fiction. 3. Prostitutes—Fiction.
4. Hong Kong (China)—Fiction. I. Title.
PR6025.A79275W67 2012
823'.912—dc23 2011031965

Printed in the United States of America
Set in Granjon
Designed by Elke Sigal

The World of Suzie Wong

1

The Girls

Chapter One

She came through the turnstile and joined the crowd waiting for the ferry: the women in cotton pyjama suits, the men with felt slippers and gold teeth. Her hair was tied behind her head in a pony tail, and she wore jeans—green knee-length denim jeans.

That's odd, I thought. A Chinese girl in jeans. How do you explain that?

I watched her hold out a coin to a squatting vendor in a battered old felt hat. The vendor twirled a piece of Chinese newspaper into a cone, shoveled in melon seeds, and exchanged it for the girl's ten cents. She turned away, absently picking into the seeds with red-painted nails, and stopped only a yard from me.

Probably some wealthy taipan's daughter, I thought. Or a student. Or a shopgirl—you never could tell with the Chinese.

She cracked a seed edgewise between her teeth, peeled back the shell, popped the kernel into her mouth. Next to her an old man in high-necked Chinese gown leaned on an ebony stick, stroking his white, wispy, foot-long ribbon of beard. A baby peeped from its sling on a woman's back, blinked its black contented eyes in perfect infantile security. A youth in horn-rimmed glasses and threadbare open-necked shirt held a book close to his nose. He was studying a graph. The book was called *Aerodynamics.*

The girl nipped another seed between her white even teeth. Just then her eyes caught mine. They seemed to linger, so I said, "I wish I could do that."

"Hah?"

"Crack melon seeds—I've never been able to learn."

"No talk."

She turned her face away haughtily, looking over the barrier behind which swarmed the ten-cent passengers for the lower deck: the coolies in blue tattered trousers and the remnants of shirts, the Cantonese fisherwomen in conical straw hats and shiny black suits. She chewed self-consciously.

I tried not to feel snubbed. Well, I was always hopeless at pickups, I thought. I haven't the nerve.

And then she seemed to be . . . yes, she was relenting. Giving me a secret glance from the corner of her eye. Wondering if she had misjudged me.

She looked away quickly. Stole another glance. Then said guardedly:

"Are you sailor?"

"Me a sailor? Good Lord, no!"

She relaxed a bit. "You're sure?"

"Oh, positive."

"All right, we talk if you want."

"Well, that's fine," I laughed. "But what have you got against sailors?"

"Not me—my father."

"You mean your father doesn't like sailors?"

"No. He says sailors catch too many girls, make trouble."

"So he won't let you talk to them?"

"No. He says, 'If you talk to sailor, I beat you!'"

"Well, he's probably very wise."

"Yes—wise."

The ferryboat came churning alongside and the crowd moved forward. We jostled together up the gangplank and chose one of the slatted bench seats on the covered top deck. The ferries were Chinese-owned and run, and very efficient, and we had hardly sat down before the water was churning again, the engines rumbling, the boat palpitating—and we were moving off busily past the Kowloon wharves, past anchored merchant ships, past great clusters of junks. Ahead, on the island across the channel, was Hong Kong, squeezed into a coastal strip a few hundred yards wide, with the miniature skyscrapers in the center and on either side the long water front, stretching for miles, wedged with sampans and junks; and behind rose the steep escarpment of the Peak, shedding the town and the lower social orders as it climbed, until at the higher altitudes there remained only a sprinkling of white bungalows and luxury flats inhabited by the elite.

We rounded the tip of the Kowloon peninsula, heading slantwise across the channel for Wanchai, the most populous district of Hong Kong's eastern flank. I turned to look at the girl beside me. Her face was round and smooth, her eyes long black ellipses, and her eyebrows so perfectly arched that they looked drawn—but in fact they had only been helped out with pencil at their tips. Her cheekbones were broad, with hints of Mongolia.

"Aren't you a northerner?" I said.

"Yes, Shanghai."

"But now you live in Hong Kong?"

"North Point."

"That's a good district." And it accounted for her being on this ferry, since North Point lay beyond Wanchai—the expensive suburb beyond the slums—and the Wanchai pier was the nearest ferry point.

"Yes, only I like Repulse Bay better. Nicer house."

"You mean you've got two houses?"

"Four."

"Four?" I knew that Chinese taipans, who made the richest Europeans seem like paupers, often owned two or three houses, but four was surely a record. "You mean all in Hong Kong?"

"Yes, Hong Kong. My father is very rich, you know." She looked pleased with herself, boasting with the naïveté of a child.

"Well, so I gather. And where are the other two houses?"

She counted off the first two on her fingers and went on, "Number three, Conduit Road. Number four, Peak. Number five—"

"Not *five!*"

"Yes, I forgot—number five, Happy Valley. But that's just small, you know—only ten rooms."

"Oh, nothing at all," I laughed. "And what about cars? How many of those has your father got?" The Chinese collected cars even more assiduously than houses.

"Cars? Let me think." She puckered her brow, counting on her fingers again, then gave up with a giggle. "Oh, I forget how many cars."

"I suppose you've a car of your own?"

"No, I'm too scared to drive. But I don't mind tramcars, you know—I like riding in tramcars." She proferred the ten cents' worth of melon seeds in their newspaper cone. "You want one?"

"Yes, but I honestly can't open them," I said. "You'll have to teach me."

"Try first."

I tried several, but one after another the seeds splintered between my teeth, crushing the kernels inextricably. My ineptitude sent the girl into delighted giggles; she buried her face in her hands, her pony tail comically whisking and bobbing, then recovered herself, still twinkling with merriment, and gave me a demonstration—nipping a seed edgewise, peeling back the shell, handing it to me with kernel intact.

"Well, that's exactly what I did," I said. "Yours must have been an easy one."

"No, all same."

"Then I give up. What's your name?"

"Wong Mee-ling."

"Mee-ling—that's charming."

"And you?"

"Robert Lomax—or Lomax Robert, your way."

"Lobert."

"No, 'R.'"

"Robert. Where do you live?"

"Well, actually . . ."

"Peak?"

"Well . . . yes, mid-level. I live in a boardinghouse—Sunset Lodge." Well, it was nearly true—I had lived at Sunset Lodge until a few days ago, before moving down to Wanchai. And I couldn't very well tell her about the Nam Kok—not, at least, without knowing her better.

"You work Government? Bank?"

"No, neither. I used to be a rubber planter, but I chucked it up a couple of months ago to try and paint."

"Paint?"

"Pictures." I started to feel for my sketchbook to show her, then remembered that all the sketches were of the Nam Kok and thought better of it.

"I know—artist."

"Well, I don't call myself that yet." Then, since we seemed to be getting on so well, I asked her if I could take her out to dinner one night; but she flatly refused.

"Then lunch?" I said.

"No." She shook her head firmly so that the pony tail wagged.

"But I'd love to see you again, Mee-ling. Can't we meet sometime?"

"No."

"But why not?"

"I get married soon." The marriage, she explained, had been arranged by her parents, according to Chinese custom, and she had not yet met her husband-to-be, though she had seen his photograph and thought him very good-looking. He also had plenty of money. However, even if she had not been getting married she could not have met me—for Chinese girls were not permitted the same liberty as English girls. The latter, she knew, could have boy friends—could even allow their boy friends to anticipate the role of husband—without seriously prejudicing their chance of marriage. She had even heard of one English girl, from the upper contours of the Peak, who had taken four boy friends in as many years, and then been married to a high-ranking Government official in the Hong Kong cathedral. But for a Chinese girl such behavior was unthinkable—for purity was an indispensable condition of marriage, and on the day of marriage the husband's relatives were traditionally entitled to seek proof. And if the girl was found wanting the contract would be annulled; there would be nothing left for her but the streets.

"So you see, I have never had a boy friend," Mee-ling declared solemnly. "I have never made love yet."

"No?" I said, startled by such frankness.

"No, not once."

"Well, you've still plenty of time." I wondered if this kind of conversation, at first meeting, was typically Chinese.

She looked at me innocently. "What do you call that in English?"

"Call what exactly?"

"I mean, if you have not made love—not with anybody."

"Well, you call it 'being a virgin,'" I said.

"'Virgin'? Like that?"

"Yes."

"Yes, virgin—that's me."

She said this pointing to herself with a red fingernail. I burst out laughing.

"Mee-ling, you're marvelous!" I said. "Anyhow, now we've got that point cleared up, won't you have dinner with me? I mean, if I promise not to try and spoil your record?"

She shook her head again stubbornly. "No."

"But I'd love to paint you."

"No. We say good-by in a minute."

The boat shuddered through its frame as the engines went into reverse. It nudged against the Wanchai pier. The gangplank clanged down and I followed Mee-ling off the boat in the crush of passengers. We paused outside on the quay where a group of rickshaw men sat idly between the down-tilted shafts of their rickshaws. Only a hundred yards along the quay was the Nam Kok, and I could see the blue neon sign over the entrance, and my corner balcony on the top floor, and my easel standing out on the balcony with the white-square of canvas: the painting of Gwenny that I had started this morning.

Mee-ling followed my glance.

"What's that place?"

"Which . . . ?" I said vaguely. Then I quickly reclaimed her attention, saying, "Where are you going now?"

"Hennessy Road."

"To catch a tram?"

"No, there is a car to meet me in Hennessy Road."

"Can I come with you to the car?"

"No, the driver might tell my father."

"And I suppose your father would beat you?"

"Yes—perhaps."

"And you won't be a devil and change your mind about dinner?"

"No. I go now."

She held out her hand for a formal good-by, gave a sudden little giggle as I took it, as if at the daring of our encounter, then turned and bolted off down the side street to Hennessy Road, her heels flying, her plume of hair bobbing. She looked back, briefly fluttered a hand at me, then was swallowed up by the food stalls and rickshaws and pedestrian swarms.

Gone, I thought, gone. *Partir c'est mourir un peu.* . . . And I turned away and crossed the quay to the Nam Kok; and as soon as I got up to my balcony

I stood the drawing board on the easel over the canvas of Gwenny, found a piece of charcoal on the cluttered table, and made a quick sketch of Mee-ling while the memory was still fresh. I sketched her with that mischievous-innocent look in her eyes, one hand holding the melon seeds, the other pointing to herself; and underneath I wrote, "Yes, virgin—that's me."

It was not very good, but it made me smile, and I kept it. I have just looked at it again now. It is very smudged, and has been torn—by Mee-ling herself, who did not like it—and repaired with Scotch tape. But it still amuses me, because it was my first sketch of her. And I have been wondering how many times I have sketched and painted her since. Well, I could never count. But probably more times than there are melon seeds in that cornet—and more times than there are hairs in that pony-tail plume.

Chapter Two

It was because of George Wheeler that I started to draw.

Wheeler, the manager of the Bukit Merah Rubber Estate in Malaya, lived alone in a huge gloomy bungalow submerged in an ocean of rubber trees. He was an unhappy and frustrated man. And the day I arrived out from England to start work as an assistant he addressed me as follows:

"You'll find me a pretty easy-going boss on the whole—but there's one thing I will not tolerate on this estate. And that's miscegenation."

I said uncomfortably, "I'm not quite sure what that means."

"Messing about with native women."

I glanced round the somber cage of mosquito wire that was his living room. The shelves were cluttered with books on mountaineering, the walls covered with pictures of mountaineering feats torn from magazines. Clearly Wheeler found an outlet for his emotions in dreaming of the conquest of glittering peaks. But how, I wondered, did others fare under his prohibition?

I soon found out: it had affected his assistants in various ways. It had caused my predecessor, a Pole, to propose through the post to a pen-friend in Glasgow whom he had never met; the girl had come out, they had been married, and now they were over at Kuantan, still behaving like lovebirds and awaiting their third child. Less happy, however, had been the effect on Ted Willis, one of my fellow assistants: already too introverted, he had turned even more in upon himself, becoming at the age of twenty-four a virtual recluse, and probably an emotional cripple for life. As for dear old Tubby Penfold, my other colleague, it had simply caused him to increase his repertoire of smutty stories and to embroider them with more detail; though occasionally he would relieve himself in some more extravagant fashion, as when once, suddenly bursting in upon me with broad and triumphant grins, he described an encounter with a Tamil woman whom he had found hanging round the smoking shed: "Black as your hat, mind you, and with those bloody great dingle-dangle things in her nose—but fairly gasping for it . . . My God, nothing like a good old knee-trembler to set you up!" I knew it was fantasy but pretended to believe him, and my belief made him almost as happy as if it had been true.

The first time I really felt the effect of the prohibition on myself was about a month after my arrival, when I fell in love with a Malay girl.

She was not employed on the estate, but would walk past my bungalow several times a day, and always at mealtimes when I was on the verandah. Was this only coincidence? I suspected otherwise, because of her wicked laughing eyes and the provocative swing of her hips when she knew I watched her. Her skin was like warm honey. I became obsessed by her, and all day long out on the estate I would be yearning for the next glimpse of her, and making plans for possessing her without the knowledge of Wheeler. A dozen times I nearly ran out to her; then fear of losing my job would prevail. Eventually she stopped coming. I had not even spoken to her, yet despair went to the depths of my soul.

After that the days seemed to drag, the evenings to be interminable with nothing to fill them but Tubby Penfold's smut. Oh, that cavernous emptiness after the early tropical sundown! I began to drink more than was good for me, to bridge the hours with stupor. I saw the red light. "At this rate," I thought one evening, "I shall go to pieces within a year. I must do something—find a hobby." And I took an old exercise book and a ball-point pen, and began to draw.

I had never drawn or painted before in my life, except at school, and then only under compulsion in weekly art classes, and without distinction. I had regarded the "arty boys" as a race apart, peculiar and to be deplored. In the holidays, as a cultural duty, I had visited the main London galleries and been bored: my lingering memories were not of the pictures but of the spectators, who had interested me much more. And only in the Royal Academy had there stirred in me a single critical thought: why on earth, I had wondered, were all the portraits so stodgy? Why were all the subjects so tidied up, so woodenly posed? Why were they never caught in a moment of life? There was more character, more expression, more meaning, in one uncertainly peering spectator's face than in any dozen of the faces in frames.

I had left school during the war and gone straight into the army, and within a year found myself in India. When the war ended I had been upcountry in Burma; and one day I had stood watching a Burmese woman washing clothes in the Irrawaddy, squatting by the water with her bright red *longyi* taut over her thighs. A Dakota aircraft had come down river, splitting the sky with its din. The woman had paid no attention until it was right overhead; then, still pummeling at the washing, she had lifted her face and given it a brief, indifferent, almost contemptuous glance—the glance of a Burmese villager who for four years had watched foreign armies fighting their seesaw battle, passing back and forth with their massive noisy machines for destruction, inflicting on each other the most hideous mass slaughter—and who was still washing clothes in the Irrawaddy as she had been washing them since childhood, no better and no worse off than she had been before. And then suddenly I had found myself filled with elation; for that glance, that tilt of the head as the hands went on pounding, had seemed to me extraordinarily beautiful in their depth of meaning, their expression of truth. If only I could have captured and preserved that moment! How much it would have told about Burma, about war, about people, about life! But already the noise of the Dakota was fading; the woman's eyes had returned to her washing; the moment had gone.

Soon afterwards I had bought a camera from a fellow officer in the mess; for there had been other such moments, such scenes, and it had seemed to me that in these, rather than in the Shwe Dagon Pagoda or the crumbling monuments of Pagan, had lain the real beauty of Burma and the real meaning of the country's life, and I had been determined to capture them. I had taken photographs by the score. But among all these photographs not more than a dozen had caught the look, the gesture, the moment at which I had aimed; and these, indeed, had been the most disappointing of all, for nothing that I had expected was to be found in them. They had turned out empty, flat, devoid of meaning. But why, why? Since they were true records of moments that had moved me, why weren't they moving in themselves?

And then I had begun to understand. A moment could never be complete in itself, since it belonged to a context of movement and mood, and only in this context had meaning; and moreover part of this context was the observer himself, interpreting the moment in the light of his own mind—his own personality and knowledge. Thus when I had seen the Burmese woman by the Irrawaddy it was not her actual expression that had moved me, but what this had suggested to me when filtered through my own vision: when fused with my own experience, my own hatred of destruction and war. And on another person standing at my side, the moment would have made a different impression. Indeed on a dozen people, it would have made a dozen different impressions.

And so it was that very belatedly—for no doubt most people had taken it for granted since childhood—I discovered the first, and possibly the only, truth about art: that its function was not to say, "This is how X looked at a given moment," but, "This is how X looked to me."

Soon my demobilization papers came through and I returned to England. I had loved the East, and wandering round London again, chilly in my new suit, I felt miserable and lost. My parents were dead; I had no training for a career; no feeling of roots, of belonging. Then my uncle took me into his estate agency in Sloane Street, promising me eventual partnership if I proved myself worthy. I gritted my teeth, went to night school, slogged at homework, and in the office began to use, with increasing familiarity, words like leasehold, tithe, non-basement, low out-goings, parquet flooring, maisonette. "I hate this life, but I've got to show I can do it," I thought. "I've got to pass my exams." But I had no sooner done so than I threw it all up to go planting in Malaya; and though my kindly, disappointed uncle said, "I'm afraid you may regret it," I knew when I caught my first nostalgic whiff of the East that he had been wrong. I had been three parts dead in London, catching buses in Sloane Square; now suddenly I had become wholly alive again, all my senses alert. And once more I began to feel elated by those fleeting moments of beauty: by those gestures, those expressions, those little scenes of native life. If only, I thought, I had been an artist! . . . And thus it was that in my third month at Bukit Merah, after the Malay girl had ceased her tantalizing walks, I took the exercise book and the ball-point pen and started to draw.

And almost at once, though I had no illusion about the crudity of my first scribblings, I felt myself to have a real facility. It was a strange, an almost uncanny sensation. It was as if I had sat down at a typewriter for the first time and found my fingers familiar with the keys—like the feeling of "I have been here before." And at the same time it was tremendously exciting. I had always thought, "I'm not a bad all-rounder, but there's nothing at which I'm *really* good," and I had envied those with a bent, a talent, some metier at which they could excel. And now at last I had found a métier of my own. And it was as if, by accident, I had pulled open a drawer that I had always thought to be empty, and found it to contain a treasure that could alter the course of my whole life.

Soon drawing had become a total preoccupation: I thought of nothing else day or night. I carried a sketchbook in my pocket while out on the estate, and all the time I would be watching for moments to sneak away and record impressions, and counting the hours until the lunch break or until the evening when I could indulge my passion freely. Every moment of spare time had become infinitely precious. I was hungry for knowledge, for instruction. I racked my brains for any morsel of advice that I might have retained accidentally from those wasted art classes at school. I sent to Singapore and London for art books of every description. I devoured them avidly; found myself moved, enchanted, thrilled, by the reproductions of pictures whose originals, twelve years ago in the London galleries, had left me cold. Even newspaper cartoons, pictorial letterheads, held new interest for me, as I studied them to see how their effect had been achieved. And I no longer thought about the Malay girl who had walked past my bungalow. My frustrated emotions had been canalized. I was pouring into my sketchbook all the energy that, but for George Wheeler's prohibition, I would have spent in making love.

I discarded styles unsuited to me, and by the end of a year was working comfortably in a style of my own. I had also started drawing in color, first using children's crayons from the local Chinese store, then pastels sent from England. And now I began a new adventure into the world of oils.

Wheeler, despite the number of times he had caught me sketching in working hours, was well-disposed toward my hobby, which he thought clean-minded; indeed I was his favorite assistant, for he had little use for

Tubby Penfold, whose mind so uncleanly dwelt on girls. He even asked me to paint a picture for him. It was Coronation year, and Everest had just been climbed: he wanted me to reconstruct on canvas the moment of conquest at the summit, and had collected magazine photographs of Hillary and Tensing for me to use as models. I had neither the taste nor the capability for such an assignment, but expediently promised to do my best; and I duly produced a work of prodigious falsity, that nevertheless delighted him. And he hung it on his bedroom wall, so that he could relive the Himalayan epic in bed.

A week later, still purring over my Everest effort, he showed me an item in a London newspaper: a gossip columnist's interview with a woman painter whose first exhibition had just opened at a private gallery, Ullman's, in the West End. And all Mayfair was gasping with astonishment, for the woman, who was in her mid-thirties, had only taken up painting the previous year.

"And you've been at it longer than that now," Wheeler said. "Why don't you send them some of your efforts?"

"I'm not good enough yet," I said; though a more accurate rendering of my thoughts might have been, "I think I'm pretty good myself, but I'm not sure that others will think so, and I'm scared stiff of putting myself to the test."

"Well, have a shot—you've nothing to lose."

I took no more persuading, and promptly dispatched a quantity of pastel drawings and two oils at enormous expense by air. But they were not even acknowledged. It was the last I saw or heard of them for eight months.

And I did after all have something to lose—my self-confidence. The blood rushed to my cheeks when I thought of my presumption in sending my pictures to London—how well I could imagine the derision with which they had been received! I dared not even write to ask for their return. My belief in myself was shaken. And it was therefore no mere chance—since to restore self-esteem a man will often turn to a woman—that during this period I became engaged to Stella.

Stella Plowden was twenty-four and moderately pretty, which by upcountry Malayan standards meant ravingly beautiful; and when she came out with her mother to stay on the next estate to Bukit Merah the bachelors converged on her—from a radius of a hundred miles. I joined in the stampede, with the advantage not only of proximity but also of the bandits—for after one suitor, incautiously motoring Stella-wards overnight, had been ambushed and shot dead, the ardor of other far-flung competitors had noticeably cooled. I proposed to her on Christmas Day; on Boxing Day was accepted; and by early New Year had already become aware of gnawing doubts. However, it was not until April that I had the courage to break it off.

The chief cause of friction between us was my painting. It hurt Stella that I should continue to sketch and paint Malays more than herself. She could not understand. Now that I had a willing model, impeccably white-skinned and not unattractive, why should I go on wasting my talents on natives? She did not admit to this grievance for a time, but I could not help being aware of it, for whenever I showed her my work she would become moody and make edged remarks, and start picking on my faults—on every fault except the one which was actually upsetting her. Eventually, however, she came out with it: it was not, she explained, that she wanted to be painted—indeed she could think of nothing more utterly boring—but that my apparent lack of interest in her was so humiliating. Only this morning her mother had asked her if I was painting her portrait, and she had been obliged to reply, "No, he's painting some Malay girl." She could have died of shame.

We began to bicker at every meeting; and it was always the same arguments that were repeated, the same accusations, though each time a little more bitterly. And finally, one day on a picnic, came the showdown, after I had defiantly sketched three Malay women passing with jack fruit and the usual row had begun.

"What's the matter with me?" Stella demanded. "Am I so ugly or something?"

"No, of course not."

"But it's so insulting—and so unnatural."

"To paint Malays?"

"Yes, especially when nine times out of ten you pick on the girls. It's disgusting."

"But they're so beautiful—they've got such grace."

"My God, listen to you! And you pretend there's nothing in it!"

"Of course there's nothing in it." We went at it hammer and tongs for another ten minutes, trying to hurt each other, then were silent. I began to feel ashamed of what I had said and presently tried to make amends, saying, "Anyhow, I'd like to sketch you now."

"All right, wait a minute." She reached for her handbag.

"No, don't move! Just as you are—it's marvelous!"

"Don't be a fool."

And then, as she manipulated comb and cosmetics and began to preen herself, everything inside me exploded. "You silly bitch!" I wanted to shout. "You silly, vain, self-conscious bitch! *Now* can't you see why I paint Malay girls? Can't you see the difference? Can't you see they've got an innocence that you've lost?"

She arranged her skirt, and then herself, in a chocolate-box pose.

"All right, I'm ready now."

"Fine," I said, and sketched her. And the next day I told her I did not think I was the sort of husband she wanted, and we had better break it off.

She was very upset. "But what shall I tell people?" she kept saying. "What shall I tell people?" And although I despised her at the time for this characteristic concern with what other people would think, I came afterwards to judge her less harshly, for the fear to lose face was natural enough and among whom was it stronger than the oriental races themselves? And also in retrospect I came to realize that Stella's grievance about my painting, which I had so self-righteously dismissed as mere vanity on her part, had been perfectly justified. The creative impulse had its roots in sexuality, and it was no more chance that I enjoyed painting Malay women than that other artists enjoyed painting nudes. (For any painter who claimed that the female body only interested him as "abstract form" was talking rubbish—he might as well paint pillows.) They aroused in me feelings which, denied direct expression, had found expression in another form, and which gave to my pictures whatever merit they might possess; such feelings as Stella had never aroused. And of course she had known it. "If he paints Malay women and not me, he can't love me," had been her instinctive reaction, and I had thought the argument unsubtle, only proving her abysmal ignorance of the higher motives of art. But of course she had been right. I had never loved her—never for a moment.

A few weeks after breaking with Stella I received a letter from London. It was from the Ullman Gallery, where I had sent my pictures, and contained a check for sixty-three pounds.

The letter itself was signed by Roy Ullman, Director, who apologized that the check was no larger owing to gallery fees and cost of framing. He gave no explanation for not having written before, but went on to say that he had included fourteen of my pictures in a group exhibition for the work of several new young painters—though only, he admitted, after some hesitation. However, as the attached clippings would show, the vigor and the intensity of feeling of my pictures had more than made up for the weakness of composition and the frequent clumsiness of technique. And he went on, "In fact one may say without exaggeration that they stole the show, and you may congratulate yourself on a magnificent triumph. However . . ." However, he now recommended that I should not exhibit again for another year, during which time I would undoubtedly develop beyond recognition. And he finished, "You have a really exciting and unusual talent, and I know we can expect great things of you."

My first extravagant excitement at this letter was followed by the conviction of destiny and genius, and the natural acceptance of myself as a superior being. This period lasted a week, during which I not only felt myself to be taller but evidently, due to buoyancy of spirits, actually appeared to be so—for both George Wheeler and Tubby Penfold remarked independently, and in some puzzlement, that I seemed suddenly to be overtowering them. The next week, however, they were both remarking that I had shrunk back to normal. And I fancied myself that it was to even less than normal—for trying hard to live up to my inflated estimate of myself, I was finding myself altogether devoid of inspiration and talent. I could achieve nothing; my conviction was no longer of genius, but of mediocrity; I was plunged in despair. Even the phrasing of Ullman's letter, to which I resorted in the hope of encouragement, now seemed empty and insincere; what, after all, had he to lose? And what, at best, was the "triumph," except a momentary stir among the culture snobs of Mayfair, before they moved on to the next stir, the next discovery, the next fashion? And as for the check, which in my initial surprise had seemed a fortune—it now dwindled to a mere pittance, as I thought of it in terms of time and effort and the elusiveness of inspiration.

My despair and inability to work lasted for most of two months; then the pendulum settled back somewhere about the middle. I was neither a genius nor a mediocrity, but possessed a certain gift that only patience and hard work could bring to fruition. And thus chastened, I found my spirit stirring again, the creative impulse returning.

Then one weekend, a month or so later, I went down to Singapore. It was a year since I had been anywhere larger than Kuala Lumpur and the huge city strangely excited me. I roved through the Chinese street markets, dined and watched cabaret at the Cathay, then wandered for hours round one of the great, glittering, tawdry Chinese entertainment parks, where Cantonese opera rubbed shoulders with open-air boxing, Chinese strip tease with bumping cars; and I danced with a taxi girl in one of the dance halls. Two days later I returned north by train, dreading the thought of going back to those endless, monotonous acres of gray-trunked trees, and to the drudgery of work that claimed so much of my time and kept me from painting; and I began to toy with the notion of leaving Bukit Merah. I had saved nearly four hundred pounds since I had been in Malaya. If I was careful I could spin it out for a year—a year to do nothing but paint. And while I was turning this over in my mind an army major in my carriage suddenly sighed and said, "My word, I wish I was back in Hong Kong!"

"Why?" I asked him.

"Singapore's all right, only it's the sort of town you find anywhere. But Hong Kong's really China. Take a minute's stroll from the center and you won't see a European. And oh, my word, it's beautiful!"

"Yes, so I've heard." And I remembered the gardener we'd had at home when I was a child, the gardener who had been no good at gardening because he was really a sailor, and on whose brown knotted arms had been tattooed, among the fading blue Chinese dragons, the word *Hongkong;* and who had been the unchallenged hero of my boyhood as he leaned on his spade and talked of opium dens, and gunboats, and firecrackers, and the Pearl (which was a river), and Chinese funerals with six brass bands and professional mourners in white hoods like the Ku Klux Klan, weeping and wailing and gnashing their teeth; and who sometimes, at the most exciting moment, would say, "But no more about that, or I'll be in trouble with your father"—oh, what realms of mystery lay beyond those words!

"Yes, my goodness," the Major said. "When you get a fleet of junks coming into that harbor in full sail, proud as bloody schooners . . . Well, you've got to see it for yourself. Oh, yes, my word—you ought to see Hong Kong."

"I shall," I said; for I had suddenly made up my mind. "You'll go up for leave?"

"No, to live."

I broke my news to George Wheeler as soon as I got back. He was not at all pleased, for he had paid me well to learn the job and had expected me to stay longer; but when he saw that I could not be shaken he put a good face on it, smiling grimly and saying, "Well, I suppose if you're going to be famous one day, I'd better be nice to you. Have a stengah?"

And when I was relaxed with the whisky, and he was as relaxed as his chronic inner tautness allowed, I laughed and said, "Anyhow, you've only yourself to blame. If it hadn't been for you I might never have started painting."

"What do you mean?"

"That ban on miscegenation."

He looked puzzled for a minute, trying to work out the connection, and then said, "Oh, nonsense. You'd never have gone with a native girl. You're not that sort."

"Well, actually—" I had been going to tell him about the girl with the laughing eyes and provocative hips who had walked past my bungalow, but he interrupted.

"Of course you're not—you're too clean-minded. I'd know that just from your Everest picture. That's a beautiful piece of work. Only a decent clean-minded chap could have painted a picture like that."

And then, since it would have ruined the picture for him to know the truth, I held my tongue after all, and just said, "Well, I'm glad you liked it."

"It's a work of art."

A new assistant was engaged locally. His name was Hewitt-Begg, and after his initial interview with Wheeler he told me, "This girl business doesn't really worry me, old man. I dabble in yoga." And so he did, squatting cross-legged in a loincloth, his pink and white English torso stiff as a ramrod, his finger pressed to his nose, making the most alarming noises as he breathed in through one nostril and out through the other, timing each respiration by a watch placed in front of him on the floor.

I remained a couple of weeks to show him the ropes, then Wheeler ran me in his car to Port Swettenham, where I embarked on a tramp. It was called the *Nigger Minstrel,* and was bound for Malacca, Singapore, Manila—and Hong Kong.

Chapter Three

I had no idea, when I first discovered it, that there was anything odd about the Nam Kok.

It was my fifth week in Hong Kong, and I had been to call at a house on the escarpment behind Wanchai, following up an advertisement for a room to let. The advertiser had been a Mrs. Ma, and I had found her flat on the second floor; but the moment she had opened the door, and I had glimpsed behind her, in the small living room, the usual abundance of children, grandparents, cousins, aunts—they must have numbered nearly a dozen souls—I had known that it would be no use, that there would be no privacy for me to paint; and I had been relieved when Mrs. Ma had told me that the room had already been taken by a Chinese. She had been sorry: she had wished she had known I was coming, for she would have liked an English guest so that she and her husband could have improved their English. She had insisted, anyhow, on rewarding my wasted journey with a cup of tea, which I had drunk while sitting stiffly on a hard, straight-backed chair, my presence scarcely noticed by the relatives seated about the room.

"Well, perhaps I can get something down in Wanchai," I said. "It's one of the few districts I haven't tried yet."

Mrs. Ma, who was very neat and bird-like, tittered with merriment as if I had made a joke. "You wouldn't like Wanchai," she said.

"Why not?"

"It's very noisy. . . . No Europeans live in Wanchai—only Chinese."

"That's what I want," I said. "The trouble with my present place is that there are only English." I told her about Sunset Lodge, which was at the lowest contour of the Peak at which a European could respectably live, and where I had been living until now—not for respectability, but because I had not been able to find anywhere cheaper. And I told her about the other residents: about the bridge players whose sessions began at eleven o'clock every morning in the lounge and continued all day; about the sad wistful wives who said, "Of course we're spoiled out here," but really wished themselves back in Sutton; about the feuding middle-aged ladies, and about the garrulous ladies who laid in wait for you, trapped you, and then turned their flow of talk onto you like a hose; and about how I had taken to entering by the kitchens to reach my room without being caught. It sounded quite funny when I told it, but really wasn't. I had become almost desperate; for by now a whole month of my year had gone by and I had still not settled to work, I had done nothing. At first Hong Kong, with its teeming, jostling populace, its atmosphere tingling with activity and excitement, had been too stimulating, too confusing; the impressions had whirled in my head too swiftly to record. "I must let it take shape," I had thought. "I'll be all right in a week or two." But nothing had taken shape; I had been able to find no center of interest, no point of beginning; and I had begun to wonder in dismay if I should have chucked up rubber planting at all. Then I had begun to understand. My work had always depended on sympathetic feeling, on a sense of identity with the people I sketched or drew; and here I was a mere spectator in the streets, making my occasional sorties from another world. A great wall divided me from the Chinese—how could it be otherwise, living in Sunset Lodge? And thus I had begun another room hunt—for I had given up once in despair—and again taken trams from district to district, trudged from street to street, only to be reminded again everywhere, by the swarming pedestrians, by the quantities of washing hung out overhead, that this was the most overcrowded city in the world. Only a few years ago, at the end of the war, the population had been barely half a million; but since the revolution in China, from which the refugees had come flocking across the border in their hordes, it had swollen to two and a half million, and some thought to three million by now—who could tell? And when the first corners had packed themselves into every available room—each divided into ten, fifteen, twenty "bed-spaces"—there had been nothing left for the remainder but the empty sites and the hillsides, and such shanties as they could build from threadbare sacking, flattened tins, and treasured gleanings of wood. And if indeed any room did become vacant now it would be let at an inflated rental that no legislation could restrain. And so for a second time I had found nothing within my means, and dispirited and footsore had once more given up; and it was only Mrs. Ma's advertisement that had brought me out again this afternoon.

I put down the little decorated cup and said, "It was delicious tea. You were very kind."

"Not at all, not at all," she tittered politely. "The tea was very poor."

"No, it was delicious." I rose to go.

"I hope you are not really going down to Wanchai?" she said anxiously, coming to the door. "It is too noisy—too dirty. The people in Wanchai are so poor, you will get such a bad impression of the Chinese. You won't go?"

"Well, perhaps not."

But I did go nevertheless—descending the escarpment by the long steep flights of steps that dropped straight down into the oldest part of Wanchai: into the teeming alleyways with the litter-filled gutters, the pavement vendors, the street stalls, the excitement and bustle. The sun slanted brilliantly down, making deeply contrasting patterns of light and shade and giving the overhead washing the gaiety of bunting. I saw a post office and went in, thinking the clerk would speak English; but when I asked him about rooms he shook his head and said, "No, sorry. No sell."

"I don't want to buy anything," I said. "I'm just looking for a room."

"Sorry. Only sell stamp."

I crossed Hennessy Road, with its clattering trams and its two huge modernesque cinemas showing American films, and came out on the water front by the Mission to Seamen. Next to the Mission was a big hotel called the Luk Kwok, famous for Chinese wedding receptions and obviously too expensive for me even to try. Further along the quay shirtless, barefoot coolies were unloading junks, filing back and forth along the gangplanks like trails of ants. Sampans tied up among the junks tossed sickeningly in the wash of passing boats. Across the road from the quay were narrow open-fronted shops, between which dark staircases led up to crowded tenement rooms; and along the pavement children played hopscotch while shoveling rice into their mouths from bowls, for all Chinese children seemed to eat on the move.

I sat at the top of a flight of steps leading down to the water. A month gone, I thought. A whole month gone, and I've done nothing. I must take myself in hand. I must bully myself.

But no, that's no use, I thought. I've already been bullying myself and it doesn't work. You can't bully yourself to paint. It's like bullying yourself not to hear a ticking clock. The harder you try, the more the sound fastens itself into your ears.

Sometimes will power is its own enemy, I thought. You can't paint by will power.

Yes, relax, I thought. It's only when you relax, when you're not trying to grab what you want, that you suddenly find it's there. . . .

I leaned on the sun-warmed stone. A rickshaw went by, the coolie's broad grimy feet making a slapping sound on the road. Then my eyes fell on an illuminated sign among the shops. The blue neon tubes were twisted into the complicated, decorative shapes of Chinese characters. I recognized the last two. They meant hotel.

Well, that's more my cup of tea, I thought. And right on the water front. Of course, it would be perfect. So perfect that there must be a snag. Still, there's no harm in trying.

I got up and crossed the quay, and turned into the entrance under the blue neon. And still not a suspicion passed my mind. Indeed the hall gave the impression of such solid respectability, with the middle-aged clerk behind the reception counter, the old-fashioned rope-operated lift, the potted palms at the foot of the stairs, that I was reminded of some old family hotel in Bloomsbury, and felt discouraged. It was all wrong for the water front of Wanchai—and anyhow would probably be too expensive after all.

I approached the desk and asked the clerk, "How much are rooms by the month?"

"Month?"

The clerk's fingers paused over the beads of his abacus: he had been making calculations from figures in his ledger, as though playing some musical instrument from a score. His Chinese gown, like a gray priest's cassock, gave him an old-fashioned appearance in keeping with the potted palms, the antiquated lift. His head was shaven, and he had several silver teeth.

"Month?" he repeated.

"Yes, don't you have monthly terms?"

"How long you want to stay?"

"Well, it would be a month at least. . . ."

He gave me an odd look, then dubiously began a new calculation on the abacus. The beads clicked up and down under his finger tips.

"Two hundred and seventy dollars," he announced at last. "A month?"

"Yes—month."

The Hong Kong dollar was worth one shilling and threepence, so that was about seventeen pounds—a little dearer than Sunset Lodge, but with cheap meals I could just afford it. I asked to see a room, and the clerk called one of the floor boys on the telephone while I went to the lift. The liftman lounged inside against the mirror reading a Chinese newspaper. He folded the newspaper, crashed the gate shut, yanked on the rope, and we rumbled upward, our passage punctuated at each landing by a loud metallic clank. On the third and topmost landing, where I alighted, a miniature radio on the floor boy's desk was emitting the falsetto screeches of Cantonese opera. The floor boy, a smiling fresh-faced youth of about twenty, dressed in a white jacket, wide-legged cotton trousers, and felt slippers, led me down the corridor and unlocked the door of the end room.

"Very pretty room, sir," he grinned.

It was not pretty, but it was clean and perfectly adequate, with a wide hard bed, a cheap dressing table and wardrobe, and the inevitable enamel spittoon on the floor. There was also a telephone and a padded basket for a teapot: I remembered hearing that in Chinese hotels a constant supply of green tea was provided free of charge. I could almost live on tea; it would be a great saving.

"And a pretty view, sir."

He opened the doors onto the balcony, which was roofed over but beautifully light: a perfect studio. And the view was indeed superb, for the balcony was on a corner and commanded an immense panorama. On one side it looked out over the roof tops of Wanchai, behind which rose the skyscrapers of Hong Kong and the Peak, while in front was the harbor scattered with ships of every shape and size: cargo boats, liners, warships, ferryboats, tramps, junks, sampans, walla-wallas, and numberless comic, graceless, rusting mongrels—some lying at anchor, some in ponderous movement, some bustling about busily, crisscrossing the harbor with their wakes. And across the harbor, so close that I could count the windows of the Peninsula Hotel, was the water front of Kowloon, with a backdrop of tall bare hills stretching away into China.

I said, "This'll do fine."

"My name is Tong Kwok-tai, sir," the floor boy grinned deferentially. "Will you please correct my bad English?"

"There's nothing to correct, Ah Tong."

"You are too kind, sir." And as we turned back into the room he said, "You have a girl here, sir?"

"A girl? No."

I supposed that by "here" he meant Hong Kong and still did not realize. I went down again in the rumbling lift, and paid the clerk a deposit to make sure of the room. He wrote out a receipt in Chinese. I could hear the muffled sound of dance music coming from a swing door leading off the hall. I nodded to the door, asking the clerk, "What's in there?"

"Bar."

"Good, I'll have a beer."

I turned away across the hall, and just then the door swung open and a Royal Navy matelot came out. He was small, wiry, and darkly tanned by the sun. He wore a hat with H.M.S. *Pallas* in gold letters round the brim.

He cocked his head at me in casual salutation.

"Good Lord, the Navy!" I laughed. "The last thing I expected to meet here!"

He gave me an odd look like the clerk. "Well, you won't meet much else here, mate," he said. "Not at the Nam Kok."

"No? You mean there aren't any Chinese here?"

"Only the girls," he said. "The girls are all Chinese."

The door swung open again at this moment and a Chinese girl came scurrying out, laughing and saying to the matelot, "Hey, you left me." She wore high heels and a cheongsam with tall collar and split skirt. She was very pretty.

"And they're a decent lot, too, if you treat them proper," the matelot said proprietorially. "Eh, Nelly? Isn't that right?"

"Sure, we're plenty nice," the girl acceded cheerfully, tugging at his hand. "Come on, you talk too much. You make me chokka."

"No, you won't do better than this place nowhere, mate," the matelot said. They went off, the matelot swaggering a little, the girl balancing on her high heels.

I watched them cross the hall, grinning to myself. Well, I am an idiot, I thought. I ought to have guessed from the clerk's face when I asked for a room. A room for a month! I suppose he's only used to letting rooms by the hour. And I turned and went through the swing door into the bar.

Inside it was dim after the daylight of the hall. The windows were curtained and the room lit like a night club with rosy diffused light. I paused while my eyes adjusted themselves. Then the scene began to take shape: the bar counter in the corner; the huge walnut-and-chromium juke box playing "Seven Lonely Days"; the Chinese waiters carrying trays of beer among the tables; and the sailors at the tables; and the girls.

Yes, that sailor was right, I thought. I won't do better than here.

Yes, this is what I've been waiting for. This is the point of contact. This is where I'll be able to start.

And I went across to an empty table, and ordered a beer.

II

"Actually, I am not very popular with the sailors," said Gwenny Lee. "I am too thin. Too skinny."

"But you're very pretty, Gwenny."

"No, I'm much too skinny. And I have no sex appeal. It is sex appeal that really matters."

She clicked away with her knitting needles. The juke box was playing "You Can't Tell a Waltz from a Tango," the second favorite to "Seven Lonely Days" which had just been played three times in succession. The grizzled, middle-aged matelot at the next table comfortably sucked at his pipe, with the calm satisfaction of a man at his own fireside, while a girl snuggled kittenishly in his arms. The atmosphere was smoky and the table tops smelled of spilt beer. It was still early and there were not more than a dozen sailors scattered round the tables; they were all English, except for three Americans who Gwenny had explained were regulars from the U.S. Station Ship—there were no visiting American ships in port at present. The girls outnumbered the sailors, and at one table five girls sat by themselves looking bored.

Gwenny Lee broke off her knitting to free some more wool from the ball in the bag beside her. She had joined me at my table soon after I had sat down, and we had been talking for an hour. She was a thin girl of twenty-six with a pale triangular face and gentle eyes. She wore a Western-style cotton dress, instead of the cheongsam worn by most of the girls, and a crucifix on a thin gold chain round her neck: she was a Catholic, educated at a mission school in China. Now she lived in one room in Wanchai with her mother and sister, whom she supported financially. She was determined that her sister should stay respectable and make a good marriage; and once this happened, she would be able to give up working at the Nam Kok.

"Yes, it is sex appeal that counts," she went on philosophically. "Some girls who are not at all pretty make much more money than I do. That girl, for instance—Typhoo." She nodded to a girl across the room. "She is not pretty, but she has sex appeal. Also, of course, she is not so skinny."

"You're not as bad as all that, Gwenny."

"Oh, yes, look." She put down her knitting—it was a yellow jumper that she was making for her sister—and pushed up the sleeve of her cardigan. Her arm was pathetically thin and shapeless. "I always have to wear something to hide my arms. It is very annoying in summer when it is hot."

"You must appeal to some men very much, Gwenny," I said.

"Well, sometimes. I had one boy friend called Chuck. He was an American. His ship stayed in Hong Kong five days, and I was very fond of him. I took him to the Tiger Balm Pagoda and the Peak. He was very nice. Sometime I will show you the letter he wrote me." She picked up the beer bottle on the table and drained it into my glass. "You would like another San Mig?"

"Yes, but won't you have something, too?"

"No, Chinese women don't drink much, you know. None of the girls here drink." She beckoned a waiter and ordered a San Mig, then said, "I think I will fetch that letter now. I would like you to see it."

"Isn't that a nuisance, Gwenny?"

"No, I live quite near. And it is such a nice letter. I think you will enjoy reading it."

She left her knitting on the table and went out through the door onto the quay. The record on the juke box came to an end and Typhoo, the girl whom Gwenny had pointed out, got up and held out her hand to her matelot companion for a coin, wiggling the fingers impatiently. She was as ugly as a little monkey, but had a beautiful figure and legs. The split in her skirt rose to immodest heights and showed a long white sliver of thigh. The matelot gave her a coin. She noticed as she turned away that he was still wearing his hat and playfully grabbed it, giving him a great broad grin over her shoulder as she stuffed it on her own head. She sauntered over to the juke box and inserted the coin. She pressed one of the buttons to select a record, then stood back to watch the mechanical antics behind the glass, her legs planted firmly apart, her scarlet-nailed hands on her hips, her split skirt gaping, her little monkey's face craned towards the machine, her eyes like two bright-pointed blackberries, and the matelot's hat sitting rakish but forgotten on her head.

Look at that, I thought. Look at that face, at that stance. A Chinese girl in an English sailor's hat gazing into an American juke box. What more could you want than that?

A matelot at a near-by table noticed her gaping skirt. He nudged his companion, winked, and dipped his forefinger in his beer. He leaned over from his chair and ran the wet finger down the sliver of Typhoo's thigh. Typhoo turned on him furiously.

"Hey, what you think I am? Street girl?"

At that moment the music from the juke box burst upon the room, drowning the rest of her vituperation. She gesticulated at him for a minute, then made a face of "Pouf! You're beneath my contempt," and walked away. She sat down at her table and began to tell her own matelot about it, with an expression that suggested she was saying indignantly, "Some of your friends make me sick. I've got pride, you know! What do they think I am?"

I sat smoking and sipping the cool beer. Presently Gwenny returned, taking from her handbag an envelope that was rather grubby and dog-eared. She handed it to me across the table, saying, "You will see, it is a very nice letter. He was a very nice boy."

The envelope was addressed to *Miss Gwenny Lee, Nam Kok Hotel (Bar), Wanchai, Hong Kong, China*. The postmark was over a year old, and the letter inside was disintegrating along the folds like an Indian bearer's testimonial.

Gwenny watched, glowing with pleasure, as I began to read.

Dear Gwenny.

Well, don't die of shock, I expect you will to get a letter after all this time, anyhow it's never too late to keep a promise so here goes.

Well, Gwenny, I sure was a lucky fellow meeting a girl like you, especially just after getting that letter from my girl back home, when I was feeling so sore. She was no good that girl, Gwenny. I only wish she could have met you. I guess she thinks Chinese girls still wear grass skirts or something, she'd have got a big surprise to find someone as swell as you. I had to hide in the heads when we left Hong Kong ("No kidding!") so as the other fellows wouldn't see me cry. Well, we've been in about every port out East since then and I won't say I haven't looked at another girl, because I know you wouldn't believe me, but I've not met another to touch you, Gwenny, and that's honest to God.

Now for the good news, we just heard we're heading back for the old U.S. next month, but wish we could have called at Hong Kong again first.

Well, good-by, Gwenny, you really are a swell girl, so thanks again.

Chuck.

Gwenny smiled at me over her knitting.

"Well?" she said. "Don't you think it is a nice letter?"

"Very nice, Gwenny. You must have been very kind to him."

"Of course some of the girls have many letters. Suzie, my best girl friend, has had five. She had one only last week. It was very passionate. It was from somebody called Joe. But she could not remember him because there are so many sailors called Joe." She broke off, looking at me. "What's the matter?"

I nodded towards the door from the quay, which had just swung open to admit a posse of four naval policemen, two British and two American, equipped with boots, gaiters, armbands, and truncheons. They filed into the bar briskly and aggressively.

"What on earth is it?" I said in alarm. "A raid?"

Gwenny gave them a brief glance. "Oh, it's only the S.P.'s," she said, and resumed her knitting.

"Only?"

"They are very nice. They only come round to see there is no fighting."

The patrol, consisting of one officer and one sergeant from each navy, had divided into national pairs. The two American S.P.'s strolled past our table. Just then one of the sailors from the American Station Ship caught sight of them and called out, "Hi, there!" He had his arm round a girl. He stretched out his other arm to pull up an extra chair, but could not reach it without relinquishing the girl, so extended his leg and pulled up the chair with his foot. The Sergeant sat down, while the Officer pulled up another chair for himself, saying, "Well, boys? How are we doing?"

The two British S.P.'s chose an empty table on the other side of the bar. The Sergeant pulled out a chair for the Officer, then they both seated themselves stiffly, removed their caps, placed them upside down on the table, and took out their handkerchiefs. They methodically mopped their brows. The matelots at neighboring tables looked sheepish and pretended not to notice them.

The manager of the bar limped out from behind the bar counter. His slight limp, in conjunction with his shaved head and black suit, made him look a trifle sinister, like a Chinese version of Goebbels, though according to Gwenny he was very kind-hearted and popular with the girls. He approached the two British S.P.'s rather obsequiously, offering them a drink on the house, but they shook their heads, and he limped over to the Americans, who refused likewise.

"But hey, come here, feller," the Sergeant said, catching him by his sleeve as he was turning away. "You got any more of those chopsticks with the name of this dive on, like you gave the Lootenant? O.K., but they gotta have the name on, see? I want 'em for a souvenir." The manager limped away and returned with the chopsticks, and the Sergeant said, "Yeah, those'll do, I guess."

Gwenny glanced at me over her knitting and said, "I have never met an artist before. But I once saw a film about an artist at the Roxy. It was very beautiful. He also painted in a bar. But he was a dwarf."

"I expect it was Toulouse-Lautrec," I said.

"I don't remember his name. But I remember reading in the newspaper that the actor had to walk on his knees. He wore boots on his knees instead of his feet. It was very clever."

"I didn't see the film, but I've seen his drawings in a book," I said. "They were wonderful."

"I'm sure yours are better."

"I wish they were, Gwenny," I laughed.

"If I was a painter, I would paint pictures of hills. Why don't you paint hills? Why do you want to paint inside a bar?"

"Because I'm really only interested in people," I said. "I think there's more beauty in people."

"It is funny your coming to live here. Nobody has ever lived here before. I must introduce you to the other girls—they will be very interested."

Later several of the girls came and joined us, including Typhoo, Little Alice, and Wednesday Lulu. Little Alice was a plump little partridge of a girl, loaded with bangles and dangling earrings, who shook like a jelly with perpetual giggles. Wednesday Lulu was silent and watchful, with a round smooth face in which her eyes looked like slits cut from an alabaster mask. She never spoke without deliberation. Typhoo, however, gabbled irrepressibly, and was presently launched into an account of a curious experience the night before, when she had been told by one of the waiters that there was a man outside the bar who wanted a girl but refused to come in. Typhoo had gone out onto the quay and found the man seated in a rickshaw. He had been the captain of a merchant ship. She had been very impressed.

"Sure, he was proper ship captain—big man," she said. She talked with the vivacity and gesticulations of a Latin. "Sure, proper big man. He say, 'How much all night?' I say, 'Hundred Hong Kong dollar,' because a big man like that must get plenty lot of money. But he get chokka, he say, 'What you take me for? Yankee? Me no Yankee—me English. I give you thirty Hong Kong dollar.' I say, 'What for? Short-time?' He say, 'No, all night.' I say, 'I know you're ship captain but you must be crazy in the head!'"

They had finally compromised at sixty dollars—about four pounds—and had gone up to one of the rooms. Presently, after the Captain had worked off his first ardor, Typhoo had felt like a gossip with her girl friends before settling down for the night, and had asked the Captain to excuse her for half an hour. However, upon reaching the bar she had found herself without her handbag, which she had left upstairs—and which contained, among other items, the Captain's sixty dollars paid in advance. But after all, she had thought, a ship's captain was a man to be trusted. She wouldn't bother to go back for it. However, half an hour later, returning to duty, she had been greeted on the landing by the floor boy, announcing, "Typhoo, your boy friend went off twenty minutes ago." Well! So he had pinched the money after all! A ship's captain—a big man like that! She had dashed along to the room. Her handbag had still been on the dressing table where she had left it. She had wrenched it open—and gaped in astonishment. The money was still there—every cent of it!

And now Typhoo was really worried. If he had not stolen anything, why on earth had he gone off? She could not understand.

"He pay out plenty money altogether, you know," she said. "Rickshaw, ten dollar. Room, ten dollar. Make-lovey, sixty dollar. Altogether eighty dollar! All right, then why he run off after one short-time? Why? What happen?"

Little Alice was simmering with giggles. "Maybe he no like the way you make lovey," she said, and the giggles boiled over.

Typhoo grinned. "Everybody like the way I make lovey. Plenty boys tell me, 'Sure, you got a funny face, Typhoo, but I sooner have a short-time with you than all night with a big-bosom Yankee film star!'"

Wednesday Lulu, who had been thinking very hard, said carefully, "I think he had a wife."

"That ship captain?" Typhoo said. "Sure, he told me. He got a wife back in England."

"Then perhaps it was like this," Wednesday Lulu said solemnly. "First he wants a girl very badly, so he forgets about his wife. He catches a girl, makes love. Then inside he feels different. He remembers his wife. He thinks, 'I'm bad, very bad!' He feels very ashamed. So he runs off."

"Maybe you not so crazy," Typhoo said, impressed. "Yes, he was nice man, that ship captain. He got plenty good heart."

"Yes, I think that's right," Gwenny nodded. And she turned to me to elucidate. "You see, often sailors will take a girl all night, because they have been a long time without a girl and think they are very strong. But their strength goes quickly."

"Sure, every sailor same-same," Typhoo grinned. "He think, 'Minute my ship reach Hong Kong, I catch girl, make love nine, ten, twelve times.' What happen? He makes love once, twice—finish!"

"Yes, that's right," Gwenny said. "Finish."

"He just go to sleep—and snore-snore!" She laid her head on her hands as though on a pillow and distorted her face hideously in imitation of a sailor snoring; then grinned again. "Then morning-time he wake up and think, 'Hey, me crazy! That snore-snore cost me forty, fifty dollars! I gotta make up!' So he poke girl friend in the rib and say, 'Hey, come on, sweetie! We make love ten more times—we gotta be plenty quick!' So what happen? He make love one more time—then finish! Go back ship!"

"It's a good thing it's like that," Gwenny smiled. "It would be awful otherwise."

"You crazy or something?" Little Alice's giggles boiled up again. "You all crazy? If my boy friend go to sleep, I hit him! I say, 'Hey, come on! Me sex-starve!'" And her plump little body shook, her earrings danced and bobbed.

"You got plenty cheek, taking sailors' money," Typhoo said. "You enjoy make-lovey so much, why you don't pay sailors?"

Just then there was an influx of matelots through the door from the quay, fifteen or twenty in a bunch. The girls fell silent, watching them. The matelots sat down at three or four empty tables, ordering San Migs from the waiters and casting sideways glances at the girls, but not letting their glances linger or catching the girls' eyes in case they should get landed with girls they did not want. Presently all the girls except Gwenny drifted away from my table, hovering round the sailors, asking politely if they could join them, then sitting down rather stiffly in their high-necked cheongsams, demure and attentive, lighting the sailors' cigarettes and pouring their beer. The sailors were awkward for a bit and then began to unbend.

"Gwenny, aren't I keeping you?" I said.

"Oh, no," she said quickly, dropping her eyes to her knitting.

"Oughtn't you to be making some money?" I had already told her that I would not be having a girl, because although I thought several of them very attractive, I did not see how it would work out if I was living among them.

"Well, perhaps I should really go and work," Gwenny said, relieved that I had suggested it. "Only it seems rude to leave you."

"Of course it isn't."

"Anyhow, I may not have any luck."

However, half an hour later I saw her rise from a table with a big, clumsy, tow-haired matelot. She led the way to the door, looking rather delicate and skinny, though very neat and poised; so poised that you might have thought she was going in to dinner at Government House. The matelot shambled after her. They went through into the hall and the door swung to and fro behind them. The juke box was playing "Seven Lonely Days." The record came to an end and a matelot went over, put in a coin, and pressed a button. It was for the same record over again. He left the juke box to its manipulations and went back to his table. I caught the waiter's eye and tapped my glass, and he went off to fetch me another beer.

III

I did no serious work in the bar for the first few days, because as soon as I started to sketch the girls would cluster round to watch, leaving me scarcely room to breathe. I amused them with quick portraits of themselves and of a few favorite boy friends. Then the novelty wore off and they began to take my presence for granted, and no longer became self-conscious if they knew I was sketching them. I usually went down to the bar about eleven or twelve in the morning, when the girls were starting to arrive, and they would sit round my table and talk until business warmed up. I also ate all my meals in the bar. I could get a dish of fried rice, with meat or prawns, for a dollar or so, and it was all I needed to keep me going. The tea served with meals did not cost anything. Tea was always served free in China.

The Nam Kok was not technically a brothel, for brothels were illegal in Hong Kong, and it made its profit only from the rooms, which were sometimes let several times over in the course of twenty-four hours. The girls lived outside, made their own prices with the sailors, and kept what they earned; but they provided the hotel with its lifeblood, in the form of occupants for the rooms, and the bar was placed at their disposal as a hunting ground, on condition that they did not take their pickups elsewhere. This was sometimes a temptation, since the Nam Kok rooms were expensive, costing ten dollars a night with no reduction for shorter periods, and if a sailor was short of cash a girl might suggest slipping off to one of the many hotels in the neighborhood that charged only five dollars a night, or three dollars an hour. This would require leaving the bar separately and meeting again outside on the quay, in order not to arouse the suspicion of the manager. Nevertheless a girl would sometimes be caught, and punished by rustication from the bar—a week for her first offense, a fortnight for her second, and total expulsion for her third.

Once, before the war, there had been proper brothels in Hong Kong, and it was said that the police had approved of them, since they had enabled prostitution to be controlled and a check kept on disease. Then a certain lady politician at home, hearing that licensed immorality still existed in the Empire, had raised her scandalized voice in the House; and soon word had been hurried out from Westminster, and the brothels shut down. And so the girls had gone out into the streets, just as in London itself, and had taken their men up alleyways and into back rooms, and disease had spread uncontrolled. But now that licenses were no longer formally issued we could pretend it did not happen, wash our hands of it. Morality had been saved.

And then there had sprung up places like the Nam Kok, satisfying the letter of the law if not its spirit; and the police, one supposed, turned a blind eye, for the sailors would find the girls somehow, and the girls the sailors, and here at least there could be control of a sort. This, of course, had to remain invisible, since there could be no conditions officially laid down for an activity that was not supposed to occur at all; there could be no ordinance about it, no direct communication between police and hotel. But the Nam Kok itself, only too aware of its equivocal status, expediently toed what it supposed to be the invisible line; which entailed, in particular, obliging the girls to attend the Wanchai Female Hygiene Clinic for weekly examinations, and to satisfy the floor boys, before being allowed into any of the rooms, that their clinic cards were stamped up to date. And if this house rule had been allowed to lapse, with a consequent increase of casualties among sailors, I have no doubt that, for all the invisibility of control, the hotel would have found itself promptly and unceremoniously placed out of bounds, or otherwise caused to shut down.

The girls, on the whole, gave the sailors their money's worth, and often much more. There was a code of honor among them according to which, once a sailor had committed himself by taking a girl upstairs, he thereafter became her property, to be reclaimed by her on his subsequent visits to the bar, and eschewed by the rest. They despised the "butterfly" who liked a change of girl at each visit, and only the less scrupulous girls would contravene the code to oblige him. And their greatest pride and delight was to have a "regular" boy friend, which meant the same boy friend for three or four days, or for whatever period his ship was in port; and a girl thus engaged would usually go far beyond her commercial obligations, providing not only sex but something like affection, besides all those little feminine attentions which were the lonely sailor's need. And she would boast of him to her girl friends, become jealous of rivals, and bestow presents on him—if not actually shed tears—when he left.

They were mostly generous, loyal to one another, and easily amused; though like all social outcasts they suffered from over-sensitive pride, and were touchy about slights. And if a sailor showed lack of respect, a girl would retort, "What do you think I am? A street girl?" For a bar girl considered herself as superior, socially, to a street girl, as a respectable woman would consider herself superior to a whore.

The girls originated in about equal numbers from Canton and Shanghai, and most of the quarrels or jealousies arising in the bar were between girls of these two factions. Language itself divided them, for their provincial dialects were like different tongues; and since few knew Mandarin, the *lingua franca* of the bar was English. (Though if this proved inadequate to convey some fine point they could always fall back on writing, since the Chinese written characters, at least, were universal.) Each faction was equally convinced of its own natural superiority, and despised what it supposed to be the provincial characteristics of the other. However, the day-to-day intercourse of the two factions was quite amiable, and it was only in a crisis that enmity would come out.

The girls I came to know best, apart from Gwenny and Typhoo, were Wednesday Lulu, Minnie Ho, and Jeannie Chen. Jeannie was a luscious-looking little creature with chalk-white face, crimson splodge of a mouth, and great masses of black hair about her shoulders. She wore a black split skirt stretched tautly over undulating hips, black stockings, and enormously high heels—the only girl who dressed the part, for none of the others, if met out in the street, would have given a hint of their profession. Across the room, one gasped at Jeannie's voluptuousness. However, at close quarters—and each time I found myself at her side it came with a fresh little shock—she turned out to be so incredibly tiny that she no longer seemed quite real, but only a scale model that was not meant to be touched. Nor was her nature what, from first appearances, one might have expected, for despite the dress and crushed-strawberry mouth, which looked ill-tempered and pouting, she was one of the shyest and most sweet-natured of the girls in the bar.

And Minnie Ho, whom on my first evening I had seen snuggling in the arms of the middle-aged matelot, was the most cuddlesome and kittenish. She could not even cross the bar without flinging her arms round a sailor or two *en passant* and briefly nuzzling in their necks; and once ensconced with a man she could not bear to break away even to go upstairs. She could not live without cuddling, and in the absence of sailors would simply cuddle up with another girl. She would also cuddle up with me if I happened to be handy: enfolding herself round my arm, rubbing her cheek against my shoulder, and looking up at me with such pathetic appeal, such helpless adoration, that in order to keep my head I had to remind myself sternly that the same treatment was meted out indiscriminately to a dozen sailors a day.

She was understandably much in demand and could have done very well for herself; but she had no head for business. Once, wrapped round my arm after returning from a short-time with a matelot, she suddenly put her hand to her mouth and exclaimed, "Oh, I am stupid!"

"What's the matter?" I asked.

"I forgot to ask him for any money."

I laughed, finding this charming. But Minnie was so ashamed of the mental lapse that she begged me to tell nobody, afraid that the other girls would make fun of her for being so foolish.

Wednesday Lulu was the only girl in the bar not wholly Chinese: her father had been Japanese, her mother a Chinese prostitute in Shanghai. She adored her mother, whom she now supported with remittances sent to

Shanghai through the Bank of China, and while telling me about this the tears had begun to roll out of her long, black, rimless Sino-Japanese eyes. She was worried that the money was not getting through, and was in a dilemma about whether to stay in Hong Kong, or return to China to be near her mother, and accept a decent though less remunerative job under the communists.

Wednesday Lulu, despite her unpromising origin, was the most stubbornly honest and high-principled of the girls, and nothing in the world would have induced her to act against conscience. One night an American from the Station Ship, whose regular girl friend was otherwise engaged, had wanted her to go upstairs, offering her staggering financial reward. The regular girl friend was one of the least popular Cantonese and herself unscrupulous in such matters, and the other Shanghai girls had urged Lulu to accept. But it would have been unethical. She had refused.

Wednesday Lulu's curious name had been devised to distinguish her from another Lulu in the bar—a rather garrulous, quarrelsome, and unpopular Cantonese, masochistically inclined, to whom the other girls would refer any sailors making those sadistic demands which to all of them except the Cantonese Lulu were anathema. The similar names had been confusing, especially over requests for "Lulu" on the bar telephone, and various frivolous and unsatisfactory epithets had been suggested—like Sit-down Lulu and Stand-up Lulu, which drew attention a little maliciously to the Cantonese girl's reluctance, after a vigorous session upstairs, to be seated. Finally they had consulted Fifi Chan, a rather big-boned, heavily built girl with Rabelaisian vulgarity and wide, generous grin, who was a natural mimic and the bar's acknowledged wit and comedienne. Fifi had thought for a moment, then asked the two girls on what days they went to the Wanchai Clinic for their weekly medical inspections. They had told her.

"All right," Fifi said. "Call yourselves Wednesday Lulu and Saturday Lulu."

And thus they had been known ever since.

There were also two Alices in the bar, but here the choice of distinguishing epithets had presented no difficulty owing to the difference in their heights, which had made them automatically Big and Little.

Big Alice, who was only twenty-four, was a heavy heroin smoker, and like most addicts had become sluttish, usually appearing in the bar in a grubby man's shirt with untidily rolled sleeves, and with her unhealthy pasty face devoid of make-up. However, sometimes she would go to the opposite extreme, turning up in some fussily patterned cheongsam in which she looked absurdly overdressed, and with her face now plastered too thickly with powder and rouge, her eyes grotesquely blackened, and her lips smeared carelessly with lipstick beyond their natural outline. Curiously, though, she enjoyed considerable success with the sailors, some of whom perhaps, intimidated by the smarter girls, found her sluttishness more homely. She also had a seduction technique of her own: instead of joining the sailors at their tables she would sit alone, choose a victim, and fix him steadily with her eyes. And her eyes could be extraordinarily disturbing; they had a quality of their own which was a mixture of the hypnotic and sexy. The sailor who found himself held by them would grow uneasy; he would try and ignore her, then find himself drawn; and presently, no matter that he was with another girl, he would get up on the pretext of going to the lavatory, and stop as if accidentally at Big Alice's table; and in five minutes they would be on their way upstairs.

It was thus hardly surprising that Big Alice, who at one time or another had stolen boy friends from nearly every girl, should have been unpopular with the Shanghai faction and her fellow Cantonese alike.

Little Alice, the plump little giggler, was one of the girls most in demand in the bar, though her nature was less agreeable than I had supposed at first encounter: she was, in fact, shallow, irresponsible, and mean. She had had three babies, and for this her parsimony had mainly accounted; for while other girls who found themselves pregnant would go to a Chinese doctor for an illegal injection, regarding the four hundred dollars' expenditure as an overhead expense of their trade, Little Alice had always resisted making the painful disbursement until too late. Yet unlike the others, and untypical of the Chinese who as a rule adored children, she had no use for babies, and had given away two for adoption. The third had died before she had got round to making arrangements—no doubt from neglect.

Little Alice's three passions were eating cream-filled chocolates, going to the cinema, and buying new clothes. Every day she would appear with some new item of clothing or jewelry, and she would discard clothes that she did not like after a single wearing; but she gave nothing away and once, when Gwenny had offered to buy a month-old brocade jacket from her, Little Alice had charged her the full shop price.

Her selfishness was unique among the girls. And almost unique, too, was her taste in sailors: for while most of the girls preferred older men, who were kinder and less trouble, Little Alice liked boys of twenty, or if possible under. Herself twenty-six, she would put up her price for men much her senior, and offend middle-aged matelots by making it clear, with giggles at their expense, that she only took them on sufferance. On the other hand if a sailor was sufficiently callow, and was out of funds, she would oblige him for nothing.

The girls were all in their early or mid-twenties except for two; and both of these, Doris and old Lily Lou, were on the wrong side of forty.

Lily Lou claimed to be only forty-one, and would whisper this figure huskily into my ear, adding, "But the girls think I'm only thirty-seven—you won't tell them my secret, will you?" She would wink conspiratorially, and pat my hand. "Good boy! Good boy!" In fact the girls knew perfectly well, and so did I, that she was not a day under fifty.

I could not help liking old Lily Lou. She reminded me of an old theater pro, who had grown up in a narrow professional world, took pride in the old-fashioned thoroughness of her technique, and looked down on the present-day youngsters for skimping their job. She remembered her own training in a smart brothel in Shanghai—oh, in those days you'd got to know how to please a man, you'd got to take trouble and time. It had been a real vocation; none of these modern girls would have lasted a minute. "They've got no mystery, dear," she would whisper huskily, confidentially, patting my hand. "And that's what a man likes—mystery." And she would smile her carefully enigmatic smile that, despite the old whore's shabbiness and over-rouged cheeks, could still just pass for mystery in the low diffused light of the bar.

Lily Lou was the only girl besides Little Alice who sought out younger men; though in her case it was from expedience, since she appeared to succeed with them most. Doubtless she was more skilled than the younger girls with the inexperienced and shy, and more cozy; and in addition, of course, she appealed to the pocket, for as you grew older, mystery or no mystery, your prices had to drop. She would tell the other girls that she never took less than ten dollars. But they all exaggerated themselves, out of pride, about their minimum prices; and they knew perfectly well that old Lily Lou, at a pinch, would go upstairs for five.

And then Doris . . . Doris Woo was a little over forty, with a remarkably smooth complexion for her age and not bad-looking, but with the misfortune to wear glasses. She favored the rimless kind, presumably in the belief that these were more easily overlooked.

She was also hard—hard in the calculating, commercial way that was characteristic of some Chinese women. She was much harder than old Lily Lou, although she had only been at the game for a few years since she had come as a refugee from Pekin. She had no friends in the bar and always chose a table by herself—sitting very erectly, and turning her head with abrupt little movements as she surveyed the room for likely business, looking like a schoolmistress watching for notes being passed under desks. She had little success, and would sometimes sit for twelve hours in the bar, from noon till midnight, and go home without having made a cent—and poorer by the cost of her meals. She probably found, on the average, four or five clients a week. These were usually sailors who were too polite, too weak-willed, or too drunk to turn her down, or who, on a busy night, found themselves left with no alternative; though occasionally some sailor with a fetish about schoolmistresses or glasses would take her for choice.

Doris was even more unpopular among the other girls than the heroin addict Big Alice. I thought their hostility toward her was ungenerous, and told them so, saying I was sure that a little kindness toward her would work wonders; but I received only cynical looks, and even the kindly Gwenny seemed unpersuaded. Then one morning, returning from town, I found myself beside Doris on top of the tram; and grasping this opportunity to prove what kindness could achieve, I invited her to have lunch with me. I suggested a little restaurant close to the tram stop in Hennessy Road where we had alighted; I had been there already and knew we could eat well for a few dollars. She accepted the invitation in principle but thought the restaurant looked sordid; and proposing an alternative, she coaxed me into taking a taxi to reach it. At the restaurant she disappeared on the pretext of making a telephone call, though in fact, I had no doubt, to arrange commission for herself on the meal; and when she returned I found that without consulting me she had already given the order. The dishes began to arrive. They continued to arrive in fairly rapid succession for an hour. Finally I was presented with the bill. It was forty-eight dollars.

Blackmail, I decided as I paid up, could hardly go further. But it could, and did. For we were no sooner outside the restaurant than Doris, using that coaxing tone that was meant to be attractively feminine but that was in fact as hard as nails, urged me to "lend" her five dollars: she wanted a taxi back to the Nam Kok.

I decided that the time had come for a stand.

"I've never used a taxi before this morning," I said. "I can't afford it. Why not take a tram?"

She flushed, and sudden anger glittered in her eyes behind the rimless glasses.

"I'm a business girl," she said nastily. "You're supposed to pay for my time. I've wasted nearly two hours with you."

I suddenly could not bear to enter into argument. I felt in my pocket. I had nothing left but a few coins and a ten-dollar note. "There," I said coldly, and handed her the ten dollars. She took it without gratitude, still in a huff, and walked away briskly across the road. An oncoming tram narrowly missed her. And I was so angry at being exploited, my vanity was so hurt, that I half wished it had run her down.

And it was not until weeks later that I really forgave her: not until one night when, glancing at Doris as she sat alone in her usual erect, schoolmarm way, I happened to notice with surprise that her eyes were closed, and that there were tears running from under the lids behind the rimless glasses.

"Look," I said, pointing her out to Gwenny. "What's the matter with Doris?"

"It's her children—you know she has two?"

"Yes," I said. "Are they ill or something?"

"No, but she has no money. She's only had one short-time in the last week."

I gave Gwenny ten dollars, asking her to slip them somehow into Doris's bag. It was conscience money because my effort at kindness had been so feeble, and so short-lived—as if one invitation to lunch could cancel out years of bitterness and despair.

Chapter Four

The lunch with Doris had occurred only about ten days after I had moved into the Nam Kok. And it was on that same day that another extraordinary thing happened.

I had been so ruffled by Doris's behavior that my work that afternoon had been worse than indifferent, and at five o'clock I decided to pack up. There was a film I wanted to see at the New York. I couldn't afford it—but what was another couple of dollars after the debacle at lunch? I cleaned my hands with paraffin and then washed them in the basin. I looked round for the towel. It was on the back of the armchair. The seat of the chair was cluttered with odd sketches and drawings, and as I dried my hands my eye fell on the charcoal sketch at the top. It was the sketch of Mee-ling——the little virgin of the ferry.

It was not yet a week since our encounter, and despite the absorbing interest of the Nam Kok she had kept returning to my mind. That round enchanting little face. That look of mischievous innocence. That absurd pony tail—and those knee-length jeans. And only two days ago I had thought I recognized her on the quay, in a crowd of ferry passengers disgorging from the pier. I had been astonished at my own excitement. I had dashed toward her, but had tripped over the gangplank of a junk and sprawled headlong—and by the time I had picked myself up she was being whisked off in a rickshaw. The pain in my shin had not stopped me racing in pursuit. I had shouted her name, and the rickshaw coolie had looked back over his shoulder and slowed his pace.

"Mee-ling!" I had called again.

"Hah?" A girl's puzzled face had looked out of the rickshaw. A fringe and two gold teeth. I had made a mistake.

"I'm awfully sorry—I thought it was somebody else."

"Hah?"

"It doesn't matter."

I had left her staring after me in bewilderment. I had felt very foolish—and my shin had ached all the more because I had hurt it for nothing.

I finished drying my hands, smiling at the caption under the sketch, "Yes, virgin—that's me." I was still musing about her as I left the room. I handed the key to Ah Tong who was talking to the liftman. Somebody was calling the lift from downstairs and there was an angry buzzing. The buzzing became continuous as we rumbled downward. We reached the ground floor and the liftman clanked open the gates. A sailor and a girl were waiting outside, the girl with her hand on the bell-push. She gave it a couple of final jabs to express her indignation at being kept waiting. I had not seen her before during my ten days' residence, but several girls had been away because of illness or because they had "regular" boy friends, and new faces were still turning up. She looked pretty, if at the moment rather cross. I stepped out of the lift. I passed close to her, glancing to see her better—and stopped dead.

"Mee-ling!"

It was absurd, incredible—and yet there could be no mistake. It was Mee-ling. Mee-ling with her hair loose on her shoulders instead of in a pony tail. Mee-ling in a cheongsam instead of jeans. But unquestionably Mee-ling.

She seemed not to hear.

"Mee-ling!" I repeated.

The girl glanced round. She looked at me blankly. She seemed to recognize neither me nor her own name. She turned away and entered the lift, saying something to the liftman in Chinese—it sounded like a passing rebuke for his slackness. The sailor entered behind her. And then there was a loud metallic clank as the gate shut them off.

I stood staring in bewilderment. Well, either that girl is Mee-ling, I thought, or I am going out of my mind. And I turned and went outside.

I walked slowly along the quay, determined to take it calmly. It was true that it was the second time this had happened—but this time it had been different. I had been only a yard from her. And it had been Mee-ling—I was positive.

In that case there were two possibilities. Either she had taken to this profession in the last few days, since our meeting on the ferry, or else everything she had told me on the ferry had been invented.

But no girl who'd been a virgin a week ago would have buzzed so impatiently for the lift—would have been in such a hurry to get upstairs. No, that girl at the lift had known her way around; she could have gone through the routine with her eyes closed. So that ruled out the first possibility.

Therefore everything she told me on the ferry must have been make-believe: the rich father, the five houses, the uncountable number of cars, the arranged marriage. All invented.

But no, that was impossible, I thought. There had been too many convincing details—as when she had said that she enjoyed riding in trams. If it had all been a boast, a fantasy, she would have pretended to disdain trams. Such touches were authentic—she couldn't have been inventing.

So that ruled out the second possibility—and proved that, after all, the girl could not have been Mee-ling. I had again been mistaken.

Well, I must watch my step, I thought. No more accosting, or I'll get a bad reputation. And with this matter settled, I walked up to Hennessy Road and took a tram along to the cinema.

I walked back after the cinema. It was nearly ten o'clock when I reached the quay, but many of the shops were still open. There was a busy noise of sewing machines coming from the shirt maker's. Four thin young men in shirt sleeves were working at the back under a naked bulb. In the workshop next door a man was welding: the bright white glare of the welding torch threw shadows among the ceiling-high stacks of metal junk. Farther on a red neon sign glowed over a lighted doorway. There was a great clatter like the noise of a factory that grew deafening as I approached—the most familiar noise of the Hong Kong night, the noise of mah-jongg. I glanced inside at the packed smoky room, where the players sat clicking the white bricks on the hard-topped tables. The clatter faded as I walked on. I passed the naval tailor's with the glass window and the fat beaming proprietor in the doorway and the blackboard beside him with WELCOME TO ALL MEMBERS OF in white paint at the top, and three numbers chalked below—the numbers of the three American ships in port. There were a few more shops and then the blue neon sign of the Nam Kok. I could see Minnie Ho standing like a stray kitten outside the bar entrance. I knew that as soon as she noticed me she would say, "Oh, Robert! Please will you take me in!" It was a cry I heard several times a day, because the girls were not allowed to enter the bar without an escort: thus could the law be technically satisfied that they were not entering for the purpose of soliciting, and that the Nam Kok was not a brothel. The bar manager insisted on meticulous observance of the rule, and would shoo out any girl who tried to slip in unnoticed without a man. My frequent presence had thus become very useful to the girls. In the mornings they would peer through the glass door to see if I was in the bar, and then tap on the glass to attract my attention, and I would go out and escort them inside—sometimes half a dozen at once. It saved them the long dreary wait for the first sailor to appear.

Minnie suddenly recognized me approaching.

"Oh, Robert! Please will you take me in!" It was like a kitten's plaintive mew.

"All right, Minnie."

The moment I came within reach she entwined herself round my arm and snuggled against me, sighing, "Oh, Robert, you are sweet," infinitely grateful and relieved because loneliness had been ended, human contact restored. I pushed open the door and we went inside. The bar was crowded and very noisy and there were several near-drunks. Minnie spotted a familiar face, squeezed against me gratefully, kissed the tips of two fingers, transferred the kiss to the tip of my nose, giggled, and made off.

I saw Gwenny sitting with some Americans. I sat down at the emptiest table, occupied by only one matelot who was slumped forward with his face buried in his arms. I caught the waiter as he passed and said, "Small San Mig."

The sailor lifted his bleary face.

"Fred?" he said. He tried to focus his eyes.

"Sorry," I said.

"Where's Fred? Where's my mate?"

"I don't know, I've only just come."

"Fred's my mate. We're like brothers, we are, Fred and me." An American sailor knocked against the table. "Fred?"

The American went on. The matelot grunted and his eyes began to close again inexorably. He dropped his face back onto his arms. Just then I noticed the girl I had seen getting into the lift. She was sitting with an American sailor on the bench seat of an alcove table, making teasingly amorous play with him. She entwined his arm and took his hand, pretending to read his palm. She looked less like Mee-ling now. It was true that there was a similarity in the round smooth face and the black ellipses of the eyes—she was probably also a northerner. But it was absurd of me to have made the mistake.

A girl was squeezing behind my chair. It was Fifi, the comedienne.

"Hey, *Chow-fan,* you're too fat," she grinned at me. *Chow-fan* meant fried rice. It was her nickname for me because I practically lived on it.

"Fifi, who's that girl over there?" I asked her, indicating the girl I had mistaken for Mee-ling.

"That girl? Suzie."

"Oh, it's *Suzie!*"

"Sure, she's just come back. Her regular boy friend went off this morning. Why, you like her?"

"No, I just wondered."

"If you want a girl friend, you take me," she grinned.

"You'd make me laugh too much, Fifi."

"Well, what else you go to bed for? Not that same dirty business like everybody else?"

"Get off with you."

So it was Suzie. Gwenny's girl friend. In fact Gwenny's heroine—because twice when there had been long spells with no ships, and business had been in the doldrums, she had helped Gwenny out financially: she was one of the girls most in demand, and made two or three times as much money as Gwenny herself. Gwenny adored her and had never stopped singing her praises to me. She had been longing for Suzie's return so that she could introduce us: she had been away over a fortnight, devoting herself to a boy friend whose ship was undergoing repairs.

Just then Gwenny came over to join me. She sat down next to the matelot slumped over the table; he was groaning now but she did not notice. She was too excited.

"My girl friend's back," she said. "You know—Suzie. She's back."

"Yes, over there—I've seen her," I said.

"You haven't spoken to her yet?" She looked anxious.

"Oh, no."

She smiled in relief: she had so looked forward to introducing us, to showing us off to each other. "What do you think of her? Don't you think she is pretty?"

I looked across at the girl again. The American had been seized by sudden violent passion and was thrusting her back into the corner to kiss her and the girl was struggling, though only half-heartedly as if she found it no more than tiresome. There was not much to be seen of her but her kicking legs and her thigh through the split skirt. I laughed. "Well, she's got beautiful legs, anyhow."

"But don't you think she is the prettiest girl in the bar?"

"Well, I don't know . . ."

"Oh, she is! She is lovely! You will see when I introduce you!"

The black-suited manager limped hurriedly toward them. In the bar the decencies had to be preserved—they were sailing close enough to the wind without this kind of thing. He tapped the sailor on the shoulder, nervously grinning: he knew how easily sailors turned nasty. He reserved the scolding for Suzie, shook an admonishing finger at her. Suzie expostulated. The sailor waved a big weary hand and cocked his head at the ceiling, as if saying, "Oh, beat it—we're going upstairs in a minute anyhow." The manager retired, satisfied. Suzie looked fed up, snapped open her bag, began to dab at her face. The sailor leaned to kiss the side of her neck. She brushed him off irritably.

"She has a temper," Gwenny said proudly. And she giggled, "Once she threw a beer bottle at a sailor. He was a terrible brute—it was very brave of her."

"Did she miss?"

"Oh no, she hit him. Here, on the forehead. He was knocked out for ten minutes."

"What did he say when he came round?"

"He made the manager telephone to the police. The manager pretended to telephone, but put his finger somewhere so that the telephone did not work, because he likes Suzie very much."

"Is she sad that her boy friend's gone?"

"Oh, yes, of course. She said he was not particularly nice—but she was very sad."

"Why, if he wasn't nice?"

"Well, it is much better to have only one boy friend, even if he is not very nice. She hated coming back to the bar. You know what she said to me this morning? She said, 'Gwenny, you don't know how I hate short-times—I wish there was a law against them!'"

"Perhaps that's why she looked so fed up when I saw her going upstairs this afternoon," I said. I watched Suzie and the American approaching. She looked more like Mee-ling again when she was standing up, and I had another momentary start of uncertainty. Then I saw she was taller. Of course—much taller. She led the way between the tables. She looked very bored and as though oblivious of the American following behind.

"But you didn't speak to her this afternoon?" Gwenny said.

"Not really," I said. "Only a word—I'd thought for a moment she was a girl I'd met on the ferry."

"But she wasn't?"

"No, not by a long chalk," I laughed. "The girl on the ferry was a very diff—"

I suddenly broke off. Because at that moment Suzie, passing the table at which Typhoo was irrepressibly holding forth, had picked a drinking-straw from a bunch on the service table and flippantly planted it, unnoticed, in Typhoo's hair—and then turned away with a mischievous giggle.

And it was Mee-ling giggling as she watched me crack melon seeds. Mee-ling giggling as she said good-by on the quay.

It was Mee-ling.

I knew it now beyond doubt. Suzie was Mee-ling.

"Gwenny, what's her real name?" I asked, though I already knew the answer.

"Suzie Wong."

"I mean her real Chinese name."

"Wong Mee-ling."

Yes, of course. Wong Mee-ling. The girl who was forbidden to speak to sailors. I might have guessed it before from that little touch. It was the first thing she'd know about good girls, that they didn't speak to sailors.

Gwenny noticed them as they went out through the swing door into the hall.

"Oh, what a pity, they're going upstairs," she said. "Never mind, I'll introduce you when she comes down. I expect she's only gone up for a short-time."

I remembered my sketch of Mee-ling, and her wide innocent eyes as she had pointed to herself saying, "Yes, virgin—that's me." And now she had gone up for a short-time. I burst out laughing.

Gwenny looked at me in surprise.

"What's the matter?" she said.

"Nothing, Gwenny—except that I'm such an awful fool. And I'd always rather prided myself on being able to see into people's souls!"

"I think you are very understanding."

"Well, I'm trusting, anyhow," I laughed. "You could have told me you were Mme. Chiang Kai-shek and I'd have swallowed it, Gwenny. That's one thing about me—I'll swallow anything I'm told."

II

Actually Suzie Wong, alias Wong Mee-ling, did not reappear that night after all, and I did not see her again until the next morning, when she came into the bar about lunchtime. She was dressed exactly as she had been dressed on the ferry, in the green denim jeans and her hair in a pony tail. I suspected that this was no accident, but a gesture of defiance.

She sauntered past my table, pretending not to see me.

"Suzie!"

She took no notice but went on. However, Suzie's behavior was full of surprises, and a few minutes later she sauntered up again of her own accord.

"You mind if I sit down?"

"Of course not, Suzie."

Her manner neither admitted nor denied recognition. Her face was expressionless. I had often thought how absurd was the popular Western notion of Chinese inscrutability—many Chinese were positively Gallic in their vivacity of expression—but now Suzie came close to it. Only her eyes belied her casual indifference. I could see the deep and careful thought going on behind them.

"You live in this hotel?" she asked in a polite automatic tone.

"Yes, that's right."

"What floor?"

"Third."

"What room number?"

"Three-one-six."

"I know, corner room," she nodded. "You like it here?"

"I like it very much."

"How long you stay?"

She kept up the polite trivialities for several minutes, then all at once switched to another key.

"All right." She held me with a bold, level gaze. "You know something? I told you lies on that boat. All lies."

This sudden interruption of the trivial evasions with absolute bluntness took me aback, though later I was to grow used to it. It was her standard form of procedure when there was anything on her mind: first the five minutes of preliminaries, then all at once that bold direct gaze and the blunt announcement. The gaze was always quite unflinching and would be maintained for minutes on end. I had never known anybody with a more direct look than Suzie. It was one of the reasons that I found her so difficult to deceive.

"Well, don't worry about it, Suzie," I said. "I'm always telling lies. I don't mind a bit."

"You know why I told those lies?"

"You don't have to explain unless you want."

"Yes, I want." Her eyes held mine evenly. "You ever go to the cinema?"

"The cinema? Yes, often."

"Then say one day you go to the cinema and see a film. And the hero-man is very rich. Very good-looking. And he has a big car. And a beautiful girl friend. And they go into the mountains where everything looks beautiful—and there is snow. And they are very happy. All right. You believe everything true?"

"I believe while I'm watching it," I said. "I believe enough to enjoy it."

"Yes. Only you know the hero-man is only pretending. You know maybe from the newspaper that really he is very unhappy—just got divorce from his wife. And you know the film was made up in somebody's head. You know it is just a story, like Chinese opera. You believe—but you don't believe."

"That's quite true, Suzie."

"All right. So sometimes I make up a story in my head. And I believe—and I don't believe."

And she went on to elaborate this explanation with a lucidity that took my breath away. She had known exactly what she was doing. What was she in reality? A social outcast engaged in a dirty job; a bad girl who could never get married. And what did she want to be? A rich girl of good family; a good girl with virginity intact and marriage in store. And playing this fantasy role with a stranger, and making him believe in it, she could believe in it herself—believe in it enough to supply authentic detail, like the rich girl's enjoyment of riding in tramcars. Believe in it in the same way that she could believe in a film. Believe—and not believe.

"But you never did a dirty job like me," she said when she had finished. "I don't think you understand."

"Of course I understand, Suzie."

"No." She had suddenly withdrawn again, as if regretting what she had told me. She looked almost hostile. "I don't think so. You're a big man. Good class—I know. You never understand."

"But everybody makes up stories for themselves, Suzie," I said. "We're all pretending to ourselves all the time about something or other—only we're not usually honest enough to admit it like you."

She gave me a shrewd, watchful look from the corner of her eye. I suddenly realized that there had been a hint of patronization in my tone: the blessedly tolerant fellow from a superior world patronizing the clever little water-front whore—oh, damn nice girls, some of 'em, damn nice!

Awful!

And she had caught it. She was as sharp as blazes, the little smooth-faced mischievously innocent Suzie-Mee-ling. She had caught it all right.

"No." She shook her head. "You never understand."

"Well, perhaps not, Suzie. Anyhow, let's have some lunch."

"No."

I laughed. "I'm not letting you off this time. I've learned my lesson."

She eyed me suspiciously. "Why you want to invite me?"

"Why? Well, I don't know. I suppose because I rather like you."

"No—you lie."

"Really? And how do you know if I like you or not?"

"You like Mee-ling. You like that virgin girl on the boat. But I'm Suzie. I do dirty job. Go upstairs with sailors."

"That doesn't stop you feeling hungry," I said. "Come on, what shall we eat?"

But she went on, determined now to rub my nose in it. "You know how long I do this job? Six years—since seventeen years old."

"That makes you twenty-three. You don't look it, Suzie."

"Six years. Six years I go with men—make 'lovely.'" She used the pidgin expression to make it sound worse.

"There must have been an awful lot of men in that time. I wonder how many?"

"I don't know. I never counted. Maybe two thousand."

"Good Lord!" I laughed.

"Why you laugh?"

"You must admit, it's terribly funny, Suzie. I mean, that you really took me in about being a virgin—and now you tell me you've made love with two thousand men!"

"Maybe three thousand—four thousand."

"Well, I can only say that more women ought to try it, because you look marvelous on it. I suppose it's partly that indestructible Chinese complexion. Look at you, that lovely smooth skin!"

"Yes—smooth. So you can't see how much dirt inside."

"Oh, stop it, Suzie! Come on, I want to try a new dish—what do you recommend?"

"I don't know. I go now."

"Suzie, sit down."

"No, I got my job to do. I got to make 'lovey-lovey.' You go and find Mee-ling—go and find virgin girl."

And she went off and sat down with an American Negro sailor who had just come into the bar.

III

The next evening at ten o'clock my telephone rang.

"Hello, this is Molly."

"Who?"

"Molly." There were voices and music in the background that sounded like the bar downstairs, but I knew no girl of that name at the Nam Kok. And the voice continued, "What, you forget me already? You catch me last week!"

"It certainly wasn't me."

"Yes! Make lovey all night!"

"I did nothing of the kind!"

"Yes, you just forget! Butterfly! Catch too many girls!" There was a splutter of delighted giggles, followed by a clatter as the receiver was dropped. Then another clatter as it was picked up again.

"Hello, this is Gwenny," said Gwenny's familiar voice. "That was Suzie—did you guess? We were just having a joke."

"Well, I'm delighted," I laughed. "I didn't know that Suzie and I were even on speaking terms."

"Oh yes, I have told her you are really very nice and not stuck-up, and she is sorry about yesterday. Now she would like to see you." Her voice abruptly faded as the receiver was snatched from her hand.

"Hello," said the first voice, cheekily pleased with itself. "What are you doing now?"

"Nothing."

"All right. I come and see you."

When she appeared, about twenty minutes later, the cheeky high spirits of the telephone call had deserted her, though for a time she tried to maintain the mood artificially, sauntering round the room and inspecting its contents with a rather false bravado, demanding, "What's that for?" and

"How much did that cost?" She was wearing a silk cheongsam with high, tight-fitting collar, which although very smart was too sophisticated for her: I thought the pony tail and jeans better suited to her style. She had also put on too much make-up, and I suspected that this titivation accounted for the delay in her coming upstairs. I wondered rather uncomfortably if she was out to impress me.

I poured out two glasses of tea and we took them onto the balcony, leaning on the balustrade to look at the lights of the harbor. She fell silent. We watched two ferryboats crawling towards each other like luminous caterpillars. Their noses appeared to join as they drew level and they became a single long caterpillar that rapidly contracted to the length of one, expanded again, then was torn apart in the middle. The two halves crawled away in opposite directions. We turned our attention to the Peak, picking out the moving light of the Peak tramcar as it began its descent from the top. Lower down the escarpment the thickly clustered lights were like a cascade of jewels tipped from a casket. And below was the great glittering jewel heap of Hong Kong, fringed by the emeralds, rubies, and sapphires of neon along the water front.

"I go now," Suzie said.

"But you've only just come."

"I got to work, you know. Maybe I can get two more short-times tonight." She was laying it on thick again.

"Why did you come up and see me, Suzie?" I asked, puzzled.

She shrugged evasively. "No reason. I just get tired of that bar sometimes. Too much smoke. It gives me headache." She turned off the balcony, but halfway across the room paused as her eye fell on something under my bed. "What's that? Gramophone?"

"No, it's a tape recorder." It was an obsolescent model that I hired very cheaply for practicing Chinese intonation, though my use of it had been sadly sporadic.

"What's it for?"

"Well, it's like a gramophone, but you make your own records."

She nodded indifferently, not taking it in; she had lost interest. However, I thought the tape recorder might break the ice and I pulled it out from under the bed, opened the lid, attached the lead from the microphone on the dressing table, and switched on. Soon the quivering green light appeared. I switched over to "Recording" and the reels of tape began to revolve.

"I know," Suzie said. "Cinema. You make film."

"No, it's not film."

"I go now."

"Wait just a moment."

I kept her talking for another minute or two about going to the cinema, then reversed the tape and switched over to "Loudspeaker." I had run the tape back too far and first there issued a series of curious noises like bad farmyard imitations, which Suzie clearly failed to recognize as my attempts to master the elusive Chinese tones. They stopped abruptly. There was crackling. Then Suzie's voice said, "I know. Cinema. You make film."

A queer sigh. Then a pause—one of those pauses that make you wonder, when listening to recorded conversation, what on earth you could have been doing. And then my voice said, "No, it's not film."

"I go now," said Suzie's voice.

Suzie gazed blankly at the instrument. She had not yet recognized the voices distorted by the loudspeaker.

"Radio?" she said.

"No, Suzie. That's us."

I pointed to the microphone. She had seen plenty of microphones in films and understood at once. She glanced back sharply at the recorder.

"Yes, I go often," her voice was saying, "I go to the Roxy, Princes, Majestic, New York—every cinema."

She looked startled.

"Me?" she said. "That's me?"

"Yes."

She listened in disbelief—for nothing sounds more improbable than one's own voice when heard for the first time; it might be the voice of a perfect stranger, and it is a shock to realize that this stranger has been one's spokesman all one's life. Then she giggled, beginning to enjoy herself; but at that moment there was a perfunctory oscillation and the voices stopped.

"Finish?" she inquired anxiously.

"You can hear it again if you like."

"Yes—again."

I reset the tape and once more our conversation began to unfold. Suzie sat on the edge of the bed clutching a pillow to stop herself giggling. However, it was too much for her: soon her giggles were out of control and she was rolling about on the bed with her face buried in the pillow, and I was laughing helplessly in sympathy.

The recording ended and she looked up from the pillow, pink with merriment.

"Again!"

"Let's do another, Suzie. Can you sing?"

"Yes, I know Pekin songs, Shanghai songs—plenty of songs."

She became serious, required a private rehearsal, and scuttled out onto the balcony, shutting the door behind her so that I should not hear. Ten minutes later she reappeared.

"I sing you a Pekin country song," she announced. "It's about a boy cloud who falls in love with a girl cloud. But the girl cloud says, 'You're no good—you've not got a good heart. I wait for some boy with a good heart.' So the boy cloud feels very sad. He starts to cry, and his tears make rain—because that's all rain is, just a cloud crying. Well, down below sits an old man. He is very hungry, because there is no water for the rice paddy. The soil is hard like stone. The rice will not grow. Then he sees the rain falling down. He feels happy. So the girl cloud tells the boy cloud, 'You did a good thing. Maybe you're not so bad as I thought.' So in the end they get married."

She was nervous in front of the microphone, and after listening, head cocked critically, to the playback of her first attempt, she said "No good. I sing again."

And the second time she sang charmingly, in a funny high-pitched little voice that went on and on, with that characteristic monotony of Mandarin songs. She listened to the playback, decided she could do no better, and promptly lost interest in the recorder. But it had done its job—the ice was broken.

We drank tea and chattered.

"I show you my room sometime," she said, sitting on the edge of the bed swinging her legs. "Then you can see my baby."

"Your *baby?*"

"Yes, very nice baby."

"But Suzie, don't be ridiculous!" I laughed. "It's not your *own?*"

"Yes—my baby. Half-caste."

"Who was the father, Suzie?"

"My boy friend. English policeman—only he disappeared off to Borneo."

"But is it a boy or a girl?"

"Boy—very good-looking. Soon one year old. I like him very much."

"I'm sure you do."

"Yes. Some girls don't like half-caste baby. They give away. But I like my baby. I will never give him away."

"And who looks after him when you're working?"

"My amah. Oh yes, I pay her plenty of money, my amah." She looked worried. "Only my baby coughs too much, you know. Cough-cough! Cough-cough! You think my amah leaves him in a draft?"

"I don't know, Suzie."

"I think so. I think she leaves him in a draft."

Presently I rang the bell for a fresh supply of tea, and Ah Tong came in with a new teapot. While he was exchanging it for the old teapot in the padded container I noticed Suzie stealing glances at me from the corner of her eye, as if estimating my state of readiness to bear something that she had to say. Ah Tong departed, closing the door. Suzie chattered inconsequentially for another minute or two, then broke off and fixed me with that level gaze. "You know why I come to your room?" she said.

"I've no idea, Suzie."

"Then I will tell you. This evening I go upstairs with a sailor, come down again, say good-by in the hall. I come back into the bar. Another sailor pulls my arm. 'Yum-yum,' he says. 'Pretty girl! Come and sit on my knee.' I sit on his knee. 'Yum-yum,' he says. 'How much for short-time?' I say, 'Hundred dollars.'"

"That was a bit steep!"

"Yes—steep. So he says, 'Go to hell.' Good. I get off his knee. I go and sit down with Gwenny. 'Suzie, what's the matter?' she says. 'You unhappy?' I say, 'Yes—unhappy.' I tell her I don't like sailor who says 'Yum-yum.' I don't like short-time. I like a regular boy friend, like I had last week. Same boy every day. Then Gwenny says, 'Suzie, you know something? I think

Robert likes you. I think he likes you very much.' We begin to laugh. We ring you on the telephone. I come upstairs—and feel scared."

"Why did you feel scared, Suzie?"

"I think, 'This Robert, he's a big man. Important. He has nice hair-brush. Nice pyjama. Nice everything. He doesn't want dirty little yum-yum girl.' I want to run away. Then you play the machine. I laugh—stop feeling scared."

"And stop feeling like a dirty little yum-yum girl?"

"No, still feel like dirty little yum-yum girl. Only I think, 'If he likes me, good. If he doesn't like me, then nothing to do.' All right. You like me?"

"I like you very much, Suzie."

"Then you like me for regular girl friend?"

I laughed. "If I had any girl friend, Suzie, I'd have you. But I can't afford one."

"I'd work for you very cheap. One month—six hundred dollars."

"But Suzie, that's a fortune!"

"I'd work very hard—come any time you want. Never go with other boy friends."

"I know, but I couldn't nearly afford it."

She looked thoughtful, making some calculation on her fingers. "All right—I come for five hundred dollars."

"Suzie, I'll tell you the truth," I said. "I'm not really a big man at all. I'm terribly poor—I've only got six hundred dollars a month to live on altogether."

She stared at me. "Six hundred? A month?"

"Yes, a month."

"That all?"

"That's all."

"For room? Chow? Everything?"

"Everything."

"Then no good."

"No."

"No." And she sat looking crestfallen, picking disconsolately at her nails. A minute went by. Then she looked up. "All right. You like me to stay tonight?"

"I can't afford even that, Suzie." My budget had not yet recovered from the lunch with Doris.

"I like you," she said. "You're good man. I stay for nothing."

"Suzie, it's terribly sweet of you," I said. "And I'm very tempted. But I'd only make myself miserable. I couldn't bear it tomorrow, when I'd have to sit and watch you going upstairs with sailors."

"Then I go now."

She got up. I went with her to the door.

"You're not going down to the bar again, Suzie?" I said.

"No."

"Where are you going?"

"Home—see my baby. I get worried about his cough."

She went off down the corridor. The lift gate clanked open and Typhoo came out, fumbling in her bag for her clinic card. A matelot came out behind her. He stood waiting while Ah Tong inspected Typhoo's card, making an entry in his ledger. He watched Suzie approaching, a cigarette drooping from his mouth, his eyes narrowed against the smoke. His eyes roved up and down her figure; he was comparing her with Typhoo, wondering if she might have suited him better. Suzie disappeared into the lift. The gates clanked behind her. The matelot turned back to Typhoo.

I went back into my room. I heard Typhoo and the matelot come down the corridor and enter the room opposite. The door banged shut. I could still hear their muffled chatter through the slatted ventilators in the walls. I started the tape recorder. Suzie's high-pitched monotonous little voice began to sing the Mandarin song.

"The boy cloud feels very sad, so he starts to cry. That's all rain is, just a cloud crying. . . . So in the end they get married."

I got into bed. I was glad she had not gone back to the bar. I would have to get used to it, of course. But I was glad she had not gone tonight.

Chapter Five

Suzie thereafter would drop in at my room at all hours of the day and night—and when she was not dropping in she would be telephoning.

The telephone calls were made for no reason at all, except that she had a passion for telephones and could not see one without itching to use it. She would ring me from all over Hong Kong.

"Hello! This is Molly!" The Molly joke was perennial and growing increasingly vulgar.

"Hello, Molly."

"You gave me a bad time last night!" (She always shouted on the telephone, and I had to hold the instrument six inches from my ear.) "You're too big for a little Chinese girl! Yes! You nearly killed me!"

"Really, Molly? I noticed you didn't complain last night."

"You kept me too busy!" She giggled, then abruptly abandoned Molly and became Suzie again. "I just been to the Roxy with my boy friend. He's waiting outside the shop. All right. I go now."

In the bar she claimed me as her "No. 1 boy friend" and was inclined to monopolize me; and (shades of Stella!) she would regard with deep suspicion any girl whom I appeared to favor in my sketching. The other girls naturally supposed, from her visits to my room, that our relationship was more than platonic, and this was the source of much gratification to her pride. She begged me not to disillusion them, and was very hurt when I would not promise. But I did not care to live under false pretenses; and moreover I wanted to remain on friendly terms with them all. I began to find her possessiveness a little irksome.

Then a new girl called Betty Lau came to work in the bar. Betty was

Cantonese, though very westernized, and had modeled herself very obviously on an American film star who was famous for her waggling behind. She had achieved her object with considerable success: as she teetered along on her too high heels, her posterior undulated in so striking a manner that it drew whistles, catcalls, and hilarious remarks from the sailors, and provoked the comedienne Fifi into comical imitations. It was hypnotic. One stared in fascination, wondering how it was done: how she always managed to maintain that rhythmical slow-motion.

One day, after Betty's behind had just waggled past our table, Suzie asked me what I thought of this most unorthodox manner of progression. And failing to take warning from her watchful look, I told her that although it was so exaggerated as to be almost grotesque, my baser nature found it distinctly provocative.

Suzie was silent. And for a chatterbox like Suzie this foreboded ill. Betty had clearly fallen under suspicion.

Two days later I was drinking a San Mig before lunch when Betty, to whom I had never spoken before, sat down at my table. She fluttered her big curled eyelashes, laid a hand caressingly on my arm, and purred that she had heard of my reputation for aiding girls in trouble. I wondered in alarm what was coming next. Was she going to ask for money? Or for my help in procuring an abortion? And I muttered that my reputation had been acquired by nothing more than handing out codeine tablets for headaches.

However, my fears were at once dispelled; the big vamp act had been a steam hammer for driving in a nail. Her trouble was nothing more serious than a Northern Irish five-pound note, which she had accepted from a sailor only to find that the moneychangers would not change it. Could I help?

I offered to try my own bank, which duly obliged me the next day by exchanging the note for seventy-six dollars. I handed these over to Betty in the bar, taking care to do so while Suzie was absent, since I had already foreseen how easily this transaction might be misconstrued. However, the precaution was not enough, for a few hours later my telephone rang.

"Hello. This is Suzie."

Not Molly—that was bad.

"Hello, Suzie."

"What are you doing now?"

"Nothing."

"All right. I come and see you."

And for five minutes after entering the room she made trivial conversation, watching me from the corner of her eye. Then the direct, level look.

"You go with that Canton girl. I know everything."

"What Canton girl?" I asked innocently.

"That girl with the show-off walk. You give her seventy-six dollars."

It was typical of Suzie's careful mind that she should know the exact amount. News of the payment, I gathered, had spread round the bar, and Betty, who was a mischief-maker, had no doubt been only too delighted to let it give a wrong impression. I told Suzie the truth but she refused to believe me.

"You lie! You make love to that Canton girl!"

Her anger unbottled itself and she became a little tornado, abusing me with words picked up from sailors that I had never heard her use before. I continued to deny the accusation, and she hurled a glass at me. It exploded on the wall over the bed, scattering the bed with fragments.

"You lie! I thought you were a big man—important! But I made mistake! You're just butterfly—no good!"

"Suzie, this is ridiculous," I said. "I'm not even your proper boy friend, and you've no right to behave as if you owned me. I don't like it."

"Now you speak truth—you don't want me! You think me dirty little yum-yum girl! All right—finish! I go!" And she went.

That night she cut me in the bar. The next morning, meeting her on the quay as she was coming to the Nam Kok, I started to speak to her, but she averted her face and stalked past. This went on for several days and I found myself missing her telephone calls and visits. I realized how fond of her I had grown.

Then one morning, turning out a pocket, I came across a slip of paper from the bank recording the transaction with the five-pound note. I had forgotten ever receiving it. I rang for Ah Tong and asked him to write me some Chinese characters, which I copied onto the back of the bank slip.

They meant "I miss you very much." And that evening I gave the slip to Gwenny, to pass on to Suzie.

An hour later my telephone rang.

"Hello, this is Suzie."

"Hello, Suzie."

"What are you doing?"

"Nothing."

"All right. I come and see you."

And once more there were the five minutes of preliminaries, followed by the straight, frank look.

"You're a good man. No lie. I make mistake."

I laughed and said that I could not care less about Betty Lau. Then she explained solemnly why she had been so upset: after she had claimed me as her boy friend, my apparent liaison with Betty had caused her serious loss of face.

"I felt scared to go inside the bar, you know," she said. "I felt too much shame. I thought, 'Except for my baby, I'd kill myself!'"

"Suzie, you didn't!"

"Yes, I was so ashamed."

"Well, come and look what I've been doing."

And I showed her the oil painting of her that I was making from a sketch. The size of the canvas impressed her, and the prospect of bringing her girl friends to see it made up for the humiliation she had undergone. She became herself again. She gave a sudden mischievous giggle as she remembered throwing the glass at me.

"I nearly hit you! Whoosh!"

"Yes, and I've been pulling splinters out of myself ever since."

The giggles overcame her. She rolled about on the bed in delight.

"I bet you were chokka! You still chokka with me?"

"Yes, you little devil—thoroughly chokka," I said.

II

Sometimes in the mornings she brought her baby to see me. It was rather a puny, pathetic little infant, with something quite heart-rending about its sallow Chinese-English face; and it looked not young but middle-aged, with an expression, in repose, of bewildered despair. It was as if it knew that it was a half-caste and had nothing to look forward to except a lifetime of not-belonging.

But Suzie was marvelous with it. She would hold it on her crooked arm with a practiced and motherly ease that never failed to astonish me; it was so incongruous with her unmotherly appearance. The baby would splutter ecstatically, waving a tin rice bowl at the end of its outstretched arm, while Suzie chattered to it adoringly.

"Hey, why you still cough? Why you so naughty? Yes, naughty boy! Only you're so beautiful, I got to forgive you! Oh, yes, you're beautiful baby! Good-looking! Maybe some day you make a film star!"

We would spread a blanket on the balcony and it would crawl about in its red corduroy rompers, which had animals on the front with "Gee-gee," "Moo-cow," stitched underneath in English. And Suzie, crawling behind in her jeans, would pretend to chase it; and when she finally caught it and tickled its ribs, it would nearly choke with delight. Then she would take it down to the old blue-trousered amah waiting outside on the quay, and place it in the sling on the amah's back, where it would fall promptly asleep. She would watch the amah shuffling off, calling, "Good-by, mind you be a good baby! Yes, mind you behave!" And then she would turn and go into the bar.

She would also bring her girl friends up to see me; and with a good deal of showing off would treat them to a conducted tour of my room, showing them my pictures and possessions with emphasis on their imagined value. "This hairbrush—it's real silver, you know." (It wasn't.) "Now I show you my boy friend's cuff links—real gold. Maybe worth three hundred dollars. . . ." And pulling open a drawer, "No, don't worry, my boy friend doesn't mind . . ."

Finally there was the *pièce de résistance,* the tape recorder, on which she had fixed the fictitious price of two thousand dollars rather than admit that it was only hired; and I would be called upon to make a recording of the girl friend's voice while Suzie, behaving as if the machine had been her own invention, stage-managed the performance. Then before the girl friend had begun to feel too much at home in my room Suzie would usher

her out, explaining that I had work to do; and as they went off down the corridor I would hear her saying importantly, "My boy friend's a big man, you know. One day he will get five thousand dollars for those pictures. . . . Oh, no, each!"

And even boy friends would be brought along—usually to break the tedium when she had been engaged for "all night." Thus some unfortunate young matelot with tattooed arms and untidy hair, dragged unwillingly out of bed and dressed only in a singlet, would stand there blinking and bewildered while Suzie gave him the conducted tour, wondering nervously if I was a policeman working under cover. Then she would lose interest in him and start chattering to me, until eventually I would feel so sorry for the matelot, for whom the night had cost half a week's pay packet, that I would pack them off back to their room. On one occasion, however, I became so engrossed in argument with a young American intellectual, a law student on naval service, that we were still talking at five o'clock in the morning. Suzie had long since grown bored and retired to sleep. Finally, after nearly losing our tempers, we shook hands, both confessing that we had been vastly overstating our views. I apologized for keeping him so long away from Suzie.

"It doesn't matter," he said. "I'm not interested in her that way—if you know what I mean."

"No?" I said, astonished. "Then what on earth are you doing with her?"

"Well, it's like this. The boys on the ship think I'm a bit of a prig. So I came along with them tonight, and took a girl just to show them I was a 'regular guy.'"

"Then you'd better not tell them you sat up all night discussing communism," I said.

"You bet I won't. I'll tell them I beat all their records."

But more often, when Suzie had an all-night boy friend, she would simply abandon him and come along by herself for a chat; and if we happened to be hungry she would pick up the telephone and call a near-by restaurant. Fifteen minutes later, notwithstanding that it was two o'clock in the morning, a coolie would arrive at my door with a bamboo carrying pole over his shoulder, from which trays, as on an old-fashioned weighing scale, would be hanging fore and aft; and piled on each tray, in diminishing sizes like the weighing-scale weights, would be anything up to a dozen covered dishes, containing chicken, pork, fish, and innumerable other delicacies of which I never learned either the ingredients or the names; and the coolie would unload them on the veranda table. This delivery of meals to the door, at all hours of the day or night, was a commonplace with the Chinese, and the bill would be fantastically small considering the magnificence of the spread. Suzie would try and pay, since she was gravely concerned over my budget, and sometimes succeeded. If, however, I managed to pay myself, she would always ask me how much I had tipped the coolie.

"Fifty cents," I would have to admit. It was only about seven-pence.

"Too much. I told you before!"

"But he looks so poor, Suzie."

"Yes, and if you give fifty cents to the coolie, that's how you will look soon! You give him twenty cents next time. That'll make him plenty happy."

And it was on one of these late-night visits that I made an astonishing discovery about Suzie. I had received a laundry bill, written in Chinese, the total of which I thought excessive, and I showed it to her and asked her to read out the various items. She glanced at it only briefly.

"Nothing wrong."

"But you don't even know what I sent yet," I said.

"This laundryman is very honest. He never makes mistake."

"Well, I'm sure he's made one this time." She was usually so anxious to see that I was not cheated or overcharged for anything that her indifference puzzled me. "Anyhow, how many shirts has he charged for? And what are all those other items?"

She studied the bill in her hand. Then after a minute she looked up at me with that bold, level gaze that meant she had something difficult to say and I would have to take it or leave it.

"There's something I never told you before, because I felt too ashamed," she said.

"What's that?"

"I can't read."

"What?"

"No. I can't read—can't write."

"Not at *all,* Suzie?"

"No."

I was flabbergasted. This possibility had never even occurred to me. I knew that most of the girls in the bar were literate or semi-literate, and I had taken for granted that Suzie was the same; moreover her manners, her mentality, her very appearance and style, had suggested something more than a humble upbringing. But perhaps I had left out of account that heritage of a great civilization that was shared in some measure by all Chinese alike.

"But I've seen you write your name, Suzie," I said. I remembered her writing it in both Chinese characters and Roman alphabet—inscribing "Suzie" in the latter very laboriously, with the Z disjointed, outsize, and back-to-front.

"Yes, just my name," Suzie said. "Gwenny taught me to write my name."

"But what about that message I wrote you on the bank slip? I suppose Gwenny read that for you, too?"

"Yes. You mean this?" She opened her bag and took out the piece of paper.

"Good Lord, you've still got it!"

"Yes, I keep."

"But what for, Suzie?"

"Because of what you wrote to me. You wrote something beautiful. 'I am very unhappy without you. I miss you.' That's what Gwenny said you wrote." She looked uncertain. "Only perhaps she just made it up."

"No, she didn't, Suzie."

"That's really what you wrote?"

"Yes, really."

"Nobody ever wrote to me like that before."

"Well, I meant it. I did miss you."

"Perhaps you feel different now. Perhaps you won't care about dirty little yum-yum girl who can't read, can't write."

"Suzie, what rubbish!"

"I tried once to learn writing. Two years ago. Only too many thousand characters—too difficult."

"Didn't you ever go to school, Suzie?"

"No, my uncle never sent me to school. He was no good, you know."

And then she began to tell me about her childhood, her life; about how she had come to Hong Kong, how she had started to work at the Nam Kok. Her own father had been quite prosperous, a Shanghai junk owner and trader with business interests in the Philippines, and her only memory of him was saying good-by before his departure for Manila in one of his own junks. Suzie's mother, following the Chinese habit of consulting a fortuneteller before taking any major decision or making a journey, had previously consulted one on his behalf, and the fortuneteller had declared the day inauspicious for him to set sail. She had begged him not to go; but his business interests had outweighed his superstitions, and he had disregarded her pleas. He had never been seen or heard of again. The junk had never reached Manila; it had simply disappeared. It had probably struck a typhoon.

A year later her mother had died in some epidemic. Suzie, then five years old, had been taken into the household of her paternal uncle.

This uncle, a drunkard and good-for-nothing, already had two daughters of his own at school. According to Chinese family tradition he should have treated her equally; but proposing to keep her as servant, he considered education to be superfluous. He had also taken control of her father's business, but must either have sold it or let it go to seed: it had certainly no longer been in his hands when Suzie was grown-up.

Suzie's life in the household was only made tolerable by her uncle's second daughter, a good-natured, easy-going, rather lazy girl called Yu-lan. She was very kind to Suzie, and Suzie adored her. She became the ideal that Suzie longed to emulate.

At the time of the communist revolution in China, Yu-lan was twenty and Suzie four years younger. Soon Yu-lan was drafted into a factory; but finding the work too arduous, she obtained a permit to visit fictitious relatives in Hong Kong. Her departure was a catastrophe for Suzie, who cried for a week.

One day her uncle sent for her and asked her why she was crying.

"Because I love Second Daughter, and miss her now she is gone," Suzie said.

"You should not cry," her uncle said. "You are now grown-up. I did not notice this myself until recently, but it has begun to strike me with some force."

"I do not feel grown-up yet," Suzie said.

"Then I will make it clear to you," her uncle said. "Follow me."

She followed him into another room, where he seduced her, threatening to turn her out of the house if she uttered a sound. She was then sixteen. Her uncle was not drunk at the time.

She was ordered to her uncle's room again the next day, and then at unpredictable intervals. She was too frightened to resist. Meanwhile not only letters but also monthly remittances of fifty dollars were arriving from Yu-lan in Hong Kong. She had found work in a shop and was earning four hundred Hong Kong dollars a month.

Suzie yearned for Yu-lan and her head filled with impossible plans for running away to join her. Then one day her uncle sent for her.

"Tell me," he said. "Have you ever thought of going to join Second Daughter in Hong Kong?"

"Never," Suzie said, terrified. She thought he must have been reading her mind. "Such an idea has never entered my head."

"Then let it enter your head now," her uncle said. "Second Daughter says in this letter that she can get you a job in the same shop as herself, at four hundred Hong Kong dollars a month. And since that is excessive for your own needs, you will doubtless remember your obligation to the relatives who took you in as an orphan, and send home one hundred dollars a month through the Bank of China. This idea appeals to you?"

"It would be hard to leave home," Suzie said, still suspecting a trap.

"It will also be hard to lose you. I shall be sorry in many ways. But it would be selfish to stand in your path when you could be sending your family one hundred Hong Kong dollars a month."

Six months later, after a permit had eventually been obtained for her to leave China, Suzie set off from Shanghai by train. It was the first time in her life that she had been more than a few miles outside the city. She traveled south to Canton, where she changed trains, and a day later arrived at the frontier. She alighted and carried her bag across a suspension bridge. She had left New China behind. She was now in the British colony of Hong Kong.

Another train stood waiting. She squeezed into a carriage that was bursting with men, women, children, and pigs in baskets, feeling like a foreigner, for all her traveling companions gabbled in incomprehensible Cantonese. The train traveled through hilly country that differed little from the country on the other side of the border, with tombs dotted over the slopes and villages and paddy fields in the valleys, and presently pulled into Kowloon. She saw Yu-lan waiting on the station platform, and pushing her way through the crowds and the pigs, and forgetting that restraint was the mark of good manners, she threw herself into Yu-lan's arms with tears of joy. Then Yu-lan, always inclined to extravagance, insisted on taking a taxi, and ten minutes later they were climbing the stairs to her room in Kowloon—a small room, but her own.

Yu-lan spread herself comfortably on the bed and picked at a saucer of melon seeds. Suzie, too excited to sit down, stood looking out of the window at the bustling street. It could almost have been Shanghai.

"How far is the shop where you work?" she asked Yu-lan. "Is it in this street?"

Yu-lan laughed and nibbled at a melon seed. She dropped the shell into the spittoon. She had grown much plumper, though was prettier than ever. She was wearing a cheongsam of pure silk.

"I don't really work in a shop," she said. "I just invented that for the benefit of the family. Actually I did work in a shop for a week, but it was worse than the factory. I was expected to work all day and half the night for a hundred and fifty dollars a month. You can't possibly manage on that—not unless you're prepared to live in a bed-space, in a room with twenty other people. Besides, the shopkeepers don't like Shanghai girls who can't speak their barbarous Cantonese. They treat us like dirt. Luckily I met another Shanghai girl who was working in a dance hall and she introduced me to the manager, and I've been working there ever since. I have spoken to him about you. He was delighted when I told him you were only sixteen—I know you're seventeen now, but I exaggerated a bit—because young girls are popular in the dance halls, and most girls don't start until they're older."

"What is a dance hall?" Suzie asked.

"Like the places they had in Shanghai before the wretched communists closed them down. It's very smart and there's a Filipino band. Only rich men can afford to go. But Hong Kong's full of rich people nowadays. They pay eight dollars an hour for a partner, and the partner gets half. Four dollars an hour—just for dancing!"

"You must make a lot of money in one evening," Suzie said.

"Well, actually it doesn't always work out like that," Yu-lan said. "There are so many girls, and some evenings you don't get picked. You make the real money when you're bought out."

"'Bought out'? What does that mean?"

"Well, if a man likes you and wants to take you out, he pays eight dollars an hour for every hour before the dance hall closes, and of course you get half. Then he gives you dinner, and what he pays you is a private arrangement. It is usually about sixty dollars."

"You mean he pays you sixty dollars just for going out to dinner?"

"You are innocent, aren't you!" Yu-lan laughed good-naturedly. "Oh, no, you have to spend the night with him at a hotel. But it's not as bad as it sounds. The men are usually very nice—especially the northerners, and there are heaps of northerners here since the revolution. I was terrified at first. I hated making love. But now I quite enjoy it. And it always makes me laugh to think I'm getting paid for enjoying myself!"

Suzie said, "I don't think I would ever enjoy making love, Yu-lan." And then, since she could not keep a secret from so dear a friend, she told Yu-lan about her horrible experience with her uncle, who was Yu-lan's father.

Yu-lan was less shocked than Suzie had expected. She seemed to take it almost as a matter of course.

"Oh, my father was always rather a gay dog," she said. "Didn't you know? He spent more money on girls than on drink. You should really blame the Reds for closing down the brothels. I suppose he didn't know where to find a girl and got desperate. Still, it's an awful pity the old brute couldn't contain himself, because virginity's worth a packet if you play your cards right. It's a thousand dollars down the drain."

Suzie said, "Yu-lan, I think I would rather work in a shop."

"You'd soon change your mind if you tried living in Hong Kong on a hundred and fifty dollars a month," Yu-lan said. "And I was forgetting—you don't read or write, so you might not even get a hundred and fifty."

"Couldn't I work in the dance hall but not go and stay with men in hotels?"

"No, that's impossible. It's not supposed to be a pick-up place but of course it is, and the manager would throw you out if he found you weren't obliging the customers." Then she looked anxious. "But I don't want to influence you, Mee-ling. Honestly, I'd hate to feel responsible for you doing something you might regret. You can certainly try working in a shop. And at least you won't have to live in a room with a lot of smelly Cantonese. You can stay here as long as you like. Rent free."

However, that night in bed, when Yu-lan was out at the dance hall, Suzie did some realistic thinking. She considered the blunt fact that she had lost her virginity, that she could never marry. No amount of drudgery in a shop could restore what her uncle had taken from her. Very well, if she was denied the fruits of respectability it was pointless to try and cling to it. There was only one consideration: which was the lesser of the two evils? The drudgery of working in a shop, or the drudgery of making love?

Meanwhile at the dance hall Yu-lan was pleading a headache to a Shanghai businessman in pebble glasses who had made a fortune in Hong Kong putting up jerry-built blocks of flats. He increased his offer from eighty to eighty-five dollars. However, Yu-lan felt she could not abandon the little Mee-ling on her first night in Hong Kong, and fobbed him off with an arrangement for the following Friday. She took a rickshaw back to the room.

She found the little Mee-ling out of bed, gazing into the cheap rickety wardrobe which so unostentatiously housed her collection of beautiful clothes. There were at least a dozen silk cheongsams, several brocade jackets, a reversible jacket that could be worn either with the white lamb's wool outside and the gold-embroidered brocade inside or vice versa, and some Western-style dresses skillfully copied by a Chinese tailor from pictures in an old edition of the magazine *Vogue*.

The little Mee-ling looked boldly into her eyes and said:

"I have made up my mind. I shall work in the dance hall."

Yu-lan regarded her anxiously. "Are you sure? I'm so worried now that it won't suit you. You know, you've got to make love with all sorts of people—even old men, and Cantonese."

"Yes, I know."

"And you don't care?"

"Not if that's how the silly old fools want to spend their money," Meeling said. "I'll just close my eyes and think, 'What a nice easy way to get a new dress.'"

Chapter Six

"Suzie, it's three o'clock," I said. "What about your boy friend?"

She shrugged. "I don't care."

"You don't think he'll make trouble if he wakes up and finds you gone?"

"No, he was passed out, that boy, you know. He just made love once, then he was finished." She was sitting cross-legged on the bed in her jeans. The table by the bed was scattered with the remnants of our Chinese meal: it had been too chilly tonight to eat out on the balcony. "All right. I tell you how I got fired from the dance hall."

"Fired? You didn't really, Suzie? What for?"

"I stole money."

"Good Lord, whose?"

"Oh, lots of people's—I stole everybody's money."

She had entered the new life, it appeared, with violent abandon—burying once and for all her romantic girlhood dreams. She had hated and despised men and thought only of exploiting them. Nevertheless she had been a great success at the dance hall: she had been even more popular than Yu-lan, and seldom spent a night at home; and soon she had acquired several wealthy and regular patrons, including a young Chinese playboy and a Cantonese restaurateur. And one night, observing the restaurateur's wallet sticking out of a pocket of his jacket beside the bed, and her companion to be soundly sleeping, she had stolen six hundred dollars and concealed them in her shoe.

The restaurateur had suspected her of the theft and withdrawn his patronage; but his place had promptly been taken by an ex-minister of Chiang Kai-shek, a sixty-year-old Pekinese. And soon she was robbing her patrons whenever the opportunity occurred. Curiously, however, she had seemed to care more about the actual stealing than about the money itself. The problem of how to pick a companion's wallet would obsess her, she would lie awake all night planning subtle strategies, and perhaps in the end take some absurd and unjustifiable risk—only to tuck the gleanings into some pocket and forget all about them. She had always been coming across such wads of money among her clothes: but for all her pleasure in their discovery they might have been worthless bits of paper.

But if she had been popular with the men at the dance hall, she had been far from popular with the other girls—for at first she had been a little horror. She had flaunted her success, put on airs, considered nobody but herself; she had overdressed, and hung herself with jewelry until she looked like a Christmas tree. She had only been tolerated at all because she was still a baby, still only seventeen: several of them remembered that they themselves had started by going overboard in the same way. Then one night she had relieved the ex-minister of four hundred dollars. It was her second foray into his wallet in less than a week. He had not been able to prove anything, but he had dropped a word into the ear of the dance-hall manager. Suzie had been dismissed.

She had found another job without difficulty—this time on the Hong Kong side, in a dance hall called the Granada. Nevertheless the experience had been salutary. She had been shaken; she had been reminded that not even pretty girls of seventeen could have everything their own way. Her passion for expensive dresses and jewelry had vanished almost as suddenly as it had come. She had settled down to the job as though to any other. It had become mechanical routine.

And then something else had happened to assist the change in her. One night she had been bought out from the dance hall by an Englishman. His name was Alan Muir: he worked in a chemical firm, had a soft, burry, gentle voice, and spoke a smattering of Chinese. He took her to dinner at a restaurant before going to a hotel. However, halfway through the meal he said suddenly, "I've changed my mind. I'm not going to spend the night with you after all."

"Why not?" she asked.

"Because you're too much of the little businesswoman," he smiled. "You wouldn't enjoy it—so nor should I."

The gentleness of his tone was at such variance with his words that it was a moment or two before the insult struck home. Then Suzie's anger flared. She accused him of going back on their agreement, of trying to cheat her of the money.

"Oh, don't worry," he laughed. "I'm going to give you that 'gift' you told me you expected—we can't waste all that bargaining. Here you are. Fifty dollars."

In a way his willingness to pay up made his rejection of her more insulting, but she congratulated herself on getting the money for nothing. However, the next night, when he surprisingly turned up at the Granada again and requested her as partner, she flatly refused. Muir countered by sending for the manager, who reminded her that it was not a prerogative of employees to pick and choose. Sullenly she entered Muir's embrace on the dance floor. But soon, provoked by the humorous teasing of that deceptively gentle voice, her anger suddenly flared again. She tried to break from him, but he held her wrists. She struggled. He caught her up and carried her through the gyrating couples to the edge of the floor—only to find that he had walked straight into the arms of the manager. He grinned.

"Ah, the chap I was looking for," he said. "I want to buy this girl out."

It was only nine o'clock, which meant four hours left to pay for: thirty-two dollars. Suzie was duly given the ticket which entitled her to collect her half-share at the end of the week. However, once outside she told Muir that she would not go another step with him.

"Then I'll call the police," he said. "After all, I've paid a mint of money for you."

"I don't care."

"Anyhow, you've got to have dinner with me for your own sake."

"Why?"

"So that you can tell me how much you hate me."

The dinner ended with Suzie in tears—and secretly hoping that tonight he would take her to a hotel, because she felt strangely drawn to him. But he didn't. He only suggested meeting the next day for lunch.

The lunch was followed by several more daytime meetings; and they became so friendly that when at last he took her out to dinner again, and then afterwards to a hotel for the night, Suzie would not accept any money from him. Nevertheless he slipped fifty dollars into her bag.

The next night they met again. In the morning, when Muir had gone to the bathroom, Suzie noticed his wallet lying on the dressing table. She picked it up as if impelled by some instinct. "What on earth am I doing?" she thought. "What on earth am I doing?" It was as if she was watching somebody else: some stranger over whom she had no control. She opened the wallet and took out three hundred dollars.

Presently Muir returned. He glanced into the wallet before slipping it into his pocket. He must have noticed the missing money but said nothing. He took her hand.

"Sunday tomorrow. Let's drive over to Repulse Bay for a bathe."

She said, "I can't. I'm busy."

"Then you can un-busy yourself, because it'll do you good."

She finally agreed and they parted. She wondered what could have possessed her to take the money. It was the first time she had stolen money since she had been dismissed from the other dance hall—why on earth should she have started on Alan? Then she began to justify the theft to herself. "After all, think of the time I've spent with him," she told herself. "Why shouldn't he pay for it like anybody else?" She decided that he had been unscrupulously taking advantage of her good nature, and that she hated him for it; and the next day, at Repulse Bay, she put herself out to be nasty to him. Her nastiness only seemed to amuse him, and she began to hate him more than ever. She told him exactly what she thought of him.

He laughed. "You know why you're so cross with me, don't you? Because you took that money out of my wallet. But you were worth every cent of it. I don't mind a bit."

"You lie! I never took your money!"

"Of course you did. And I'll tell you why. Not because you wanted it, but because you wanted to punish me. To punish *men*. You hate men, don't you?"

"No."

"Yes, you do. We're all one person to you. I don't know who exactly—but I suspect the man who first seduced you."

She flushed scarlet. It was extraordinary—the blood had rushed to her cheeks before she had even had time to think. And Alan had seen it. He was now looking away, pretending he hadn't—but she had caught his shrewd glance at her face. She was furious.

"Nonsense," she said. "You talk just nonsense. My first boy friend was fine, good-looking—we loved each other very much. Yes! Good man! Good heart! Not like you!"

However, a few days later, when she was in a calmer mood, they talked about it again, and she suddenly found herself telling Alan about her uncle. She agreed that what he had said about hating men was probably true; though once she had said it, it seemed rather ridiculous to judge all men by the same yardstick. And somehow after this she lost interest in wallets. She had never stolen money again—except once at the Nam Kok from a sailor who had cheated her, and that was not really stealing so much as the summary administration of justice.

Her affair with Alan Muir continued, and she realized that for the first time in her life she had fallen in love. And now she wanted to spend all her money on presents for him; she wanted to sacrifice herself for him; she longed desperately to have a child. Her whole personality seemed to melt and glow. And she even enjoyed *making* love with him. Yes, even *making* love, even that act of utter drudgery, had become a pleasure! And indeed on every occasion it became more so; on every occasion Alan's tenderness and consideration drew a greater response, and she felt herself approaching closer to some glittering, tantalizing, mysterious summit. And at last the day arrived when she reached it, and there were great blinding flashes like the lightning you saw over China, and a great cataclysm that shook the earth, and then it was dark, and she was falling and falling and falling through the darkness, and she could hear the burry whisper of Alan's voice in her ear, though she did not know what he was saying until she asked afterwards, "What did you say?"

"I said you must remember today," he said. "It's the day you became a woman."

The day was Thursday. On Saturday they met again and he gave her a gold bangle engraved with their initials and Thursday's date. The next day, Sunday, he was bathing from a Chinese friend's launch when a shark attacked him and tore his right leg to tatters. He died before the launch reached shore.

Alan Muir had been an excellent ambassador for his nation, and thereafter Suzie showed a preference for Englishmen; and whenever they came to the Granada she would put herself forward. A few months after Alan Muir's death she was bought out by a sub-inspector of police who was seeking to make a discreet arrangement, not uncommon among bachelors in the colony, to keep a girl on call. He liked Suzie, and since he had private means and was able to afford exclusive rights, she gave up the Granada to be available as required. She spent most nights at his flat. He was in his mid-thirties, undemonstrative and inclined to brooding, though subject to unpredictable rages. His name was Gerald Parry. He inspired in Suzie no such devotion as Alan Muir. Nevertheless her attachment to him went beyond the purely financial, for her womanhood had been awakened and Parry was currently her man.

Soon she found herself pregnant. It was not by any means for the first time: often enough had she parted with four hundred dollars to a Chinese doctor. But ever since the advent of Alan Muir she had longed for a baby—even a baby that wasn't Alan's. Many of the dance girls had babies, and she had become more and more painfully envious when she heard them discussed. And she decided that this time she could not bear to lose the baby that had started inside her. She would not go for an injection.

She was still sharing the room with Yu-lan in Kowloon, but she said nothing to Yu-lan about the pregnancy; she knew that Yu-lan would think her out of her mind. Nor, for fear of his anger, did she tell Parry—until her secret began to threaten its own revelation. Then she gathered up her courage and broke the news. And she told him that she was determined to keep the child. Even if it meant the end of their relationship; she was going to keep it.

Parry listened and said nothing. He said nothing for two days. He remained brooding and cut off from her, and she waited on tenterhooks for one of those violent outbursts of temper with which his periods of brooding would commonly end. But she was due for a wonderful surprise. For on the third evening, arriving at his flat, she found herself greeted as she had never been greeted before—by a Parry whom she could hardly recognize, a Parry who was grinning, excited, tender, warm. And before she had recovered from her astonishment, he was declaring himself delighted about the child, and delighted even more by her determination to keep it: by her courage, her loyalty, her womanliness. In the past, he explained, he had suffered bitterly at the hands of women. Supposedly respectable women—yet all worthless and deceitful, all trollops. Indeed it was disgust for such a woman that had made him decide to leave England, come to Hong Kong. But now his faith had been restored. Now, at last, in a Chinese dance girl, he had found all those ideal qualities of whose existence he had despaired. He wanted to pay her the tribute she deserved. He wanted to marry her.

"No," Suzie said. "No good."

"No good? Why?"

"You marry Chinese girl, and other English people make trouble. Number One policeman make trouble. He call you to his office. He say, 'Good morning. You're fired!'"

"I'll leave the police," Parry said. "I'll go into business here. I've hundreds of contacts—and there's much more money in it."

Yu-lan was thrilled when she heard Suzie's news. She had never thought Suzie's heart had been in her work—no, she'd really been cut out for motherhood and marriage. And what wonderful fortune—an English husband! Oh, much more tractable than a Chinese husband—none of this trotting off every evening to brothels and dance halls! And she was so excited that she rushed out and bought Suzie an expensive pair of earrings as a wedding present in advance.

And now Parry was full of enthusiastic talk about their future: about where they would live, about how contemptuously he would deal with anybody who tried to snub him for marrying a Chinese. This went on for three or four months. Then Suzie noticed that he was growing less communicative, that he was having those brooding spells again. One night she asked him when he intended to resign from the police, start looking round for another job. He replied impatiently that there was no hurry: he couldn't leave the police, anyhow, until he had completed another half-year. Then he said he was tired. He sent her home.

The next night he sent her home again; and a few nights later, after further brusque dismissals, she turned up at his flat to find it full of luggage and crates.

"Where are you going?" she asked.

"Borneo." He looked at her as if she was a stranger. He took five hundred dollars out of his wallet and handed them to her. "Now get out."

"How long you go to Borneo for?"

"How long? I'm being transferred to the Borneo police—I'm going for good."

"What about getting married?"

"What's that?"

"Getting married."

He stared at her with such a convincing show of bewilderment that Suzie wondered if he had really gone mad and forgotten.

"What the devil are you talking about?" he said.

"You said we get married at English church. Live North Point. Nice flat."

His eyes blazed with anger. "What are you trying on? Blackmail?"

"No blackmail. You're father of my baby."

"That's your story. But I know you dance-hall girls—you're just a bunch of dirty tarts. All right, I'll send you fifty dollars a month for maintenance. Only don't try any funny business, or you'll regret it. Now get out!"

The baby was born two months later. Shortly afterwards she received a money order for fifty dollars. The payment continued for another three months and then stopped. She never heard of Parry again.

Soon after the arrival of Suzie's baby Yu-lan left Hong Kong to take a dance-hall job in Japan. The heyday of the Hong Kong dance halls was passing as the wealthy refugees from New China drifted away to Formosa, and the girls were feeling the pinch; but in Tokyo there was always an opening for Chinese girls, who appealed to exotic tastes. Yu-lan had been recruited along with five other girls by a little Japanese gentleman with a toothbrush moustache, who had made arrangements for their transit by air; and Suzie, prevented by the baby from going herself, said a tearful farewell at the airfield.

Until this time Suzie, who had started work again at the Granada, had continued to share Yu-lan's room in Kowloon—for the obliging and easy-going Yu-lan had thought nothing of the addition of a baby and amah, which indeed by local standards had still left the room luxuriously underpopulated. However, now that Yu-lan had gone Suzie took a room on the Hong Kong side to save the endless ferry crossings. She consulted a fortuneteller about the best day for removal, and moved strictly according to advice. Nevertheless her tenancy of the new room began unluckily: the following day she fell ill with some sort of fever. She grew worse from week to week, and lost all her flesh. She became like a skeleton. She was bedridden for three months.

During this time her savings ran low, and before she had properly recovered she went out to find work again. She took a tram to the Central District to ask for her job back at the Granada. The dance hall was on the sixth floor above a department store. The lift was out of order and she had to walk up the stairs. She arrived feeling dizzy and sick. She noticed that there was a new sign outside the dance hall, although she could not read it. She went in. It had been turned into a restaurant.

After this outing she was in bed for another three weeks. Then the amah left because Suzie could not pay her. There was no food for the baby, no money, and Suzie decided that she would have to sell her only remaining piece of jewelry: the gold bangle given her by Alan Muir on the last occasion they had met. She looked for it, but it had vanished. The amah must have taken it in lieu of wages.

She felt very ill again; but the baby was crying. She went round to a girl friend's room to borrow some money. The girl was out. She returned to the street and hung about on the corner until she was picked up by a coolie from the docks. He paid her two dollars. She was so ashamed of this episode as a "street girl" that she had never told anybody about it before. She had not even told Gwenny.

The next day she found a job in another dance hall. But there was less money nowadays, and more girls; prices had dropped. She made scarcely enough to pay the rent and the new amah.

Then one day in the street she ran into a Shanghai girl she had known at the Granada. The girl, who looked very prosperous, told her that she was now working in a hotel catering for European sailors. She much preferred it to the dance hall. There was no bossy manager to push you around, no time wasted dancing with a man all evening only to find he didn't want you. No messing about at all. You just took the boy upstairs and got on with it.

Suzie asked how long you spent upstairs.

"Oh, just a short-time," the girl said. "Sometimes you go for all night, but you really make more money with several short-times."

Suzie shook her head. She despised the girl for sinking so low. It was really prostituting oneself. The dance-hall girls did not consider themselves to be prostitutes; they were dance partners who were prepared, if they liked a man enough, to extend their favors to the bed for a gift of money. The transaction was performed decorously, with dinner as a preliminary, and was sanctified by the length of time it took: a whole night was the minimum requirement of decency. The dance girls looked down on bar girls, with their unceremonious short-times, just as bar girls looked down on street girls who picked up coolies on corners.

"I don't know how you could bring yourself to do it," Suzie said, conveniently forgetting her own shameful experience in the street.

The girl, who as it happened was Little Alice, giggled unabashed.

"I like it. The sailors are nice and young. Not old dodderers like we used to get at the Granada. I like them young." She glanced down appreciatively at the new pair of shoes that she had just bought herself. "Well, I've got to get on. There are two American ships in this morning. In case you're interested, the hotel's on the water front near the ferry."

Suzie watched her go with a mixture of pity and contempt. However, that night, after hanging about for five hours in the dance hall, she returned to her room with an empty purse. The time had again arrived to face facts. And the next day she consulted a fortuneteller about a favorable day for changing jobs.

The fortuneteller advised against the next few days, the last of the First Moon. He recommended an early day thereafter, reciting to her from his almanac that this day would be good for traveling, starting new studies, putting in doors, buying livestock, burying female relatives, and commencing new business. The luckiest period was between 3 P.M. and 6 P.M. He thought that if she followed this advice she was bound to prosper and attain success in her chosen career.

And thus a week later, on the Third Day of the Second Moon, in the afternoon, Suzie started work at the Nam Kok.

II

She picked absently at the blanket between her crossed legs. "I hated this place at first, you know," she said. "It was very hard. Sometimes I told sailors, 'You find some other girl! You're too dirty for me! Too drunk! Too bad-manners!' So the other girls told me, 'Suzie, you're stuck-up!'"

But she had got used to it. One got used to anything. One started by thinking, "Circumstances may have pitchforked me into this life—but I'm not like the others who belong to it naturally. I shall always be a stranger here. I'm different." Then the life embraced one; became one's world. One became a stranger to the worlds one had left behind.

"Yes, I suppose one can get used to anything," I said, and I thought: like the war. Like all the people who had found themselves in situations that a year or two before would have been unthinkable: living under a sky that had once been so safe, and that now rained bombs; machine-gunning those boys you had drunk beer with at Heidelberg, the brothers of the girls you had kissed at Bonn; cleaning the lavatories you had only expected to have to use. Oh, you could get used to anything, even being a sailor's whore. It would surprise the nice girls how easily they could get used to it if it came to the push; how soon they'd be chattering about positions and prices; how quickly they'd know a sailor who was out for a free fumble from a sailor good for a short-time. How quickly it became their world.

I looked at my watch. Twenty minutes ago Ah Tong had come in for Suzie. Her boy friend had waked up and demanded her return.

"Suzie, hadn't you better go?" I said.

"Soon." She leaned without uncrossing her legs to reach the teapot on the bedside table, and refilled her glass. She sipped the tea, frowning. "My baby still coughs, you know. I get worried."

"Haven't you seen a doctor about him, Suzie?"

"Yes, I took him to hospital. The hospital doctor said, 'Nothing the matter—fine baby!' But he still coughs. Cough-cough! Cough-cough!"

The telephone rang and I picked it up. It was Ah Tong speaking from his desk on the landing. He said that the sailor had been asking for Suzie again, and though he had been very polite and restrained, Ah Tong counseled her return.

"Otherwise, sir," he said, "it will give our house a bad reputation."

"That would never do, Ah Tong," I said.

Suzie rose reluctantly and went to the door.

"I go now."

"He sounds a nice boy, anyhow," I said.

Suzie shrugged indifferently. "Suzie, you're so pretty," she said like a sailor.

"Is that what he told you?"

"All sailors tell me."

"Well, don't you like it?"

"I don't care. Suzie, you're so pretty.' Then he goes away—new sailor comes. 'Suzie, you're so pretty.' What good? I want same man to say that every day, 'Suzie, you're so pretty.' Yes, same man!"

"I say it most days."

"No good. You're not proper boy friend. Don't go to bed."

"Is that so important?"

"Yes—important."

"Well, it's no use thinking about it when I can't afford it."

"I told you before. I don't want money. I go to bed for nothing. But you think, 'No good—she's just come from sailor.'"

"But surely you can understand, Suzie?"

"No. I go with sailor for job. No love. No feeling. Just like holding somebody for dance. Only take off clothes, lie down."

"It's not really the same."

"Yes, same."

"If I made love to you, I'd want to feel you belonged to me. And you wouldn't belong."

"Yes—belong. Go to bed with sailor—nothing happens inside. Nothing happens in heart. Go to bed with you—everything happens. I love. I feel beautiful. I think, 'My man.' You think, 'My girl.' We belong."

"It's not as easy as that."

"Yes, easy. So easy you don't understand." She started to go.

"Suzie, listen—"

"No listen. No good talking—your talk is more clever than dirty little yum-yum girl's. Only dirty little yum-yum girl understands love. You don't understand."

"Suzie, sit down again for a minute."

"No. I go back to sailor. Take off clothes. Give one short-time before ship sails."

"Suzie—"

"No."

And the door slammed and she was gone.

III

And after that I could not sleep but lay awake in the dark, seeing her standing there at the door and hearing her voice in my ears.

"I love. I feel beautiful. I think, 'My man.' You think, 'My girl.' We belong."

The simplicity of it, I thought; the beautiful simplicity. The simplicity of the girl who can't read, who can't write. The simplicity of the uncluttered mind, clean-cutting as a diamond.

And indestructible as a diamond. Undestroyed by two thousand or however-many-it-was men. The part of her they'd never touched. The virginity they'd never taken.

Virginity of heart.

"I love. I feel beautiful. We belong."

And I was so moved by the words that I could have cried. I could be happy with her, I thought; and my head began to fill with all those wild and fantastic notions of the sleepless dreamer in the dark. I would rescue her from the Nam Kok; I would marry her; we would go and live cheaply on one of the neighboring islands—on Cheung Chow, where the bustle and chatter of black-trousered women filled the cobbled village street, and where every evening the fishing junks with billowing sepia sails came gliding one behind the other into the arms of the harbor, and you could go away and return after half an hour and find them still coming in, and they would go on coming in until it was dark and the harbor packed solid. Or we would go and live on the monastery island of Lantao where the leisurely donging of the monastery prayer bell would sound in my ears as I painted, and where we would grow paddy and keep pigs and exchange pleasantries with the Buddhist monks, and where I would think "My girl" and she would think "My man." . . . And I was still awake, the romantic idyl still unfolding itself before me, when the amplified voice from an American warship came echoing across the silent harbor.

"Now hear this. Now hear this."

It was dawn. The stars went out over the mainland. The gray light crept into my room.

"Now hear this."

And like the images on a cinema screen when the light is let in, my idyllic fancies began to fade. I watched the cheap wardrobe, the dressing table, the remnants of our Chinese meal, take shape. Daylight, reality. And I knew that after all I would just carry on with Suzie as before: unless perhaps I tried to overcome my squeamishness about the sailors, and made love to her.

I wondered how it would work. "I suppose it's only a matter of getting used to a new convention—and one can get used to anything," I thought, and fell asleep. But the problem, as it happened, was only academic. The option was no longer open—because that day she met Ben.

2

The Men

Chapter One

Ben Jeffcoat, although Suzie met him at the Nam Kok, was not a sailor. But he had been a sailor during the war—and not just a matelot either. He had commanded a corvette, and had been awarded a D.S.O. for some action in the Atlantic in which he had lost his ship.

I do not know much about this action, since I only heard him mention it once, when he described it as "A jolly good bit of fun, actually. We gave the old Hun quite a time of it." Six months later he had lost a second ship, and had been ten days adrift on a raft. He regarded these ten days in retrospect as the finest experience of his life, since the lonely battle for survival had called into play all the best qualities of manhood.

And Ben set a great store on manhood. He talked about it often. "What the devil's the use of manhood to a civilian? A fat lot of manhood one needs for selling air-conditioners!"

Nevertheless he did very well selling air-conditioners. After the war he had acquired the Hong Kong agency for an English firm that manufactured small one-room units; and he had no sooner set up shop than the influx of refugees from China had started a building boom. Air-conditioning units had been required in vast numbers for new hotels and blocks of flats, and his percentages on sales had totted up to an enviable income. He had bought himself a house on the Peak, an unostentatious but expensive car, and a sailing dinghy for weekends. At thirty-five, he was an established and successful man.

But I knew none of this, of course, when at one o'clock in the morning he first appeared in my room. Suzie had rung up from another room to announce the visit; and when I had protested that it was far too late, she had urgently assured me that her companion was so intelligent and charming, so altogether unusual, that the opportunity of meeting him was not to be missed. She was certain that I would take him to my bosom as a soul mate.

Five minutes later she ushered into my room a tall, broad-shouldered man in tropical suit. He was in early middle age; fair, good-looking, but with features that showed signs of coarsening too early and running to seed. He stood swaying just inside the doorway, eyeing me with bleary hostility. "Humph," he grunted.

Clearly my soul mate was drunk.

I threw Suzie a look that I hoped expressed my displeasure, then steeled myself to the task of playing gracious host. I said, "You're my first civilian. I'm honored."

"Humph."

"My boy friend, Ben," Suzie cheerfully introduced. "I forget his other name." And she launched into an abbreviated version of her conducted tour, hurrying through it like a guide at an historic monument a few minutes before closing time. Ben swayed gently in the middle of the room, withdrawn behind blinking, hooded eyes. I fancied that he was not quite so drunk as he wished to appear: he was embarrassed at being confronted at the Nam Kok by a fellow countryman, and was using the intoxication as a convenient cloak behind which to hide.

Suzie finished the conducted tour abruptly, omitting the tape recorder. She picked up her bag. "All right, I go now."

I stared in alarm. "Go?"

"Yes, I just go to see my baby."

Her eyes twinkled mischievously. It dawned on me at last why she had been so anxious to bring along this great drunken lout: she wanted me to act as nursemaid while she slipped off home. I said, "You little devil!"

"I won't be long—ten minutes."

"But if you're going to your house—"

"Maybe twenty minutes." And she was gone.

I turned to the bleary swaying figure and said, "Come and sit on the balcony. I think it's warm enough." And if it isn't, I thought, so much the better. It'll help sober you up.

He sank into a balcony chair, and I seated myself in another. I asked him politely if he lived in Hong Kong.

"Humph," he said.

I decided on a less personal topic. I remarked that the harbor of Hong Kong was said to be one of the most beautiful in the world.

"Humph."

"Though I believe Rio's even more spectacular," I said. "Have you ever been to Rio?"

He said aggressively, "You're bloody curious, aren't you?"

"I'm awfully sorry."

"Humph."

Silence. I considered the possibility of retiring to bed forthwith, and was on thc point of doing so when he said suddenly, "Christ, I'm pissed. I'm pissed as a newt."

"You look a bit under the weather," I sympathized.

"First time I've been to a place like this." He shot me an aggressive glance. "You don't believe me?"

"Certainly, if you say so."

"I do say so—the first bloody time." Hc noticed his own disagreeable tone, and looked a bit ashamed. He said in a more conciliatory way, "Look, old man, can't we get a drink?"

"Oughtn't you to go steady?"

This was fatal. He exploded again aggressively. "For Christ's sake! Don't start pulling that Liz stuff on me!"

"That *what* stuff?"

"Forget it. Can't we get something sent up?"

It seemed the lesser of two evils, so I rang down to the bar. Presently one of the waiters appeared with a double whisky for Ben and a San Mig for me. Ben gave him a note and told him to keep the change. He began to relax a bit with the whisky in his hand.

"Sorry I'm being such a bastard," he said. "I always get like this when I'm drunk. I suppose that's because when I'm sober I'm the mildest bloody well-behaved bloke you could ever bloody well imagine. It's true, what I told you just now—I've lived in Hong Kong for years, and this is the first time I've ever been in a brothel. First time I've ever mucked about with a Chinese girl. In fact, let's face it, I've been a model husband to old Liz."

"So Liz is your wife."

"With a bloody vengeance, old man."

And for the next hour, since Suzie was no quicker in returning than I had expected, he treated me to an account of his marital troubles. It appeared that the biggest thorn in his wife's flesh had been his sailing dinghy. Ben hated being a businessman, and admitted that he had never really enjoyed life since the war—and only sailing, with its requirements of tactics, manual skill, and knowledge of the elements, had been able to give him anything like the satisfaction of his life in the navy. He had developed a passion for it. He had hungered for reunion with his dinghy at weekends as another man might hunger for reunion with a mistress. Sailing, however, had made Elizabeth sick. She had hated it. And she had also hated being left out of it—and so every weekend had finished up with a cataclysmic row.

Finally Ben had agreed to sail only on Saturday afternoons and to devote Sundays to Elizabeth. However, even this compromise had not brought peace. Certainly Elizabeth, who had herself suggested the new arrangement, would no longer find fault with the actual sailing itself, but she would always greet him on his return from sailing with some allied grievance: there were people coming to dinner and he was late, or he had rushed off without doing something he had promised, or he had selfishly taken the car when he could so easily have got a lift, and had thereby caused her to miss a tea party—the *only* tea party for months that she had really wanted to attend. The rows usually lasted through Sunday, and he would return to work on Monday morning feeling shattered and exhausted.

At last, in exasperation, he had decided to chuck sailing. He had sold the dinghy. He had taken to going to the Kit Kat instead.

The Kit Kat Club was situated in the Central District. It was useful for morning coffee, lunch, and companionable drinking, since there was always somebody one knew at the bar. Ben took to calling in every evening after the office. After a drink or two he would forget the time and arrive home late for dinner. The rows started again. The blunt fact was that Elizabeth could not bear him to enjoy a moment's pleasure without her. She wanted total possession. And she damn well wasn't going to get it.

The rows had grown more bitter and prolonged, and their causes more trivial and absurd. Then one night about a week ago a row had started in the car after a cocktail party. It had been over a single word—over whether Ben, in refusing an invitation to a stag party, had said, "I'm sorry, I've got to stay with old Liz," or "I'm sorry, I *want* to stay with old Liz." Elizabeth had insisted that he had said "*got*," thereby giving his friends the impression that he would gladly have abandoned her if he could, which of course was most dreadfully humiliating.

The row had continued during dinner, lapsed for an hour, then broken out again in bed, where it had outlived a crying fit by Elizabeth (much to her surprise) and continued until four o'clock in the morning. It had set off a series of rows which had broken out sporadically throughout the week. Ben, as usual, had dropped in every evening at the Kit Kat, since Elizabeth had finally agreed to this provided that he limited himself to one drink. But as with the sailing, so with the drinking—and albeit that he had kept strictly to the agreement, he would always find Elizabeth waiting for him with some grievance that indirectly reproached him for visiting the club at all. Thus tonight on his return she had complained that the cook, while trying to mend a blown fuse, had broken a dining-room chair, which would never have happened if Ben, instead of being at the Kit Kat, had been at home to mend it himself.

Ben said, "I see, so now I'm blamed because Ah Yuen is too lazy to fetch a ladder."

"I wasn't blaming you. I merely said . . ."

An hour later at dinner they were still at it. Suddenly Ben put down his knife and fork.

"Listen, we've been at this for a week now, and I'm not going through another night of it. If you go on, I'm going back to the Kit Kat."

"You started it."

"I don't care who started it. I've warned you."

"Well, if you prefer the Kit Kat to your own home—"

Ben rose without a word, left the house, and drove down to the club. There he deliberately set about getting drunk. Soon he was joined by a ship's surveyor called Wildblood, a small, rat-faced, taciturn man with thinning hair, who was married and had children but was reputed to sleep with his Chinese servant. Ben despised him. They desultorily discussed the virtues of different brands of whisky and the pro-communist statements of a brain-washed missionary who had just been released from China. Ben noticed Wildblood's eyes follow someone across the room. He looked round. It was Moira Wang, a slim beautiful girl of twenty-six who was a qualified doctor. She had been brought in by Bill Harper, an up-and-coming young left-wing politician.

"Not bad," Ben said approvingly.

Wildblood grunted, pretending to notice her for the first time. He was always at pains to conceal his interest in Chinese girls and to imply that he would not touch them with a barge pole. He said that Moira Wang was a damned Red. Why didn't she stand by her principles and go back to China for a taste of her own medicine?

"I've never had a Chinese girl," Ben said.

"Well, keep off them. They're all gold diggers—hard as nails."

They had another whisky. Moira Wang and her companion were eating a Chinese dinner at a near-by table. Ben watched them. He had reached that stage of intoxication at which, his attention concentrated supernormally on some person or object, he would perceive truths of world-shattering importance. These would come to him almost like spiritual revelations, giving him the same ecstatic sense of privilege as a prophet or saint. And now, as he watched Moira Wang wiping Harper's chopsticks for him and then helping him to some choice morsel, a new truth burst upon him with a blinding flash: that oriental women had a femininity that Western women had lost—that they were dedicated to building up masculinity, whereas Western women were dedicated to its destruction.

He continued to watch the couple at the table. The feminine tenderness of Moira Wang's manner filled him with fresh anger at the thought of Elizabeth, who for so long had starved him of his masculine due. He began to feel an almost intolerable yearning. He had never been troubled by a promiscuous desire for women. But now he hungered for a woman—for tenderness, for love. He made up his mind. He turned to Wildblood and said bluntly: "Where can I get a Chinese girl?"

Wildblood gave him a peculiar look, then avoided his eyes. "Why ask me? I wouldn't go with a Chink if you paid me."

"Come off it, Wildblood," Ben said. "You know where one can get a girl."

Wildblood said he had heard that the taxi girls at Chinese dance halls were really tarts—but he wouldn't know.

"I can't go to a dance hall," Ben said. "Too public. I've too many Chinese clients."

"Then go to a Chinese hotel. They've always got girls laid on."

"But I can't speak Chinese. I wouldn't know how to ask for one."

"You don't have to ask. Take a room in a Chink hotel, and there'll be six lined up in the corridor before you've closed the door."

"Six?"

"All shapes and sizes—take your choice." He admitted that he had been to the odd Chinese hotel in his time. Not intending to have a girl, of course—but you were obliged to take one in the end, otherwise they went on knocking on your door all night so that you couldn't get a wink.

"Tell me the name of a hotel," Ben said.

"Dozens of them. They're all brothels, these Chink places."

Now that he was faced with practicalities, Ben began to get cold feet. But his nature was stubborn. He felt committed to his decision, if only as an act of defiance against Elizabeth. He put down another double Scotch to bolster his courage, then left the club. Outside he took a taxi. He told the driver what he wanted, and presently they stopped outside a hotel in the back streets of Wanchai. It looked so sordid that he refused to go in. Next the driver brought him to the Nam Kok. He booked a room at the reception desk and went upstairs. There was no sign of any girls so he rang for the floor boy, who explained that the hotel really only catered for sailors, and that he would have to get a girl from the bar downstairs. Ben was self-conscious enough already, without having to perform this shady transaction before a crowd of matelots, and he gave the boy a hefty tip to bring some girls to the room. Then he collapsed on the bed, his head spinning.

Soon the floor boy returned with four girls, who stood in line for his inspection. He dragged himself up on his elbow and looked them over.

They all seemed dull-eyed and indifferent. They showed no signs of distaste at his drunken condition, indeed hardly bothered to look at him. He did not want any of them. His yearning had gone, and he half wished himself back at home with Elizabeth. But he still felt stubbornly committed. He pointed to the girl second from the end, who happened to be Suzie, and said, "That one."

Suzie at once brightened and seemed delighted to be chosen. She was very tender and sweet; and when he apologized for being tight, she tactfully assured him that she would hardly have known. He remembered his revelation about oriental femininity—how right he had been! Unfortunately, however, he had drunk too much. He was useless.

"I'm sorry," he said, feeling rather absurdly the need to apologize. "It's only the whisky."

"I expect you will feel all right soon," Suzie encouraged him.

But her patient ministrations had been of no avail, and presently she had given up and dragged him along, somewhat unwillingly, to my room. And now he was still feeling humiliated by his failure: he was worried that Suzie had not really believed that it was due to the whisky.

"I'm sure she did," I said. "Anyhow, it was probably the best thing. You've made your gesture of defiance, but you can still go home with a clear conscience. You've both had your cake and eaten it."

But this argument did nothing to encourage him. He sat brooding for a minute, and then said, "I still don't think she believed it was the whisky. I think she thought I was impotent."

I laughed. "Well anyhow, what on earth does it matter?"

"Perhaps I am impotent." He paused. "Listen, there's something I didn't tell you. I don't know what sort of picture you've got of Elizabeth. I've probably given you quite a wrong impression—made her out to be a sort of monster. But actually she's a damned attractive girl—bright, witty, the life and soul of every party. I'm the opposite, rather a dull old dog. A bit of a bore. I suppose that's one of the reasons I married her.

"Well, Liz used to talk a lot about sex. Make brittle, sophisticated jokes, and give the impression that she jumped into bed with men at the drop of a hat. I secretly rather admired that. I was terribly innocent and inexperienced myself. I'd been wrapped up in the Navy, besotted with it, and I'd not had a woman all through the war. I was flattered because after I met old Liz she never looked at another man. I'd ousted all her lovers. Then we got married and I found she was a virgin. There'd never been any lovers. It was all talk. She was practically frigid. And when I made demands on her, it was just wifely duty so far as she was concerned."

He drained his whisky. I reflected that probably Elizabeth's frigidity accounted for her possessiveness, for a woman who could not take possession in bed would try and take it elsewhere.

"Anyhow, it was obviously so disagreeable to her that after a time I stopped bothering her. I haven't touched her now for over a year. I can't say it's worried me much. I've always thought that this sex business was overrated. The only thing that *has* worried me, if you see what I mean, is that it hasn't worried me more. I've kept wondering if I was impotent. Of course it's absurd, because if one's not interested in sex, why should it matter? One should be thankful that one's spared from making a fool of oneself—having to go through that ridiculous performance. But it's bothered me more and more. It's mad. I can't make it out."

"I don't think it's so mad," I said. "Nobody wants to be impotent."

"Anyhow, it's become a sort of obsession. And that's one reason I decided to have a girl tonight—to prove to myself that I wasn't."

"You didn't give yourself much of a chance with that whisky."

"If it *was* the whisky. Anyhow, it was a bloody waste of that beautiful girl. Ah, talk of the devil. . . ."

Suzie had reappeared, twinkling and breathless, in the balcony door. "Sorry I took so long. My baby was so sick—cough-cough, cough-cough! I had to sing him songs. Then he went to sleep, and I ran the whole way back. Oh, I am so exhausted! Wait, I will just get some tea. . . ."

She skipped back inside, completely at home in my room. Ben watched her appreciatively through the open door. "A little enchantress," he said. And then turning back to me, "Only I don't quite see where you come in."

"I'm just a friend of the family."

"Well, look here, old man, I was just wondering—I mean, I'm not going to be any use tonight. You wouldn't mind if I saw her again?"

I said, "It wouldn't make any difference if I minded or not. She's her own boss."

"Yes, but I mean—" He broke off as Suzie reappeared with her glass of tea.

"You know what my amah just told me?" she said, bursting with high spirits. She perched herself on the balcony table and swung her legs. "She told me that today an Englishman came to the house. He looked at the drains and said 'Ugh!' Then he looked at my baby and said, 'That baby is very good-looking!'" She giggled. "'Very good-looking—a very beautiful baby.'"

Ben said, "Look here, what are you doing at twelve o'clock tomorrow?"

"Night?" Suzie said indifferently.

"No, morning."

"You only paid for all night, you know. Tomorrow you must pay more money."

"Don't worry about that."

"All right. You come and find me in the bar."

Ben said that he felt too conspicuous here, and so they arranged to meet at noon at a hotel which Suzie had often patronized when she was working at the Granada. Then he said he must go home, and since he had left his own car outside the Kit Kat, I took him round to a little back-street garage where there was a taxi and the proprietor did not mind being wakened at any hour of the night.

When I got back to my room Suzie was sitting on the bed looking at a book of London photographs. She would sit absorbed in this for hours, her brow puckered as she studied every detail of the pictures.

She held the book out to me, pointing to one of the figures in the photograph of a crowd outside Buckingham Palace. "That woman, what's she got in her hand?"

"It looks like a loaf of bread," I said. "She must have been shopping."

"Maybe she brought it for the Queen." She was always interested in the Queen. She closed the book. "All right, I go now."

"Don't forget your appointment for tomorrow morning."

"I don't think I will go. That man was too drunk. I think he will forget."

"I'm not so sure."

"Anyhow, he is no good at making love."

"Wasn't it just the whisky?"

"No, he is a big man, very strong—but too much worry up here." She tapped her head with a red fingernail. "Too much shame. He can't manage anything."

Suzie may not have read Freud, but as a psychological observer she was pretty shrewd.

Chapter Two

She had been mistaken, however, about Ben not keeping the date for the next day. He not only kept it but, when Suzie did not turn up, proceeded to the Nam Kok in a taxi, sent the driver to dig her out of the bar, and bore her off to the hotel—where they ordered a Chinese lunch in the room, went to bed, confirmed their joint suspicions that the origin of Ben's failing was something more than alcoholic, and parted with their union unconsummated but a similar appointment for the morrow. Thereafter they met at twelve o'clock every day. And towards the middle of the second week Suzie, who had no inhibitions about reporting progress to me, was able to announce with some satisfaction, "He is all right now—it was just nerves."

Meanwhile the relationship had been established on a permanent footing, for Ben had agreed to pay her one thousand dollars a month for exclusive rights. And thus Suzie, happily set up once more with a regular boy friend, had withdrawn her custom from the sailors.

I did not see Ben again myself for nearly a month after his first visit to my room, since he avoided the Nam Kok. Then one morning as I was strolling through the Central District I heard my name called, and saw Ben grinning at me from a car pulled up at some traffic lights. He leaned over from the steering wheel to open the passenger's door. "Quick, man, jump in—the lights are changing."

I climbed in beside him, astonished by his affability. I had supposed that my knowledge of his personal affairs might make him feel embarrassed about meeting me again.

"That door properly shut?" The car shot forward. "Sorry to kidnap you, old man, but it's awfully good to see you. You're not busy? Fine, come and have a coffee at the Kit Kat. I'm meeting old Liz."

"Won't that make it a bit difficult?"

"Difficult? Why?"

"I mean, how will you introduce me?"

"Oh, we'll think of something. No, I've been wanting you to meet her. I've had a guilty conscience ever since that night in your room when I did nothing but run her down. Of course I was tight as a coot. Actually she's a damn good sort, old Liz. I'm sure you'll like her enormously."

This surprised me even more than his affability. He spoke with such warmth and enthusiasm that one would have supposed him to be the most faithful and adoring of husbands; yet I knew for a fact that in less than two hours' time, at twelve o'clock, he would be meeting Suzie for his regular lunchtime tryst. Moreover he knew that I knew—so how on earth could he talk of Elizabeth so shamelessly?

"Yes, I'm sure that you two'll get on like a house on fire. God, isn't it the devil, this parking. . . ." We were cruising round looking for somewhere to put the car. "I've been nabbed twice this month already. I can't get away with it like old Liz. She's marvelous—you ought to see her." He grinned with uxorious admiration. "She just turns on the old charm, and the policeman's had it—melts like butter. . . ."

We finally abandoned the car in front of a "No parking" sign and made off quickly, so that if he was going to be fined he could at least get his money's worth of parking first. We entered a near-by building and went up to the Kit Kat on the first floor. It was a single room with a long polished bar, a dart board and pin table, and a number of dining tables with table lamps decorated with English pub signs. The place was deserted except for a waiter and two women having coffee. We sat down at the sign of the Marquis of Granby, and Ben grinned across the table at me, looking ten years younger than at our first meeting, and said, "Well, old chap, I certainly bless my luck in stumbling on the Nam Kok that night."

I said, "We're always glad to hear from satisfied customers."

"Suzie's a marvelous girl, you know—marvelous." Sober, with eager boyish look and plummy wardroom voice, he was the typical naval officer again; and indeed his dark suit, with white starched collar and neatly knotted black tie, gave almost the impression of naval uniform.

"Yes, she's a little charmer," I said.

"I don't mind telling you, it's changed my whole life." He glanced to make sure that the waiter was out of earshot, then inclined towards me confidentially, as if to tell me about the fantastic performance of the ship's new radar. "You see, the fact is, old boy, I was brought up to believe that sex was shameful and dirty—a hole-in-the-corner business that decent chaps had as little to do with as possible. But that's all rubbish. Because it's something bloody marvelous—something that, instead of being ashamed about, we should go down on our knees and thank God for."

I laughed. "Well, coming from a man who a few weeks ago was talking of 'that ridiculous performance' . . . !"

"I was talking through my hat. Because those psychology chaps are absolutely right when they say that sex is behind everything. I know that now from my own experience. I know that it can affect one's whole outlook—how one feels, how one behaves. I mean, why are some people such bastards? Why are they so bitter and disagreeable? Because they're all twisted and dried up inside—because they're frustrated. And in my opinion half the world's troubles are due to just that—to frustration." And he went on to say that it was all the fault of our narrow and unenlightened upbringing. He was horrified to think how long he himself had struggled in darkness and ignorance. His own first sexual experience had been at the age of nineteen with a London prostitute. He had gone with her because he had been ashamed of his virginity. She had asked for two pounds, then demanded another pound before she would properly undress. He had not got another. "All right, then, dear, hurry up," she had said, and he had been out in the street again within ten minutes of leaving it. For months afterwards he had lived in fear of disease. Then he had had a fumbling affair with an inexperienced girl of his own age and lived in fear of her having a baby. Soon after this he had joined the Navy. He had decided that sex was a sport for the lower deck, and had had nothing more to do with women until he had met Elizabeth. The marriage had kept him in ignorance of the true importance of sex for another seven years—and only the advent of Suzie had at last brought him enlightenment. And since the fruits yielded by the lunchtime lunch sessions were still increasing in proportion to their growing knowledge of each other, even more wonderful joys lay ahead.

"But what about Elizabeth?" I asked. "You haven't told her about Suzie?"

"Told old Liz? Oh, my dear chap! Oh, good Lord, no!"

"But how are you getting along with her?"

"Marvelously."

I waited for an explanation of this paradox, but just then Ben caught sight of the door opening and his face lit up with pleasure.

"Ah, good old Liz! And she's brought Binkie. Here, Binks boy! Binks, Binks, Binks!"

Elizabeth let her dog off the lead and it scampered towards us, skidding on the polished floor. It was a Scottie with an absurd, sad, long face. It looked very old. It rolled on its back by Ben's chair, its paws in the air. Ben scratched its pink tummy.

"Silly boy! Silly Binks! Wouldn't think he was only a puppy, would you? How's that, Binks—nice scratchy-turn?"

"Sorry I'm late, darling," Elizabeth said, sailing up. "And I can't stay a second. I promised to meet Gwen Mathers at the hairdresser's—she wants to copy my hair style. Oh, Binkie darling, look at you! You really are a Thurber dog!" Her manner was brightly artificial, and I fancied that she was acting a little for my benefit. She was in her early thirties, good-looking, and dressed in a coat and skirt of such stylishness, and with all her accouterments so perfectly matching and in place, that she might have stepped straight out of a fashion plate.

"What the devil's a 'Thurber' dog?" Ben said.

"Darling, you're so uneducated! He's that marvelous man who draws nothing but ridiculous dogs like Binkie. Now I can't bear the suspense a minute longer. I'm waiting to be introduced to your *fascinating* friend." She flashed her smile at me. It was as beautifully tailored as her clothes.

"Good Lord, I forgot!" He introduced us, saying that he had met me in the Kit Kat, and that I was an artist living somewhere down in the slums of Wanchai.

"How perfectly thrilling!" Elizabeth exclaimed. "Isn't Wanchai nothing but brothels? You don't *live* in a brothel, do you?"

"No, just in a hotel," I said, sticking to the legal truth.

"What a pity! I'd *adore* to live in a brothel—I mean, what heaven to be absolutely surrounded by rampant men! Now I've simply got to rush. Darling, shall I meet you for lunch?"

"Sorry, I'm tied up for a business lunch," Ben said.

"Not another? You must be doing an awful lot of business these days. Never mind, you'll be able to afford a new dress for me. You can hear the whole of Hong Kong groaning every time I reappear in these ghastly old rags. Well, 'by, darling." She kissed his forehead, and he smiled and squeezed her hand. "Come on, Binks. No, no more scratchy-turn you're coming on the lead."

When she had gone Ben smiled at me a trifle smugly, like any proud paterfamilias after a display of family affection and unity.

"Ben, you're a disgrace to the Royal Navy," I said. "I don't know how you get away with it."

"With what, old boy?"

"Fooling Elizabeth."

"I'm not fooling her. I mean, not about my feelings for her. I've never been more fond of her. And of course she realizes it, and she's changed out of recognition. She's even suggested that I should take up sailing again—buy another dinghy. But I don't care tuppence about sailing now. It was just a sex substitute."

"Ben, you're too good to be true," I laughed. "But I still don't understand about Elizabeth. Why, she's positively glowing!"

"I *could* explain it." He regarded me with a faint superior smile, as the seasoned officer would regard the midshipman, wondering if he was yet ready for initiation into some esoteric shipboard mystery. "Only I'm afraid it'll shock you."

"One gets pretty shock-proof living at the Nam Kok," I said.

"You may be shocked all the same. The fact is that I've resumed full marital relations with old Liz."

"You mean, while you're still carrying on with Suzie?"

"Of course."

"Good Lord! Well, I suppose if it's working. . . ."

"It is."

And he proceeded to describe the events of the previous weekend. Since he had no opportunity to meet Suzie on Saturdays or Sundays he had come to dread the weekends, which had seemed to stretch before him like a great arid desert that had to be crossed before reaching the oasis of

Monday noon. Then last Saturday afternoon he and Elizabeth had set out with another couple for a picnic by the sea. In the car Ben had made some thoughtless remark about envying a certain young bachelor his freedom: and later, after their friends had wandered off along the beach, Elizabeth had angrily taken him to task for it. Here she was running his house for him, slaving for him, sacrificing herself for him by living in a Godforsaken colony—and all for what? Just to be humiliated in front of their friends by being told that he would rather be a bachelor.

Ben thought for a minute and then said, "Yes, I realize now. It was a beastly thing to say. I'm terribly sorry, Liz."

Elizabeth stared at him. The wind had been taken out of her sails. Several times recently the same improbable thing had happened—instead of growing angry, arguing back at her, he had admitted the justice of her complaints. But she had still not grown used to it.

"Well, you should be more careful what you say," she said rather lamely.

"Yes, I really should."

They lay in silence. He reflected that a month ago the quarrel would have lasted twenty-four hours and left him more exhausted than a running battle with a U-boat; and he was at a loss to understand his own former perversity. Why had he found it so impossible ever to admit that Elizabeth might be right? And even supposing she wasn't, what did it matter? Wasn't it worth giving way just for the sake of peace?

She was lying on her back on a towel. He looked at her. "What a lovely profile you've got, Liz."

"What *are* you talking about?"

"I'd forgotten. I think I first fell in love with you because of your profile."

Elizabeth laughed and said she did not know what had suddenly possessed him, but he could not fail to notice her glow of pleasure. It was Suzie who had taught him to pay compliments. He had never formerly paid compliments to girls, because if a girl was pretty she was probably quite conceited enough already, and if she wasn't pretty—well, it was just downright dishonest. He had never complimented Suzie. However, this had not deterred Suzie from paying him compliments, and not a day had passed without her picking on some quality in him that she professed to admire; and although he had sometimes suspected her of exaggeration, he had invariably been touched and pleased—for the wish to flatter was a flattery in itself. And it was largely due to her compliments that he had overcome his impotence. He had been in dread of her ridicule—but so far from making fun of him, she had congratulated him on the virility that she had felt certain was latent in him, and had even pretended to dread its release, since it would undoubtedly overpower a little Chinese girl like herself. Such suggestions had been like the touch of a magic wand. His strength had risen to meet them.

And now he had learnt to use the magic wand himself. He had learnt that often a compliment would help to soften a personality, give it warmth. He looked at Elizabeth again. Something almost like tenderness had come into her face.

She smiled at him and stood up. "Let's go and bathe."

And the sight of her standing there in her bathing costume had a strange effect on him. He felt quite stirred. He could not have been more astonished, for he had thought that his feelings for her were long since jaded, and he had never expected to be stirred by her in this way again. He chased after her into the sea. He caught her and they struggled playfully. Then they saw the other couple returning along the beach.

"Thank God you've come!" Elizabeth shouted to them in her gay brittle way. "My husband was just about to rape me!"

This struck a jarring note with Ben. It was that familiar sophisticated talk which Elizabeth thought rather smart, and that always included a liberal spattering of words like "rape," "brothel," "seduce"—and that had now turned an intimate and rather wonderful event into a cocktail-party joke. His desire was promptly extinguished.

But in the back of the friend's car going home Elizabeth suddenly took his hand. Perhaps she had remembered his compliment. His desire for her rushed back—overwhelmed him. And they had no sooner reached home than, ignoring her protests that she must immediately feed Binkie, he took her by storm.

He had learned much about the art of love-making from Suzie and he gave Elizabeth the benefit of his new accomplishment. It found the beginnings of response in her, an incipient passion. She was no less surprised than Ben.

"What on earth's happened to you?" she asked afterwards, with a puzzled laugh. "You never behaved like that before."

"I know, I've been a rotten lover."

"Well, what's made you change?"

"I was worried about it. I bought one of those books."

"You'd better let me see it."

"I was so ashamed of it that I threw it away."

On Sunday he was overcome again, and made love to her half an hour before guests were due to arrive for lunch. During the meal one guest remarked that Elizabeth looked radiant. Another found her unusually quiet. Ben himself noticed that throughout the meal she never said "rape," "brothel," or "seduce," or made any brittle witticism about sex. And since then, despite the resumption of relations with Suzie on Monday, they had not looked back.

I laughed and said, "Well, I'm damned. And that's the man who a month ago was impotent!"

"You're joking about it now," Ben said. "But I could see you really were shocked."

"Yes, I was a bit at first."

"I don't blame you. But look at it this way. What was our marriage worth before? Nothing. All right, is it better now or not?"

"It certainly appears so."

"And let's face it—man is a polygamous animal. Of course in Europe we try and blind ourselves to the fact. Bloody stupid—why don't we accept it as a basic truth, like these Orientals? Their attitude is much more sensible. All the rich Chinese chaps keep mistresses, and it's considered perfectly respectable. They do exactly as I'm doing. All right, so look at it statistically. On the one hand there are a few thousand Europeans in Hong Kong whom my behavior would scandalize—and on the other hand several million Chinese who would accept it as perfectly natural. It makes one think." He flicked his wrist with a decisive movement to look at his watch. "Lord, look at the time!"

I smiled to myself. Nearly eight bells—time to go on the bridge.

"And I've a couple of letters to dictate before I meet Suzie." He pushed back his chair. "By the way, I suppose she's really behaving herself—keeping off sailors?"

“Yes, she’s been very faithful to you,” I said.

“I imagine so. Now, you’ll excuse me if I shoot off?”

“Go ahead,” I said. “And I hope you haven’t been pinched for parking.”

“That’d be too bad.” He gave a suave naval grin. “Still, when one’s got this sex business taped, and a marvelous girl like that lined up—well, I mean, old boy, what’s the odd fine?”

Chapter Three

When I had told Ben at the Kit Kat that Suzie was behaving herself it had been perfectly true. But only a few days later she blotted her copybook.

It happened one evening when she was in the bar and a matelot came over to seek her favors. Since the advent of Ben, whom she met only at lunchtime, she had been at a loose end in the evenings, and she had been in the habit of spending them either gossiping with me in my room or with her girl friends downstairs; and whenever a sailor had approached her, she had simply apologized and explained that she was "resting." However, this particular matelot refused to be shaken off. He had been her boy friend eight months before, when his ship had last called at Hong Kong; and he earnestly assured her that for those eight months he had done little else but think of her and look forward to this return visit.

He was Irish, and his tongue persuasive. And as added inducement he offered her twice the sum that he had paid her before.

Suzie thought of her baby's future. And since the matter, financially speaking, concerned her baby more than herself, she was not sure that she had any right to refuse on his behalf. Besides, the matelot had been her boy friend before Ben, which gave him a sort of prior claim.

"All right," she said, and upstairs they went.

And after falling once it made the offense hardly worse to fall again, and she occasionally did so. She would not deliberately offer herself; but if a sailor approached her and she liked the look of him, and if she could bring herself to interrupt her gossip, she would let herself be persuaded.

I thought this very naughty of her and told her so. She was very cross. She told me to mind my own business. Then she relented and apologized for being rude, and explained that she would never dream of deceiving a boy friend whom she respected—but the fact was that she did not respect Ben. She thought he had no strength of character.

"The Navy wouldn't agree with you," I told her. "He got a very good decoration in the war. He was a hero."

But she was stubbornly indifferent to the Admiralty's estimate of him. "No, he is weak. Oh, I know, he has a big strong body. He has plenty of muscle and a big chest. But there is nothing inside that big chest except a little heart about so big"—and she held up her little fingernail.

"I think he's got a very good heart," I said. "Anyhow, that's no excuse for taking his money under false pretenses. You're cheating him."

"Yes—cheating."

"And aren't you ashamed of yourself?"

"No."

About a week later, however, an incident occurred that caused her to revise her estimate of Ben, and that put an abrupt end to her infidelities. It began, so far as I was concerned, at about eleven o'clock one evening when I had just got into bed, and there was a sudden loud banging on the door. I thought it must be a drunk. "Who is it?" I demanded.

"Ben."

He entered without further invitation, slammed the door, and stood looming over the end of my bed, with an aggressive aspect that suggested he had been drinking. However, he was nothing like so drunk as he had been on his first visit and was perfectly in command of himself. His chin purposefully jutted, as if the enemy had just been sighted and he stood grimly on the bridge giving orders for action stations.

He said, "You'd better get dressed, old boy. We've got a job to do."

"What on earth's happened, Ben?"

"It's that little bitch of mine. She's with a sailor."

"Good Lord! Well, what are you going to do?"

"Fish her out."

"But you can't go—"

"Come on, man, get cracking. We can talk while you get your things on."

I began to dress, playing for time. Meanwhile Ben explained that this evening he had been to a stag party given by a rich Chinese client in one of those huge expensive Chinese restaurants the size of department stores. There had been lashings of whisky to wash down the fabulous food, and the usual little Chinese hostesses to joke and flirt with the guests. The attentions of these girls had reminded him of Suzie; he had begun to feel a longing for her that had become almost unbearable; and as soon as the party had broken up—Chinese dinners were never prolonged beyond the end of the food—he had driven down to the Nam Kok and, emboldened by the whisky, walked straight into the bar. Not finding Suzie herself there, he had asked one of the girls where she was; but the girl, evidently a friend of Suzie's, had disclaimed all knowledge of her whereabouts. He had repeated the question to a second girl with "a waggling bloody bottom like a voodoo dancer," who had been more forthcoming, and had revealed that Suzie had just gone upstairs with an American.

I said, "That was obviously Betty Lau. Of course, she'd have no compunction about doing Suzie in the eye."

"Look, man, can't you get a move on?"

"Ben, we can't just go barging into some room—"

"Why not?"

"What's the point? The harm's done now."

"You leave that to me, and just get dressed."

"Ben, I'm having nothing to do with it."

"All right, if you haven't the guts—I'll do the job myself."

And turning away disdainfully, he strode from the room.

Several minutes passed. Then Ah Tong entered in a state of perturbation to report that Ben had been grilling him to find out in which room Suzie was installed, and that on his assurance that she was not on this floor had gone to pursue his search on the floors below. Ah Tong, perceiving Ben's dangerous mood, was fearful of what might happen when he found her. He begged me to try and restrain him from violence.

I reluctantly agreed to do what I could and set forth in pursuit. I found him leaving the floor boy's desk on the lower landing.

"Ah, you've thought better of it," he said, walking briskly past me toward the stairs. "Well, she's not on this floor," so that leaves only the floor below."

I said, "Listen, Ben, I know what we can do. If we can find out her room number, you can speak to her on the telephone." And I added, to try and impress him with the effectiveness of this measure, "She'll get the most awful shock when she hears you."

"I've no intention of speaking to her on the telephone." We reached the first floor landing, and he strode up to the floor boy's desk. "Suzie Wong, what room's she in?"

"Uh?"

"You heard me. Suzie Wong."

The floor boy shook his head. He was looking at a Chinese film magazine with pictures of American stars. I never came to this floor and I did not know him.

"Not here." He had shifty eyes and was obviously lying.

Ben was about to make some retort when his attention was distracted by a door opening down the corridor. The tiny luscious Jeannie came out, ushered by a gangling American sailor. The sailor paused at the door of the next room, adjusting his round white sailor's cap from the back with one hand, and thumping on the door with the other. "Hey, Hank!"

A girl's voice replied from within, "What you want? Hank's busy."

"Hey, that you, Fifi? Tell Hank we're just gonna have chow."

Hank's voice from inside said, "Hey, Joe!"

"Yeah? That you, Hank?"

"Yeah, where you gonna eat chow?"

Jeannie put her face close to the door and said, "Hey, Fifi! I take Joe to the Victory. You going to bring Hank?"

"Sure," called back Fifi. "He make me plenty hungry!"

"O.K.," said Joe. "See you later, Hank."

"O.K., see you later, Joe."

Joe lifted his hand behind his head, screwed his hat round again, and pushed it so far forward that it was almost resting on the bridge of his nose. He had to tilt his head well back to see under the brim. Jeannie took his arm. They came toward us and turned down the stairs.

"Christ, what a place to live!" Ben exclaimed. He turned back to the floor boy. "Now, where's that girl? I'm from the police."

"Uh?"

"Police."

He pulled out his wallet without removing his eyes from the floor boy, opened it, and tossed it on the desk. There was a cellophane partition inside, and behind it an official printed document. I gazed in astonishment. Ben's authoritative manner was so convincing that for a moment I was almost taken in, and began to wonder if he was really engaged in some mission quite different from what I had supposed.

Then I peered at the wallet more closely. The document was his driving license.

The floor boy, however, gave it only one brief glance. He turned white about the gills.

"Number Fourteen, sir," he muttered.

Ben repocketed the wallet and started down the corridor, followed by myself and the floor boy. The floor boy was dancing and tripping in agitation. In common with the manager and entire staff of the Nam Kok he lived in holy fear of the civil police.

There was a murmur of voices through the ventilator of the room occupied by Fifi and Hank. An elderly amah with tiny slit eyes and huge prognathous mouth with gold teeth was entering the room that had just been vacated. She wore a blue jacket, black cotton trousers, white socks, and black felt slippers. She carried clean sheets over her arm. She threw the sheets on the bed and closed the door. No. 14 was two doors farther along. Ben raised his knuckles and knocked stoutly.

"Police."

There was an outbreak of whispering inside, followed by sounds of panic-stricken activity. Ben tried the handle. The door was bolted.

"I'll give you ten seconds to open up."

The floor boy rapped anxiously on the door, holding his head close to the panel and giving agitated exhortations in Cantonese. I had given up all thought of intervening, except as a last expedient in the event of threat to human life. I stood by helplessly, and not without admiration for Ben's suave performance.

Ben looked at his watch. "Five seconds to go."

The door opened a few inches. Behind the crack stood a young man hitching at his trousers. He was squat and hefty, with broad shoulders, tattooed arms, a chest as furry as a gorilla's, and a tiny upturned baby's nose. Despite the nose, he looked a tough customer.

Ben gave the door a violent kick. It swung back with a crash. Suzie stood by the bed in cotton brassiere and knickers. She was on the point of reaching for her cheongsam on the chair, but the crash of the door sent her scrambling back into the bed. She squatted with the sheet pulled protectively up to her neck. She caught sight of Ben for the first time, as he entered the room with myself and the floor boy behind, and a look of utter astonishment came over her face—a look so comically exaggerated that I could never remember it afterwards without a sputter of laughter. Her eyes, naturally elliptical, became as round as saucers. Her eyebrows rose in prodigious arches. Her jaw dropped. Her mouth fell open. It was straight out of stock—the stock of some ham actor playing melodrama in repertory.

"Gee," said the sailor.

His voice was high and squeaky and soft as butter. It matched the turned-up baby's nose and not the gorilla chest. It made him suddenly seem quite harmless.

Ben said, "Get dressed and beat it."

"Gee, sir, we ain't been doing nothing wrong." He cleared his voice on a falsetto note and felt a bit braver. "I ain't never heard of no law, sir, that said a feller could come bustin' in when a feller was—"

"Beat it." Ben gave him a confidential wink. "This girl's been peddling drugs."

"Gee!"

Suzie at last found her voice. She began to scream abuse at Ben, alternating it with indignant outbursts of Chinese at the floor boy. Ben ignored her. He turned to the sailor who was hurriedly finishing his dressing, and asked, "How much did you pay her?"

"Well, sir, I was on an all-nighter—"

"How much?"

"Hundred Hong Kong dollars, sir."

"She bloody rooked you." He took out his wallet and handed the sailor a large pink hundred-dollar note.

"Don't you take it!" Suzie screamed. "He lies! He's not a policeman—he's my boy friend! You make him get out!"

The sailor said nervously, "I ain't gonna get mixed up in nothing. I just wanna keep my nose clean, see, that's all."

"You're scared!"

She tried to urge him to battle. The sailor stood grinning uneasily like a huge absurd baby. He scratched the back of his head with one hand, and stared in disbelief at the hundred-dollar note in the other.

"Gee, sir! I never heard of no American cop giving a feller his money back for a lay."

"Hop it."

The sailor went off sheepishly, looking at the money and scratching his head. Suzie continued her tirade against Ben. She needed her hands for gesticulating and the sheet had fallen to her knees.

"What you think I am? Your slave girl? I'm nobody's slave girl! You got no right to come into this room—my boy friend paid for this room all night!"

Ben said, "Shut up."

"No! You shut up! Get out! Go to hell!"

Ben advanced towards the bed. He made an unhurried grab at her. Suzie's spate of invective was interrupted and she struggled violently. She wriggled free and escaped across the bed. Ben leaned over without effort and caught her ankle. He dragged her back across the bed like a lizard by its tail. She looked quite tiny beside Ben's large looming figure. She kicked and lashed about with her arms. He pinioned her arms, and she twisted her head and dug her teeth into his hand. He forced her head back, his hand dripping blood where she had bitten it, and rolled her onto her face. He leaned over her on his elbow, securing her with his weight under the angle of his arm, and raising his free hand, he began to spank her.

He spanked her long and hard. Suzie yelled blue murder. The screams must have resounded throughout the Nam Kok. But it was only after it was over, and Suzie lay there crying like a child, that I glanced round and saw the tier of astonished gaping faces in the doorway—the faces of the gold-toothed amah, three sailors, and Fife, Wednesday Lulu, and Gwenny Ching.

II

It was an hour later. The three of us were seated in a little restaurant in Hennessy Road that specialized in Pekin food. We had ordered a single plate of *pin-pan,* a kind of Chinese hors d'oeuvres, most of which Ben had polished off single-handed while Suzie and I, who were neither of us hungry, had sat sipping tea and nibbling at melon seeds.

Ben said, "I'm not an expert on Chinese cooking. But on the whole I prefer Pekin style to Cantonese."

The conversation had also been largely a single-handed effort on Ben's part. He courteously pretended not to notice Suzie's sullen lack of response. He was still behaving with perfect aplomb—the skipper who, after carrying out the unpleasant duty of punishing a recalcitrant officer, now considered the offense expiated and the incident closed. Never might the Royal Navy have been prouder of him.

"More tea?" he asked Suzie, but she shook her head. He glanced with a faint smile at the handkerchief wrapped round his hand where she had bitten him. "That's going to take a bit of explaining. I'll just have to keep it covered, and say I got it caught in a door."

Suzie glanced at the hand surreptitiously. She looked anxious. Then she remembered that she was still supposed to be sulking; for although she no longer felt like sulking, her pride demanded that she keep it up. And she tried not very successfully to look pleased she had hurt him.

"How's the time?" The skipper jerked up his cuff. "I say, I must get cracking!"

Suzie watched him rise, longing to know whether or not she had been relieved of her duties, but too proud to ask. Ben paid the bill and we followed him out to his car. He got into the driving seat, slammed the door, leaned his elbow out of the open window.

"I'll have to buzz off—leave you two to get back under your own steam."

He withdrew the elbow, started up. Suzie could bear it no longer. She said, trying hard to sound indifferent, "You want me tomorrow?"

"Want you tomorrow?" Ben regarded her with an appearance of blank astonishment. (Really frightened the life out of the young puppy! Silly mugwump doesn't realize he's indispensable to the ship!) "Certainly I want you tomorrow. Why not?"

"You're not angry with me?" She could hardly believe it.

"No, we'll forget it. But you're to keep out of that bar in future. Right out of it—understand?" And he put the car in gear and shot off.

Suzie and I stood staring after the car in silence. I could feel the radiation of her joy. We began to walk along the empty street. The pavement was littered with bits of paper, old cigarette packets, discarded fruit rind. Between two shops a woman and two children lay asleep on sacking. Round them were stacked all their household possessions: tins, cooking pans, wooden boxes. The woman clutched an old cornflake packet tied with string. We walked on past shuttered shop fronts, past a cinema, past more homeless sleepers nursing their little claims of stone pavement from passing feet. We entered the flood of light from a modern shopwindow: banked with shoes, it bared its breast to the empty pavement, the silent roadway. We paused, momentarily hypnotized by its unreality, by its absurd refusal to admit that it was night and that everybody had gone to bed.

I said, "That reminds me, Suzie. I need some new shoes."

"Yes," she said absently.

"Or sandals might be cheaper. How d'you like those?"

I pointed into the dazzling Aladdin's cave of footwear. As a rule Suzie held strong views about what I wore, and she had admonished me to buy nothing without her approval; but now she gave only a brief vague glance towards the sandals. I do not think she even saw them. "Yes, very nice," she said automatically. And then with a sudden giggle, "He hurt me, you know! That spanking really hurt!"

"I bet it did."

"It hurt to sit down in that restaurant. I wanted to ask for a cushion, then I thought, 'No, that will show him how much it hurt—and I will lose face!'"

"Do you really like those sandals?"

She said rather impatiently, "Yes, I told you—very much." And then, "Yes, he's really strong, that man. Woosh! Woosh! Plenty of muscle!"

"Well, you always said so."

"But I made a mistake about him before. I thought he had only a small heart. But I think he must have a big heart—because I cheated him, I did a very nasty thing, but he said, 'That's all right, we just forget it. I forgive you.' He must have a big heart to say that."

"I'm delighted to hear it."

"'Just forget it, Suzie.' I think that is very beautiful. It was beautiful to say that."

We walked on, out of the light again, back into the shadows, Suzie's arm brushing against mine. But she was walking in another world; a world where I could not follow. I had ceased to exist for her. I could have slipped away down a side street and she would not have noticed. Or cared.

I felt a dull ache over my heart.

But it's nonsense to feel hurt, I thought. That strong-arm stuff always goes down with the simple type of girl. See them falling in swoons at the cinema over Tarzan: their ideal man. It's exactly what you'd expect with her lack of education, her illiteracy. And frankly, if that's the sort of girl she is, who cares? I shan't pay her the compliment of feeling hurt. . . .

The ache was worse. I think it was the first time I had really been jealous of Suzie.

Chapter Four

Thereafter Suzie kept strictly to the rules of the game. She had been speaking nothing less than the truth when she had said that if she respected a man she would not dream of deceiving him; and now that she respected Ben, I do not think that anything could have shaken her fidelity—nothing, at any rate, short of a guarantee for her baby's education at the best school in Hong Kong, followed by three years at Oxford and a starring role in a Hollywood film.

And the spanking had become one of the proudest events of her life. For in the water-front world, where girls were shared and recommended to friends ("You can't go wrong with Typhoo, mate—she does you real proud. . . ."), a boy friend who jealously demanded fidelity, and who in order to enforce it would descend on the Nam Kok by private car, impersonate a policeman, throw out a sailor, and turn a girl over his knees, had the romantic appeal of Prince Charming, Gary Cooper, and the heir of the Tiger Balm Millions rolled into one.

And now Suzie would tell me, "You know, last night I stayed awake just to think about Ben. I thought, 'If I got to sleep I may dream about him or I may not—so I had better stay awake to make sure.'" And she would say, "I wonder if I am in love with him? What do you think, Robert? You think I am in love?"

"Of course, head over heels."

"Yes, I think so," she would nod pensively. And then add with satisfaction, "And I hate his wife! I hate that woman very much, so I must be in love!"

She had even made herself believe, on the strength of odd remarks of Ben's, that one day he might divorce Elizabeth and marry her; and she asked me endless questions about London, so that when he took her to England she would not shame him with her ignorance.

"Suzie, I shouldn't count on it too much," I told her. I had come to terms with my jealousy by now, and hated to think of the disappointment that must follow such extravagant hopes.

"But Ben has promised. He has told me often, 'Suzie, I want to show you London. You will look so pretty in London with your Chinese skin! Yes, one day I will take you, and show you everything, and we will get married in—' I forget where, but it was some big old famous church where the Queen got married in."

"Westminster Abbey?"

"Yes, Westminster Abbey! He says, 'We will pretend you are a Chinese princess.'"

I was sure that these had been no more than Ben's idle musings as he lay replete on the bed at lunchtime in the little Chinese hotel, and that he had not intended her to take them seriously. I pointed out that it might be very difficult for him to get a divorce. But she gaily reassured me, "Oh, don't worry, Ben knows all the big people in Hong Kong. He only has to tell the Number One Top Englishman, 'Good morning, Mr. Governor, my wife is no good; I want a divorce,' and the Number One will say, 'Very good, I will ask someone to fix it while we have some lunch.'" And she held up the book of London photographs, which now fascinated her more than ever, and pointed to a picture of a beefeater at the Tower of London. "Look at that man—how fat! I will tell him when I go to London, 'Hey, you're too fat, you eat too much!'" She twinkled happily, then suddenly started back from the book with an "Ouch!" of pretended pain.

"Good Lord, Suzie! What's the matter?"

"This beefeater just told me, 'You're too cheeky!' and stuck me with that spike!"

She still came to visit me every day but obediently kept clear of the bar; for although she had pleaded with Ben to repeal his harsh edict, which deprived her of so much enjoyable gossip with her girl friends, Ben had firmly refused. However, to keep her out of mischief in the evenings he had granted her permission to work at a new dance hall in the Central District. This had a mixed Chinese and European clientele and was more or less respectable, since no obligation was placed on the girls to extend favors off the dance floor. Suzie loved dancing, and would go along most evenings, making ten or twelve dollars for enjoying herself—or a good deal more if she was bought out and taken to dinner. However, she never accepted a dinner invitation without first making it clear that there would be nothing else doing, and she never allowed a patron to run her home in his car. She had learned by experience that, by the time you had convinced him that you meant what you said, it was less trouble to take a tram.

The dance hall was called the Astoria. And it was through Suzie working at the Astoria that, to my eternal regret, Rodney Tessler came into our lives. Or at least into my life—since Suzie was too wrapped up in Ben to be much aware of him.

It began exactly as it had begun with Ben, with a late night telephone call from Suzie—this time from a restaurant in town where she had been taken to dinner. Her partner, I gathered, was proving difficult to shake off, despite her usual clear warning beforehand: he had turned quite nasty, and she had no good to say for him, except that he was intelligent and "good class," and also passionately interested in painting. This had transpired during dinner, when she had told him about me. She thought he was a painter himself, she was not sure. Anyhow he had begged to be brought along to meet me and see my work; and if I was agreeable she would be delighted, since it would give her a chance to slip out on him.

I hesitated, and then said doubtfully, "All right, bring him along." I rang off in a state of some perturbation. So far nobody had seen my Nam Kok pictures except Ah Tong and Suzie, and a few other girls and sailors, whose praise had never failed to delight me, but whose adverse comments had always been easy enough to dismiss—"After all, they're just Philistines." I hastily looked through my finished pictures. A few minutes ago I would have found no difficulty in persuading myself of their merit; I could even have believed that in one or two I had soared to the most breath-taking heights of artistic achievement. But now, seeing them through the eyes of a hypercritical stranger, all my self-confidence abruptly vanished, and they became distorted by my fears into a pathetic collection of meaningless daubs.

Oh God, I thought miserably, I wish I'd never said he could come. And I hurriedly hid the worst of them, and arranged the others in the most effective order for display, though in apparently casual disorder to conceal evidence of such nervous preparation.

Twenty minutes later, a knock on the door—and Suzie entered with a young man whose crew-cut hair indicated an American. He wore a gabardine suit of expensive but unassuming English cut, a silk shirt with small embroidered monogram on the pocket, a neat spotted bow tie, and suede shoes. He looked about twenty-five or -six.

He held out his hand to me with a charming, frank, boyish smile. "Glad to meet you, Bob. They do call you Bob, I suppose?"

The hand was soft and manicured, with a gold signet ring. His voice had a mild American twang. But I think that without either the accent or the crew cut I would have guessed his nationality. It was in the readiness of the handshake, the blandness of the smile, that seemed jointly to declare, "I'm an American, and proud of it, and when you shake hands with me you are not just shaking hands with an individual, but with America itself—with the Empire State, and nation-wide television, and General Motors, and the American democratic constitution."

I found such openness disarming, and felt an instant liking for him. I wondered why Suzie had been so disparaging.

"I'm not usually called Bob," I smiled. "But I don't mind a bit."

"Well, I hope you won't mind if I call you Red by mistake."

"Red?"

"You see, Bob, I used to have a classmate who was a namesake of yours—Red Lomax. And ever since I heard your name was Lomax, I've been thinking of you as Red. But I don't think you'd mind my mixing you up if you'd known him, because he was a very fine person—a very, very fine person—and so far as that goes, I think that you two have got a good deal in common."

"I'm flattered."

"Well, you should have heard the build-up that Suzie gave you. I wondered if you employed her as publicity agent, but now I've met you I can see it was all true. And I really mean that, Red." He realized the stupid mistake. He flicked his fingers in exasperation, then grinned and said, "Now, you keep out of this, Red, d'you hear? We all know you're a great guy, but just now Bob and I are busy talking—and as a matter of fact we're getting on very well, and I've got a feeling that Bob and I are going to be very, very good friends."

I was a little puzzled by this pantomime, for I was almost sure that he had called me Red on purpose. However, I soon forgot about it as he began to admire my room, and the panoramic view from the balcony, with that genuine warmth of appreciation that makes Americans the most delightful guests in the world. I thought him charming. I gathered that he himself was staying at the Gloucester, the most expensive hotel in Hong Kong; and he was very fed up because he had found it so booked up on his arrival a few days ago that he had been obliged to take a suite. It was not the expense that bothered him, but the size. He felt lonely and quite lost in it. And while all that period furniture and ormolu would have been fine in the Ritz, Paris, they were the last thing you wanted here. No, in Hong Kong you wanted atmosphere—like this place. He was crazy about this room of mine.

Then he said, "Look, Bob, may I use your bathroom? It's all this Chinese tea you drink with meals here. It runs straight through you."

"I'm afraid I've no private bathroom," I apologized.

"You expect too much, Bob! I'd swap my private bathroom at the Gloucester for this view any time you like—with an ormolu clock thrown in."

I took him outside and directed him down the corridor, explaining that he could take his choice between Chinese-style and Western-style. I recommended the Chinese-style as more hygienic. Then I closed the door and turned back to Suzie. I said, "But he's very nice, Suzie. Why don't you like him?"

"He got angry because I wouldn't go to bed. He said horrible things."

"That chap? I'm astonished."

"He gets horrible when he is angry. I was scared."

"Well, you skip off. I'll deal with him."

Suzie suggested that to avoid offending him I should explain that she had just gone round to see her baby, and would be coming back. Then she would ring up to say she could not come back after all because the baby was sick. I thought this unnecessarily complicated, but there was no time to argue so I agreed and dispatched her. A minute later Rodney returned. He said, "Hullo, where's our friend?"

I explained, saying she would be back in half an hour, and meanwhile he must make himself at home. He smiled gratefully, and with such friendly warmth that I felt quite ashamed to be deceiving him.

"That's very nice of you, Bob. I can see you've got a real gift for hospitality and friendship—and nowadays that's something one certainly does appreciate."

"Why the 'nowadays'?" I said.

"Well, don't let's kid ourselves, the American stock's pretty low at present. Particularly out here, with our China policy, and Chiang Kai-shek sinking British ships, and all the usual American hysteria about the commies. But you've got to remember, Bob, we're still a young country. We've still a lot to learn. And so far as diplomacy is concerned, we're just a lot of bunglers compared with you British."

"We've done our fair share of bungling," I said, though I was liking him better every minute.

"That's just your British modesty. Now, Bob, what about these pictures? Because I've been very, very much looking forward to seeing what you've been doing."

He explained that he was not a painter himself, but had always been interested in painting above all else. The interest ran in the family, for his mother had one of the finest art collections in New York: and as a matter of fact he was going to pick up one or two little pieces for her in Italy, when he finally reached there on his round-the-world trip. "You see, my mother was a Mitford, and it was her father who started Mitford's in New York. But he died a couple of years back, and my uncle's running the show now." He saw that I looked blank and smiled. "You don't know Mitford's? Well, I guess that means you've never been to New York, because it's practically an institution there. In fact there's a joke about it, that no American artist goes past it without lifting his hat—because it's put so many of them on their feet."

"What is it—a gallery?"

"It started as a gallery. But now it publishes art books as well, and runs an agency side, like an agency for writers or actors. You should get them to handle your work over there, Bob."

"Wait till you see it."

"Well, if that pastel study against the wardrobe is anything to go by, I'm going to like it a lot."

And as I began to place my pictures one after another on the easel for his inspection, feeling that I was baring my soul to him, he was indeed warmly appreciative. He obviously knew a great deal about painting. He used words I did not understand and compared me with artists of whom I had never heard. But his comments showed a real percipience that gave weight to his praise and made me purr with delight.

"Of course, I'm bound to admit, Bob," he said, "that so far as modern painting's concerned I'm biased in favor of the abstract. In fact I've often thought that representational art was dead as the dodo. But there's certainly nothing dead about your work. It's intensively alive. Look at that one, for instance—those girls and that sailor. They're so alive that I can hear them thinking. And what's more important, I can hear you thinking, too!" And he pressed me to send a selection to Mitford's, offering to write to his uncle and tell him about me.

"Mind you, I'm not promising anything, Bob. You must remember that their attitude is basically commercial—what can they make out of you? But my guess is that this stuff will knock them sideways. And I'll be very surprised if they don't—" He broke off. The telephone had begun to ring. He stiffened a little as he watched me pick it up.

"Hullo, this is Suzie!" the instrument vibrated in my ear; for Suzie always shouted on the telephone, as if she had little faith in it. "That man still there?"

I had to keep the instrument pressed hard against my ear to muffle the words from Rodney. Her voice pierced my eardrum, and the pain was so acute that I feared lifelong injury. I muttered hurried regrets, as though at the news of her baby, and rang off.

Rodney said at once, "That was Suzie, wasn't it?"

I turned back to him, and for a moment was aghast at the change that had come over him. He was standing quite rigid, with every muscle in his body tensed like a dog watching a rabbit hole. The blood had drained from his face, and he no longer looked young but middle-aged. There were little angry glinting lights in his eyes.

"Yes, that's right, she rang up to say—" I began, but he interrupted.

"All right, I can guess." He spoke with a kind of deadly patience and control. "I can guess, Bob. She's not coming back, is she?"

"No, she's awfully sorry, but her baby's ill."

He said carefully, "Balls."

"I know it's had a cough. She's been very worried for a long time."

"I said balls, Bob."

We stared at each other. The little pink angry fires in his eyes gave him such a dangerous mad-dog look that I now understood why Suzie had said she was scared. He went on, with that same painstaking control, "Now, that was a very nasty trick she played on me, Bob. A very, very nasty trick. And I am not going to let her get away with it, so I would be very much obliged, Bob, if you would tell me where she lives."

"Rodney, you really can't—"

"I asked you a question, Bob. Perhaps you didn't hear, so I shall repeat it. Would you kindly tell me where she lives?"

"I've no idea," I lied.

"Now, I thought you were my friend, Bob. I thought that this evening I had made a real friend, and I was doing my best to reciprocate. But evidently I was mistaken. Evidently you are not my friend, and have got something against me, or you would answer my question."

"I've nothing against you."

"Then please don't lie to me, Bob. Where does she live?"

"I'm sorry, I can't tell you."

And when I continued to refuse he relaxed the control on himself and gave way to violent rage. His face became flushed and distorted with spite and he submitted me to a stream of abuse, accusing me of taking a dislike to him the moment he entered the room, and of only being nice to him because of what I could get out of him. It was no use trying to protest; I could not get a word in edgeways. I stood helplessly, until after five minutes or so the storm began to pass. A few minutes later he dropped into a chair, buried his face in his hands, and began to sob with self-pity.

"I'm sorry, Bob," he cried. "Oh, God, I'm sorry, I'm sorry, I'm sorry. I wanted so much to be friends with you. And now I've messed it up. I've ruined it. Now you just despise me."

I assured him to the contrary. Very soon he had begun to cheer up, and five minutes later he was quite himself again, grinning at me with that boyish charm as if the scene had never taken place. He said, "You know, you're great, Bob. I like you very, very much. And now I'm going to ask you a very personal question. What was your first impression of me? Now, think carefully. What was your very first impression when I came through that door?"

I said, "Well, I guessed that you were American from your crew cut—and I thought how quietly dressed you were for an American. I mean, you weren't wearing a picture tie, or anything like that."

"Go on."

"Well, I thought how charming and friendly you were, and how self-assured—"

"Sorry to interrupt, Bob. You did say self-assured?"

"Yes, extremely—the way you asked me if you could call me Bob, and told me about the chap who was my namesake, and so on."

He looked gratified, as if this was exactly what he had wanted me to say. "Now, it's very, very interesting that you should say that, Bob. Because two years ago, if I'd had to walk into a room like that and meet a stranger, I'd have been too scared to open my mouth, and—well, the state of my pants would have been nobody's business. In fact I'd have sooner faced a firing squad than come in here like that. So now you know what it means to me when you tell me that you thought I was self-assured. Because I think you mean it. I think it was your honest impression. And now I'm going to let you into a secret. All the way over in the taxi I'd been in a real stew about whether to call you Mr. Lomax, or Robert, or plunge right in with Bob—and preparing that little story about your namesake."

"But it was true, wasn't it? You really did have a classmate called Lomax?"

"I've never met anybody called Lomax in my life before tonight." He smiled with satisfaction at my astonishment. "It was just a little idea that I picked up from someone back in the States—a very, very successful man, who started off as an ordinary salesman, and who told me that he put down his success to that one little trick for breaking the ice with his customers. If he saw a fellow was going to be sticky, he'd just start talking about this namesake called Red, and then call the fellow Red by mistake—and by then they'd be getting along like old buddies, and he'd make his sale."

I said, "Well, I'm damned."

"And I suppose that when I asked to use your bathroom, you thought I really wanted to go?"

"I did rather assume so."

"Well, I didn't. I didn't want to go at all. I only asked because I used to be scared to tell strangers I wanted to go to the bathroom, and I'd hold on until I was bursting. So now I just like to show myself I can do it. And every time I do something like that I say a little prayer in my heart to Dr. John Howard Salter."

"Who's that?"

"Well, Bob,' Dr. John Howard Salter is a very, very brilliant man who lives in New York, and whom I wish that some day you could meet, because he is a man for whom I have the very, very greatest respect and admiration."

Dr. John Howard Salter was a psychoanalyst, and it appeared that Rodney had spent a daily fifty minutes on Dr. Salter's couch for five days a week for the last two years. Finally Salter had advised him—or at least, since analysts never took it upon themselves actually to give advice, had enabled Rodney to see for himself—that the treatment could never wholly succeed while he continued to live at home under the disturbing influence of his possessive mother. He had also been enabled to see for himself in the process of analysis that he must cultivate to the maximum the company of the opposite sex, and let no inhibitions deter him from finding normal and regular sexual outlet. He had thus prescribed for himself a world tour, whose therapeutic advantages would include the breaking of the mother-bond, and the provision of sexual stimulation in every possible shade of skin.

He was now in his second month of travel and at his third port of call. He had previously visited Hawaii and Japan, both of which places had made ample provision not only of stimulation, but also of what Rodney called "outlets."

However, it seemed that the mere quantity of his conquests (or purchases, as they were more often) provided no answer to his basic problem of inferiority. He dreamed of women adoring him, yet believed himself unloved, unlovable; and if indeed some girl did actually show signs of liking him, he would conclude that there must be something wrong with her and disqualify her as a true test case. He seemed perversely determined to prove to himself that he was despised. And Suzie's behavior this evening had been more grist to his mill; he had becen told that dance girls would always go home with you if they liked you, so that her refusal had seemed to him a personal slight. A slight that both hurt and gratified him.

This unhappy state of mind clearly caused Rodney much distress, yet as I listened to him talking I remained quite unmoved. I felt rather ashamed of myself; for, after all, such mental suffering was as much to be pitied as physical illness. A man could no more help being neurotic than he could help being afflicted by tuberculosis or cancer. I tried hard to feel more sympathy. But it would not come.

And then I began to understand. The fact was that something did not quite ring true. He described his own mental complexities with a little too much loving analytical care, a little too much relish; and I realized now that I did not really believe in them. I suspected that they were chiefly a device to make himself more interesting. A device of his self-pity, to attract that very sympathy in which I had found myself deficient—a device to win friends and influence people. I no longer believed that two years ago he had been anything like the frightened little boy he had made out; and I no longer believed in his explanation of the namesake story, or of his visit to the bathroom. I was certain that both these little pantomimes had been performed, not for the reasons given, but for the sole purpose of arousing my interest and sympathy when he told me about them later. I even thought it possible—and the theory gave me a certain malicious amusement—that he had gone to the bathroom for perfectly natural reasons, and had duly relieved himself, and had only afterwards thought of twisting the incident to suit the needs of his self-pity.

All this, of course, meant that he was still a neurotic—but a neurotic of a different kind. A kind whose chief trouble, I suspected, was too much money and no compulsion to work. And with a pauper's satisfaction I reflected on the terrible misfortune of wealth.

I had supposed that my lack of sympathy must inevitably communicate itself to Rodney. However, apparently it did not do so, for when at length he rose to go, he warmly shook my hand, thanked me for my wonderful patience and understanding, and swore that not for years had he made a better friend; and his manner was so sincere that I began to like him again and feel guilty of misjudging him. And it was only at the very last, as we stood in the open door at the point of parting, that he dropped his bombshell.

"You know, Bob, I think I'll move out of the Gloucester and join you down here," he said. "That is, of course, if you've no objection."

The possibility of him wanting to do this had vaguely occurred to me earlier, but I had neglected to prepare any defenses, and I could only stammer unhappily that of course I had no objection at all. Oh, heavens no, I should be delighted. Except that, well, I was rather the sort of chap who liked to bury himself, and—

"Now, you needn't worry on that score, Bob," he interrupted. "Because I know that solitude is very, very precious to a painter, and I shall treat your room as if there was a plague warning on the door."

"Actually, there's another thing," I said, growing a little bolder. "You see, as the only resident here I've got a rather privileged position—"

"Sure, I gathered from Suzie that you were practically Jesus Christ to all the girls down in the bar." He smiled charmingly. "Well, you needn't be afraid that I'll horn in on that racket, because nobody's going to mistake me for Jesus Christ."

This struck uncomfortably near the mark; for however ludicrous his analogy, the ignoble truth was that I was jealous of my position among the girls, and didn't want anybody "horning in." I wanted to continue my solitary enjoyment of their esteem. I resented competition.

I deflated like a punctured tire. "Well, of course you must come here if you want."

"Thanks, Bob. That's very generous of you. And I know we're going to become very, very great friends."

And the next morning he moved in, taking a room on the same floor, next but one to mine. He was installed by nine o'clock—showing an alacrity which wasn't bad going, I thought, for such a hopeless neurotic.

II

Rodney's presence, as it turned out, made no difference to my status at the Nam Kok, though it did cause a certain wonderment at my choice of friends. For the girls, whose shrewdness in judging character never failed to astonish me, saw through him at once: they pronounced him to be a phony, and not to be trusted farther than you could throw the juke box. However, taking cynical approval of his prodigious wealth, they set themselves out to be nice to him, while all the time watching him from withdrawn half-amused little eyes, keeping all but their bodies locked up from him. They nicknamed him "The Butterfly"—and indeed never before had there been seen in the bar such an unequivocal flutterer. He was the butterfly to end all butterflies—a self-proclaimed butterfly who made no secret of his tendency to lose interest in a girl after he had slept with her once. He called this "my little peculiarity."

And his sexual capacity was astonishing. The girls, who after all should have known, declared it to be a phenomenon, and it had soon become a humorous yardstick by which others were judged, and the subject of numberless jokes. He pursued love-making joylessly, with that dogged perseverance with which other men pursue their careers, as though under some obligation to get through the work however much, at times, it might go against the grain; and he discussed his activities in a matter-of-fact manner like the day's affairs at the office. He seemed virtually indifferent to his partner's age, shape, or size: the only condition he imposed was novelty. And thus in a remarkably short time he had disposed of all the Nam Kok girls who were willing, including even old Lily Lou and Doris of the Rimless Glasses—both of whom, indeed, survived their innings, whereas the poor Gwenny Ching was thrown out of his room after only half an hour, for what he afterwards described to me as "lack of imagination and bone laziness," and replaced by another girl summoned by telephone from the bar.

He paid the girls on the whole generously; but now and again he would suffer an acute attack of meanness, when he would haggle over fifty cents, lose his temper, accuse girls of trying to exploit him, and swear never to touch any of the mercenary bitches again. He would also, at such times, accuse waiters of shortchanging him—though if I happened to be with him, he would take good care to disappear before the arrival of the bill. These attacks occurred unpredictably and also became a stock joke among the girls, who claimed they could tell if it was one of his mean days the moment he entered the bar: they said it made his face look pinched and cold.

There were only two girls who refused to go with Rodney. One of these, Wednesday Lulu, had refused on principle, since his prior liaison with several of her girl friends would have made her own relationship with him practically incestuous. The other dissident, Minnie Ho, had simply taken an intense dislike to him: an astonishing departure for Minnie, who usually bestowed her kittenish affections indiscriminately, and whom I had never known to take a dislike to anybody before. However, she could not bear so much as to speak to Rodney; and if he sat down at her table she would become petrified, like a hypnotized rabbit awaiting the strike of a snake.

These two girls, who became known as "the conscientious objectors," were a constant source of vexation to Rodney. He discussed them with me interminably, brooded about them, and finally resorted to various highly involved tricks to try and break down their resistance. On one occasion he engaged a room on another floor, and somehow had word conveyed to Minnie that an old sailor boy friend awaited her there. The unsuspecting Minnie duly arrived upstairs; but after the first minute of total petrification she unfroze, and proving that the affectionate little kitten had the makings of a tigress, scratched his face and fled.

Rodney afterwards explained to me that the scratches had been inflicted by a drunken matelot who had assaulted him in the street. This was unlikely enough in itself; and in any case he must have known that the truth was bound to reach my ears in the bar. Yet for days he kept stubbornly returning to this absurd story, each time adding fresh description as though to make it convincing by the sheer weight of detail. He even insisted on taking me out for a walk to show me the exact spot where the incident was supposed to have occurred; and on another occasion he pointed to a sailor passing in a rickshaw, claiming to recognize the man as his assailant.

"Well, there's a policeman over there," I said. "Why not have him arrested?"

"I've no witnesses. He would just deny it."

I knew better than to declare my disbelief outright. It would have meant an emotional scene, with bitter accusations of disloyalty and betrayal of friendship, and no doubt even tears. And in the end I would have to pretend to believe him about the drunken matelot just for the sake of peace.

But if the two conscientious objectors were thorns in Rodney's flesh, it was still Suzie who preoccupied him most. Now I never saw her alone. He had somehow wheedled from me a promise that whenever she came to see me I would let him know; and although it was a promise I would have had little compunction about breaking, he left me no opportunity to do so, for he would always manage to recognize her step in the corridor, and would be out of his room in a flash, before she had reached my door. And if he happened at that moment to be ensconced with another girl, no matter: Suzie came first, and he would simply abandon the other girl and come hurrying to join us. He had become quite obsessed with her. He declared himself wildly in love, and said she was the only girl he had met since leaving America to whom his "little peculiarity" would not apply. He called her "my Goddess."

One night, after Rodney had been at the Nam Kok a month or so, Suzie dropped into my room about eleven o'clock. She closed the door with a look of disgust.

"What's the matter, Suzie?"

"I just saw that butterfly man go into his room with a street girl."

Suzie characteristically avoided using the proper names of people she disliked, and just as Betty Lau was always "that Canton girl," so Rodney was always "that butterfly man." She had recognized the street girl by her cotton pyjamas, a form of dress disdained by dance girls and bar girls. In fact it was by no means Rodney's first, since by now he had exhausted the resources of the Nam Kok, and with a peculiar preference for girls of the lowest class, he had resorted to the streets rather than the dance halls. But it was the first that had come to Suzie's notice.

She shuddered. "Ugh, he is filthy!"

Just then Rodney came in. He pretended to be struck dumb at the sight of Suzie's beauty, and fell to his knees at her feet—a pantomime that by now had become a familiar accompaniment to his entrance. He kissed her hand.

"My Goddess!"

Suzie withdrew her hand contemptuously. She said, "You better get back to that street girl."

"What street girl?"

"That street girl in your room. You can't keep a street girl waiting, you know. They're too busy with all those coolies from the docks."

"I never had a street girl in my life."

Suzie ignored him and began to talk to me. Presently she mentioned that tomorrow, since Ben had a business lunch, she would not be keeping her usual lunchtime appointment; and Rodney, trying to regain favor, proposed a picnic and bathing party, for which he would provide a hired car and packed lunch from a restaurant.

Suzie, after first declining, finally agreed on condition that I would also agree to come. I had been hesitating on account of work but let myself be persuaded. However, Suzie had no sooner left us to go home than Rodney, speaking mysteriously of some proposition that he wanted to make to her, begged me to cry off the next morning at the moment of departure so that he might have Suzie to himself; and when I refused to take part in such trickery, he made a minor scene, which was only brought to an end by my agreement to a compromise: I would go along for the picnic, but after lunch would feel overcome by a need for solitude and retire, leaving them alone for a minimum period of half an hour. And my peace thus purchased, I was allowed to go to bed.

The next morning a huge sleek Buick stood awaiting our pleasure outside the Nam Kok. The chromium head lamps glittered in the sun; the polished body work shone like a mirror, reflecting the astonished faces of Little Alice and old Lily Lou, who were waiting on the pavement for an escort into the bar.

A uniformed Chinese chauffeur held open the rear door. We sank into—no, not sank, but floated upon—the buoyant cushioning; waved our good-bys; and bouncing in gently sprung luxury, were borne up the twisting escarpment road. We crossed the shoulder of the Peak and began the descent to the south coast of the island. We passed through Repulse Bay with its big hotels, its modern white houses and flats, its crowded popular beach, its fake English castle built by a Chinese millionaire, and somewhere beyond found a charming little beach to ourselves.

Suzie, who adored bathing, put on her costume and dashed first into the sea. We followed her. She swam and splashed and laughed; but all her enjoyment was directed at me, as if she was not even aware of Rodney's existence. We had a tremendous splashing match. It continued until we were both rendered helpless by laughter. Then Rodney, struggling manfully against his discomfiture, shouted, "Come on, I'll take you on next," and submitted Suzie to a tentative spray.

Suzie stopped laughing. She looked at him coldly. "What's the matter? You want to drown me or something?" And turning her back on him, she laughingly resumed her sport with me.

Rodney showed more resilience than usual. He refused to be daunted. And as we extended ourselves on the sunny beach he fell on his knees before Suzie, indulging his taste for histrionics, and kissed her pink-tipped feet.

"My beautiful Goddess! I prostrate myself!"

Suzie gave him a brief contemptuous glance, withdrew her feet from his reach, and turned away as if she had already forgotten him. Rodney was left kneeling there absurdly. I was afraid for a moment that he was going to cry. And I was so sorry for him that for the next half-hour, as we ate the superb cold buffet that he had provided at prodigious cost, I made a persistent effort to manipulate the conversation so that Suzie was obliged to recognize his existence. She gradually forgot her hostility; and by the end of the meal she was speaking to him quite naturally and warmly. I decided that the time had arrived to carry out the terms of my agreement with Rodney. I got up.

"Nature calls," I said, and made for the rocks.

I found a comfortable niche in the rocks, and was soon lulled into a doze by the suck and surge of the water. I was wakened by a sudden loud gollop-gollop as the tide invaded some new chasm in the rocks and then noisily withdrew. I looked at my watch. Three quarters of an hour had passed. I decided to interpret the terms of the contract generously, and lay for another fifteen minutes, then aroused myself and started back.

I met Suzie scrambling over the rocks in search of me. She scolded me indignantly. "What happened? Why did you go off like that, and leave me with that terrible butterfly man? I am very angry. No, don't laugh! I mean it!"

"I'm awfully sorry, Suzie. But he was so anxious to have you alone."

"Yes, you know what for? He wants to take me to—where's Bangkok?"

"Thailand."

"Yes—Thailand—he wants to take me there. He offered me three thousand dollars a month." She stopped being angry and giggled. "Yes, honestly. He told me, 'I will give you three thousand dollars—three times what you get now from Ben.'"

I stared at her. "Suzie, you didn't accept?"

"Accept?" She looked disgusted. "Pouf! You think I would accept to go away with that butterfly man?"

"I'm so glad, Suzie. I was quite scared for a minute. I'd have missed you."

"I wouldn't go with that man, not for ten thousand dollars. I told him, 'Why don't you take that street girl—give her a rest from those coolies?'"

Her refusal, I gathered, had sent Rodney into a tantrum: he had pleaded with her, wept, and finally turned nasty, calling her a cheat, an ingrate, a dirty little sailor's whore. There had been such a dangerous light in his eyes that she had been quite scared; she had quickly made her escape, and come to look for me. Now she thought it likely that we should find he had gone off in dudgeon in the car, and left us stranded.

However, as we climbed over the last rocks we saw him still lying there on the beach. He rose at our approach, grinned, and stood at military attention before Suzie. He performed a mock salute.

"Lieutenant Tessler reporting. He wishes to apologize, and say that he is very, very sorry for the way he spoke to his Goddess. I guess he just got so sore he didn't know what he was saying. O.K., is he forgiven? One nod for 'no,' two for 'yes.'" Suzie vaguely shrugged assent. "Well, that's good enough for me. And if that guy Tessler ever speaks to you like that again, just let me know and I'll wring his neck myself."

I said, trying to help lighten the atmosphere, "Well, Lieutenant Tessler certainly did us proud with that lunch. It was a triumph."

Rodney ignored me and, turning to Suzie, said, "What about another bathe?" I stared in puzzlement, uncertain for a moment whether or not this was a deliberate snub. But he continued to avoid my eyes. I realized that he had not looked at me once since we had rejoined him.

I. laughed and said, "Oh, dear, I'm not in the doghouse now, am I?" Rodney kept his face turned away, pretending not to hear. I said, "Oh, come off it, Rodney. What am I supposed to have done?"

He gave me a brief look, his eyes glassy and remote. "Nothing that I know of," he said. And turning back to Suzie, he forced a casual grin and said, "Now, come on, I want to see you in that bathing costume again, because I don't mind telling you, it makes you look very, very cute."

An hour later as we started home he was still ignoring me. Suzie sat between us in the back seat of the Buick, and he tried to hold her attention with a flow of conversation. Suzie hardly listened: she was silent and pensive, absorbed in thoughts of her own. Presently she interrupted him, turning to me and saying, "I must go to my fortuneteller this evening. You want to come?"

Rodney said quickly, "Sure, we'll go this evening—that'll be fine."

Suzie ignored him, and went on, "I think I will go to that Tibetan monk. It is a long way, but he speaks Shanghai. None of the fortunetellers in Wanchai speak Shanghai, and it is very important with a fortune to understand properly. It is no good running risks."

There followed an absurd three-cornered conversation in which Rodney and I addressed ourselves to Suzie but not to each other, and Rodney took no account of any remark that I made unless Suzie relayed it—but in which it was somehow established that we would drop Suzie in Wanchai, so that she could go back to her room and see her baby, and that she would pick us up later at the Nam Kok, when we would proceed to the fortuneteller's in a threesome.

Suzie's street was too narrow for a car, and we dropped her at the nearest point in Hennessy Road; then Rodney and I drove back in silence. The silence continued in the lift at the Nam Kok, and we separated in silence to our respective rooms. I knew that Rodney was incapable of keeping his grievance to himself much longer, and waited for something to happen.

I did not have to wait long. After five minutes there was a knock on the door and Ah Tong entered, looking uncomfortable and puzzled, as if he suspected that he was being made the victim of some practical joke. He handed me a letter. He said, "From your friend, sir."

He stood watching curiously as I opened the envelope. Inside was a note in Rodney's small, neat, rather old-fashioned hand, with big twirling capital letters like an illuminated manuscript. The message occupied a perfect square, about the area of four postage stamps, in the dead center of the page.

May I take it that, according to the arrangement made in the car, I am to escort Suzie to the fortuneteller alone, and that you will not continue to interfere and to willfully spoil our pleasure?

Rodney Tessler.

I laughed, and told Ah Tong to hang on a moment. And I scribbled underneath:

No, you may not take it, you silly old idiot!
P.S. Thank God somebody else splits infinitives!

I dispatched this reply with the bewildered Ah Tong, who ten minutes later returned with another sealed envelope, and his face now pained to a really pitiable degree by his frustrated curiosity. I drew out a fresh sheet of notepaper and read:

Then may I ask you to remember the many acts of friendship I have shown you in the past (and which you have made no effort to reciprocate) and to stand down as a personal favor?

May I also ask you, when writing insulting remarks, to enclose them in an envelope so that they cannot be read by hotel servants?

Rodney Tessler.

I wrote my reply underneath:

I refuse to stand down because this is an old date with Suzie, and I refuse to pass any more notes because (a) it's childish, and (b) it's wearing out poor old Ah Tong's slipper leather.

P.S. No insults, so no envelope.

I handed the note to Ah Tong, who hesitated and then said, "Sir, please excuse me. You have quarreled with your friend?"

I laughed, "I'm afraid so, Ah Tong."

"Sir, what about?"

"Well, that's the trouble. I'm not quite sure."

Ah Tong departed, now with a determined, almost evangelical expression, as if he conceived it his mission to act as peacemaker, and would not rest until he had seen us reconciled. However, Rodney must have dismissed him, to his great disappointment, for he did not return; and when, after a further fifteen minutes or so, there was another knock on my door, this time it was Rodney himself who entered.

He closed the door and stood there stiffly. He said, "Well, Bob, I've decided to sink my pride, and throw myself on your mercy. The fact is, Bob, I love that girl. I'm terribly, terribly in love with her, Bob, and it's making me—oh, God, if you knew—if you knew how unhappy. . . ." And he began to cry.

His tears always weakened me, and I waited until they were over to tell him that I didn't care a damn about the fortuneteller, that of course I would stand down; but before the opportunity presented itself, he was seized in the midst of the tears by a sudden fresh attack of fury, and he submitted me to a stream of violent abuse, during the course of which I learned for the first time the nature of my supposed offense on the beach: it appeared that, although shamelessly riding in his hired car and eating his food, I had persistently tried to turn Suzie against him. The diabolical tactics that I had employed to this end included telling her—he claimed to have overheard me whispering——that he made a habit of entertaining street girls; subtly distracting her during lunch from paying him any attention; and carefully choosing the moment of greatest disruption to carry out my bargain and leave them alone.

I said wearily, "Rodney, you know that's all rubbish. You had no luck with Suzie, so you want to put all the blame on me. Well, I can't stand it. It's too exhausting. Go and find somebody else to quarrel with."

There followed an excruciating half-hour in which, his face ugly and distorted with spite, he continued to belabor me with abuse, preventing all possibility of escape by planting himself grimly before the door—until finally, his rage working itself out, he arrived at the recommendation that I should depart forthwith for London, Vienna, or New York, and place myself in the hands of a psychoanalyst. This conclusion of Rodney's, that he himself was perfectly balanced and that I was really the neurotic, had recently become his standard ending for every scene, so that I welcomed its arrival as the herald of my release. Five minutes later we were shaking hands and agreeing to visit the fortuneteller in a threesome as originally planned. And in the midst of this scene of amity Suzie arrived to collect us.

The Buick had remained at our disposal, and once more we climbed into the back. Rodney was now behaving so congenially that Suzie chattered to us both without discrimination; and all went well until we had passed through the business center of Hong Kong and were entering the Western District, when I suddenly became aware of a familiar tension.

I glanced across at Rodney. And sure enough, he was sitting once more with every muscle taut, and with that familiar tense, set look on his face. And just then, as I wondered what on earth had started him off again, he leaned forward and tapped the driver on the shoulder and ordered him to stop. The driver slowed down, looking for somewhere to pull in to the side; but the cars were parked along the pavement without a gap.

"I told you to stop!" Rodney snapped furiously.

"What's the matter?" Suzie said, in the same bewilderment as myself. "What's happened?"

Rodney ignored her. The driver obediently brought the car to a standstill in midstream, blocking the traffic behind, and sat waiting indifferently.

Rodney got out and slammed the door. He went to the driver's window, taking out his wallet.

"Drop these people where they want to go, then pack up," he said.

He handed the driver some money, then came and stuck his head through the back window, his face pinched and spiteful, his eyes glinting with hate. His hand on the door trembled.

"That's what you want, isn't it?" he said. "That's what you've been waiting for all day—just to get rid of me? Well, I hope you're happy now. Though my God, when I think what I've—"

He suddenly bit his lip and closed his eyes as though from an unbearable access of self-pity. He turned away quickly and crossed the road without regard for traffic. He disappeared along the pavement in the crowd.

Suzie and I stared at one another. I said, "But what on earth was all that about, Suzie? What suddenly upset him?"

"I don't know. I was being very nice to him."

There was an angry blaring of horns from the cars piled up behind us. The chauffeur was indifferently lighting a cigarette. I told him to drive on, and he unhurriedly threw away the match, lodged the cigarette in an ashtray, put the car in gear.

"I was being very nice," Suzie said. "Didn't you see?" She was indignant now that so much niceness had been wasted. "And after that street girl! He was lucky I even spoke to him, never mind being so nice."

"You didn't put your hand on my knee while we were talking, did you?"

"No, I never touched you."

"Then it must have been something we said."

But a post-mortem of our conversation revealed nothing that could possibly have offended Rodney, and we decided that it must have been something quite imaginary, or else simply that his distemper had come round automatically, like a point on a wheel, in the endless cycle of his moods. I was only worried, since he had looked so distraught, that he might have gone off to do something desperate, like commit suicide; but when I suggested this possibility to Suzie, she shook her head. "No, he won't kill himself. Not today."

"He's the sort of person who would, just to make us feel bad about it," I said. "Anyhow, what makes you so sure he won't?"

"I just know. I could tell."

She spoke with the conviction that told me her sixth sense had been in operation. This sixth sense of Suzie's, like the sharpened sense of smell that counterbalances blindness, counterbalanced her illiteracy. It often afforded her astonishing flashes of insight; and although these flashes occurred unpredictably, and never to order, whenever they did occur they proved unerring, and I had come to place in them an implicit trust.

"Well, thank God for that," I said. "We needn't worry about him." I glanced out of the window. We were now passing through the oldest part of Hong Kong, where the margin of land between sea and escarpment was barely a hundred yards wide. Short streets led down to the quay, and I caught a glimpse of the *Fatshan,* the steamer that plied between Hong Kong and the Portuguese colony of Macao, and of forests of swaying junk masts. "Aren't we nearly there, Suzie?"

"Yes, soon."

"By the way, what are you going to see the fortuneteller about?" I knew that she never paid such a visit without some particular problem on her mind.

"I just want to ask him something," she said evasively. And she added, "I may tell you afterwards."

"All right, Suzie."

"Driver, stop! We must walk now—up that hill."

We dismissed the driver and turned up a side street, a narrow canyon packed with stalls and pedestrians that soared up out of sight like a switchback, ending somewhere among the houses at mid-level on the escarpment. It was turned almost into a tunnel by the ceiling of washing on bamboo poles. It rose in a series of flights of steps, each flight steeper than the last, and we climbed slowly, keeping pace with a sedan chair carried on the shoulders of four coolies. Inside sat a tiny old Chinese woman fluttering a cheap paper fan. We reached an intersecting road and turned off through a vegetable market, and past an open site that at first glance appeared to be a rubbish dump, and at second glance a gigantic rabbit warren because of the holes in the rubbish like burrows, and at third glance a human warren, which is what it was—a colony of squatters' huts made from old sacking, rotting wood, and flattened-out tins. The road seethed with humanity. Beyond the warren of rubbish was a warren of concrete: a block of tenements, into which we turned. I followed Suzie up a concrete staircase. It was strewn with litter and stained by spittle. The building resounded with voices, the cries of children, the clatter of mah-jongg. We turned down a dark narrow concrete passage and Suzie knocked at a door. A blue close-shaven scalp appeared amidst a waft of cooking—and under the scalp, a broad friendly grin. The door opened farther, revealing the fortuneteller's faded, food-stained orange robe, tattered at the extremities where it trailed on the floor. He shook our hands and invited us inside, grinning and fussing and chattering in the dialect of Shanghai. He was himself a native of Shanghai: the Tibetan guise had only been adopted to give himself a professional *cachet*.

The room was partitioned with sacking, from behind which came the hushed voices of a numerous family that had been admonished to keep quiet, and also the aura of frying fat which now fought with the smell of incense from burning joss sticks for the domination of our nostrils. The joss sticks were stuck like fireworks into an old soup tin filled with sand on the fortuneteller's cheap little table. Near them was a pile of tattered almanacs, a Tibetan rosary, the shell of a tortoise. The table was squeezed into a corner of the cubicle, for most of the space was occupied by a huge black wooden settee, elaborately carved and inlaid with ivory; and here the fortuneteller made me sit, while Suzie sat on a chair at the table, and he himself behind the table on a wooden box. He hooked a pair of horn-rimmed glasses over his ears and the session began.

It lasted nearly an hour. It was conducted with great solemnity, and no traditional method of divination was omitted. The fortuneteller pored over astrological charts and consulted almanacs; he read Suzie's palm and felt the bumps of her head; he watched her shake a cylinder of spills until one fell out onto the floor, then looked up its number in a key; he examined the fateful positions of two banana-shaped pieces of wood which she had cast upon the table.

Meanwhile my discomfort on the flat-seated straight-backed settee mounted with the steep curve of compound interest. I wriggled and squirmed on the flat unyielding wood. Then all at once I realized that I was under scrutiny: a child's eye was watching me from a hole in the canvas partition. I challenged it with a bold stare, and it sheepishly withdrew. I looked away. Presently, from the corner of my eye, I saw it return. I challenged it again, and again it disappeared. And this game continued for nearly fifteen minutes, providing a welcome distraction from the cruel torture of the settee; and we were still playing it when Suzie turned round in her chair.

"All right—finished!"

Her face glowed with satisfaction: evidently the session had been a success. She opened her bag and gave the fortuneteller a five-dollar note. He grinned us to the door. I turned abruptly in the door and gave a last wink to the eye at the hole: it shot back in surprise. We went back down the spittle-stained stairs and out into the street. Suzie glowed in silence, nursing her secret happiness. We strolled past the squatters' rubbish warren, through the market. The road was littered with trodden cabbage leaves, the air laden with heavy decayed-vegetable smells.

Suzie said, "I am going to England."

"What? *What* did you say, Suzie?"

"I am going to England." She glowed. "In three years' time."

"Good Lord, Suzie! Are you really?"

"Yes, my fortuneteller just told me. Ben will take me. He will divorce his wife in Hong Kong, then take me to England."

"Well, how marvelous! Is that what you went to find out?"

"Yes, I had got scared. I was scared that Ben had finished with me." And she explained that recently he had put off their lunchtime meetings so often on account of business lunches that she had grown suspicious. She had been afraid that he had fallen out of love with her; she had even begun to wonder if he was keeping another Chinese girl. She had been so worried about it that at night she had lain tossing and turning and been unable to sleep. It had been like that for nearly two weeks.

I said, "But Suzie, I'd no idea! Why didn't you tell me?"

"I was ashamed. I didn't want to lose face."

"Suzie, how absurd—to feel that with me!"

"If it was true, it would have been a terrible loss of face. I would have wanted to kill myself. But it is all right, he still loves me. My fortuneteller got four signs." She purred with satisfaction. "Yes, four! He told me, 'I only need one sign really, but I got four. I got one sign in your horoscope, one sign in your hand, and one sign in the numbered sticks. Then you threw the two pieces of wood, and they said, Yes, we agree. So that is four signs altogether that your boy friend loves you'!"

"Well, no wonder you're looking so pleased with yourself."

"And he got two signs about going to England. Only he was not quite sure about the three years. He said it might only be two and a half years, or it might be three and a half."

We turned down the steps. It was dusk and most of the washing had been taken in, leaving the bare bamboo poles jutting horizontally overhead. Far below the canyon was discharging its stream of pedestrians into the broad river of the street. Trams clanked past. The noise of the city came up to our ears like the noise of a busy factory.

Suzie said, "What dress shall I wear in England? You think Chinese dress would look best, or English dress?"

"You've plenty of time to think about that, Suzie," I said. "Three years is a long time."

"No, it will go very quickly. What do you think, Robert?"

"I think you should stick to Chinese dress. You'd be a sensation in London."

"Yes," she nodded. "I think Chinese dress, too."

The last light went quickly: it was dark when we reached the bottom of the steps. The neon signs along the main road leaped on and off, flashing out their messages in red, green, white, pink, blue. They said: Don't mourn the sun. The sun is a spoilsport, and now that it is out of the way we can enjoy ourselves, get on with the night's gaiety.

A tram came along, clattering and sparking. We climbed to the top deck and were carried jolting along between the swarming pavements and cliffs of neon; into the dim quiet streets of the Central District that had begun to die its nightly death; out again into the lights, the neon, the swarms of Wanchai.

"I don't want to go to that dance hall tonight," Suzie said. "I feel too happy."

"We'll have dinner somewhere."

"Yes, let's go to that Pekin place." She giggled. "That place where we went after Ben spanked me."

At the restaurant she wanted to sit at the same table as before: it brought Ben nearer. She talked about Ben and about going to England all through dinner. Her happiness made her look very radiant and pretty; but she was remote from me, in a dream world that I could not enter, and it was as though there was a sheet of plate glass between us. After the meal I asked her if she would like me to walk home with her; and she said, "If you want—you can walk home with me if you want." She did not care one way or the other.

"No, I think I'll get back," I said.

"All right, good night, Robert. I shall sleep tonight!"

"Yes, sleep well, Suzie."

I strolled down the street to the water front. The stalls along the pavement were lit by the white glare of pressure lamps. I stopped at a fruit stall where there were laichees hung in bunches from the wooden posts and joists: as a child in England I had sometimes been given tinned laichees as a special treat, but I had not eaten fresh laichees until I had come to Hong Kong. They were as succulent as the best hothouse grapes. The stall keeper unhooked a bunch, and weighed it, and put it in a paper bag. I took a loose one from the bag and shelled it as I walked along. A flock of half a dozen rickshaws overtook me. They contained a party of sailors. When I turned the corner onto the water front they were paying off the rickshaw men outside the Nam Kok. They went into the bar. I passed the bar entrance and went through the main entrance into the hall. I stood waiting for the lift and thinking about Rodney. I thought: I hope Suzie was right about him not committing suicide. I hope he hasn't cut his wrist, or hung himself from the ceiling.

But just then the lift came down, and the gate clanked open, and inside stood Rodney.

He came out quickly, his crew-cut head lowered, not seeing where he was going, and walked straight into me, nearly knocking the paper bag out of my hand. Several laichees rolled on the floor.

He started to apologize. "I say, I'm awfully—" He stopped as he recognized me. His eyes turned hostile. Then they became glazed and remote as he canceled out the recognition, tried to look as if I wasn't there. He turned away abruptly. He went through the swing door into the bar.

I smiled to myself. Well, that's better than finding him hanging, I thought. He may be a pain in the neck, but I'd be sorry to find him hanging. I'd feel there was something I could have done.

I picked up the fallen laichees and went into the lift. The liftman heaved on the rope. We rumbled slowly upwards, causing that sudden mysterious "clank" as we passed each floor.

Chapter Five

It was two days later that Suzie turned up at my room, at the unusual hour of three o'clock in the afternoon, looking white and shaken. She could not have looked more ghastly if she had just seen a judge put on a black cap and heard herself sentenced to death.

"Suzie! What's happened?"

"Nothing."

She pretended to look at a painting leaning against the wall. She said, "When did you do that?"

"That picture? Several weeks ago."

She nodded, tense and bottled up. I knew that she must have just come from a lunchtime appointment with Ben, and I thought I could guess what had happened: Ben had given her the brush-off. I had been half expecting it. The more I had thought about those business lunches of Ben's, the less I had believed in them; and I had not been able to share Suzie's faith in the fortuneteller.

She looked at the canvas on the easel. "Who's that?"

"You."

She nodded vaguely. She said, "I just met Ben."

"Oh, yes?"

"We're finished."

I said inadequately, "Suzie, I'm awfully sorry."

"My fortuneteller must have made a mistake. Ben just told me, 'Suzie, we've got to finish—because my wife has found out everything.' Oh, yes, we only have to finish because of his wife. He still loves me, you know." I knew she did not believe this; she was only saying it to save her pride. She realized that her voice had lacked conviction, and added, "Oh, yes, he still loves me. He told me, 'I love you terribly, Suzie—I never loved anybody so much in my life.'" She stood tensely, her face white and taut. "All right, I go to the cinema now."

"The cinema? Suzie, stay and talk for a bit—I'll get some fresh tea."

"No, I want to go to the cinema. I hear the film at the Roxy is very good. A musical film—you heard about it, didn't you?"

"I don't think so."

"Oh, everybody is talking about that film—I don't want to miss it." She went to the door, trying to look as though nothing mattered to her except the film.

"Can I come with you, Suzie?"

"No, I will go alone. I don't think that film would interest you." She opened the door, then paused and said unconvincingly, "It's just the money I care about, that's all. That's the only reason I mind finishing. Of course I'd have been hurt if he didn't love me still—but he only finished because of his wife. You believe that, don't you?"

"Of course, Suzie," I lied.

"Oh, yes, don't worry, it was only because of his wife. He still loves me very much—you needn't worry about that." And she went out stiffly, and closed the door.

II

Ben extended his legs from the balcony chair, laid his hands complacently on his stomach, and said, "Of course the most important factor in the relationship between a man and a woman is mental companionship. The physical side doesn't matter a damn—not a tuppeny damn." He gave me a glance and said tolerantly, "All right, you can smile. You can smile all you want, old chap, it doesn't bother me."

"I'm sorry, I was just remembering that morning at the Kit Kat, when you'd just discovered that lack of sex was responsible for all human ills."

"I was talking nonsense—absolute nonsense. I was suffering an attack of delayed adolescence, that's all. I was like a kid with a new toy. But I can't say I regret the experience. I'm sure it was very necessary for my development. It gave me a sense of values. And I know now that it's all rubbish, this fuss that chaps make about sex."

I said, "Like the fuss that chaps in the desert make about water."

"I'm not quite with you."

"I mean the chap who's just had a surfeit of water is inclined to underrate its importance to those without it."

"Well, I don't care what you say. I've got this business all worked out now. And I've no doubt you'll learn for yourself one day." He had never been more pompous. "Anyhow, you must admit that old Liz has behaved marvelously over the whole affair—absolutely bloody marvelously."

He had rung up only a few minutes after Suzie had left the room and asked if he could drop in to see me. He had felt he owed me some explanation of what had happened. It was apparently quite true that Elizabeth now knew about Suzie, for he had told her himself the night before—not by way of confession, but in order to hurt her. It seemed that the marital bliss about which he had told me at the Kit Kat had been short-lived, and the old domestic frictions had long since returned; they had begun to have rows again with increasing frequency, and these had culminated in a major row last night after a cocktail party at their own house. During the course of this Ben, well primed with drink, had been provoked by some wounding remark of Elizabeth's into seizing upon the most lethal weapon in his armory with which to retaliate. And he had told her all about his lunchtime betrayals with Suzie.

At first Elizabeth had refused to believe him. Then she had turned as white as a sheet, and without another word had gone to her bedroom. Fifteen minutes later he had heard her drive off in the car. He had helped himself to another whisky, muttering "Good riddance." But by midnight, when she had still not returned, he had begun to grow anxious. He had been filled with remorse. He had spent the next hour telephoning friends and hotels, but nobody had seen her. Then he had remembered her once saying, as they had walked together along a cliff-top on the far side of the island, "If ever I wanted to kill myself, this is where I would do it." He had been convinced that she had committed suicide. He had been seized by panic. He had summoned a taxi by telephone, driven across the island to the cliffs, and searched for two hours among the rocks at their foot. He had returned home empty-handed as daylight broke, to find still no sign of her at the house, and had set off again to make a round of the police stations.

He had finally got back to the house again at about eight-thirty, guilt-stricken and in despair—only to be greeted on the doorstep by Elizabeth herself.

"Oh, hullo, darling," she had smiled, with the same casual composure with which she might have greeted him on his return from the office. Then she had noticed his disheveled appearance, and exclaimed in apparent astonishment, "Good heavens, what on earth have you been doing?"

She herself had spent the night with friends, who at her request had denied her presence when Ben had rung up at midnight to inquire for her. They had been horrified to hear of her terrible ordeal, and had offered her sleeping tablets upon retiring. But she had refused them. She hated having to fall back on drugs—it seemed somehow so weak-minded.

"And as a matter of fact I never slept better," she told Ben brightly. "And oh, by the way," she held out a letter, "here's my ultimatum."

The ultimatum, written on the friends' notepaper after the good night's sleep, had laid down her conditions for continuing to live with him. These had included, in addition to a number of other minor restrictions on his activities, a complete ban on after-office drinking at the Kit Kat, and of course the immediate dismissal of Suzie. However, she had made one concession. She had come to realize, she had explained, that her objection to his sailing had been very shortsighted, and had no doubt partly accounted for his kicking over the traces and so shamefully demeaning himself with the Chinese girl; and accordingly she had decided to allow him to resume his sailing on Saturday afternoons.

"Absolutely marvelous," Ben repeated. "Yes, there's no doubt that old Liz has certainly turned out tops. I don't believe that one woman in a hundred would have behaved so well. No, let's go further—let's say not one in a thousand."

I was silent. I thought it might have augured better for their future if Elizabeth had behaved a little less well.

Ben went on complacently, "And it's made the turning point of our marriage—no doubt about that. We've both learned our lesson. We shall be able to make a real go of it now—on the basis of mental companionship. Of course I realize that it's all been very hard on Suzie. But I don't mind telling you, I'd decided to finish with her anyhow."

"Yes, I gathered you'd been cooling off a bit," I said.

"Well, let's face it, old chap, a relationship of that kind is doomed from the start—because there's no mental companionship whatsoever. I'm not blaming Suzie, mind you. Considering her profession and upbringing, she's a very decent girl. It's not her fault that she never went to school, that she's illiterate. But we'd nothing in common—nothing to talk about."

"We always find plenty," I said.

"Frankly, I can't imagine what. Mention anything you like—business, politics, sailing, something you've read in the newspaper—and what do you get? Blank looks. Do you know, I found out the other day she hadn't even heard of Winston Churchill."

"I'm astonished," I said. "Are you sure?"

"My dear chap, positive. I said, 'Come off it, you must have heard of Winston Churchill—British Prime Minister during the war.' But she didn't even know what a Prime Minister was."

"Well, she's heard of Mao Tse-tung and Sun Yat-sen and Ching Ming—which is probably more than you have."

"I know the first two. I don't know that last chap."

"It's not a chap. It's the Chinese festival for honoring the ancestral spirits."

"Oh, I know what you mean now—and a damned nuisance it is, too, because the Chinese staff in the office expect a day's holiday on full pay, and we have to shut down the office while they all troop up to the cemeteries with buckets and mops to clean the graves. Well, frankly, old chap, that just goes to prove my point. Because let's face it, you can't have mental companionship with a girl who's been brought up to believe in all that ancestor-worship nonsense—it's just bloody barbaric."

And it was only later, as he was leaving, that a chink momentarily appeared in the armor of his pomposity and revealed the doubts lurking below. He had just risen from the balcony chair, and glancing over the balustrade he noticed a sailing boat from the Yacht Club skimming along the water close to the quay, its wind-taut sails gleaming white in the sun. His eyes shone with eager anticipation. "That's what I'll be doing on Sunday," he said.

I said, "I thought your license was only for Saturday afternoons."

And I had no sooner spoken than I saw that he had realized the significance of his own mistake: he had unconsciously wished that it might indeed have been Sunday, when he could have sailed all day: that it might have been both Saturday afternoon and Sunday, and that it might have been in freedom, whenever he chose, and without a license to be obtained.

He said, "That's right, Saturday. I meant Saturday." But his eyes no longer shone, they were confused.

And just then his attention was caught by something else in the harbor: the winking light of an Aldis lamp on the bridge of a cruiser. Anchored over towards the Kowloon side, it was flashing a message to H.M.S. *Tamus,* the shore station in Hong Kong. Ben watched, his lips silently shaping each letter that was winked out.

And then I noticed his eyes again; all their confusion had gone, and had been replaced by a look of calm and untroubled satisfaction such as I had never seen in them before—the look of a skipper on his bridge when he feels the ship under his control and knows himself master of its destiny: the look of a man engaged in a man's job. And I knew that for a moment he was back in the Navy—back in a life of clear-cut relationships, clear-cut objectives, clear-cut orders to give and obey. Back in a life with no women, no nagging, no untidy emotions, no sex.

The light gave a few last quick winks and went out. He paused another moment then turned away. The look of satisfaction had gone from his eyes, the confusion had returned.

He took out his wallet. He said, "Do me a favor, will you? I tried to give Suzie some money, but she wouldn't take a cent. But you could take her out to dinner for me—get her mind off it a bit."

He gave me a hundred-dollar note. He opened the door, then paused again.

"You know to tell the truth I never thought she cared a damn about me," he said. "I always thought she was really in love with you. The way she talked about you—well, I mean, one would have thought her head over heels."

"I expect that was before the spanking," I said. "It was that Tarzan stuff that did the trick."

"Well, I don't know."

"Of course it did. It made her your slave. You ought to try it out on Elizabeth."

"On old Liz? My dear chap, I wouldn't dream—" He broke off and smiled. "Well, it would be something to do on Sunday. I'll have to give it a thought."

III

"That man is no good! No, I pity any girl who gets mixed up with that man! Nothing but lie, lie, lie! 'Suzie, you're so sweet!' he says. 'Suzie, you're so pretty! I shall divorce my wife, Suzie! I shall take you to London, Suzie!' Yes, he said that fifty, a hundred times! And now he pushes me out!"

Suzie exploded about my room as unpredictably as a firecracker. She had not been to the cinema, but had walked about the streets brooding for nearly three hours; and though she had returned with her feelings still bottled up, and still pretending not to feel hurt, I had seen that she was not far from bursting point, and had done everything I could to provoke the burst; and by the end of ten minutes her injured feelings had begun to come out. And when once Suzie gave vent to her feelings, she could throw as theatrical a scene as any prima donna: the tense white-faced little figure in jeans had turned improbably into a tornado, and another five minutes had seen the end of my ash tray, which now lay about the room in a thousand scattered fragments. She had hurled it against the wall to help out expression.

I thought this a very healthy sign and was delighted. However, I had taken warning from the ash tray, and worked my way round the room surreptitiously concealing other breakable items.

"Yes, pushes me out! And tries to give me money!" She slashed at the bed with a paintbrush that I had overlooked, leaving some pink paint from the brush on the blanket, and some hairs from the blanket on the brush. She had not noticed what she was holding, and there was already paint on her hands, her jeans, her face.

"Suzie, you'd better let me have—"

She ignored me. "Yes, he tried to give me money! I told him, 'You think I'm a street girl or something? You keep your filthy money!'"

"Good for you, Suzie." In her first version of the incident, before she had really got going, she had described her refusal of the money as dignified and polite. But the exaggeration was pardonable.

"Yes, I'm going to make trouble for that man! Tomorrow I'm going to his office, I'm going to tell everybody 'Your boss is no good! I was a virgin, a good girl, and your boss seduced me!'"

She momentarily made herself believe that this was true, and her indignation renewed itself. She thought of other ways she could punish him. She would also go to his house and expose him to his servants. And best of all, she would write a letter to the Number One Top Englishman of Hong Kong—at least I would write the letter from her dictation—recounting the episode of the spanking, when Ben had masqueraded as a policeman. He would undoubtedly be sent to gaol for this offense—"Yes, they'll put him in the monkey-house! For maybe two, three years! That will serve him right!"

However, the discovery that she wielded the power to send him to gaol slightly awed her. Her anger noticeably subsided.

"Let's hope he gets three years," I said encouragingly. "It'll be well deserved."

She said doubtfully, "Yes, he deserves a bad time, that man." She was not sure that she liked to hear me disparaging Ben; it was her own privilege. It made her want to defend him. And a few minutes later she was doing so, and diverting all the blame to the evil influence of Elizabeth. But she had blown off nearly all her steam; she was almost back to normal.

I said, "Suzie, have you seen your face? Look in the mirror."

She did so, and sullenly resisted a smile. "What, that bit of paint? I don't care." But soon she was managing to smile at herself, and saying, "Well, suppose I did go to his office? They wouldn't know I wasn't a virgin—I could make plenty of trouble for him!"

"I still like the idea of the letter to the Governor best."

She glanced at me a trifle anxiously, afraid I might try and hold her to her threat. "No, that's no good—that wouldn't punish his wife. It's his wife who ought to go to the monkey-house." She looked at her hands and giggled. "I'm in a mess!"

"Here, catch." I threw her the turpentine rag. "And you must be frightfully hungry after all that, aren't you, Suzie?"

"No, I couldn't eat anything."

"Well, you've got to try. Because I had none of your scruples about accepting Ben's money, and I've got a hundred dollars just for taking you out to dinner. So come on, let's go and enjoy ourselves."

She consented without much enthusiasm, and after she had cleaned herself up we set off. Ah Tong was just going off duty, and as we waited at the lift he grinned and said, "Your friend has gone out. You are safe, sir."

"Thank God for that," I said.

Rodney had still not spoken to either Suzie or myself since the scene in the car two days ago, and Ah Tong, who saw no hope of being able to reconcile us, had taken to reporting Rodney's movements to me, so that as far as possible I could avoid the embarrassment of running into him.

"That stupid butterfly man!" Suzie fluttered her hands like a butterfly. "You know, I feel better now. Yes, I feel quite hungry!"

"That's marvelous, Suzie. Where shall we go?"

"Some small place. No, I think some big place. Yes, let's go to some big stuck-up place with music, and make that man give us a good time!"

We settled on a restaurant in Kowloon where there was dancing and cabaret, and since this meant that Suzie would have to change we arranged to meet in three quarters of an hour at the ferry. I went back to my room to put on jacket and tie, and then passed the time strolling along the quay. I arrived first at the ferry and stood watching three men and a woman playing mah-jongg in a sampan tied up near the pier. It was dark and they played by the light of a hurricane lamp, squatting round a low packing case, indifferent to the little vessel's bobbing and lurching. It made me seasick even to watch and I turned away, just as Suzie came up in a rickshaw. She wore a little Chinese brocade jacket over a plain white silk cheongsam, and white shoes. She carried a gold handbag to match the gold thread of the brocade. Her nails were freshly painted.

"Suzie, you look marvelous," I said. "And you've been so quick about it."

"I'm so angry—I tore my stocking getting into that rickshaw." She craned backwards to examine one of her nylons.

"Have you dabbed it with spit?"

"Spit?"

"Don't you know? I'll show you on the boat."

She held my arm as we went to the turnstile. "I feel happy now, you know! I feel beautiful!"

Her gaiety was a trifle forced, and the hurt was still visible underneath; but she had accepted the situation now as a *fait accompli,* and had made up her mind that she was not going to let it get her down. And on the ferry she gaily pretended that we were on a steamer bound for America, and waved her handkerchief as though to Ben, saying, "Good-by! Good-by! So sorry to leave you, only I'm off to marry a rich Yankee!" And when we disembarked on the other side, she said, "I never knew there were so many Chinese in New York—it looks just like Kowloon!"

We decided that on Ben's money we could afford a taxi, but there was no taxi to be seen so we took two rickshaws. We turned into Nathan Road, twisting in and out of the congested buses and cars, the rickshaw men keeping up a steady jog trot, their broad bare calloused feet padding the hard city street. The shirt of my man was in holes, I could see his shoulder blades working. We halted at traffic lights, turned off to the left, stopped outside a building with a red neon sign. The sign cast a glow on the pavement. The sign went out and the glow vanished; then, as the Chinese characters came alight again one by one the glow reappeared, becoming redder each moment like the reflection of a fire being fanned by the wind. We went up in the lift to the restaurant on the top floor, where the Chinese manager in white dinner jacket led us through the crowded room. There were parties of both Chinese and Europeans at the tables, many in evening dress, and there was a dance floor and a Filipino band. Suzie followed the manager with poise: in her early days in the dance halls she had been brought often to such places, and she was more accustomed than I was to their sophistication.

The manager took us to a table within a few feet of the band. I was about to accept it meekly, but Suzie said, "There is too much noise here. There is a better table over there."

"It is reserved," the manager grinned. "You see the notice—Reserved.'"

"We will go deaf at this table," Suzie said.

"I am sorry, it is the only table."

"All right, we will go somewhere else. You charge a big price in this restaurant, and we are not going to pay a big price to go deaf."

"Well, perhaps the party that reserved the other table will not turn up. I will take a chance."

He took us to the reserved table, removed the sign, deferentially lit my cigarette, and gestured to a waiter who was busy at another table to come and attend us. After he had gone I laughed and said, "He was fearfully impressed, Suzie—and so am I. You've got such aplomb."

"What does that mean, 'aplomb'?"

"It means you could wipe the floor with any other woman in this room." I nodded to the menu that the waiter had put into her hands. "Now, what do you fancy?"

She gave me an odd look, and I suddenly remembered that she could not read the menu. I laughed and said, "Suzie, how ridiculous of me! Well, that just goes to show. You've got so much aplomb that I'd completely forgotten."

"And now you feel ashamed of me."

"Ashamed! Suzie, if you say anything like that again I'll turn you upside down and spank you like Ben—because I'm so proud of you that I have to keep looking round to make sure that people are watching us."

I did really feel proud of her, for I thought she looked lovelier than I had ever seen her in the white silk cheongsam, with the black smooth hair falling to her shoulders and framing the little white face with the high Mongolian cheekbones and the long black elliptical eyes. And then there was a kind of old-fashioned primness and modesty about her appearance, due partly to her prim erect Chinese manner of sitting without leaning against the back of the chair, and partly to the tall collar of her cheongsam, reminiscent of those high neckbands worn by Victorian ladies to effect the maximum concealment of skin; and this appearance amused and enchanted me, all the more so because of its incongruity.

Suzie said, "They are eating Pekin duck over there. You like Pekin duck?"

"I only had it once, it's so expensive—but I loved it. And let's have some Chinese wine."

"Hot?"

"Oh, yes, hot."

The food was delicious, but Suzie had become rather silent and preoccupied and ate little, and we did not talk much, except to discuss the Pekinese singer who had appeared at the microphone with the Filipino band. She wore a long shiny black cheongsam with sequins, and looked like a beautiful stiff china doll, and she sang with doll-like mannerisms as if she was operated by strings. The collar of her cheongsam was even stiffer and taller than Suzie's, and made her look like a giraffe-woman with elongated neck. She had appeared first in a jacket of white fluffy fur, that you wanted to blow like the fluff of a dandelion to see how many blows it took to make it disappear; and this now lay behind her on the grand piano like a gigantic powder puff of swan's-down. She looked no more than twenty-five across the room, but according to Suzie she was at least forty, and was the concubine of a rich businessman who had brought her out of China with his wife and children before the revolution.

She sang Mandarin songs in a small squeaky plaintive voice, going on and on with that characteristic Mandarin monotony, with the same tone and the same stiff doll-like mannerisms whether the songs were happy or sad.

"I think you sing just as well, Suzie," I said. "And you certainly manage to look more human about it. But I suppose it's remarkable that she can sing at all in that collar."

"It is very smart, that collar," Suzie said, a little envious that it was taller than her own. "Oh yes, a tall collar is very smart."

"Let's dance."

I was a poor dancer but Suzie, like many dance girls, danced beautifully; and moreover she had that art of transmitting her skill, while seeming to remain all the time passive and as light as a feather, so that her partner might believe it his own. And as I abandoned myself to this beguiling illusion, and seemed to blossom with new talent, my usual self-consciousness on the dance floor miraculously vanished. I had never enjoyed dancing so much before. And whereas before I had always been puzzled by the vast enjoyment that ballroom dancing apparently gave to others, now all at once, as the rhythm spun round us a silken thread and sealed us together inside a cocoon, and our limbs moved intricately and magically together like the limbs of a single being, the secret revealed itself: we had created a unity that answered the yearning of loneliness. We had been two imperfect halves that had come together and made a perfect whole; and this merging of selves had no parallel except in the act of making love.

The music ended; the silken cocoon that had held us together as a single being was suddenly gone; we fell apart. The perfect whole had split again into its two imperfect halves. It was like the shock of amputation; and in my solitary imperfection I felt self-conscious and awkward and rather absurd. I sensed that Suzie, too, had felt a kind of amputation. We returned to the table in silence. We did not talk for several minutes.

And then Suzie said, looking me evenly in the eyes: "You think Ben will be happy now with his wife?"

"I rather doubt it, Suzie," I said. "Not for long."

"Why not?"

"Well, I think Elizabeth's bound to start nagging and becoming over-possessive again."

"You blame her? You think it is all her fault?"

"I think it's mostly her fault. Don't you?"

She shook her head. "No."

"But I thought you did," I said, surprised. "In my room you were blaming her for everything."

"I was still upset in your room. I said anything that came into my head. But I don't think it is her fault. I think she is very unhappy, his wife."

And she proceeded to express her view which, summed up in terms that she herself would probably not have understood, was to the effect that Elizabeth's nagging and over-possessiveness were due to her feeling insecure and unloved, and that Ben's incapacity to feel real love for any woman was basically at fault. She realized now that she had become blinded to Ben's character by her infatuation, and that her first judgment of him had been correct.

"He is not a bad man," she said. "He doesn't want to hurt anybody, you know. He is good, nice, kind. But he has got a small heart—too small to hold much feeling. Maybe just enough for himself, but not enough feeling to give out to anybody. He couldn't really love anybody, that man."

"You're awfully bright, aren't you, Suzie?" It was not the first time that her perception had proved more acute than my own; and I found the truth of her observations all the more astonishing when I remembered that she had not even met Elizabeth. "Anyhow, if that's how you feel about Ben, perhaps you won't mind so much about what's happened."

"I still feel hurt, you know. My pride is hurt, because he made me lose face. I feel hurt just like I did when the father of my baby left me, and went away to Borneo. I did not love him either, it was just hurt pride."

Presently we got up to dance again. As I followed Suzie out between the tables I heard someone call, "Hullo there!" and saw one of the assistants from the bank where I had my account. He was a young Scotsman called Hamilton, who was always very friendly in the bank, and ready to help with one's troubles. I smiled "Hullo" and went on, because I was too impatient to reach the dance floor to stop and talk. I watched Suzie's back as she went ahead of me, with the white silk cheongsam molded into her waist and out over her hips, taut as a cheongsam should be, and the smooth black brushed hair ending in uneven little tails. I felt very touched by the little tails of hair, I did not know why. Then she was slipping into my arms, and a moment later the miracle had happened again, and the rhythm had enfolded us in a cocoon, and the two imperfect halves had merged together into the perfect whole; and we floated in our element of music as a sea gull floats in the air, soaring, turning, hovering, and there was no time any longer, no place, only the joy of movement as a single being.

And when the dance ended I could not bear the sudden dismemberment and kept hold of Suzie's hand as we left the floor. Then I remembered Gordon Hamilton from the bank, and released her to go back to our table while I went over to exchange a polite word. He wore a black tie and kilt, and had rather an absurd handle-bar mustache, but nice amused twinkling little eyes. He introduced me to his wife, who wore a long evening dress, and then his eyes twinkled and he said, "I've just been telling Isobel about that water-front place where you live. I hope you didn't mind me giving away your secret."

"It's no secret," I said.

"It sounds absolutely intriguing," his wife said, in the tones of a nice well-brought-up young girl being determinedly broad-minded. And as added reassurance that she belonged to the modern generation, not to her mother's, she gave me an eager smile, as though linking us in conspiracy against our unenlightened parents.

"I say, you've got a smasher in tow tonight," Hamilton twinkled. "And you were certainly doing all right on that dance floor!"

"Practically indecent," his wife said, because the modern generation was permitted such remarks.

"A real corker," Hamilton said. "What is she? Some rich old taipan's daughter? Bags of money and her own car?"

"I'm afraid not."

"Well, don't tell me she's one of your water-front girls—not a corker like that?"

I was about to deny it but hesitated, something inside me protesting against the simple lie. I said, "Yes, she is, as a matter of fact."

"Good God! I say!" Hamilton grinned and rolled his eyes and pulled at the handle-bar mustache. "Well, well! If I wasn't a married man—hum-hum!"

His wife looked completely mystified and said, "I'm sorry to be so stupid, but she isn't—I mean, of course she isn't, but I thought for a minute you meant she was one of the girls from your hotel."

"That's just what he's told us," Hamilton said. "That's what she is."

"But I thought they were—I mean—well, for the sailors. . . ." The full horror began to dawn. She remembered us dancing and glanced at the dance floor, then flushed and became confused; and I felt very sorry for her, because she meant well and was now upset because she was afraid she had embarrassed me with her stupid lack of tact.

"Don't worry, Isobel's still a bit innocent," Hamilton winked, trying to make light of it. "I'll have to teach her the facts of life."

I said good-by and left them, hoping that Suzie had not noticed the glances in her direction and guessed that we had been discussing her. Then I saw her watching me as I approached, her face expressionless, and I knew that she had seen.

I sat down, and after a minute she said, "You were talking about me?"

"Yes, it's a man from the bank. He said he thought you were a 'corker.'"

She said, "That woman kept looking at me."

"That's his wife."

"She was thinking, 'That girl's dirty. She's a dirty little yum-yum girl.' You told her?"

"I told her you worked at the Nam Kok."

"Why? Why did you tell her?"

"I don't know, Suzie. I just found that somehow I couldn't tell her a lie about you. I don't know why."

She was silent, her face still without expression, except for her eyes, which showed the careful deliberate thought going on somewhere behind. The silence continued a long time, and I turned to watch the beautiful giraffe-necked Pekinese doll, whose squeaky monotone in amplification was again being carried on the flood of music that swamped the room. Then I looked back at Suzie, and to my astonishment saw on her face a glow of satisfaction, a secret smile.

"Suzie!" I laughed. "I thought you were angry with me!"

She shook her head. "No."

"Well, you've every right to be. Anyhow, that's marvelous—now we can have another dance."

She hesitated, as though puzzled. "You want to dance again?"

"Certainly. Don't you?"

"Yes."

We had several more dances, and when we went out to the dance floor Suzie walked quite slowly, taking the shortest route past the Hamiltons' table instead of avoiding them by a longer way round, and keeping herself very straight and poised, and holding up her chin to show she was not ashamed; and when the dances ended we came back holding hands. Her face still wore that secret glow, but I could not understand what had caused it.

We had a last dance, then I paid the bill and we went down in the lift, and walked along the pavement looking for a taxi and still holding hands. There was no taxi to be seen, and Suzie found it difficult to walk in her high heels, so I called two rickshaws from across the road.

"I wish they had double rickshaws, then I wouldn't have to let go of your hand," I said.

"You would rather go by bus?"

"Which would you rather? Bus or rickshaw?"

"Bus—keep hands."

I gave the rickshaw men a dollar between them for coming across the road, which Suzie thought needless extravagance, although I still had half Ben's money left over. We went round the corner to the bus stop in Nathan Road and caught a double-decker bus, which was exactly like a London bus except that it was green instead of red; and we climbed up the narrow steep stairs to the top deck and sat in the front left-hand seat, which in London buses had always been my favorite: front for view, and left-hand for comfort, since in the right-hand seats you were tilted out into the gangway by the camber of the road.

Suzie still radiated that glow of satisfaction and wore that secret smile, and I said, "Suzie, I wish you'd tell me why you've been looking so pleased with yourself."

She said, "Because of what you told that Englishwoman. Because you told her I was a dirty little yum-yum girl."

"I didn't put it quite in that way. Anyhow, what's so good about that?"

"'My girl friend is a bad girl, she does a dirty job,' you said—or something like that. Only you didn't look ashamed. You looked proud, as if you were talking of some decent good girl. And then you asked me to dance. You took me out to dance in front of that Englishwoman, and held my hand. Yes, held the hand of a dirty little yum-yum girl in front of that Englishwoman! And you still didn't look ashamed, you looked as proud as if I was some princess! So I felt very good. I don't think anybody ever made me feel so good before."

I could not say anything for a minute. I just squeezed her hand and said, "Suzie, my sweet."

"'My sweet.'" She giggled.

"Suzie, the only reason I looked proud was because I really was proud of you. In fact, I think that's why I couldn't tell a lie about you. I was so proud of you as you were, that I couldn't pretend you were anything else."

"Ben was not proud of me. He was ashamed. Once we went out to a restaurant, and he was so scared and ashamed that his face got wet with fright, and he kept dropping things, and saying, 'Suzie, I think that's somebody I know! Suzie, you better hide! Suzie, what shall I do! Suzie, you think they'll know you're a bad girl?'"

"I know, Suzie, but it was different for Ben. He was in business here and he'd got a wife, so he had to worry about things that I don't."

"But he never felt proud, not even alone with me. He never felt love, happiness, anything very much. Oh, I got so bored with that man! He never had anything to talk about!" I remembered Ben's identical complaint and burst out laughing. She gave me a puzzled look. "What's the matter?"

"Nothing, I just remembered something Ben said. And that reminds me, Suzie—you've heard of Winston Churchill, haven't you?"

"Say that again."

"Winston Churchill."

"Where's that? America?"

"Suzie, really! It isn't a place, it's a person."

"I never heard that name."

I remembered that English names were often pronounced so differently in Chinese that you could not recognize them, for the pronunciation depended on whatever written characters were chosen to represent them; and this choice was made arbitrarily, with aptness of meaning often counting for more than phonetic resemblance. So I repeated "Winston Churchill" with random variations of pronunciation and tone.

Suddenly light dawned on Suzie's face.

"You don't mean ———?" She said something that sounded like *"One-shoe Chee-chee,"* but with inflections running up and down the whole gamut of the Chinese scale.

I said, "Yes, I suppose I do."

She looked at me as if I must be very stupid. "Then why didn't you say so? Why did you give him that funny name?"

"Well, anyhow, who is he?"

"*One-shoe Chee-chee*? He is England's Number One Top Man—only he is finished now. He always smokes a big fat cigar. And he is a big fat man with a big white face. Oh, yes, I told Gwenny once, when we saw him at the cinema, 'That *One-shoe Chee-chee* looks just like my baby!'"

I laughed and put an arm round her and kissed her, and said, "Bless you, Suzie! I wish Ben could have heard that!" She snuggled against me. We were silent for a minute. And then she said:

"Robert? You know what Ben used to say?"

"What was that?"

"He used to say, 'Suzie, you aren't in love with me. You're in love with Robert. You must be crazy about Robert, the way you talk about him.'"

"Yes, he told me that. But I'm afraid it isn't true."

"Yes—true."

"Suzie, here's the ferry. If we don't look out we'll be whipped off to the depot."

We caught the last Wanchai ferry. The illuminated signs along the Hong Kong water front had nearly all gone out, but there was a cruise ship in the Kowloon wharf strung with colored lights from stem to stern, and the name of the ship glowed on the funnel in green neon script. We sat a little apart, keeping our clasped hands out of sight on the seat between us, because Suzie said that the Chinese considered it very ill-mannered to show affection in public. We slid alongside the Wanchai pier and I followed Suzie down the gangplank and out through the turnstile. She paused on the way for me to catch her up. Her hair was invisible in the darkness and I could only see her white face and white dress and white shoes.

I took her hands and said, "Suzie, will you come back to my room?"

She turned her white face up to me. She said, "You mean to sleep? You want me to sleep with you?"

"Yes, that's what I meant. I've wanted you so much all evening. I was rather ashamed of myself earlier, because it was so soon after Ben. But we've been so close tonight that nothing else matters, and I don't feel ashamed any more. So will you come?"

She laid her forehead against me so that the top of her head was under my chin. She said, "I want to come," but uncertainly, as if only in order not to disappoint me.

"What's the matter, Suzie? Is it Ben?"

"No, not Ben. It's so silly, I don't want to say."

"Tell me, Suzie."

"All right." She paused. "Say I had been an ordinary girl you had taken out this evening—an ordinary English girl. And say you liked her and wanted her to come back and sleep. You think she would have come?"

"I don't know. No, I expect she'd have refused."

She nodded her head against me. "I know it's silly. But I want to be like an ordinary girl for you. I want to refuse."

I laughed, "Suzie, you're adorable."

"I knew you would laugh."

"I'm not really laughing—not like that."

"I will accept tomorrow. I only want to refuse once, so that I can remember I did it. You understand?"

"Of course."

"Then I am sorry I must refuse, Robert," she said formally. "It was a lovely evening, and I like you very much. But I am a good girl, you know. I am still a virgin. And so I am sorry, I can't sleep with you."

"I'm terribly disappointed, Suzie. You're sure I couldn't persuade you?"

"No, I'm sorry."

"You wouldn't like to come up just to look at my pictures? That is, if I promise to behave—well, to try and behave myself."

"No, Robert, I like you too much. I am scared of myself. I must go home."

"I suppose I can see you home?"

"Yes, you can take me home. You can take me just to the door."

IV

And so it was not that night but the next that we walked together along the water front to the Nam Kok to become lovers. We had been to the cinema, and afterwards had walked back along Hennessy Road under the arcades, past the crowded cafes and electric-lit shops, and down Lincoln Street with the hissing of pressure lamps in the food stalls and the men squatting like chimpanzees along the benches noisily sucking at soup, and along the water front past the workshops and the mah-jongg rooms and the naval tailors and "WELCOME TO ALL MEMBERS OF H.M.S. *Athene,*" and through the shadows at the edge of the quay; and then I had stopped, my heart in my mouth, to watch a drunken man tottering up the gangplank of a junk, sprawling headlong on the narrow plank but somehow not falling in, then picking himself up and lurching onward, like the circus clown on the tightrope when he pretends to miss his footing to scare you and saves himself by a hairsbreadth. I watched until he had gained the deck and sprawled out of sight into safety, then turned away to rejoin Suzie, but stopped as I caught sight of her—and stood rooted.

For she had paused to wait for me a few yards along the quay in a pool of pale livid light from an electric street lamp—a light that had the same mysterious quality as the shaft of light that thrusts like some heavenly illumination through a gap in a thundercloud, and that, shining on her face and hands and her legs below the skirt of her cheongsam, invested her with a complete unreality; and the sight of her provoked in my mind some shadow of a memory, like a flitting bird that for a moment or two I could not catch to identify. Then all at once I trapped it: it was the memory of a picture from my childhood—a rather sickly colored plate in the illustrated Bible that I had been given when I first went to school, showing a miracle performed in a street of Jerusalem. In the foreground was the shoulder and lifted hand of Jesus, and beyond him a white wall with a barred window, with two ragged lepers squatting at its foot, their bodies disfigured and eaten away by disease, and in front of them a third begger who a moment ago had been like them, but who now stood straight and whole—and illumined by this same livid, unearthly light in which Suzie stood under the street lamp.

And I was momentarily seized by the fantastic notion that another miracle had occurred; that Suzie, who had wanted to love as a virgin, had had her innocence restored, that she now stood there in perfect purity, miraculously cleansed of her uncle's rape and the contamination of her trade as the leper had been cleansed of disease. For her face was luminous, it shone with a virginal beauty; and she seemed to wear that same expression that I remembered on the face of the beggar, an expression partly of humility, partly of wonderment.

And I was so moved with wonderment myself that for a while I could only stare. She did not move, but watched me as if she understood.

And then I went to her and held her, and began to kiss the white upturned virginal face, and she accepted the kisses without returning them, holding her face still and smiling a little—until a sudden loud resonant burping from the ferry's hooter made us both glance over toward the pier, and reality returned, and I knew that there had been no miracle, no physical restoration, no super-natural cleaning of the slate.

Yet as we continued along the quay, out of the lamplight and into the shadows again, I was still aware of some luminous quality about her, some radiation. And then, as if her own thoughts had been following some similar train to mine, though I had not once spoken since I had turned to see her under the lamp, she said:

"Robert, you know something? I have been pretending all day that you are my first man. I know it is not true—but I feel it is true." And she added with a shy little laugh, "And I feel scared. Isn't it funny? As if it was the first time, and I didn't know what to do."

I said, "I feel rather scared, too."

"I am very scared."

And I thought: there has been a miracle after all. Not a miracle in her body to make her intact again, but a miracle in her heart. Because love is a miracle: a miracle that rubs out the past, cleanses the heart, fills it with a virginal mystery and wonderment. It is Suzie's own miracle, the miracle of belief. And because she wants me to be her first man, I am the first, and for me, too, the past is nothing.

We crossed the road towards the Nam Kok. We walked a little apart. For now that we were soon to become lovers our old sense of familiarity had gone: we seemed almost strangers to each other, as familiar houses will seem strange when approached by new paths. We entered the hall, and I saw thankfully that it was empty: our mood was so delicately balanced that I was scared of it being upset, and as we stood waiting for the lift I prayed that no sailors or girls would come out of the bar, and that we should get upstairs without meeting any dull-eyed love-emptied couples coming out of rooms—without any reminders of Suzie's past. I only wished now that I had thought of taking her to another hotel, where we would have avoided all such risks.

The lift came down, the gate opened—it was empty except for the liftman. I breathed a sigh of relief and followed Suzie inside.

And then to my anguish, as we clanked past the first floor, we heard the sound of raised angry voices. The noise grew louder and more jarring as we rumbled upward—until the gate opened on the third floor and we were hit by the full force of it, and stepped out into the midst of the most violent and impassioned scene that I had ever witnessed at the Nam Kok.

The row involved, of all people, Wednesday Lulu, who was struggling to free herself from the grasp of the bar manager and two other girls, who were only just succeeding with their combined efforts in keeping her pinioned. Her face was ugly with rage as she screamed abuse at a sailor. The sailor, who was also purple-faced with rage and half drunk, was trying to shout her down with a methodical repetition of that single four-letter word which means simply love-making, and yet which for some reason is commonly used for the most violent expression of insult or contempt.

The corridor was blocked by girls and sailors who had emerged from their rooms to watch in various states of undress. It was impossible to get past to my room, and we stood outside the lift gazing at the scene in dismay. I had never before seen Wednesday Lulu anything but quiet and self-controlled, nor heard her speak other than gently. And now, as her rage rendered her almost inarticulate, she resorted to that same four-letter word as the sailor, hurling it back at him with the same methodical repetition.

The manager was also shouting in his effort to make peace, but his voice was drowned by the other two. The four-letter word flew senselessly between them, slashed harder each time, like a tennis ball between two demented, epileptic players.

The sailor began to move away, still shouting the word. Just then Wednesday Lulu broke free and threw herself at him. He staggered under her unexpected assault: she battered wildly at his face with her hands. The manager and girls and a couple of matelots grabbed at her, ripping her cheongsam. They dragged her off. The sailor spat and brushed himself disdainfully. Little Alice, who was watching from the doorway closest to the lift, suddenly broke into giggles. She pulled at the hand of her matelot, a small crook-boned youth with darkly tanned chest, saying, "Hey, come on, Jackie, what's so interesting?" She pulled him back into the room. The matelot began to close the door, but noticed Suzie and stuck out his grinning face again.

"Hey, Suzie!"

Suzie turned and looked towards him, her face expressionless.

"Jack," he grinned. "You remember me—Jack. Jackie Boy. *Athene,* last June. Well, be seeing you, eh?"

He closed the door. Suzie turned her expressionless face back to the scene in the corridor. The sailor was moving off again. He stopped and hurled his parting shot over his shoulder, to the effect that so far as he was concerned Wednesday Lulu, the manager, the whole mucking lot of them, could go and make love to themselves in four letters. He went off down the stairs.

The spectators began to disperse. The manager and Wednesday Lulu and a few others stood in a group in the corridor holding a post-mortem, angry and red-faced and shouting. We pushed past. I followed unhappily behind Suzie, feeling jarred and soiled, and wondering if we should ever recapture our mood.

But I had no sooner closed the door of my room, muffling the voices in the corridor, and turned to see Suzie standing there in the middle of the room, white-faced and half shy as though she had never been in the room before, than I knew that we should quite easily do so, and that the scene outside had not been the disaster I had feared; for there was still that luminous quality, that wonderment about her, that meant that the miracle had withstood the assault: that it had survived the ugly rage-distorted face of Wednesday Lulu, the half-dressed sailors, the four-letter word, the encounter with Jack from the *Athene* last June: that her feelings were still intact.

I rang the bell and the No. 2 floor boy brought tea. We took our glasses out onto the balcony and leaned on the balustrade. Across the harbor lights glowed in the windows of the Peninsula, and hung in garlands on the cruise ship. The neon name on the funnel was a smudge of green.

"That ship is still there," Suzie said.

"Yes, I think it goes tomorrow."

She said, "I am still scared."

"So am I. But we'll be all right, won't we?"

"Yes."

"Let's go to bed, Suzie."

She did not move, and presently I went inside and pottered for a while and then got into bed myself. Suzie was still at the balustrade. She came in without looking at me and stood at the dressing table, idly touching my hairbrush, my books, the new ash tray with which Ah Tong had replaced the one she had broken yesterday. She picked up the brush and pensively brushed her hair, looking at herself in the mirror. Then she put down the brush and began to undo the hooks and eyes of her collar; and after she had freed the collar, she felt for the zip-fastener under her armpit. She drew down the zip a short way and then stopped.

"Robert, please put off the light."

I laughed. "You aren't shy about undressing?"

"Yes, shy—with you."

I turned off the switch over the bed. I could see Suzie's silhouette against the sky in the open balcony door—the sky over the mainland, the sky of China.

She stepped out of her cheongsam. Her hair fell forward across her face as she leaned to remove her stockings. She came and slipped into bed beside me. Her body was cool and unknown, and nobody had touched it before, because it had been cleansed by a miracle and remembered no touch. And I thought: this is the moment of beginning, and it is the loveliest moment of all. And then the two imperfect halves had come together again to make their whole.

And then a strange thing happened; for at the moment of perfect unity, the moment at which there is no self-consciousness and no division of joy, Suzie burst into great sobs, so violent and cataclysmic that it was as though she was being shaken by some force outside herself; and I was half afraid, for her body seemed too tiny and fragile to be able to bear it.

And then the sobs had passed, and we had fallen apart into our halves again, and she was lying alone and abandoned and gently crying.

Later she stirred and felt for my hand. She said, "Robert, that was funny, I never cried like that before."

"It was rather wonderful."

"But of course, I forgot—I never had a man before, did I? You are my first man."

"Yes, no wonder you cried."

"I was all right for a virgin, wasn't I?"

"You were marvelous for a virgin."

"The best virgin you ever had?"

"I never had a virgin before. I never had any girl before."

"I'm the first girl you ever had?"

"Yes, of course, you're the first girl, and I'm the first man, and the world has only just begun."

Chapter Six

I woke in the morning at nine o'clock. Suzie was still asleep and I stretched over her to the bedside table for a novel and started to read, but I could not concentrate because I was too happy, so I laid down the book and watched Suzie sleeping. Her face was as peaceful as a child's, and the lids smooth over the eyes, and the lashes spread like little Japanese fans so that I could count each hair. I wondered if she was dreaming, and what Chinese dreams were like. I hoped they were like Chinese poetry, full of wicket gates and rock pools and chirruping cicadas, and warm rice wine and love.

She did not move for an hour. Then she stirred and sighed and rolled over and settled herself comfortably in another position.

"Come on, Suzie darling," I said. "Wake up."

She purred like a sleeping kitten and said, "'Darling.'"

"Wake up."

She rolled over again and snuggled against me. She giggled and shivered deliciously, and said, "Very beautiful."

"What's beautiful?"

"'Darling.' Deep voice very beautiful. Boom-boom!"

"I'm going to get some tea. Watch Ah Tong's face when he comes in."

I rang the bell by the bed. Suzie pulled the sheet up to her chin without opening her eyes. Ah Tong knocked and came in with the teapot. He saw Suzie and stopped, his eyes like saucers. Then he remembered himself and crossed to the bedside table, averting his eyes from the bed and struggling to keep his face wooden. He exchanged the new teapot for the old pot in the padded basket. I decided that I had tortured him enough and said, "That surprised you, didn't it, Ah Tong?"

He looked up and saw me laughing. His face exploded into grins of relief.

"Yes, sir. I am happy, sir."

I knew that Ah Tong was really happy because it had worried him that I did not have a girl. He had suspected either that there was something wrong with me, or else that I was an agent of the police; but now I was in bed with a girl like anybody else, and so all was well. He poured out two glasses of tea, happily grinning, and left the room. Suzie had not opened her eyes.

"'Darling,'" she purred. "Boom-boom!"

At eleven o'clock Ah Tong came in again with my laundry. He was still grinning. He reported that Rodney had asked him if Suzie was still with me, and that he had tactfully pleaded ignorance.

"How did he know she was here in the first place?" I asked.

"Number Two floor boy told him last night, sir."

He went out. Suzie sat up and said, "Hey, what's the time? I must go and see my baby."

"Can I come with you?"

"No!"

"Why not?"

"Because you didn't say 'darling.'"

"Can I come with you, darling?"

"Boom-boom! Yes, all right."

We dressed and walked round to her room. Her white evening cheong-sam and embroidered jacket were conspicuous in the morning, especially as we entered the narrow teeming back streets. Suzie's room was in a corner building at the intersection of two streets, above a paper shop selling paper articles for providing dead relatives with the wherewithal for the next world. The gaily colored paper models were hung out for display over the pavement like Christmas decorations: paper clothes, houses, junks, cars, and bundles of million-dollar notes for financial provisions, which could be transmitted to dispossessed spirits by the simple expedient of burning. There were more paper shops in Wanchai than grocers. Suzie thought it possibly unlucky to be living over one, though it was better than living over the shop next door, which sold coffins.

The entrance to her house was between the coffin shop and the paper shop. I followed her up the steep narrow stairs. The house was rickety and old, and the landings littered with rubbish. There was a smell of cooking and urine and close-packed humanity. The rooms on the two lower landings were each occupied by ten or fifteen people, and through the open doors I could see children shoveling rice into their mouths from bowls, mothers suckling their infants, old listless bearded men lying like corpses. There was a din of voices and quarreling. We climbed the last dark staircase to the top where the two rooms were both let to single tenants, and the landing swept. We entered Suzie's room. It was small and fastidiously clean, but the walls and little balcony were stacked high with nameless junk. The Chinese were collectors, and Suzie typically could not bear to throw anything away: not an empty bottle, not a tin, not an old cardboard box, not a piece of string.

The amah was squatting on the floor mending one of Suzie's cheongsams. The baby was playing with an old tin. It saw Suzie and beat the tin on the floor, grinning and dribbling ecstatically. Suzie gathered it into her arms, indifferent to the dribbles that smeared her white silk dress. She chattered to it adoringly in Chinese.

"He's looking marvelous, Suzie," I said, though it always hurt me to see that sallow pathetic little Eurasian face. And it still seemed to me very underdeveloped for its age.

"He still coughs, you know," Suzie said. "Cough-cough-cough! Hey, why you cough, my naughty baby?" She tickled its ribs so that it spluttered afresh. "Yes, my beautiful! My good-looking! You speak nicely to my boy friend, and maybe one day he will take your picture."

I remembered that I had once promised to take her baby's photograph, but my camera was broken and not worth mending. So I suggested that we should take him to a professional photographer's; I had been trying all morning to think of some present I could give her, and this was the ideal solution.

Suzie was delighted by the idea, and spent several minutes over the choice of cheongsam in which to be photographed with the baby. She changed for decency's sake behind a blanket held up by the amah. The amah was also to come along, and the old woman showed her pleasure at this prospect with great broad silver-toothed grins. Her brown old peasant's face was finely matted with wrinkles, but her little black beady eyes were as clear as a girl's. She wore a blue jacket, black baggy cotton trousers, and black felt slippers; her gray hair was knotted in a bun held by a big cheap plastic comb. Suzie was very fond of the old woman but thought her stupid, and often impatiently snapped at her. The amah accepted her scoldings without resentment, because although Suzie was such a slip of a thing, she had made money, wore beautiful silk, and could afford a room of her own. She felt great admiration for Suzie's success in her job with the foreign sailors.

The amah folded the blanket, then put the baby into a carrier-sling on her back. The baby promptly fell asleep sucking its thumb.

"You ready, good-looking?" Suzie said. "All right, we go now."

We walked down the narrow alleyway to Hennessy Road, the amah shuffling behind. There were several photographers in the locality, and we stopped before the first. The central showpiece in the window was a tinted portrait of a young English sailor with straw-colored hair, washy-pink cheeks, and angelic blue-tinted eyes. The surrounding pictures were all of Chinese couples sitting in stiff conventional European poses, the girls with crinkly newly permed hair, and the young men with their hair smarmed and glossy, and their ties and white collars and breast-pocket handkerchiefs all neatly in place. Only the Chinese physiognomy of the sitters distinguished the window from its many counterparts around the main-line railway stations in London.

"This looks very nice," Suzie said, and we went inside.

The photographer was a self-important Chinese youth with patent-leather hair, an American twang, and a bullying professional manner. Suzie, however, knew exactly what she wanted, and she firmly put him in his place. She arranged the poses herself, told the offended young man when to press the button, and scolded him when he was not ready.

"What's the matter? You expect my baby to sit still while you fiddle? No, wait now. I must make him laugh again." And she quickly did so—for she seemed able to produce almost any expression on its face to order, making it laugh, smile, look solemn, or furrow its brows in concentrated thought.

The photographs were all taken against a sentimental crudely painted back-cloth of terrace, balustrade, flower-urn, and marble pavilion. Suzie arranged several poses of the baby alone, then of herself and the baby, then of the baby and amah. Finally I was roped in, and made to stand behind the chair while Suzie seated herself with the baby on her lap.

"But it'll look as if I'm the father, Suzie," I protested.

"Yes. You mind?"

"No, I'd be very flattered."

She giggled. "And I will tell my baby, 'That man is your father. That's why you're so good-looking!'"

"You'll have to say it with more conviction than that. Now stop making me laugh, or I'll spoil the picture."

Afterwards I only just managed to snatch her bag out of her hand in time to stop her paying the deposit. I took the receipt and we left the shop. The amah shuffled off with the baby once more asleep in the sling. We stood on the pavement, the trams rattling past in the brilliant sunshine.

"What shall we do now, Suzie?"

"Cinema?"

"No, let's just get on the top of a tram and stay there until it stops."

"All right."

We boarded a tram for Shaukiwan, the junk-building village, but a few minutes later I remembered that it was Saturday and that there would be a race meeting in the afternoon. Suzie had never been to the races and said she would like to go, so we got off the tram and took another tram going back into town. We got off in the Central District and had lunch in a big Cantonese restaurant where a succession of girls came round the tables with trays of dishes and you helped yourself as you pleased. There were thirty or forty girls with as many different dishes, including sliced chicken and duck, shark's-fin soup, pork pieces, fried prawns, and a variety of Cantonese specialties in circular wooden steamers, and the girls were passing all the time.

We had a dozen dishes between us and afterwards a girl came and counted the empty plates and steamers and made out the bill. I had known this sort of restaurant to be inexpensive, but the total came to even less than I had expected.

"That leaves all the more to lose on the horses," I said. "Come on, Suzie, let's go and try our luck."

The racecourse was in Happy Valley, behind Wanchai. It was overlooked by big new apartment blocks, and by squatters' huts clinging to every ledge of the escarpment. Inside the circular track were football fields with games in progress. The first race had finished when we arrived and women in black trousers and wide conical straw hats were spread out in line across the track, pressing down loosened turf with their bare feet. A brass band with uniformed Chinese bandsmen was playing *Poet and Peasant*.

The grandstand and enclosures were packed. There were many English businessmen and their wives, and army officers with hacking jackets and shooting sticks, but they were swallowed up by the Chinese crowds. Many of the Chinese were very rich. They wore high-necked Chinese gowns or well-tailored English suits, and their wives wore pretty cheongsams and trailed tantalizing whiffs of Paris perfume.

"Too many pretty girls," Suzie said. "I am scared to lose you."

"Nonsense, Suzie. You knock them all into cocked hats."

"I keep hold of your hand, in case you turn butterfly."

There were no bookmakers on the course and we went over to the Tote. I had no difficulty in explaining the betting to Suzie because gambling is in the Chinese blood, and she had often gambled at mah-jongg and fan-tan and other games. We each put five dollars on a horse. I backed a horse called Misgiving, because it exactly described my state of mind in parting with the five dollars, and Suzie backed No. 7, because seven was her lucky number for the day.

We left the Tote and made our way toward the rail. Suzie suddenly tightened her grip on my hand.

"That butterfly man!"

I saw Rodney coming towards us, absorbed in his race card. He wore a pale green sharkskin suit, a green-spotted bow tie, and suede shoes. He had evidently just paid a visit to the barber for his hair was freshly cropped—cropped so short, in fact, that it looked as if his skull had been painted with gum arabic and the hair sprinkled on from a little packet.

"Quick, Suzie, he hasn't seen us," I said.

However, just then Rodney glanced up from his race card. I tried to look as if we had not been hoping to avoid him, and said, "Well, hello!"

Rodney walked past, cutting us dead.

"He is no good, that man," Suzie said.

"Never mind, we're not going to let him spoil our day."

We stood behind the crowd at the rail, waiting for the race to begin. Suzie, with a woman's intense interest in other women, absorbed herself in a study of our female neighbors. She examined their faces, their hair styles, their jewels, their dresses, their shoes. Presently there was a shout from the crowd.

"Here we go, Suzie!"

She reluctantly withdrew her gaze from a pretty Chinese girl with diamond clip and urchin-style hair; but soon the horses had diminished into a stream of moving specks beyond the football fields, and so she resumed her study.

A minute or two later the bobbing jockeys reappeared over the heads in front of us and passed between the winning posts. Suzie's horse, No. 7, was towards the back.

"Who won?" Suzie said. "Your horse?"

"I haven't spotted mine yet." But just then Misgiving came frisking past without his rider, looking very naughty and pleased with himself. "No, mine's last. I think his jockey's given up racing and gone to join the footballers."

Suzie pulled my arm and nodded towards the girl with the urchin hair. "Smart," she said. "Don't you think that girl's hair is smart?"

"Yes, but don't start getting ideas, because I'm not letting you cut yours off."

"She smells beautiful, too. That is very beautiful scent."

"Now, what do you fancy for the next race?"

"Number Seven."

She stuck to No. 7 all afternoon and won twice. The first time her horse was second favorite and the gleanings small, but the second time it was an outsider and she won two hundred dollars. I had one winner and ended up only ten dollars down. We managed to avoid running into Rodney again, except once when I found myself jostled against him in the crowd. We both kept our eyes averted, like secret agents in a film when they meet accidentally and pretend not to recognize one another. We did not see him again.

Suzie's second win was in the penultimate race, and after we had collected her winnings we left to escape the stampede. We walked back to Wanchai because there were already queues for the trams. On the way I went into a shop for cigarettes and when I came out Suzie had vanished. I looked round for several minutes, half anxious and half piqued because she had gone off without telling me. Then I saw her come out of a shop.

"I thought I'd lost you," I said testily. "What were you doing?"

"I just bought myself some scent."

"Scent?"

"Like that short-hair girl."

She held up her little parcel. She looked so pleased with herself that I laughed and forgot my anger. We crossed Hennessy Road and walked down to the water front.

As we turned the corner to the Nam Kok a taxi stopped outside and Rodney got out. We waited, giving him time to go up in the lift, and then followed. When we got upstairs his door was ajar, so we tiptoed past and let ourselves quietly into my room. I rang the bell for tea, and we took the pot onto the balcony.

"You like to see my scent?" Suzie said. She handed me the parcel. "You open."

I removed the string and brown paper. It did not contain scent after all, but a little silver box.

"It's beautiful, Suzie," I said. "But I don't understand. Why did you say it was scent?"

"For surprise. It's for you."

"Me? Suzie, don't be ridiculous!"

"Yes, it is a present."

"Suzie, you're mad! You must have paid a fortune for it!"

"I paid nothing. Number Seven horse paid."

"I don't know what to say, Suzie. I wish you hadn't done it."

"Look, I bought it to match hairbrush." She took the box and I followed her inside, where she laid the box beside my hairbrush on the dressing table. "Both silver."

"But the hairbrush isn't really silver at all."

"No? Then good thing Number Seven horse gave you this box. Because you are a big, important man—you need proper silver."

"Suzie, bless you."

"You can use this box for cigarettes. Or buttons. Yes, I think for buttons—when a button falls off you can put it inside this box, then I will come along and sew it on. You understand?"

I kissed her, feeling terribly touched. Then I broke away and went over to the door to lock it, but stopped with my hand on the bolt. The bottom part of the door was a ventilator with downward-sloping slats, so that you could see out but not in—and now through the slats I saw the bottom of a pair of green sharkskin trousers and a pair of suede shoes. They remained perfectly still. I waited a moment, then closed the bolt sharply and walked away. Just then there was a knock. I returned to the door and opened it.

"May I come in?" Rodney said.

"Yes, if you want."

He entered with set face and glazed eyes and went out to the balcony. He dropped into a chair with his face in his hands. Suzie and I stood watching him.

"If you'd known, you'd never have done it," he said. "You'd never have been so unkind."

"If we'd known what?" I said.

"How much you were hurting me. I've cried myself to sleep every night."

"I'm sorry, Rodney."

He kept his face in his hands. "All right," he said. "You win. You're the only friends I've got and I need your friendship. So I've got to take it on your terms." He lifted his face and stood up, feet together, and extended his hand with military formality. "All right, let's shake on it, Bob." We shook hands solemnly, then he shook hands with Suzie. "I wish you both luck. I hope you'll both be very, very happy."

"Well, thanks," I said awkwardly.

"And now thank God that's over." He shook his head as if he was coming round from a nasty dream, scratching his bristly crew-cut scalp with both hands. Then he looked up at Suzie with a coaxing grin, like a little boy who has been naughty but knows he can win everybody round again with a little charm. "Now, supposing a fellow wanted a cup of tea—how would he set about getting round you?"

Suzie glanced at me, then went inside for another glass. Rodney sat down again, puckered his brow, and leaned across the table towards me. "Look, Bob, there's something I want to ask you," he said, with the earnest humility of a student addressing a learned professor. "Now, don't get angry with me—remember I'm just a stupid hysterical American. But I confess it's got me beat. All right, now to start—how far would you say it is from here to the China border?"

"I suppose about thirty miles," I said.

"About thirty miles. O.K. Right. And what's the population of Red China?"

"Say four hundred million."

"Say four hundred million. O.K. Right. So that makes four hundred million Reds thirty miles away across the border—as against a few thousand of you British sitting here in Hong Kong. And yet to judge by that race track this afternoon, there's not a goddam one of you turning a hair. Well now, Bob, what I want to know is this. Just how the hell is it done? And are you crazy—or am I?"

He was still there after an hour. Suzie had retired into the room and was sighing heavily, banging down glasses, and throwing me challenging looks that said, "If you were half a man, you'd throw him out!"

Finally I rose and began to pace the balcony impatiently. Rodney ignored the hint, and also the mounting crescendo of angry noises from Suzie within, and continued to talk and ask me absurd questions, as though defying me to reject his olive branch and again offend him.

I gave him ten more minutes to leave of his own accord. And when the ten minutes were up and he had still not moved I told him bluntly that I wanted to work and must throw him out.

The glazed, hostile look returned to his eyes.

"I'm sorry, Bob, I was enjoying our discussion. And I thought that maybe you'd want to show me that my friendship meant something to you. But evidently I was mistaken." And without looking at either of us, he marched from the room.

I quietly bolted the door behind him. Later Suzie went out for an hour to see her baby, and after she came back we had dinner sent up from the restaurant round the corner. We were in bed about ten.

Twenty minutes later there was a knock on the door.

I gripped Suzie tightly. We closed our eyes, tensed, trying to fortify ourselves against the interruption and keep our mood intact. I knew that Rodney could see the light through the ventilator but there was nothing to be done.

"I've brought you a bottle of Scotch," Rodney said. "I thought it might come in handy."

Pause. We lay in agony.

"I'll just hand it over—I won't stay," Rodney said.

Please go away, we silently begged him. Please, please go away. But we could hear him standing there outside, his breathing growing heavier, more emotional, more hating.

"All right, if that's the way you want it," he said. "And this time let's make it final."

He went away. We heard his door close. We were still held by the lingering tension. We did not speak for a long time.

II

I did not go out for the next two days because I did not want to break the spell of enchantment, and Suzie only went out for odd hours to see her baby. In the mornings she brought the baby back to the room, and we spread the blanket for it on the balcony. It was beginning to walk, and we crouched on either side and let it stagger between us, waving its arms and dribbling and sometimes sprawling on its tummy. It choked with delight as Suzie grabbed it and tickled its ribs.

"Hey, you got to learn to walk properly if you want to be a film star! Yes, you got to grow up big, strong, good-looking, like Gary Cooper! And talk with a deep voice like my boy friend, and tell your girl friend, 'Hello, darling'—boom-boom, like that!"

At twelve o'clock she took the baby downstairs and handed it over to the amah waiting below on the quay. And then the coolie came with our lunch on his carrying-pole, and Ah Tong brought the bottle of rice wine which we had given him to warm.

The second morning Ah Tong stayed for five or ten minutes talking to Suzie in his native Cantonese, which by now Suzie herself spoke about as well as English; and after he had gone I asked her what they had been saying.

At first she was evasive; but when I pressed her, she told me that Ah Tong had been curious to know why, although we had been friends so long, we had only just become lovers.

"And what did you tell him?" I asked.

"I told him the truth. I told him I wanted to go to bed, only you said, 'No, not while you go with sailors.'"

I was silent. This came too near to breaking the spell. What were we going to do? I had tried to give Suzie money but she had refused it; and when I had slipped some notes into her purse, they had turned up later in one of my pockets. I knew that she must be spending her own savings; dipping into the tin which she kept hidden under the floor boards of her room. This tin contained about three thousand dollars—money carefully husbanded for her child's education, to keep him from growing up illiterate like herself. She even had dreams of saving enough money eventually to send him to the University of Hong Kong. She liked to add something to the tin every week. And it upset me to think that now on my account she was taking money out.

Then Ah Tong returned with a fresh pot of tea, providing a welcome distraction. I put the awkward problem out of my mind, and abandoned myself once more to the spell. There was only Suzie and myself and this room and nothing outside existed. And I remained in this state of illusory bliss for the rest of the day.

The next morning we sat in bed drinking tea until nearly eleven, and then Suzie got up and dressed.

"Suzie, you'll bring your baby again this morning, won't you?" I said.

She shook her head. "No."

"No? Why not?"

"Not today."

I watched her in puzzlement as she finished her dressing. She went to the door and paused. "All right, I come back tonight."

"Tonight? Suzie, what on earth are you talking about?"

"Holiday finish." She held my eyes with that level gaze. "Now I go back to work."

"Suzie, don't be absurd! Come here and sit down. We've got to talk."

"No good talking."

She opened the door. I jumped up and slammed it shut.

"Suzie, you're not just going like that. We'll think of something. We'll borrow some money from somewhere. We could borrow from Ben."

She shook her head again. "No. We borrow money, and maybe our holiday will last one more week—then finish again, just like today."

"It'd give us time to think. We might find you a job."

"Yes, one hundred dollars a month."

"You could get more than that."

"No. I can't read, can't write. One hundred dollars."

"I could make it up to three hundred. You could just manage."

"Yes—manage. And watch my baby grow up a coolie boy. Watch him carry lunch for people. Get hard shoulder from carry-pole."

"Suzie, we must at least think it over—think what's best to do."

"No, I think too much already. I think all day, all night, about what to do. But there is nothing to do." She opened the door again. "All right, I go now. I come back at ten o'clock. Or maybe eleven, it depends." And the door closed behind her.

I lay for a long time on the bed. Then I could not stand being alone in the room any longer, and I went out and walked about the streets until it was time for lunch. I did not want any lunch but it was something to do. I went into a cafe and ordered a dish of fried meat dumplings for a dollar. There were a dozen dumplings on the plate but I could only eat two. I sat for an hour drinking tea. I paid the bill and went out again into Hennessy Road. I did not know what to do with myself. I was afraid to go back to the Nam Kok in case I ran into Suzie with a sailor. Then I saw a cinema and went in and bought a ticket. I thought the film might distract me. It was an American film and had just begun. Soon the hero caught his girl kissing another man and went nearly berserk. My God, I thought, if that's what a bit of kissing does to you, how would you feel if you knew your girl was upstairs with a sailor? Then there was a newsreel, with a naval review at Portsmouth and the sailors lined up with beautiful precision on the deck of a cruiser, and I thought: I wonder how many of you have been out East. I wonder how many of you have been to the Nam Kok. I wonder how many have been with Suzie. And then there was a Donald Duck, and I thought: well, ducks are promiscuous. I suppose they don't mind their girls waddling off for short-times.

After the cinema I went back to the Nam Kok. The lift was waiting and I went up without meeting anybody and closed my door with relief.

Later business began to warm up and I could hear the lift gate clanking every few minutes and couples coming down the corridors and going into rooms and the doors shutting. Sometimes I could still hear them after the door was shut. I knew that Suzie would not come to my floor if she could help it. But every time I heard a girl's voice it sounded like Suzie's, and finally I could not stand it any more and went out to another cinema. I came back at half-past nine and sat out on the balcony. But the balcony was worse than the room for noises, because the doors onto the neighboring balconies were all open, so I moved back inside. A few minutes later there was a tap on the door and Suzie came in.

She came in naturally, as if nothing had happened, like any ordinary girl returning from work and feeling glad to get home. Only I knew that she was only acting to try and make me believe it was like that, and that inside she was tensed up, waiting to know how I felt.

"I finished early tonight," she said. "That bar was too noisy. I got tired."

I did not say anything. She took off her brocade jacket and slipped it on a hanger. She hooked the hanger over the rail in the wardrobe, on the left side where she always hung her clothes. She closed the wardrobe door, avoiding my eyes. She pretended to examine her hand.

"I got a splinter this morning, only I can't find it. Can you see a splinter?" She held her hand out to me.

I said, "Suzie, it's no good."

She withdrew her hand and lifted her face, and looked at me with her eyes steady.

"You don't want me?" she said.

"Of course I want you, Suzie. But not like this. Can't you understand?"

"No." She shook her head. "I don't understand. You loved me yesterday, didn't you?"

"Yes, very much."

"And I am just the same person as yesterday. I went away to do my job, and now I come back, and nothing has changed. I am just the same person."

"I still can't bear it, Suzie."

"All right—we finish."

She turned and went back to the wardrobe. She pulled open the door and removed her jacket. The hanger swung emptily on the rail. She put on the jacket without looking at me. She closed the wardrobe again and went to the door.

"Suzie!"

"Yes?"

We stood looking at each other. "Suzie, this is awful."

She turned away and opened the door, then hesitated and looked at me again.

"I love you very much, you know, Robert. I love you as much as my baby—maybe more. Only you're a big grown-up man, and my baby is just small. My baby needs me. So I must think of my baby first. You understand?"

"Yes, Suzie."

"All right; I go now."

She went out and closed the door. I listened to her steps fading down the corridor. A sailor raised his voice, arguing truculently with Ah Tong. "Sonofabitch, you . . ." The clank of the lift gates. A sudden muffled outbreak of giggles—Little Alice. Nobody else giggled quite like Little Alice. I went out onto the balcony. The wicker chair creaked as I sat down. The giggles suddenly stopped. A door slammed. A merchant ship slid silently out of the harbor, trailing pale ghostly smoke like ectoplasm under the great cool quicksilver disk of the moon.

The next day I did not see Suzie. I stayed in my room all day waiting for her knock but she did not come. I did not go down to the bar. I was afraid to see her with the sailors.

The next day was the same. And the next. But on the following day I could bear it no longer and made up my mind to go and find her. I went to the door. Just then there was a knock and Ah Tong came in with a fresh teapot. He looked uneasy and avoided my eyes. I asked him what was the matter.

"Nothing, sir."

"Then why daren't you look at me, Ah Tong?"

He turned his eyes to me reluctantly. "You know Mr. Tessler has left, sir?"

"Rodney—left?"

"Yes, this morning, sir."

I said, "Go on, Ah Tong."

He dropped his eyes.

"He has taken your girl friend, sir. They have gone to Bangkok."

Chapter Seven

Actually Ah Tong was mistaken because, although Rodney intended to take Suzie to Bangkok, they had not yet left the Colony. I heard this later from Gwenny, who had seen them just before their departure from the Nam Kok. It seemed that Suzie, not trusting Rodney, and foreseeing the possibility of finding herself abandoned in a strange country, had prudently insisted on a trial period with him first; and so they had gone to stay at a small hotel in the New Territories, about twelve miles outside Kowloon. This hotel was on an attractive part of the mainland coast, and was popular with Europeans and Chinese alike, especially with honeymoon and weekending couples. Suzie had taken along the baby and amah, and had installed them in a room in a fishing village near by.

In a way it was worse that they were still in the neighborhood, and I think I would have preferred it if they had gone right away. Every night I dreamed of Suzie. I dreamed that she had come back, and that I stood working at my easel while she sat cross-legged on the bed with mischievously twinkling eyes. And one night I dreamed that we were at the races again, holding hands in the crowd, and that Rodney appeared ahead of us—a huge lean grotesque Rodney like some half-starved bird of prey—and that I clung to Suzie in terror of him taking her away; but he went past in the crowd and the terror left me, and I was happy again with Suzie still at my side—until I awoke to find it was morning and it had all been a dream. I felt out across the bed to make sure. Yes, empty—gone. I thought of the new day stretching bleakly ahead without her, and the familiar ache came back into my heart; and I closed my eyes and tried to sleep again, to make the day shorter and anesthetize the ache for another hour.

And then when sleep would no longer come I would feed myself on the hope of her dropping in—for since she was only a few miles from Kowloon, surely she would be coming into town for shopping or a film? And in that case wasn't she certain to pay me a visit? And each day, finding half a dozen plausible reasons why she should have chosen this particular day to come into town, I would listen for her arrival, stiffening with tension at every clank of the lift gate, and again and again seeming to recognize her approaching steps. And when once the steps came on right up to my door and were followed by a knock, my heart flew into my mouth, and I dashed across the room in wild grinning excitement, knocking a glass to the floor where it exploded in smithereens, and flung open the door—only to be confronted by Ah Tong, gaping as though he thought I must have gone off my head.

And then one morning I woke up possessed by a new mood—a mood of revulsion for the Nam Kok, and for everybody and everything concerned with it. It was a mood that lasted a long time.

Hitherto I had looked upon the Nam Kok through romantic eyes. I had felt a real affection for it, and above all for the girls; for though it was true that their occupation, the repeated and meaningless offering of their bodies for sexual intercourse with strangers, was essentially degrading, I had never ceased to marvel at how stubbornly they had resisted that degradation; at how they had retained their good manners, their sensitivity, their pride; at how from the supposedly barren soil of commercial sex there could spring such flowers of kindness, tenderness, generosity, love. Nor was it only in Suzie that I had found innocence of heart.

And I had felt no less tolerantly disposed toward the sailors—I had seen their crude sensual search as being not so much for sexual gratification as an end in itself, but as a means to another end: a respite from loneliness. And I had taken no offense at their drunkenness, their carnality; for one had in one's own heart the seeds of all men's behavior, and if one's life had been different—if different circumstances had fertilized those seeds, if they had been blown upon by different winds, known a different and less kindly sun—it might easily have been that one set of seeds would have grown instead of another, that one would have been as crude and as drunk as the worst of them. I had once seen a drunken lout nearly throttle a girl who had refused to go upstairs with him, and had thought, "It could have been me," and so been able to feel pity. Afterward the girl had pleaded with the bar manager not to hand the man over to the naval police, saying, "He's just done thirty days in the cells, and we don't want him sent back." And I had been touched to the depths; because it was not only the sailor that she had saved from going back to the cells. It was also me.

But now all that pity was gone. Now my feelings had swung to the other extreme, and I saw the sailors as stupid and brutalized, and their drunkenness and their indiscriminate loveless love-making as shameful to the human race. And even the girls had turned sour on me: I saw the qualities that I had admired in them as being only skin-deep, or else mere pretenses cynically adopted as useful tools for their trade. The good manners were only a deceptive oriental façade; the kindness, the tenderness, the generosity, were but a veneer that thinly covered insensitivity and greed. Innocence of heart? Here I had made my most elementary mistake of all, confusing innocence with ignorance.

This revulsion was accompanied by a complete inability to work; for my work had depended upon a sympathetic feeling for my surroundings, and upon whatever resources I could find in myself of pity and compassion—resources that had never, indeed, been enough, but that were now altogether exhausted. My vision had become fogged by disillusion; and my past work now seemed to me so sentimental, so false, so meretricious, that I could not even look at it without nausea. I lost all impulse to continue. A few weeks ago, standing with palette and brush before a canvas, I had known exactly what I had wanted to achieve, however limited my ability to achieve it; but now I would stand staring at a canvas blankly, without compulsion or motive. It was like setting out on a journey without a map, to a destination in which I had no interest—and at the first excuse I gave up.

One day I received a letter from New York: it was from Mitford's, the gallery-agency owned by Rodney's uncle. Two months previously, when we had still been on comparatively good terms, Rodney had written to his uncle about me, and in reply his uncle had invited me to send samples of my work; and I had duly shipped off a selection of pastels and oils. I had received a formal acknowledgment of their arrival two days after Rodney's departure, and now came this letter, bearing the signature of Henry C. Weinbaum, whose name also appeared at the top of the paper as codirector with Rodney's uncle. It ran to two pages, and was full of effusive praise. My style, my draftsmanship, the originality of my subject matter, all came in for their share of hyperbole. Moreover it promised me a one-man show in New York if I would send enough material. The writer also suggested very diffidently—for far be it from Mr. Weinbaum, who knew so well the nature of the creative impulse, to try and jog an artist's elbow—that one or two more general pictures of Hong Kong might help to give the other work a background and place the Nam Kok in perspective.

A month ago this letter would have sent me sky-high. But now, in my state of revulsion and disillusion, I read it cynically—indeed had to make an effort to read it at all, for any reference to my pictures filled me with the same sort of nausea as the pictures themselves. I found the phraseology suspiciously overfulsome; and the emphasis on the subject matter clearly indicated an interest in sensation rather than art. Not even the prospect of making money could shake me from apathy. And I put the letter aside unanswered, thinking, "I'll try and knock something up for them one day."

Nor did my disenchantment end with the Nam Kok and my work. It spread to the whole of Wanchai. Now in these teeming streets, which had once so stimulated and delighted me, I felt self-consciously alien, divided by a thousand barriers from the busy, noisy, spitting Chinese. I began to long for the European company that I had formerly eschewed, and only pride prevented me from ringing up those English acquaintances whom I had once so summarily dismissed as bores. Now their very dullness held nostalgia for me, for it was so comfortable, so familiar, so English. And then one day in the bank Gordon Hamilton came over to chat, stroking his handle-bar mustache, and when he said presently, "You must come and have dinner," I was so grateful for the invitation that I could have flung my arms round his neck.

Then I remembered our last meeting in the Kowloon restaurant and said doubtfully, "But what about your wife? I don't think she exactly approved of me."

"Don't worry, she was thoroughly ashamed of herself after that evening," Hamilton twinkled. "In fact she kept me awake half the night, saying 'Those poor water-front girls, I wonder what one could do to help them?' I told her, 'I don't know, but I bet they make far more money than I do at the bank, so I can think of plenty of ways they could help us.' No, Isobel will be delighted. Make it Thursday about eight."

"I'll look forward," I said with a great deal more truth than he could have possibly known.

Two evenings later I took the Peak tram to a mid-level station and made my way to the Hamiltons' flat, which for a bank assistant's residence was uncommonly spacious and expensively furnished, for his wife had money of her own. I found that it was to be a dinner party for a dozen people. Isobel Hamilton greeted me warmly, trying anxiously to make amends for the offense she was afraid she had caused me; she gave me a drink, chatted for a time, and released me among the other guests.

And then there began to unfold all those threadbare little patterns of colonial cocktail-party conversation that I knew so well: that I had known first in Malaya, then during my first weeks in Hong Kong. I had the sensation of stepping back into a room where a gramophone had been endlessly playing. The grooves were perhaps a little more worn, the needle a little more blunted—but it was the same old record, and I knew every topic, every phrase. I knew with deadly certainty that no unexpected word would be uttered, no fresh viewpoint expressed. And now that the dullness became a reality, my nostalgia died within me.

Presently we went in to dinner. And at table the conversation turned to the discussion of a girl of mixed Chinese and English blood who had gone to Oxford, achieved almost unheard-of scholastic honors, qualified as a barrister, and returned to Hong Kong to practice her profession and to advance the cause of her fellow Eurasians. There were random contributions from all the guests.

"Of course she's as clever as a cartload of monkeys. But that chip on her shoulder stands out a mile."

"I met her once. Too damned uppish."

"That's the trouble with Eurasians. If you're nice to them, they just take advantage and begin to think they're as good as you."

"Personally I wouldn't have her inside my house."

"Nor would I, though mind you I'm always polite to her if I meet her in the street. I think one *should* be polite. I told her the other day, 'My dear, you can't help being—well, you know what I mean—it's not your fault. Of course I know some people are very narrow and prejudiced—but I was brought up to believe in good manners, and I always treat Eurasians exactly like anybody else.'"

"You know she's supposed to be having an affair with Dick Kitteridge?"

"*Supposed?* My dear, she's quite flagrant about it—you don't think she could resist showing off such a feather in her cap?"

"Somebody asked me the other day, 'Why shouldn't one marry a Eurasian?' Of course he was a young man just out from home, and rather 'pink.' I said, 'Are you trying to be funny?' He said, 'No.' I said, 'Well, because one doesn't.' He said, 'I wonder what Jesus Christ would have said to that?' I said, 'I don't know, and frankly, although I'm a good Christian, I don't care—because far too many people pass opinions without ever having been to China, and He couldn't possibly have judged unless He'd lived there as long as I have.'"

And this lack of charity for fellow human beings—for a minority of unhappy, race-less people fathered by ourselves—seemed to me an incomparably worse sin than any to be found at the Nam Kok; and my respect and affection for the Nam Kok girls, who were in the main incapable of such intolerance and inhumanity, came back to me in a great overwhelming flood.

We adjourned to the drawing room. Soon another guest arrived, a man in his sixties with white hair, a brown wrinkled face like an ancient tortoise, shrewd twinkling eyes, and an old-world courtesy. His name was O'Neill, and he was an "old China-hand" who had just come out of China after closing down his business under pressure from the communists; he was spending a fortnight in Hong Kong before sailing for England. He had pleaded another engagement that had prevented him from dropping in earlier, though I suspected that this had only been an excuse to shorten an evening that he had feared might prove tedious. Somehow the conversation turned once more to Eurasians, and soon the whole catalogue of colonial platitudes was being resurrected. O'Neill listened for a time and then, turning to Gordon Hamilton, said in a voice loud enough for all to hear, "Well, now that I'm leaving China for good I suppose I can come out with it. My grandmother was Chinese."

There was a shocked silence. Everybody stared at him. It was true that there was a hint of Chinese in that wrinkled tortoise face and those dark twinkling eyes, though perhaps no more than in many another old China-hand—for long residence in China had a curious way of imprinting itself on the features.

"I'm rather pleased with myself for getting away with it for thirty years," O'Neill went on, speaking to Hamilton as though unaware of the sensation he had caused.

Then the woman who had been brought up to good manners, and who had reassured the Eurasian girl that she always treated Eurasians exactly like anybody else, said, "Anyhow, Mr. O'Neill, I'm sure your grandmother came from a good-class family. That does make a difference."

"No, as a matter of fact she was my grandfather's wife's amah."

While this sank in there was another silence, broken only by the rattling of skeletons in the cupboard—two skeletons now, the twin skeletons of Chinese blood and illegitimacy.

At last one of the guests, a matron with loud downright voice, decided that the time had come to change the subject.

"Hilda, I told you that I couldn't play bridge tomorrow, didn't I?" she boomed across the room. "I hate letting you down, but it's my day at the Services' Club. And it does mean so much to those poor lonely boys to see a real Englishwoman's face behind the tea counter."

Half an hour later O'Neill, saying that he was an old man and liked early nights, took his leave, and I made an excuse to depart with him. We strolled together along the road that led to the mid-level station on the Peak tram, with the lights of Hong Kong and the harbor spread below.

"Were you pulling their legs?" I asked him. "Or was your grandmother really Chinese?"

He chuckled. "One of my grandmothers came from Richmond, and the other from Bury St. Edmunds. No, I'm afraid I was just having a lark. I've rather a schoolboy sense of humor, and I couldn't resist it."

I laughed. "It was a terrible shock to them. To think you'd been allowed to get away with it for thirty years!"

"Of course you don't want to take those people too seriously. They don't mean so much nowadays. That mentality's as doomed as the Empire which bred it—and which they have somehow got the impression bred the Empire, though of course it did nothing of the kind. In fact it has done a great deal, with its inflexibility, to hasten the losing of it. With due apologies to our hosts, I am afraid that most of our fellow guests tonight were second-raters. And the real Empire builders, in their own way, were first-raters."

We became so absorbed in conversation that to prolong it we walked down into the town instead of taking the Peak tram; and when we reached the Gloucester, where O'Neill was staying, he invited me in for a nightcap. I thought him charming, and by now had begun to tell him about the Nam Kok and Suzie. Over the whisky I described our last meeting in my room, and when I had finished, he said, "Of course you were mad to let her go! Quite mad!"

I watched his twinkling eyes, not sure whether or not he was pulling my leg. "You mean I was mad not to take her, sailors and all?"

"Certainly! Mad as a hatter! She sounds to me a girl of quite remarkable character, and obviously devoted to you—and speaking as one for whom the greatest pleasures of life have always been derived from the opposite sex, I know that such a girl is not to be sneezed at. Naturally there is always some drawback or other, whether a taste for expensive jewelry, or a husband, or lack of a husband—which of course can be much worse, if she starts to fancy you for the role. And it seems to me that as drawbacks go, a few sailors are really quite trivial."

I laughed. "I don't believe you mean a word of it. I'm sure that if you'd been in my place you'd have behaved in exactly the same way."

"Nonsense, my dear fellow. I was once in a very similar situation and did nothing of the kind. The lady was an actress in Chinese opera in Hankow, and I assure you very bonny. She was the concubine of a rich old gentleman, who was by no means too old, however, to enjoy her. She had also taken on a second rich gentleman, purely for financial reasons, since she was supporting a dozen members of her family. She then fell in love with me, an attitude which I heartily reciprocated.

"Now, naturally she did not tell the first rich gentleman about the second rich gentleman or myself—and indeed, if he had ever found out he would have been most displeased, for as the first comer, he was in the position of husband. On the other hand the second rich gentleman, in the position of lover, knew all about the first rich gentleman, and of course had no objection whatsoever—in fact it gave him a certain satisfaction to think that he was daily making the other a cuckold. But he naturally knew nothing about me, and if he had done so he would have taken the strongest exception.

"As for myself, the last arrival on the scene, I knew about them both and had no objection to either. In fact I thoroughly approved, since they relieved me of any financial burden and kept the lady out of mischief, while presenting no rivalry for her deeper affections."

"And supposing she'd taken a fourth lover?"

He twinkled. "I should have been extremely angry. However, that only goes to support my contention that the act of making love has no intrinsic importance, and that its importance depends entirely on the point of view. And in my opinion you should have been no more discouraged by those sailors than I was by my Hankow lady's two rich patrons; and indeed you might have derived the same satisfaction from contemplating their financial advantages."

I laughed. "You're an old cynic."

"On the contrary, I am an incorrigible romantic. There is nothing in the world that touches me more than to see two young people in love. And since I myself am too old to participate without making a tedious old fool of myself, nothing delights me more than to give them advice: which usually amounts to telling them not to expect every circumstance to be perfect, not to waste their precious youth because of trivial difficulties, and—in short—to get on with it."

"Well, I'm afraid it's too late for me to do much about it now," I said.

I met O'Neill several more times during the next ten days, and finally went to the boat to see him off when he sailed for England. After he had gone I felt that I had lost my only real friend in Hong Kong, and was plunged back into depression. His parting advice to me had been, "Go and grab that girl back—or else forget about her and take another girl. But at all events make up your mind to do one or the other, and do it resolutely." I knew this was good advice, and considered the former alternative of grabbing Suzie back; but although it would have been a fine dramatic gesture, I still did not think I could reconcile myself to the sailors, and we should simply have found ourselves back in the same situation as before. Then go down to the bar and take one of the other girls? No, it would somehow be a breach of faith. It would cost their respect for me.

So I did nothing, but continued to wake each morning with a sickening dread of the day stretching bleakly before me, and to wait longingly for the knock on the door.

Then one day I heard from Typhoo that she had met Suzie in town. She had come up for a day's shopping, and had told Typhoo that she did not intend to pay me a visit; she had decided that while living with Rodney it was better not to do so. And so now there was no longer even hope to sustain me, and I fell into a worse state of desolation than I had ever experienced before, a spiritual vacuum in which all seemed futility, a dark night of the soul. It was not a negative state, but as positive as some sickness: I could feel the ache of it like poison in my blood. I tried to make myself work—stood staring, pastel in hand, at an unfinished drawing on the easel, wondering blankly what to do with it, feeling already exhausted by the effort of overcoming my inertia enough to make myself stand there at all. Blackness enveloped my mind. I gave up and went out, and walked the streets carrying my desolation about with me like a shroud. I came back and sat alone on the balcony. The magnificence of the view meant nothing to me; I would have derived as much pleasure from a brick wall. I opened a book, but lacked the concentration to read. Nobody came. Nobody was going to come. I heard voices behind the wooden partition dividing my balcony from its neighbor: a man whispering, a girl giggling. I closed my eyes. I had no existence except as an ache. The long, long ache of loneliness.

And then I could no longer bear it, and I thought: I will take O'Neill's advice. I will be resolute. I will go down and get a girl, and bring this loneliness to an end. And then my interest in life will come back, I shall be able to work again.

I went downstairs to the bar. I felt as guilty as if I was intending to pick a friend's pocket. I sat down at a table, and Gwenny came over to chat.

No, I thought, not Gwenny. I know Gwenny too well. Like a sister.

I watched Wednesday Lulu go to the juke box, put in a coin, press a button. She is very pretty, I thought. She is beautiful. I could grow very fond of her. But what about her principles? She would say I was Suzie's boy friend and refuse me, and I would feel ashamed because I had asked. No, it couldn't be Wednesday Lulu.

Gwenny said, "Oh, good, there is Fifi—I must pay her back the five dollars I borrowed last night for mah-jongg. Will you excuse me?"

She went away. I saw Typhoo sauntering among the tables. Typhoo with her ugly little monkey's face and her shiny blackberry eyes. Typhoo with her sparkle and her long beautiful legs and her naughty split skirt and long sliver of thigh.

Yes, Typhoo, I thought. Typhoo is the medicine I need.

I caught her eye. She came over, grinning, and sat down. Round the edge of the table I could see her long thigh through the gape of the skirt. We talked for a bit, then I told her I would like her to come to my room. She looked puzzled. She said, "But you're Suzie's boy friend."

"She's been gone a long time now, Typhoo."

She was silent, preoccupied. I had never known Typhoo silent. Then she said doubtfully, "All right, but—" She broke off as Doris Woo passed the table. She was ashamed of the conversation and did not want to be overheard.

"But what, Typhoo?"

"But you better go up first," she said. "I don't want anybody to see."

"Why not?"

"I don't want anybody to see, that's all."

I left her sitting there and went back to my room. I was afraid she would not come. I wanted her to come very much now, for I found her attractive and liked her, and was certain she offered the solution I sought. After the dark night of the soul—Typhoo the dawn.

There was a knock on the door and she came in, still very subdued. We drank tea and talked until we both felt more at ease. I told her that I knew her too well to discuss money, and would just give her a present. I took her bag and opened it and slipped in some notes. She looked embarrassed and said nothing. She sauntered to the dressing table and lifted the silver box.

"Suzie give you this?"

"Yes, Typhoo."

She nodded, looking worried. We went out to the balcony and leaned on the balustrade and she began to cheer up again, and was soon chattering brightly and grinning her wide monkey grin. I held her hand and we returned inside. She withdrew her hand to open her bag. She routed in the bag, but could not find what she was looking for and snapped it shut.

"I forgot something important," she said. "I must fetch it. You don't mind waiting two minutes?"

She went away, closing the door. Five minutes went by and she had not come back. I became anxious. Then I noticed some money on the dressing table under the corner of Suzie's silver box. I counted the notes: it was the money that I had put into Typhoo's bag.

I stood staring at the notes in my hand. The telephone rang and I picked it up. It was Typhoo calling from the bar.

"I just want to say I'm sorry," she said. "But I like Suzie. She's my friend."

"But Typhoo, for heaven's sake! She's gone off with my friend—or so-called!"

"That's different. That's her job. You're Suzie's real boy friend."

"A lot of good that's doing me now!"

"All right, you catch another girl. Not me, that's all. I don't want Suzie's boy friend to catch me."

She rang off, and I slammed down the receiver. I was very angry. You little whore, I thought. You little sailor's whore how dare you trick me like that? Why couldn't you tell me to my face instead of sneaking off, telling me over the telephone? Were you afraid I'd have raped you?

And getting on your high horse like that, I thought. A little sailor's whore like Typhoo getting on her high horse and turning me down, throwing my money back in my face. The bloody cheek of it.

I kept up the anger as long as I could, because it was easier to bear than the humiliation which was buried underneath. But finally the anger subsided, and the humiliation was still there. And I knew that I did not have the courage to go down to the bar again, ask another girl, risk another refusal.

So much for my bold resolution, I thought. And I went out to the cinema which, since I had failed to get a girl, offered the only hope of distraction. I took a seat in the back circle. In front of me sat a sailor and a Chinese girl, who had evidently been westernized out of all her Chinese inhibitions, and they were petting and fondling. The girl's hair hung to her shoulders; in silhouette against the screen she might have been Suzie. And I was filled with such an unbearable yearning that after a while, although it meant disturbing a dozen people, I had to change my seat.

It was dark and drizzling when I left the cinema. I walked through the drizzle along the greasy pavements. The yearning still possessed me, I yearned with all my being.

There are always street girls, I thought. I could pick up a street girl.

I turned down a street where the girls stood in doorways, some because of the drizzle, others because they were old and the doorways dark. A girl said "Hello," and the shadowy figure looked slim and young. A bar of yellow light slanted across her shoulder. "Hello, you English?"—and she made a little hopeful movement towards me, and a triangle of cheek caught the light, and the flesh was sagging and painted and old. I hurried on down the street, and turned along the water front toward the Nam Kok.

I saw a girl walking ahead of me under an umbrella—the silhouette of her neat ankles against the wet shine of the pavement, and her slender waist, and her abundant shoulder-length hair.

But it's no good, I thought, she's not a street girl. She's probably making for the ferry. And I tried to suppress the fresh waves of yearning that the sight of her had provoked.

And then all at once I recognized her: the slow teetering on the high heels, the waggling of the buttocks. She was just passing the main entrance of the Nam Kok. She went on to the bar entrance and stopped, collapsing her umbrella.

Well, that's all right, I thought. Betty Lau's all right. Betty Lau won't have any scruples about Suzie.

She cupped a hand over her eyes to peer through the glass door. She rapped on the glass with the fingers of the other hand, trying to attract the attention of a sailor inside so that he would come out and take her in. She heard my approaching footsteps and looked round. She began to smile and flutter her big eyelashes and coo, "Oh, Robert!" She laid a caressing hand on my arm.

"Robert, you're always so sweet. You'll take me in, won't you?"

"Yes, of course, Betty," I said. "But through the other door."

Chapter Eight

Betty Lau was one of those girls, probably more common to the West than to China, who compensate for frigidity with an exaggerated outward display of sex; who exude an aura of enticement, hinting that at the first sign of temptation they are already lost, and who lead men on indiscriminately, dangling their sexual promise before the nose like a carrot, right up to the bedroom door—only to utter a cry of outraged virtue and slam the door in their victim's face.

Betty Lau did not slam the door in my face because it was her bread and butter not to do so; but once sure of me, she shed the outward display like a superfluous garment and became mercenary, cold, impatient, wooden. I overcame my inner recoil and acquitted myself. Later, as she prepared to leave, she donned that invisible sexual garment again with her clothes; for now, having played out my role as a victim, I had returned to the status of a potential victim who must be re-attracted. Yet her change of manner was quite unconscious, a conditioned response, and it did not occur to her what she was doing. Nor did it occur to her that she had failed to please me: she had paid up on demand, and since she had always been frigid, she did not know that payment could be made in more than one way.

But now I was only disgusted by that empty display: by that low husky voice, those intimate lingering looks, those fluttering eyelashes. And I could not even bring myself to look at that gross suggestive waggling as she went out of the door.

I did not have Betty to my room again, nor any other girl, but the harm was done. Betty displayed my scalp indefatigably, so that by the next day there was not a girl at the Nam Kok left in ignorance of what had occurred. Moreover she exploited the incident in every way possible to discountenance

Suzie, taking pains to give the impression that she had replaced Suzie in my affections and that our affair still went on; and whenever I appeared in the bar she would eagerly greet me, sit down with me, and appear to be exercising a permanent girl friend's rights of possession.

I do not think the other girls were altogether deceived by this; but it made little difference, for my single lapse had been enough in itself to destroy their special regard for me. They remained polite, and if they found me alone and not monopolized by Betty they would still come over and talk, for they were too well-mannered not to try and bide their change of feeling; but they no longer asked favors, discussed Suzie, or joked with me at their ease. And even Gwenny, the most conscientious of them all in matters of friendship, was subtly changed in her manner. I had appeared to her before as a superior being, and now I had turned out after all to be no different from the sailors.

I began to avoid the bar as much as possible, and took to going on long walks by myself over the hills behind the town. Gradually the worst of my desolation passed; my interest in life re-awoke. And one day, to my infinite joy, I discovered inside myself a tiny flicker of flame—a flicker from the ashes of that fire which I had feared had gone out, and which alone could make painting more than meaningless drudgery; and which indeed was the only part of myself for which I jealously cared, the only ingredient of my nature that enabled me to think, "I would rather be myself than anyone else." I nurtured the flame with tenderness and love. And soon I was working again; and digging out that letter from Mitford's, I re-read it with as much pleasure as if it had only just arrived, and answered it with a promise of some more pictures within a month, including one or two "background" pictures such as Mr. Weinbaum had suggested.

One day I was sketching near the Central District, with one of these pictures in mind, when I saw a European girl struggling to start a little Morris car with the handle. I went over to help, but at the second swing sprained my wrist, thereby bringing my manly intervention to an abrupt and ignominious end. Next I investigated the engine to try and revive the self-starter, but found the leads eaten right through with acid spilled from the battery, so that we were obliged to call in a garage.

A mechanic arrived and began to tinker. "Come and have some

coffee," I said to the girl; because I thought her quite pretty, with merry brown eyes and a mouth made for laughing, and I had been thinking of saying this for some time.

We went into the Dairy Farm Cafe near by. She had noticed my sketchbook, and after asking about it she said, "I thought artists were always hopelessly unpractical. But you seemed to know an awful lot about cars."

"I used to have my own car when I was planting in Malaya. What do you do?"

"I'm at St. Margaret's."

"What's that, a school? You're not a schoolmistress?"

"No, it's a hospital. I'm a nurse."

Her name was Kay Fletcher. We met again that night for a Chinese dinner, and then again four days later; and then we began meeting every other evening, and always on her weekly day off. I told her about the Nam Kok and Suzie, and she did not seem to mind, though she was shocked to hear of O'Neill's recommendation that I should take on Suzie regardless of sailors. However, I did not tell her about Betty. I was too ashamed of the episode and wanted to forget it myself; and besides, I was afraid that if I did so, and explained how much I had needed a girl in that way, she would apply the situation to herself, and suppose that I must either be restraining myself or else did not want her. Whereas in fact neither was true, and I just wanted to let matters take their course.

One evening we went over to Kowloon to see Mandarin opera, and afterwards, walking back down Nathan Road to the main ferry, Kay stopped at a shopwindow and pointed to a tartan bush-shirt, saying, "That's what you need. You haven't got a single shirt in a state of repair—at least if you have, you never wear it with me. And that sort won't show up the dirt."

"That sounds rather a backhanded remark," I said. "Well, all right, it looks cheap enough."

It was an Indian shop and still open despite the late hour; but the shirt in the window was too small for me, and there was none of my size in stock. The fat Indian proprietor beamed, rubbed his hands, and said, "I will get it for you by tomorrow. You will come again tomorrow afternoon, isn't it?"

Outside Kay said, "I should give him until the day after tomorrow to be on the safe side."

"Or until the day after that."

In fact I forgot all about the shirt for nearly a week, and then went over to Kowloon one afternoon on the main ferry. The shop was only a few hundred yards from the pier, in a street running alongside the Peninsula Hotel. The Indian recognized me at once as I entered. He beamed, shook my hand, and said, "You come for the shirt, isn't it?"

"That's right."

"Please come again tomorrow."

I told him that it was too much bother to keep coming over, but he reduced the price to persuade me, and indeed finally reduced it so far, while still clearly content with his margin of profit, that I felt chagrined to remember my meek acceptance of the first price he had asked. And so eventually I promised to return, and extending my hand for another damp flabby squeeze, I left the shop.

Across the street stood an airline bus, parked outside the Airways Terminal which was at this end of the Peninsula Hotel, and the sight of it made me think of Suzie and Rodney; I wondered if they had gone to Bangkok yet, or were still out in the New Territories. And this thought had no sooner occurred than I caught sight of a familiar figure standing on the hotel steps—Rodney himself!

But at that moment another airline bus pulled up, blocking him from view, and I knew I must have been mistaken. Obviously my brain had been playing that familiar trick of pinning on a stranger the image of the person who had just been in mind.

Still, it was worth making sure. I crossed the road, passing between the two parked buses onto the pavement. The man still stood on the steps, but now with his back turned. I took in the suede shoes, the English-tailored suit, the familiar shape of the head under the *en brosse* hair. I had not been mistaken after all—it *was* Rodney. And I fancied that he must have seen me and turned away to avoid recognition, for although he stood staring so fixedly through the open doorway, there was nothing to be seen there but an empty hall.

"Rodney!"

My voice acted like a starter's pistol: he shot forward without looking round and disappeared inside. A hostess, who stood on the pavement checking passengers into the bus, glanced up and said, "Now where's Mr. Tessler off to?"

I ran after him up the steps. He was standing with his back turned before a showcase of Chinese silks, a Pan-American airbag slung from his shoulder. I caught his arm.

"Rodney!"

He turned unwillingly. His eyes were remote, glazed, hostile. "Oh, hello, it's you."

"Rodney, are you off somewhere?"

"Sure, I'm just off now," he said. "I'm just leaving."

I saw Bangkok stamped on the airline tag attached to his bag. "Where's Suzie?" I said.

"Look, I'm sorry. I've got to beat it now," he said. He turned away toward the entrance, but I held his arm.

"Rodney, where's Suzie?"

The air hostess appeared at the top of the steps and said, "Oh, Mr. Tessler, do you mind?"

"I'm coming right now," Rodney said.

"Rodney," I said, still holding him. "Where is she?"

He turned on me with a sudden flush of anger. "Listen, I don't know, and I don't care—and I've got no time to stand here talking crap."

He jerked himself free. He ran down the steps, past the hostess, across the pavement, into the bus. I followed down the steps and asked the hostess, "Can I go on the bus to the airport?"

"You're welcome, but it's five dollars."

Rodney was furious when he saw me getting on the bus and would not make room for me on the seat, so I took the seat behind. I leaned over to talk to him but he turned away his face. He would not speak a word all the way out to the airport. However, at the airport I still clung to him, following him out of the bus and into the departure hall, and I kept on badgering him while his ticket was examined and his baggage weighed. The clerk said, "You've half an hour before you'll be wanted in Customs, Mr. Tessler. You can get coffee in the lounge," and I followed him into the lounge and sat down with him at a table. I was still badgering him, and after a minute he buried his face in his hands and began to shake as if he was crying, and he said through his hands, his voice emotional and muffled, "All right, if you want to know—she despises me."

"Suzie?"

"They'll ask me back home what I did in Hong Kong. I'll tell them, 'I slept with dirty little water-front whores—and they despised me.'"

It appeared that for the first week or two he and Suzie had not got on too badly; but he had become increasingly jealous of her, until he could not even bear her out of his sight. The chief object of his jealousy had been her baby, for when she went to visit it in the village she would never allow him to go with her; and he had begun to throw scenes, accusing her of not going to see the baby at all, but of going to meet a Chinese lover.

He had known this to be untrue, because once he had followed her into the village, watched her enter the house where the amah and baby were staying, waited for them to come out, then followed them down to the beach. However, later, telling her that he had followed her, he had declared that he had seen her go into another house and come out with a man. He had embellished this absurd story with elaborate circumstantial detail, in the same way that, after his abortive attempt to seduce Minnie Ho, he had embellished his story about the drunken sailor who attacked him; and just as then he had claimed in my presence to recognize his assailant in the street, so now he had actually pointed out to Suzie some passer-by in the village, maintaining that it was the man with whom he had seen her leave the house. The fatuity of such an invention, since Suzie had naturally not known the man from Adam, had been perfectly obvious even to himself; yet somehow he had found himself caught up in it, and once involved in the story, had felt obliged to continue doggedly with his fanciful elaborations. Perhaps he had subconsciously wanted to make her hate and despise him; and if so, he had certainly succeeded, for soon he had seen hatred and contempt in her every look. He had tried to counter this by making her a generous gift of money, in addition to her agreed allowance; but had promptly stolen it back from her and accused her of losing it, and of not being sufficiently impressed by the gift to look after it better. It seemed that he had to show himself that not even his money was appreciated; that not even his money could save him from being despised.

Finally his behavior had become too much for Suzie, and after he had twice frustrated her open attempts to leave him, she had resorted to subterfuge and one morning had simply disappeared with amah and baby. He had been furious. He had found a suitcase missing, and had determined to prosecute her for theft and get her sent to gaol. But he had no sooner formulated this vindictive plan than the local taxi driver, who had driven Suzie into Kowloon, had turned up with the suitcase, and Suzie's apologies for having had to make use of it in the haste of her departure.

That had been two weeks ago. Rodney had returned to Kowloon and put up at the Peninsula; and deciding that the time had arrived to move on to the next stage of his world tour, he had booked the first available air passage to Bangkok. A few nights later he had run into Suzie in Nathan Road. He had begged her to come back to him, and had been ready to cancel his onward flight if she had agreed; but she had categorically refused. She had told him that she had taken a room in Kowloon, and was working in a Kowloon bar. He had let her go, followed her, but lost her in the crowd. It was the last time he had seen her.

I asked Rodney, "Didn't she say anything more about the bar where she was working?"

"No, but I gathered that it was a pick-up place."

"But I don't understand," I said. "If she was going to do that sort of job again, why didn't she come back to the Nam Kok?"

Rodney was about to say something but changed his mind. He dropped his eyes and said with a careless shrug, "I couldn't tell you."

Just then there was a crackle from the loud-speaker on the wall, and a woman's voice requested all passengers on the Pan-American flight for Bangkok, Rangoon, and Calcutta to proceed to the Customs. Rodney got up, hitching the airbag over his shoulder. "All right, good-by, Bob."

I said, "Rodney, are you sure you don't know why she didn't come back to the Nam Kok?"

"I just told you I didn't know, Bob."

"I just wondered."

"I'm sorry you should think I'm a liar." He turned away but then hesitated. "Oh, what the hell, anyway. If you want to know, it was because of you that she didn't go back."

"Because of me?"

"She'd heard that you were having an affair with Betty Lau. She didn't like it."

"I see. Thanks for telling me, Rodney. So now we're both in the same boat."

"What do you mean?"

"I mean she now despises me, too."

"Of course she doesn't," he said quickly, almost jealously, as if being despised was an honor that he could not allow me to share. "If that's all it was, she'd have gone back. No, don't worry, she's crazy about you. I'm the only one she despises."

"Well, if you insist," I laughed. "I don't want to spoil your fun."

I held out my hand to him. He ignored it, his eyes hostile again. "I don't think I like that remark, Bob."

"Rodney, come off it. I was only—"

"That was a very, very nasty remark, Bob. And I'm sorry you made it, because I thought I was leaving behind a friend in Hong Kong—just one friend. But evidently I was mistaken." He turned abruptly and disappeared through the door into the Customs.

I smiled grimly to myself. No, of course, I thought, he couldn't have gone away thinking he'd left behind a friend. His self-pity was a jealous mistress. It wouldn't allow him any friends.

I went outside and stood at the wire-mesh fence, and when the passengers came out of the building and started across the tarmac to the aircraft I called "Rodney!" and waved, to give him the option of a friendlier memory to take away; but although several passengers turned their heads, Rodney did not look round. He continued doggedly towards the aircraft. I waved again as the aircraft took off, in case he was watching from a window. It climbed steeply, circling at the same time, and flew back parallel to the Hong Kong water front, its shadow following it across the harbor like a swift skimming fish. I watched until it was out of sight. Then I took the bus back to Kowloon to look for Suzie.

II

There were many pick-up bars round Nathan Road and I went first to one called the Windmill. I had been to a cinema to pass the time, because nothing happened in the bars until the evening, and it was now seven o'clock. The Windmill was a poky little place with a dozen cramped glass-topped tables, with cheap cruets on the tables and a blackboard on the bar counter chalked with the prices of fried fish, eggs-and-bacon, eggs-on-chips. A gramophone played with tinny desperation. Two soldiers and a bored-looking Chinese girl sat at a table in gloomy silence as if waiting for something to happen. There were no sailors in Kowloon. It was out of bounds to matelots, who had to seek their enjoyments on the Hong Kong side, and reserved as the playground for soldiers stationed out in the New Territories.

The girl watched me as I sat down. She caught my eye and gave me a discreet smile of complicity, like a wife's smile to her lover when tied to her husband's side, because there was nothing doing with the soldiers. A minute later she excused herself to the soldiers and came over, now with a smile which contained about the same mixture of the friendly and the professional as the smile of the air hostess outside the Air Terminal this afternoon. I supposed that their jobs called for many of the same qualities; only the bar hostess did not get a uniform thrown in, and had to go on being nice to amorous patrons beyond the point at which the air hostess was expected to draw the line.

"I'm looking for a girl called Suzie," I told her. "There's no Suzie working here?"

She shook her head, but said that at the O.K. Club, where she sometimes worked if business at the Windmill was slack, there was a new girl who had started only two weeks ago; and though she could not remember the new girl's name for certain, she thought it was Suzie. Yes, now it was coming back. Yes, she was sure it was Suzie.

I suspected that this recollection came only from her anxiety to please, but since the O.K. Club was near by I went there next. It was bigger than the Windmill and at the bar counter half a dozen girls stood idle. I sat down, and three came up at once with stiff false smiles. The others hovered just behind as alternative choice, with the same false bright smiles and their eyes all ready to be caught like the eyes of auctioneers. I explained my mission, and on the discovery that I was not after all a prospective client they abruptly shed their professional manner, and relaxed, and were no longer stiff automatons who at the press of the right button would mechanically smile, catch your eye, take off their clothes, lie down on a bed, but quite nice human ordinary girls. I asked them about Suzie and there was a shaking of six heads; and then I asked which of them was the new girl, and one of them answered, "Me—my name is Lulu."

I burst out laughing, and the six little painted Chinese faces stared at me in perplexity.

"You must be Monday Lulu," I said.

I told them about Wednesday Lulu and Saturday Lulu at the Nam Kok; and when I explained the reason for the choice of days there was such a twittering of laughter behind hands, such blushes, that one might have taken them for a bunch of little virgins. Then they put their heads together over the problem of finding Suzie. They were very anxious to help because they were all romantic, perhaps more romantic than most girls owing to the anti-romantic nature of their professional love-making; and there was nothing more romantic than a man looking for a certain girl and refusing to settle for any other. One of them fetched pencil and paper, and I wrote down the names of bars while they stood round ransacking their brains. Then a second list had to be made, with the names in convenient order for me to visit; and this completed, I set out for the topmost on the list under the escort of Lulu, who had insisted that by myself I should never find it. She took me to the entrance, said good-by on the pavement outside, giggled "Monday Lulu!" behind her hand, and scuttled away.

I went into six or seven more bars. They were all small, each with only a few girls and soldiers, and not attached to hotels like the Nam Kok. The girls were paid commission on the drinks bought them by the soldiers, so-called cocktails that were neat Coca-cola but the price of neat gin; and sometimes the soldiers would take them round to some near-by hotel. In one bar I waited for half an hour while a girl called Suzie was fetched from outside, only to be confronted by a girl about four feet tall and fatter than any Chinese I had ever seen. Her body was perfectly spherical, and surmounted by another smaller sphere that was her head, while from the sleeveless armholes of her cheongsam extended the exuberant rounded flesh of her arms, with creased joints at the wrists like a doll's, and then plump miniature hands covered with rings. She gave the impression that she had been blown up with a bicycle pump, and that with another blow she would have burst. She looked about forty. She also had a very nasty temper, and was not at all pleased at being disturbed for a false alarm, and I left her giving the manager a piece of her mind. Outside I took a rickshaw, because by now I was footsore after so much tramping around—and it was at the next bar that my search came to an end.

It was called the Happy Room, and was the smartest place I had yet visited. It was like a small night club, with dance floor, alcove tables, and subdued rose lighting. Not more than two or three tables were occupied, and one of these only by waiting girls, and two girls dancing together were in sole possession of the dance floor. I sat down and a girl came over; and when I asked her my usual question she said, "Yes, there is a girl called Suzie here."

"Suzie Wong?" I said, remembering the time I had waited at my last port of call before the little blown-up football bladder of a Suzie had appeared.

"Yes, Wong Mee-ling. She is out at the back playing mah-jongg with the other girls—it is so quiet tonight, it is terrible. I will fetch her."

She went out through a velvet-curtained doorway. A minute or two later the gramophone behind the bar began to play "Seven Lonely Days," the perennial favorite at the Nam Kok which Suzie and I had come to regard as our signature tune, and which I could not hear without being swamped by nostalgic memories. It was too improbable to suppose that it was being played now only by chance, and I was certain that Suzie must have requested it; and I was filled with happy relief, for she would not have made this sentimental gesture unless she had been glad to hear I had come.

Then she appeared. She paused for a moment, holding up the velvet curtain; and although she was visible only in silhouette, against a dirty backstage brick wall lit by a single naked bulb, her very outline, with the hair loose on her shoulders, and the curves of her waist and hips, was so familiar that it instantly brought her as close as if she had already walked into my arms—and I was overwhelmed by a flood of emotion beyond all my expectations for this moment of reunion.

She came into the room, dropping the curtain behind her and shutting off the bleak little passage, the damp-stained bricks. She could not see me in the subdued light. She paused again, looking round. I stood up and caught her attention. She came slowly across the dance floor.

"Hullo, Suzie." She stood stiffly without speaking and I was suddenly no longer sure of her mood, no longer sure that "Seven Lonely Days" was being played at her bidding. And to reassure myself, I said, "Listen, our signature tune."

She cocked her head a little, listening. She had not even noticed it. And now that she did so, she was indifferent. It had been a coincidence after all.

She said coldly, "Why you come here?"

"Suzie, sit down, and then we can talk properly."

She hesitated, then sat down stiffly and tentatively on the edge of the seat. Her face was indistinct in the roseate gloom, but I guessed from her mood that it was expressionless, and her eyes watchful, secretive, betraying nothing of her thoughts. The waiter came up and asked what we would drink, and Suzie shook her head; but I ordered a cocktail for her, and a San Mig for myself.

"A bit of Coca-Cola won't do you any harm," I said.

She said, "Why you come here?"

"Because I've missed you, Suzie. You've no idea how much I've missed you."

"Why you lie to me? You have got some girl friend to keep you company, haven't you?"

"You mean Betty Lau?"

"I don't know," she said, her pride demanding the pretense. "I only just heard you had some girl with you. I never heard her name. I didn't care. It doesn't bother me if you have a girl."

"Suzie, that's all rubbish about Betty."

"It wasn't rubbish, what I heard. And I think it was that girl I heard about: yes, I remember now, it was that Canton girl. I heard she was your regular girl friend."

"She was nothing of the kind. It's quite true that she came to my room once, because I was terribly lonely after you'd gone away, and I couldn't work, and I knew she was about the only girl who wouldn't refuse me out of loyalty to you. But it was awful. I hated every moment of it. And she's never been inside my room again."

"Why you tell me so many lies?"

"I'm not telling you lies, Suzie."

"Yes! Lies! You always wanted that Canton girl. I remember you told me once, 'That Canton girl excites me very much. She is very sexy, that girl. I go nearly mad with excitement when I see that show-off way she walks!'"

"I didn't put it quite like that," I said. "Anyhow, I was out of my mind, because it was like going to bed with a sack of rice. And now I can't even look at that waggling walk. It makes me quite sick."

"Then why you keep her for girl friend?"

"I don't, Suzie."

"Yes. Everybody tells me you keep her."

"And so that's why you didn't come back to the Nam Kok?"

She hesitated. Then she lifted her face, so that although I could not see her eyes I knew they were fixed on me boldly, and said, "Yes, all right. That is why. I was too ashamed to go back. I would lose too much face. I would sooner die than go back to the Nam Kok."

The waiter came with the drinks. He put the cocktail glass in front of Suzie, with an olive on a stick in the dark red liquid to make it look more like a cocktail, and filled the beer glass from the bottle of San Mig and put the glass and bottle in front of me, and went away.

"Suzie, please listen to me for a minute," I said. And I told her again about Betty, and about my feelings for her, and about her pretense that I was still her boy friend, until I had made Suzie understand that I was speaking the truth. But it seemed to make no difference.

"All right, I believe you," she said, her tone no warmer than before. "There, are you happy now?"

"No, I'm not, Suzie—not while you're still bristling at me like a hedgehog. And I don't feel very happy about you working here, because you can't be making much money."

"Today is Friday. It is only empty because it is Friday."

"Is it much better on other nights?"

"Yes, some nights it is very busy. I get plenty of money. I get I don't know how much just from drinks, without even going to a hotel." She realized that her voice had lacked conviction, and added, "Anyhow, I saved plenty of money from that butterfly man. I saved nearly two thousand dollars."

"Suzie, why don't you come back to the Nam Kok?"

"No, I will never go back. I will stay here in the Happy Room."

And nothing I could say would change her or make her relax with me; and though I asked her to dance, hoping to rediscover on the dance floor that same magic that had united us once before, she quite firmly refused. However, she did eventually agree to let me accompany her home, and we took a bus to Jordan Road and then a ferry to Wanchai; for she was not living in Kowloon after all, but was back in her old room in Wanchai above the paper shop, which she had prudently kept on when she had gone off with Rodney. She had only told Rodney that she had moved to Kowloon so that he would not come and bother her.

I reminded her on the ferry that this was the scene of our first meeting, and sentimentally took her hand. She carefully withdrew it. She shifted a little farther away along the seat. We walked almost in silence through Wanchai, and as we said good-by outside her house, at the foot of the mean narrow little stairs, she said, "Now we finish."

"Can't I see you again, Suzie?"

"No, I would rather not. I would rather finish."

We shook hands formally, and I started back toward the water front through the narrow emptying streets. I had not really accepted the parting as final; and then as I walked, there suddenly occurred to me an excuse for seeing her again. I still had in my drawer those photographs that we had had taken that morning in Hennessy Road: I had collected them after she had gone off with Rodney, and she had never seen them. And as soon as I got back to my room I took them out, removed the duplicate prints that I had ordered for myself, and returned the others to the envelope. I decided to take them to her the next evening at the Happy Room.

The next morning I woke to torrential rain—the first rain since I had come to Hong Kong except for that one evening of drizzle when I had met Betty Lau—and Ah Tong, coming in with tea, said, "The wet has begun, sir."

I sat up in bed. "Oh, God, Ah Tong! Look!"

Through the balcony door was a scene of devastation. On one side the rain was sweeping right in, and on the other exploding on the stone balustrade in great fountains that spurted everywhere; the floor was swimming, and everything on the balcony, including a dozen canvases and all my pastels and paints, had been deluged. Together we carried everything inside, and I spent the next hour wiping and drying what I could, and rearranging the room to accommodate all the paraphernalia from outside, while still leaving myself space to work. I kept reminding myself, meanwhile, that I must ring up Kay; for I had been supposed to meet her last night, and had put her off in order to go and look for Suzie, leaving a message for her at the hospital without explanation. I did not want to ring her but eventually brought myself to do so, though I did not tell her over the phone about Suzie. I arranged to meet her for a drink at the Gloucester at half-past six before going over to Kowloon.

It was still raining at six o'clock, and since I had no mackintosh I bolted through the rain to a near-by shop and bought a green Chinese parasol for a dollar, which was as good as an umbrella and cheap enough not to matter losing. I arrived at the Gloucester before Kay, and had just ordered myself a drink when I saw her come in. She sailed up cheerfully, saying, "Well, that confirms it." And when I asked her what she meant, she said, "I had a feeling yesterday that you'd put me off because of Suzie, and now you're looking so sheepish and ashamed of yourself that I was obviously right. So for God's sake cheer up, because I've had plenty of time since yesterday to get used to it."

I told her all that had happened, and how much I had been affected by Suzie's reappearance. And I asked her if she thought I was mad to go and see Suzie again.

"Do you mean looking at it from your point of view, or mine, or hers?" she said.

"I suppose I really mean from hers," I said. "Do you think that she honestly doesn't want to see me again? Or does she secretly hope I'll be masterful and break down the barriers regardless?"

"No doubt a lot of women would favor the 'masterful and regardless' line," she said. "But from what you've told me about Suzie, I've an idea she means it."

"Then I shouldn't see her tonight. I should just put these photos in the post."

"No, you damn well go. Otherwise you'll never be sure, and you'll blame me for giving you wrong advice."

"Well, anyhow, I've got to go over to Kowloon for the shirt."

"As if you needed an excuse!"

"Kay, I don't think I should see you again until I've got Suzie out of my system."

"That's up to you. Anyhow, you'd better let me run you to the ferry in my car, because now it's really coming down in buckets."

The harbor was gray with rain, and as I crossed in the ferry other boats loomed up through the driving torrent as unexpectedly as through a fog. At the Kowloon pier I decided extravagantly to take a taxi to avoid being soaked before I reached the Happy Room, and on the way I stopped at the Indian shop, where the Indian beamed and shook my hand, and said he supposed I had come for my shirt, and I said that I bet he had still not got it.

"Ah, you lose, you lose!" he grinned happily, his gray round face creased to the ears, and he proudly held up the shirt. Then he wrapped it in brown paper, trying to look sad now, and saying, "But you are too clever a businessman. You are getting this shirt for less than it cost me. I am losing money."

"Then perhaps you'd rather I didn't take it?" I said hopefully; for although the shirt had looked fine in the sunny weather, the gray pounding rain outside made it seem unseasonable and offensively loud.

"Oh, no, business is business," he beamed quickly. "I must keep my promise, isn't it?"

I paid off the taxi at the Happy Room and dashed across the pavement to the shelter of the doorway, clutching the parcel with the shirt. I had already lost my dollar parasol somewhere, in Kay's car or on the ferry or in the Indian shop, I could not remember. I went inside. The rain had kept soldiers away, and the place was as empty as before. However, Suzie was one of the few girls occupied: she sat at a table with a gangling young lance corporal, with a smooth polished public-school face that looked too cherubic to have known a razor, and that unmistakable air of the upper class doing its National Service; and when I asked his permission to speak to Suzie for a minute, he politely half rose, standing awkwardly bent between bench seat and table, like a sixth former rising at his desk for the headmaster.

"Help yourself, old chap," he said. "I say, I hope I haven't pinched your girl or anything?"

"Not at all."

"I say, I'm awfully glad."

The light was too dim to look at the photographs at the table, and we went out through the velvet curtain and stood in the toilet-smelling passage under the naked bulb. Suzie was delighted I had brought the photos. She giggled as she came to the pose of her baby on all fours looking up at the camera in surprise. Then she came to the picture in which I stood like the father behind her chair. She studied it in silence, her face noncommital, then without comment put it behind the others and went on to the next. It was another of her baby alone.

"But he looks much better now, after living in that village by the sea," she said, her eyes sparkling. "Oh yes, he looks beautiful now, with great big fat pink cheeks like an Englishman—look, like this!" She blew out her own cheeks to show me. "And he has lost that cough, you know. Oh, yes, it's quite gone, that cough."

"Suzie, how marvelous!"

"He never coughs now at all. I think it was that good air by the sea. And bathing. Oh, yes, he bathed every day, you know, in the sea! Only there were too many big waves. They just came whoosh! like that and knocked him over."

She giggled happily. She was in such a good mood, so much more relaxed with me than yesterday, that I felt all the barriers between us had gone. I was only thankful that I had not taken her at her word and had decided to come. But presently, as she held up a photograph to the light and I placed my hand over hers to lift it higher, I felt such a sudden change come over her at my touch—such a palpable resistance to me—that I withdrew my hand in dismay almost as if I had been stung. And I knew that I had been mistaken before; her pleasure over the photographs had deceived me, and in fact all the barriers were still there. And I thought, Kay is right, she meant what she said. She doesn't want me. I might manage to storm the barriers if I tried hard enough, but it isn't what she wants.

I said, "All right, Suzie. I'll leave you now."

"Yes." She held my eyes. "Because one glass of wine is better spilled. You remember?"

"Yes, I remember." It was a Chinese proverb that she had once told me in another connection, and meant that it was better to drink no wine at all, than to drink only one glass with no possibility of replenishment; for the taste of the wine would only arouse a thirst for more—a thirst that, left unquenched, would give more pain than the pleasure of the one glassful had been worth.

And thus it would be if we went on meeting without becoming lovers: the whetted appetite, the denial, the pain.

"Well, good-by, Suzie. You know where to find me if ever you want me. You can always ring me if there's anything you want."

"Yes. Good-by, Robert."

I turned and went back through the velvet curtains into the pink womb of the room. I went over to the table where I had left my parcel. The lance corporal with the smooth sixth-form face rose crookedly in meticulous regard to manners.

"I say, excuse my asking, old chap," he said, "but what exactly's the form here?"

"How do you mean?"

"I mean, I'm such a frightful ignoramus about these matters. But that girl—I mean, she's absolutely wizard, really, and I was just—well, to put it bluntly, old chap, she doesn't really go the whole hog, does she?"

"You'd better ask her."

I took the parcel and went out. The street was pockmarked by the rain. I turned down Nathan Road through the gray driving streaks. The rain stung my face and pounded coldly on my shoulders. My fingers made holes in the parcel as the brown paper grew soggy in my hand.

III

The rain continued for over a week. The noise and violence of the downpour everlastingly rose and fell. Now it swelled to a great drumming, splashing crescendo; now diminished to a whispering drizzle. Even for Hong Kong's rainy season such weather was freakish. Many parts of the town were flooded; squatters' huts had been washed down the escarpment in their hundreds; the streets were long spitting gray rivers down which you caught a misty glimpse of a Chinese, barefooted under a black umbrella, hitching his cotton trousers at the knee as he dodged a lonely tram. And there was no view from my balcony but the streaking gray curtain.

The rain coincided with a dearth of naval ships in the harbor and gloom descended on the Nam Kok bar. The girls knitted, yawned in corners, fished in their handbags for coins to feed the juke box. The comedienne Fifi persevered heroically to keep up flagging spirits; but at last even Fifi's fund of comedy ran low and she subsided with a long gaping yawn, closed her eyes, murmured, "Somebody remember to wake me up for Yankee payday," and fell sound asleep. Then the heroin-smoker Big Alice, wearing a grubby wet shirt, walked in from the quay, sat down alone, hypnotized the only sailor in the place out of the arms of Jeannie, and bore him off upstairs; and everybody woke up to enjoy half an hour of good honest indignation.

One day I was in the bar, taking a mah-jongg lesson from Gwenny, when the manager said there was a call for me on the bar telephone. Only Suzie would ring me in the bar. I jumped up and raced across the room. But it was Kay.

"You're not furious with me for ringing?" she said.

"Of course not," I said. "But how did you know I was in the bar?"

"I didn't."

"Oh, I expect the switchboard guessed. Anyhow, it's nice to hear you, Kay."

"I was just wondering how you got on with Suzie the other night."

"You were quite right about her, of course. She didn't want to see me, so I've not bothered her since."

"Well, the rain's getting me down. You wouldn't like to take me out to dinner?"

"Yes, I'd love it."

We had a Chinese dinner and went to a cinema. When we came out the rain was driving down in a solid sheet. The visibility was only a few yards and we had to crawl along in the car at five miles an hour. We stopped outside the Nam Kok and sat talking until it had subsided again, because Kay had to drive home alone.

"You sounded dreadfully disappointed this morning when you found it was me on the telephone," she said.

"Oh, nonsense, Kay."

"You're a bad liar. You thought it was going to be Suzie, didn't you?"

"Well, as the call came through in the bar—"

"That means you haven't really finished with her."

"I had a feeling she might ring sometime. But it's ridiculous, because she won't. Kay, when's your next day off?"

"Thursday."

"Can we meet?"

"If Suzie doesn't ring before then."

"She won't. I'll see you Thursday."

I dashed across the pavement. I stood in the entrance and watched her drive off, her tires splashing stickily on the road. I dropped into the bar for a beer, then went upstairs. Ten minutes later the telephone rang.

"Hello. This is Suzie."

I could hardly speak. I was grinning with excitement. I had expected it to be Kay ringing to say she had got home, or could not come on Thursday, or wanted to change the time.

"Suzie!" I said. "You sound miles away! And that funny little voice!"

There was a long pause. In the background I could hear voluble Chinese voices. It sounded like a shop. My grin died as I realized that something must be wrong.

"Suzie, what is it? What's happened?"

There was another pause, then the tiny voice again.

"It's my baby," she said. "My baby is dead."

3

The Lovers

Chapter One

She was waiting on the corner of her street. She was standing out on the pavement, as if she did not notice the steady pelting rain, and her hair was plastered flat on her head and down the sides of her face, and hung on her shoulders in lank dripping rats' tails. The shiny drenched silk of her cheongsam clung to her body and round her legs, with the split skirt dragged open and nicked up round her thigh. Her white high-heeled shoes were sodden and spattered with mud. She looked as if she had just been fished out of a pond.

I ran up the center of the street toward her, my feet splashing and my wet shirt steaming with the warmth of my body from running. She had not told me anything on the telephone except that her baby was dead, and I still did not know what had happened. She did not move as I came up but stood there with her round little face expressionless and perfectly white.

"Suzie," I said. "My poor Suzie."

Her arms hung emptily at her sides. The rain trickled down her white face and dripped from her chin.

"My baby is gone," she said.

"But what happened, Suzie? Was he ill?"

"No, my amah is gone, too."

"You mean she's dead—your amah?"

"Yes, both gone."

"Suzie, how awful."

"Plenty of people are gone. Look."

She nodded up the street toward her house on the corner of the first crossing. I saw that the street was blocked by a crowd standing in the rain, their heads and umbrellas and parasols in black silhouette against moving lights beyond. We started up the street. We pushed our way among the glazed eyes and silent faces. Beyond the crowd men were working with lights and flares, above the level of the street as though on some platform. We reached the front of the crowd, where there was a rope across the street, and I saw that the platform was a pile of rubble filling most of the crossing. Then all at once I noticed that Suzie's house had gone. The whole corner had completely gone and was open to the sky, and on either side were tiers of gaping rooms, some with beds and cupboards still in place, others with furniture hanging precariously over the torn-off edges of floors. I thought for a moment that a bomb must have fallen, it was so like a scene in wartime London.

"Suzie, what ever happened?" I said.

"The house fell down."

"You mean there was some explosion?"

"No, it just fell."

"But how?"

"Rain," she said. "It just fell in the rain."

She had left the Happy Room early this evening, because on account of the rain there had been nothing doing, and had arrived back to find the house gone. It had happened about half an hour before. Now survivors were still being brought out, but they were all tenants of the lower floors, and she held out no hope for her baby and amah, who must have fallen from the top. However, she would not leave until her baby's body had been found and she could be absolutely sure.

"Let's go and ask, Suzie," I said.

We got under the rope. A Chinese policeman made as though to stop us but hesitated when he saw that I was European, and I hurried Suzie past before he changed his mind. We clambered over the rubble. The paper shop had completely vanished, and also most of the house over the coffin shop, but half the coffin shop itself was intact with the long coffins made of round hollowed tree trunks still neatly stacked inside. The excavations were being directed by Chinese and English police officers, and coolies were carrying away the rubble in wicker baskets. A body was carried past us on a stretcher but the face was mutilated and I could not tell if it was a man or a woman. There were so many bodies partially exposed in the rubble that they had to be taken in turn. The policemen worked methodically and without fuss as if they were used to doing this kind of work every day. A Chinese officer crouched over a body half-concealed under a piece of wood. He scraped away the rubble under the wood with his hands and felt for the heart. He said, "This one's still ticking over."

An English officer said, "Half a jiff, John, and I'll be with you." He was examining another half-exposed torso. "No, this one's had it." He stepped back onto the Chinese officer's hand. "Sorry, John!"

"All right. Look, we've got to shift this piece of wood."

"I believe it's part of that same blasted beam that's been holding us up over there."

Another officer said grimly, "Pity the bugger couldn't have held up the house instead." He wore the silver insignia of Commissioner. He stood looking deceptively relaxed, the water dripping from his peaked cap.

"It must be a mile long, sir," the younger officer said. "We'll have to free the ends."

The Commissioner said sharply, "Use your saw. What's your saw for? That chap's alive—get him out quick."

"Yes, sir. Hey, where's that clot with the saw . . . ?"

The Commissioner relaxed again. I went up to him and asked, "Have you got any babies out, sir?"

"Six." He was watching them choose the spot for the saw cut.

"Can we look at them?"

He glanced round, saw Suzie, gave me a mildly curious look, then decided he had no time to concern himself with us.

"Under the tarpaulin," he said, and returned his attention to the sawing.

We scrambled back down the rubble. A stretcher was being lifted into an ambulance. It contained a young man who was muttering and crying out incoherently like someone in a nightmare. His trousers were ripped and the rain was splashing on his private parts. His face had the drained-out whiteness of death. Along the street were several tarpaulins, collecting pools of water where they sagged between the bodies. A Chinese policeman nodded toward one, indicating the babies. I lifted the tarpaulin, tipping off the pools of water which came flooding back round the bodies and over our feet. There were six small corpses, all but two with faces mutilated beyond recognition. The smallest was naked and lay face down and its two buttocks were together no larger than my fist. There were two about the same size as Suzie's baby but one was a girl. Suzie stooped beside the other, lifted the hand, and examined the fingers and palm. She could not see properly because of the light. She laid down the hand and examined a foot. She suddenly bent closer, as if in recognition, then examined the hand again. An English police officer came up carrying a flashlamp and escorting a Chinese girl in cotton trousers. He saw Suzie and turned the lamp onto the child for her. Suzie immediately put down the hand and shook her head. The Chinese girl looked at the corpses and began to smirk and titter. The officer shone his lamp along the row and each seemed funnier to her than the last. I asked the officer if any children had been taken to hospital.

He said, "One girl, but I doubt if she made it." The girl in cotton trousers burst into fresh titters. He glanced at her, and then said to me, "Nerves. I used to think they were all callous bloody bastards, these Chinese—but it's just nerves. You wouldn't think it, but that girl's heart is bloody near breaking."

He shone the torch for us while we looked under the other tarpaulins for the amah, but we could not find her. There were only twenty-seven bodies so far, and four survivors in hospital, and he reckoned that there must be a good hundred casualties altogether. He said that a house had also collapsed this afternoon over in Kowloon: it had been the same as this, old property earmarked for clearance in 1939, but the war had broken out to prevent it. And then after the war the influx of refugees, doubling the population almost overnight, had prevented clearance again until new housing could be completed.

Later, as we stood watching again at the edge of the rubble, I suddenly remembered about Suzie's savings, which she had kept in a tin under her floor.

"Yes, I know," she said tonelessly, when I reminded her.

"But how much was there, Suzie?"

She shrugged. "I forget."

"There must have been an awful lot, with all you managed to save when you were with Rodney."

"Yes, I think about five thousand dollars."

"My God, that's more than three hundred pounds!"

"Yes, gone."

"It might turn up," I said.

"Not with all those coolies." Her voice was still toneless and indifferent. "Anyhow, that money was just for my baby. If my baby is finished, I don't need that money."

"Well, let's go and look."

I led her to the place where personal possessions found in the rubble were being collected under guard. There was a pile of old battered cooking tins, remnants of furniture, a few old shoes and clothes, and one clock that by some miracle was still going, though it would not continue to do so much longer out in the rain. The guard let us search through the pile, but we could not find Suzie's tin. She shrugged indifferently: the loss of the money meant nothing to her beside the loss of the baby, and I do not think it had particularly occurred to her that she had lost everything she possessed in the world except the soaked clothes she was wearing. She had even lost the handbag and umbrella that she had been carrying when she had returned from the Happy Room.

She had begun to tremble from shock or chill. Her teeth were chattering and her face and lips looked icy. I said I did not think it was any use staying, but she refused to leave.

"I wait for my baby," she said.

"Suzie, I'll wait," I said. "You go and shelter in a shop or somewhere, and get warm."

"No, I shall wait."

"All right, I'll see if I can get some brandy to warm you up."

I went off down the street that was being kept clear for police trucks and ambulances. The shops were closed, but some shopkeepers stood watching in their doorways. I could not get any brandy but I found a clothes shop and bought a big man's sweater, and took it back to Suzie and helped her put it on in the doorway. She did not really know what she was doing because her attention was fixed all the time on the rubble, and she did not notice that the sleeves were too long, so I rolled them up for her. The rain was driving into the doorway and I looked round for somewhere else she could stand to keep the sweater dry. I remembered seeing an abandoned rickshaw near the tarpaulins, so I went to find it and dragged it back over the edge of the rubble, and set it down facing the scene of operations. It had been tilted down on the traces so that no rain had blown under the hood and the seat was dry. I led Suzie across from the doorway and made her get in, and then fixed the mackintosh sheet over her knees. She did not speak a word. She sat there without moving, except for the slight chatter of her teeth, with her eyes following every stretcher that was carried down from the flare-lit rubble. I was also feeling very chilled myself and I walked around and climbed up and down the rubble to try and warm myself up, and I kept looking back and seeing Suzie's little round white face watching from under the rickshaw hood.

Presently an announcement was made from a police loudspeaker car, in Cantonese, Mandarin, and English, that no more survivors were expected to be found. Unclaimed bodies, and the bodies of those whose relatives did not wish to make private arrangements, would be buried at public expense. Facilities would be provided for identification by relatives in the morning, and although excavations would continue, people were advised to go home.

I went back to Suzie and urged her to take this advice. But she shook her head.

"I wait for my baby."

Another hour went by, and then I was suddenly shaken out of my stupor of chill as I recognized the body of the old amah carried past me on a stretcher. It seemed too much to hope that the child's body had fallen in neat proximity and would be discovered next; but only a moment or two later, as I was crossing to tell Suzie about the amah, I saw her rise from the rickshaw and start towards another stretcher that was being carried from the rubble. It was as if she had been prompted by some instinct, for she could not possibly have seen from the rickshaw what the stretcher contained. I joined her as she stopped and watched it carried past. On it lay the corpse of a baby. The body was so tiny, just a little mutilated object in the center of the stretcher, that it seemed absurd for two hefty males to be engaged in carrying it. Its face was a mess of raw flesh stuck with bits of rubble and quite unrecognizable. It had lost an arm.

Suzie followed the stretcher without taking her eyes from the baby.

The rain had stopped half an hour ago and the row of babies' corpses lay uncovered. The stretcher was lowered and its burden placed alongside the others. Suzie crouched beside it. The English officer shone his torch unsuspectingly on the mess of the face, which in the white concentrated beam of light all at once achieved a startling, almost unreal, clarity of color and detail, like some varnished, overrealistic painting of still life. He quickly pointed the torch away, and held it so that only the edge of the beam was on the body and the face was in shadow. Suzie lifted the hand and spread the tiny fingers. Then she put it down and felt for the other hand. She could not find it. She looked puzzled, like somebody who has lost something only just laid down. She began to roll the body carefully, searching for it. The officer touched her on the shoulder. He shook his head.

"No," hc said. "Gone."

Suzie stared at the baby as if she could not believe the hand had gone. The baby must have a hand. Then she noticed the torn empty shoulder from which the arm had been wrenched. She contemplated this for a moment then turned her attention to the feet. She examined each foot in turn and afterwards both together, holding her hand under the heels. She laid them carefully down.

"Yes," she said. "My baby."

She got up and began to walk away.

"Excuse me," the police officer said. "I say, hang on one minute! Hey, young lady!" Suzie stopped and looked round. "How about burial? You want to look after it yourself?"

"No," Suzie said. "Finish."

"Leave it to us, eh?"

"Yes—you bury." She turned away again.

I hurried after her. I said, "Suzie, you needn't worry about the cost of a proper funeral. I'll look after that for you."

She shook her head. "No. Finish."

"Are you sure, Suzie? You're sure it's not just a question of money?" I could not make her out. I knew that Chinese babies were never accorded the adult privilege of a funeral procession with white-cloaked mourners and brass bands, and that even well-to-do Chinese parents would simply give somebody a few dollars to cart off their dead infant; but after all

Suzie's anxiety to wait and see the corpse, I had not expected her to abandon it so unceremoniously.

However, she still shook her head. "No, not money."

"I hope not, Suzie," I said. "Because it's no use feeling scruples about borrowing from me now. I must see you on your feet again."

She glanced at her hands, as if looking for her handbag, but remembered that even that had gone. She stopped. "You don't mind lending me just ten dollars?"

"Of course not, Suzie. But you're going to need much more than that."

"I only need ten dollars now, to buy something for my baby." She saw that I looked puzzled, and said carefully, "My baby is not dead, you know. That is not my baby we saw there. That is just his body. My baby has gone somewhere else to live, and I must still look after him. I must send him presents."

I began to understand. "You mean paper presents?"

"Yes, paper. Because he will need many things in that new place where he has gone."

There were dozens of paper shops in the neighborhood, but all were shuttered and locked. Presently we found one with spaced wooden bars in place of a door. We peered inside. An oil lamp burned in front of a wall shrine with a dim yellow light. Under the shrine a man lay asleep on a wooden bed. He wore a pair of blue running shorts and a white singlet in holes. We knocked until he woke. He slipped his feet into wooden sandals and clopped across the shop. He removed one of the wooden bars to admit us. The shop was stacked with joss sticks, firecrackers, pictures of gods for household shrines, and all the paraphernalia of Chinese religious observance, with a few shelves devoted to ball-point pens, airmail envelopes, and toilet rolls. The ceiling was hung with paper models, and as Suzie made her selection the shopkeeper unhooked them with his stick. She chose a bridge to facilitate the crossing into the next world, three suits in different sizes, a bundle of dummy million-dollar notes, and a junk—since even if her baby did not wish to become a seafarer himself, he could always let out a junk very profitably on hire. She also bought a paper house about the size of a parrot cage, because if he owned his own house he could insure that it was kept in a proper state of repair and would not fall down in the rain. Only one article that she wanted was out of stock; however, at her request the shopkeeper set to work with a pair of scissors and a pot of paste to make up the deficiency, sticking oblong sheafs of yellow tissue paper into red paper covers.

"What are those, Suzie?" I asked. "Books?"

"Yes, teaching books. Those books will teach my baby to read and write, so he doesn't grow up a coolie boy." And she told the shopkeeper what title to write on the outside of each.

We were both chilled through to the bones by the time we left the shop. We walked through the silent empty streets festooned with Suzie's purchases.

I said, "Suzie, do you want to come to the Nam Kok, or would you rather find another hotel?"

"I will come to the Nam Kok," she said.

"All right, there's sure to be a room."

She was silent for a bit, and then said doubtfully, "All right."

I said, "Suzie, you can come to my room if you like. I only thought that tonight you might rather be alone."

She shook her head. "No."

"You mean you'd rather come to my room?"

"Yes, but only if you want me."

"Of course I want you."

It was half-past four when we got back to the Nam Kok. Ah Tong was asleep behind his desk. I woke him and he brought clean towels and we rubbed ourselves down until the chill had gone and our bodies glowed, and then we sat on the bed drinking hot tea. Suzie fell silent again, her eyes stricken. She looked at the bedraggled cheongsam over the back of the chair, the torn mud-spattered stockings, the ruined shoes—all that was left of her life. She turned as if for relief to the array of paper articles on the dressing table. She got up.

"All right, I send my baby his presents now. You have matches, please?"

"I've a lighter."

She took the paper models out onto the balcony and laid them down on the concrete floor. She came back into the doorway.

"I had better shut the door, or the smoke will make you cough," she said.

I got into bed. Through the glass doors I could see her squatting on her haunches, arranging the paper models in two rows in the order she intended to burn them, working very carefully and deliberately, and sometimes changing two models round to make the order right. She wore a pair of my pyjama trousers, and one of my shirts on top because I had thrown away the jacket which had gone into holes. She experimented with the lighter, then held up the first article and set it alight. She waited until the flames licked her fingers, and then dropped it, and watched between her spread knees as it burned on the floor. When the flames had died, she recovered a fragment of unburned paper the size of a postage stamp and applied the lighter to it again. The breeze on the balcony began to swirl the paper ash against the glass. She burned some bank notes and a paper suit, then returned to the room holding the lighter.

"Petrol finish," she said.

I refilled the lighter for her and she went out to the balcony and closed the door again. Ten minutes later there was only the house left. She set a light to it on the floor. The flames leaped up to twice the height of the balustrade and quickly died. She burned the few remaining fragments of paper and bamboo frame, then came back inside, hooking the door open. There was a smell of paper ash. Her eyes were now quite calm. She took off her clothes and got into bed, and I turned off the light. I could feel her lying awake in the darkness. After a time there was a soft movement and she rolled against me, and I could taste tears on her face and on her eyes. She cried for a while without making any sound. Then the tremor of her crying died and she lay quite still, and after a while she said in a little desolate voice, "You know something, Robert? I don't really believe about those presents. I don't really believe my baby will get them."

"Don't you, Suzie? But you believed when you were burning them, didn't you?"

"Half," she said. "I half-believed. You see, when I saw my baby all smashed up like that, I thought, 'If I believe that my baby is finished, I shall feel so much pain that my heart will burst. I will go mad with so much pain. So I must pretend that he is not really smashed up, but still alive somewhere, and that I must still look after him.' You understand?"

"Yes, I understand." And I remembered our first meeting on the ferry, when she had pretended to be the rich little virgin—knowing exactly what she was doing, and yet believing in the invention enough to make it work. Believing—and not believing. She had always been good at that.

"Now I have nobody to look after—only you." She clung to me tightly, burying her face in my neck. "You would like me to stay and look after you?"

"Of course I would, Suzie. You can stay as long as you like."

"I will never leave you now. Not unless you tell me, 'Suzie, go away.'"

"But I still can't afford to keep you."

"I don't want any money. It's different now. I only wanted money for my baby."

"You'll need a bit of money. You'll need clothes."

"Just one dress, that's all."

"I think I could just afford a dress."

"But I don't mind if you can't. I can just wear your shirt and stay in this room. I needn't go out."

"You'll get awfully bored."

"No, I shall be so busy looking after you. I shall sew on your buttons, and clean your shoes, and brush your hair—you like to have your hair brushed?"

"I don't know, I never tried it."

"I can shave you, too, and knit your socks. What color would you like socks?"

"I think yellow."

"Yes, I shall knit yellow socks, and do everything for you. I shall make you the best girl friend you ever had."

"I never had a girl friend like that before."

"But you want me? You're not just pretending?"

"No, I'm not pretending." She switched on the light and I said, "What's the matter, Suzie?"

"I want to see if you are pretending."

"And am I?"

She switched off the light again and lay softly against me. "No, I don't think you're pretending," she said.

Chapter Two

The days that followed were wonderfully happy, and I worked better than I had ever worked before.

Once I had been incapable of serious work with another person in the room, for I would feel self-conscious; but I found Suzie's presence comforting, and indeed it had soon become so much a habit that I could hardly work if she was not there. Her patience was infinite, and while I worked she would sit cross-legged on the bed, often for hours at a time, looking through a picture book or else simply engrossed in her own thoughts; for she had a natural aptitude for contemplation. And from time to time she would break the silence to ask a question about whatever matter was on her mind, and afterwards would sum up her conclusions.

"I think the Nam Kok must make God feel very happy," she said once, after a long cogitation about religion. "You see, I don't think God cares whether men and women get married. He doesn't make animals get married, or fish, or flowers—and there are man and woman flowers just like us, you know."

I said, "And you think we're just the same to God as animals or flowers?"

"Yes, we have got a better brain, that's all. I have got a better brain than a cat, but we have both got life inside us just the same, and maybe God likes the cat better than me. I don't see how anybody knows. We just know that he puts life inside us, and makes us want to make love, so that after we're finished there'll be plenty more cats and flowers and people to carry on. That's all he cares about, that the world is carried on. So when he looks down and sees the Nam Kok bar very busy, because the sailors all want to make love with a girl, he must rub his hands and think, 'I did a good job with those sailors. They're more interested in girls than anything.'"

I laughed. "And what about when he sees the girls going off to get injections—do you think he rubs his hands then?"

"No, I don't think he likes girls getting rid of babies. I think those injections must make God very chokka."

Every day we went out for a walk; and each walk was a new adventure, for happiness sharpens perception, and even the most familiar streets would continually yield fresh crops of discoveries. We explored alleyways and sat at street stalls eating nameless entrails, and pored over the windows of Chinese druggists with their displays of twisted roots, dried sea horses, powdered pearls, and big glass jars of pickled snakes. We spent a day in a fishing junk, went up the Peak, and giggled at the delicious concrete vulgarities of the Tiger Balm Pagoda, commemorating the successful promoter of that universal panacea. And we made a collection of characteristic Hong Kong sounds: the massage man's rattle announcing his passage down the street; the spoon seller's clatter as he manipulated a dozen porcelain spoons in his hand like a fan; the clop-clop-clop of wooden sandals echoing down an empty street at night; and of course the noise of the mah-jongg rooms. And then the noise we forgot about until the morning we were woken by ear-shattering explosions that sounded like a barrage of machine-guns, and I was convinced for a moment that the communists had crossed the border and war had begun, and then we both looked at each other and laughed and exclaimed together, "Firecrackers!"

The source of this early jubilation turned out to be three flag-bedecked junks crossing the harbor with cargoes of roistering holiday makers; and we learned presently from Ah Tong that it was the festival of Tien Hou, the patron goddess of the boat people. And provoked by the firecrackers into a festival mood ourselves, we took a bus out to a fishing village and watched the portable shrines and roasted pigs and trays of pink dumplings carried past in long processions led by lion dancers in masks; and we lit joss sticks in the temple, burned paper gifts for Tien Hou, and ate a huge lunch of roast pork, while those pernicious firecrackers continued to explode round us all day, splitting our ear drums and scorching our clothes.

I would also read to Suzie for at least an hour every day. I borrowed books from the British Counsel Library, and I got the knack of simplifying difficult words as I went along. Suzie's curiosity was voracious, and she enjoyed fiction, biography, or travel; but the greatest success of all was de Maupassant's "Boule de Suif," the story of the patriotic little French prostitute whose bourgeois traveling companions, after first scorning her, proceed to use her for their own ends, and persuade her against her own will to sleep with a Prussian officer. Suzie hung on every word. She wanted the story read again and again, and at each reading was freshly moved; and she asked endless questions about the characters as if they had been real. How had Boule de Suif started in her trade? How many clients had she had a day, and what had she charged? And what had become of her? Had she never got married?

She told the story to the other girls down in the bar, where it also achieved such a success that she was obliged to repeat it many times. But whereas de Maupassant had ended his story with the little courtesan once more scorned and in tears, Suzie eschewed such cynicism and added a romantic ending of her own; and this went further at each telling, until Boule de Suif had not only been happily married, but also blessed with a family. And here a note of tragedy crept in, for identifying herself with Boule de Suif, she related that the first child, a boy, had been involved in a coach accident, and his mother had found him dead by the roadside—mutilated, and without an arm. However, another baby was on the way, and it might have surprised de Maupassant to know that eventually his heroine became the happy mother of six.

The story impressed the girls deeply and they always crowded round when Suzie began her narrations; and it was not long before little Jeannie, with her lusciously rounded curves, was nicknamed *Wun Tun,* which meant boiled dumpling, and was the nearest equivalent to *boule de suif* in the Chinese cuisine.

Suzie now presided in the bar like a queen, conscious of the dignity and position that she had acquired by virtue of our established liaison; for such a permanent arrangement was the girls' romantic ideal, and she appeared to her old girl friends as the embodiment of success. My own fall from grace had been forgotten now that I had taken Suzie back, and the girls treated us with all the respect due a married couple. They paid social visits to our room, brought us little gifts, and tactfully withdrew when they thought we wanted to be alone. Our most frequent visitors were Gwenny Ching and a new girl called Mary Kee, who was very shy and inexperienced. Suzie had taken Mary under her wing, giving her solemn advice and worrying endlessly over the problems of her initiation. And I would watch the two girls in conclave on my balcony: Suzie very protective and motherly, and Mary slightly awed by the older girl who had made good. And I would smile to myself, thinking that they resembled nothing more than a prefect and a new girl at school.

And now Suzie, when she spoke of me to the other girls, no longer called me "my boy friend" but "my husband." She confessed this to me herself, a little ashamed of herself for taking such a liberty, saying, "I think 'my husband' sounds much nicer—only I'm sorry I didn't ask you first."

"I couldn't care less what you call me, Suzie."

"But I tell them that we will never really get married. I tell them, 'My husband is a big man. One day he will be famous. You will see his picture in the newspapers, and at the cinema in the newsreel. So he can't marry me. He will have to go off and marry an English girl.'"

"I don't know, Suzie. I haven't thought much about the future." It was the afternoon, and we were lying on the bed after making love. I was filled with that infinite tenderness for her that always came at such times; for Suzie made love with a range and maturity of feeling that was in strange contrast to the deceptive childishness of her manner, and that touched depths in me that had never been touched before, and left me with a deeper satisfaction. We lay in silence for a long time. And then Suzie said, "What does goss-something mean?"

"Gossamer?" I remembered the word in the book that I had been reading to her at lunch.

"Yes, gossamer."

I explained, and we went on to talk about spiders and how they made their webs; for spiders had always fascinated me, and in Malaya I had spent hours studying their methods of web-spinning and trying to solve the mystery of how they managed to stretch the first strand of a web between two trees. (I had discovered that they would hang suspended from the branch of one tree until the wind swung them across to the other, whereupon they would haul in the loose thread and anchor it tight; and with this aerial bridge once established, they could run back and forth at will.) Suzie listened intently and asked questions, and I fetched a piece of paper and pencil to show her the different patterns of web made by different species; and we marveled together at the nature of instinct, which enabled young spiders to spin perfect webs without teaching. Suzie's hunger for knowledge had always been a sheer delight to me, and I experienced the creative satisfaction of a pedagogue who watches a pupil's mind opening under his guidance. Her lack of education and her illiteracy were one of her greatest charms for me, and I would not for the world have had her otherwise. And so it was that suddenly, in the midst of this discussion about spiders, I thought: I am happier with Suzie than I have been with anybody before. I would like to marry her.

Until that moment I had taken for granted that marriage was out of the question—I had not even considered it. One might live with waterfront girls, but one didn't marry them. But why shouldn't I marry Suzie? I didn't care tuppence about her past—indeed it now seemed so remote from our present life that I was able to discuss her former experiences with her with complete frankness, as if we had been discussing another woman. Besides, it made her out of the ordinary, more interesting; and it made what was good and innocent in her all the better because of what it had survived.

And I was so carried away by the notion of marrying her that I was on the point of interrupting the talk about spiders and proposing to her impulsively there and then—but at that moment a voice inside me nagged, "Don't be a fool—you know you'll regret it! You only want to marry her because her ignorance inflates your ego—because she makes you feel like a god."

"Well, what's wrong with that?" I asked the inner voice defiantly. "Why shouldn't I enjoy feeling like a god? Anyhow, sometimes she makes me feel the opposite. Sometimes she makes me feel very humble, because her own vision is so much more innocent, so much fresher than mine. I learn as much from her as she learns from me. I am learning from her all the time—seeing life freshly through her eyes."

Inner voice: "All right, it might be all very fine being married to her out here—but you could never take her back to England. Your friends wouldn't have her in the house."

Me: "Then they could go to hell. But I bet some would."

Inner voice: "Yes, and treat her as a prize exhibit. 'My dear, I've the most *fascinating* couple coming to dinner. The wife was a water-front tart in Hong Kong. Yes, honestly, cross my heart . . . No, don't dress. As George said, she's probably more used to *undressing*.'"

Me: "Then I won't take her back to England. I much prefer living out East."

Inner voice: "Even out East she'll be a social handicap."

Me: "You talk as if I had social ambitions. I'm not in the colonial service. I'm a painter. And I won't be the first painter to marry his favorite model."

Inner voice: "Well, if you can't restrain your impetuosity for your own sake, restrain it for Suzie's. Don't say anything to her until you're absolutely sure. You know what you are with your sudden enthusiasms—by this time next week you'll have come to your senses."

However, during the next few days the enthusiasm, so far from abating, increasingly possessed me. Yes, I shall marry her, I thought happily; and I had just decided that at the first suitable opportunity I would ask her, when something happened that for the time being put the notion out of my head.

It was something as wonderful as it was unexpected. It was eleven o'clock in the morning, and I was busy painting at the easel when there was a knock on the door. Suzie was out on the balcony with Gwenny and Mary Kee, and she came hurrying through the room to see who it was, for she took very seriously her duty to protect me from interruption. I heard her whispering to Ah Tong. Then she closed the door again and came over to me, looking very self-important. She held out an envelope.

"This cable just came for you."

"Be an angel and open it for me, Suzie," I said, guessing how much she would enjoy performing this service in front of Gwenny and Mary.

She glowed with pride. She took good care to open the envelope in full sight of her audience. She handed me the contents. It was the longest cable I had ever seen, and I thought for a moment that it could not be meant for me at all. Then I saw that it was from Mitford's in New York. It ran to twelve lines, and the gist of it was that a well-known American pictorial magazine, with international circulation, had made an offer for my Hong Kong paintings and pastels to display as a feature. Furthermore they wanted to commission me to follow it with a "Japanese sketchbook" for which, in addition to the fee, they would pay my air passage to Japan and expenses for two months.

The combined fee for the Hong Kong work and the work to be done in Japan was stated in American dollars, and was so large that I felt sure it must have acquired a couple of extra naughts in transmission. It would have been sufficient as it stood to keep Suzie and myself at our present standard of living for over a year.

The last three lines of the cable urged me not to scorn this commercial debut in the States, since it would greatly enhance interest in any gallery exhibition that I might give later.

The persuasion was superfluous, and I promptly cabled back my unconditional acceptance, and at the same time asked for a clarification of the fee. Forty-eight hours later came the reply. The figure given had been correct. And for the first time since Rodney's departure I wished he had been there, for if it had not been for him this would never have happened, and I was so happy that I would have liked to throw my arms round his neck.

An hour later another cable arrived, advising me that a sum of money representing the return fare to Japan and the first installment of my fee had been made available for me at the Hong Kong and Shanghai Bank, and requesting me to make tracks for Japan forthwith.

I collected the money and bought a tourist-class return ticket to Tokyo at B.O.A.C. I had been paid for first-class, and with the difference I took Suzie shopping. Since the loss of all her possessions she had bought herself only a couple of cheap cheongsams and a few underclothes, for she had hated spending my money; but now we let ourselves go. We bought shoes, sandals, stockings, jeans, cheongsams, and a whole lot of other little feminine items of which she had so long been deprived. Then, loaded with parcels and paper bags, we returned to the bank to see Gordon Hamilton and open an account in Suzie's name. She received her first check book, and Hamilton told her that whenever she wanted some money she could come to him, and he would write out the check for her and she could sign it. And she sat down to inscribe a specimen signature, which she did very carefully, biting her tongue, and writing Suzie with the Z characteristically large, disjointed, and back-to-front; and Hamilton said, "Bravo, well done. I wish everybody's signature was as easy to read." And eighteen hours later I was in the aircraft, peering through the little window as we took off and catching a last glimpse of Suzie in her new jeans behind the wire-mesh fence as she jumped up and down waving good-by.

A few hours later we landed at Okinawa to refuel. We took off again shortly, and at sunset were twenty thousand feet over the sea. I watched the light drain out of the sky until all was black except for a long streak of violent blazing orange across the horizon. Then all at once I noticed a cone-shaped silhouette against the orange. "Mount Fuji," said the air hostess—and I had caught my first glimpse of Japan.

Half an hour later we landed at Haneda airport. I went into Tokyo on the airline bus and spent the night at the Imperial Hotel, and in the morning called at the local office of the magazine.

"Coke?" said the American manager. "Miss Yamaguchi, two Cokes," and we sat chatting and nursing our bottles and drinking the ice-chilled liquid through straws. But the sumptuousness of the office intimidated me, and likewise the manager's apparent assumption that I was an artist of standing. I felt like an impostor. I had started painting for pleasure and could not rid myself of my beginner's sense of guilt at being paid for doing what I enjoyed. I blushed at each mention of my enormous fee; and when the manager began to talk of my expenses in terms of living and traveling de luxe, I kept self-consciously assuring him how modest were my needs. Finally I beat him down to a daily allowance that would have sufficed for a fortnight in Hong Kong with the odd dance girl thrown in. I also beat him down on the number of places he was recommending for inclusion in my tour, for I knew that I should do my best work with the minimum movement and the maximum time to browse. There was no obligatory itinerary or theme for my drawings, and we worked out a rough plan of campaign that gave me a week in Tokyo, a month in Kyoto and the south, another week in Tokyo, then a fortnight up in the southern island of Hokkaido.

Next I moved out of the international atmosphere of the Imperial into a Japanese-style hotel. And all at once I was immersed in an alien world, and what seemed an alien age. I removed my shoes at the front door and proceeded in my socks, squatted at a foot-high table for meals, wallowed in near-boiling water in a huge sunken bath, slept on a mattress on the floor, and was dressed, undressed, and waited upon hand and foot by half-a-dozen little serving maids in pretty kimonos chirruping round me like a flock of sparrows. And at all my departures and arrivals the whole flock would be in attendance at the porch, falling to their knees and bowing with their hands spread on the matting in front of their knees and their foreheads touching the floor.

The proprietress of the hotel was an ex-geisha, a woman in her thirties and still very pretty; and on my arrival she had greeted me in kimono and old-fashioned hair style like a figure from a Japanese print.

The next day in the garden I saw a slim woman sauntering in yellow slacks. Her hair was tied in a bandanna and there was heavy Swiss jewelry on her wrists. I thought she must be an American. Then she turned and smiled, and behind all the modernity I recognized the ex-geisha.

The occupant of the next room to mine performed a similar astonishing transformation in reverse. On my first evening at the hotel I had seen him in the corridor carrying a leather dispatch case and wearing black jacket, striped trousers, and stiff white collar. Then only an hour later, passing his room when the sliding door screen stood open, I caught a glimpse of this same little businessman squatting on the mat floor, against a background of typical Japanese simplicity: a vase containing two flowers and a leaf, and a single scroll picture on the wall. And now his black suit had been replaced by a kimono, and every other vestige of the West had been shed. It might have been a scene from one of those historical Japanese films, and I half expected to see a posse of heavy-breathing Samurai leap out of hiding and butcher him before my eyes with their great curved swords.

This duality in the life of the Japanese was in evidence everywhere. It was not a very original discovery on my part but it was so fundamental, and often so amusing, that I decided to make it the theme of my drawings. And with this important matter settled I set out on my travels south.

There followed a month of utter enchantment, for I had never before been in a country that so delighted my eye, nor met with such kindness and hospitality; and my only regret was the absence of Suzie. I was astonished to find how much I missed her. Before leaving Hong Kong I had half considered broaching the subject of marriage but had not done so, for I had thought rather guiltily that in the excitement of seeing a new country and meeting new people I might begin to forget her. Yet now, traveling round by myself, I constantly suffered pangs of loneliness that the beauty of the countryside only made more acute. And at every delightful experience—as I gasped at the splendors of Nikko, or sat cross-legged eating *sukiyaki,* or wandered at night through a wood among a myriad twinkling fireflies—I told myself, "How wonderful this is, but how much more I should enjoy it if Suzie was here!" For she would have so enjoyed it herself; and her company always touched off in me a kind of childish gaiety, as I saw the world through her eyes and shared the innocence of her vision.

It was in Kyoto that I received my first post card from her, forwarded from the Tokyo office. I had left her a number of addressed cards, telling her just to sign her name on them and post them at intervals to let me know she was all right; but this first card was one that I had written as a joke, like an official form with various alternatives to leave or cross out, such as "I *adore/detest* you. Since you left I have had *no/two/six/seventy-three* sailors." She had left *adore* in the first sentence, and *seventy-three* in the second, with an asterisk drawing attention to a note in Gwenny's handwriting below:

> *This is just a joke about the sailors. I cried after you left. Please bring me a pink umbrella that you can make small if you have enough money. I have seen Japanese umbrellas, they are very nice.*
>
> *Love, Suzie.*

The signature was her own with the usual large reversed Z.

A week or two later when I returned to Tokyo there were two more cards from her at the office, both with little messages written by Gwenny. There was also a post card signed all over by a dozen of the girls, with their names in Chinese characters followed by their adopted European Christian names in brackets. In prominence were Fifi and Wednesday Lulu. I do not know what the Japanese secretaries in the office had made of this but when the manager asked me "Did you get your mail?" I fancied from the odd look he gave me that the card must have done the rounds.

I spent an afternoon in a store and bought small presents for all the girls and several for Suzie. I had no difficulty over the umbrella because there was a whole department devoted to nothing else, with a vast range of gay, modernistic patterns that made them equally suitable for sunshades. I bought one with a pink base and blue pattern like the spattering of ink from a pen, and with a collapsible handle as requested. It cost only one pound, but looked so original and smart that it would have created a sensation at Ascot.

A few days later I received another post card from Suzie, in Gwenny's handwriting.

Something terrible has happened. That Canton girl said a very bad thing that made me angry. But all the girls helped me so it is all right now. Gwenny is writing to tell you everything. That Canton girl is no good.

Love, Suzie.

I found this rather disturbing. I knew, of course, that "that Canton girl" meant Betty Lau, who had been the only fly in the ointment since Suzie's return to the Nam Kok; for after claiming me for so long as her own boy friend, Suzie's reappearance had much displeased her and she had lost no opportunity for the oblique expression of malice. Once or twice she had made remarks that had upset Suzie for days; and now clearly she had taken advantage of my absence to give her malice full rein.

I waited anxiously for the letter from Gwenny. It turned up three days later on the morning that I was due to depart for Hokkaido, and I took it across the road from the office to read in Hibiya Park. However, when I opened it I found that, although the envelope had been addressed by Gwenny, the letter itself was written in an unfamiliar hand. Evidently the gravity of the matter had called for a writer who was more at home with the language.

Dear Sir,

I am writing this letter at the request of "Gwenny" and "Suzie" who say you are a friend of theirs and wish to acquaint you with a certain matter. I wish to state first however that I have no personal connection with this matter nor with the parties concerned except that as Chief Petty Officer in H. M. Royal Navy I am interested in fair play and justice, and having entered this bar for the sole purpose of drinking, being a married man and not otherwise interested, and having observed the two above-mentioned girls to be very upset, I am glad to help these girls without in any way committing myself.

They wish me to state that at approx. 3 p.m. on 17th inst. a third party named "Betty" used insulting words to "Suzie" in this bar, provoking the latter to strike her with a pair of scissors, and to cause injury necessitating her removal to hospital. "Suzie" was detained by the police overnight, suffering discomfort, and on morning of 18th inst. appeared in the magistrate's court and was remanded on bail, this being provided in part by herself, and in part by sympathetic friends from this establishment. They further state that there is no cause for worry since it is general opinion that "Suzie's" action was justified in view of the abusive attitude of the other party. They also wish to be remembered to you.

I must finally correct any misapprehension that this letter is intended to interfere with justice, but I am satisfied that the girl "Suzie" is a very decent sort considering circumstances and was acting in good faith.

Yours truly,
R. 0. Bridges,
C.P.O.

Below this was written "*What day will you come back?*" followed by Suzie's signature. The signature was written jauntily and was frivolously surrounded with kisses.

The letter exceeded my worst fears. I found its apparent confidence far from reassuring. Obviously "general opinion," according to which Suzie's action was said to have been justified, meant nothing more than opinion in the bar—the opinion of the other girls. And the magistrate's opinion would doubtless be very different. Especially with those scissors.

The scissors worried me most of all. What on earth had she been doing with scissors in the bar? Where had they come from? Her handbag?

But she never carried scissors in her handbag. I had never seen any girl with scissors in the bar. Yet it was inconceivable that she had taken the scissors down to the bar on purpose: that the attack had been premeditated. It was out of the question.

Or was it? The more I thought about it, the less sure I became. I remembered how she had brooded after one of Betty's slighting remarks. I remembered her eyes; and now, in retrospect, I fancied that there had been a much deeper hurt in them than I had realized at the time. I had been so busy with my painting that I hadn't wanted to be bothered; I hadn't wanted to see the hurt. Yet it was not surprising that she should have been so hurt, for Betty had struck at the most sensitive part of her—at her pride.

Suzie's pride was often petty, but I had always been able to forgive her for it; for like the pride of most girls at the Nam Kok, it stood for her belief in herself and her aspirations to be something better. It stood for her refusal to submit to degradation, and the only girls who were truly degraded were those who had lost this bulwark of their pride.

And recently, since her baby had been killed, Suzie's pride had centered round her relationship with me. It was the only tangible asset she had left. And nothing in the world mattered to her more than that it should be kept intact, not only in fact but in the eyes of the other girls. And it was this very relationship with me that Betty had always so maliciously disparaged. She had caused Suzie to lose face. And when I considered what this meant to Suzie, it no longer seemed so unlikely that she should have carried her grievance as far as premeditated attack.

And I groaned to myself at my own stupidity in not foreseeing the danger: at my own selfishness in not bothering to understand her. I could probably have prevented this from happening. There was nobody more to blame than myself. And now I wondered if I ought not to return to Hong Kong at once to help her out of the mess—if I ought not to skip Hokkaido, return tomorrow.

But that would mean breaking an agreement: it would be a professional breach of faith. My first job as an artist, and I fell down on it.

But what about the breach of faith with Suzie? Wasn't my first allegiance to her . . . ?

I crossed and recrossed Hibiya Park in an agony of indecision. Finally I decided that I must go to Hokkaido and finish my job: after all, it was only another two weeks, and I might still be back in Hong Kong in time for her appearance in court, for which she had given no date in her letter. And I left the park and went over the road to the post office in the Imperial, and sent Suzie a cable telling her to contact a solicitor called Haynes. He was the only solicitor in Hong Kong whose name I knew, though I knew nothing else about him and had never met him—I had simply read his name one day in the newspaper as the defending solicitor in a rent case, and an hour later happened to see it again at the entrance of an office building in town, and because of the odd coincidence the name had stuck in my mind. And I told her not to worry, and that whatever happened I would be behind her, and sent her my love.

I also sent a cable to Haynes, and then remembered that in Suzie's cable I had not told her the date of my return. I went over to the B.O.A.C. counter in the hotel foyer to make sure of my booking in two weeks' time, then returned to the post office and sent her another cable about my arrival. And I added another reassurance, and told her about the pink umbrella, and sent some more love. And then I took a taxi back to my hotel where the flock of little sparrows went down on their knees in the porch, and I sat on the wooden step while two of them untied my laces and took off my shoes. I told the taxi to wait, and the little sparrows came twittering along to my room and helped to pack my bag; and I tied up all my Japanese drawings and gave them to the proprietress for safekeeping. Then the sparrows all went down on their knees again in the porch, giggling and shaking warning fingers and pulling illustratively at their hair, by way of telling me to behave myself with the aboriginal girls of Hokkaido who were commonly known as the Hairy Ainu; and then I got back into the taxi and drove out to the airport, and caught the plane for Hokkaido with ten minutes to spare.

Chapter Three

"Those police, you know, they gave me a bad time. Yes! They kept me in the monkey-house all night! Not the real monkey-house, but the little monkey-house at the police station, which was worse!"

We stood outside the airport building waiting for a bus into Hong Kong. The plane from Japan had been three hours late, but as I stepped out onto the tarmac I had recognized Suzie in her jeans behind the wire-mesh fence, excitedly craning on tiptoe and fluttering her hand, as if she had stood there ever since my departure two months before. During my absence full summer had arrived in Hong Kong, bringing with it a stifling heat and humidity that was worse even than Malaya. The perspiration trickled down inside my shirt. I mopped my forehead and neck with my handkerchief as Suzie exploded with indignation about her ordeal at the hands of the police.

"Oh, it was terrible, that place—all full of horrible, dirty people! Yes, those horrible police, they treated me just like a street girl!"

I said, "Suzie, what about Betty? Is she all right?"

"That Canton girl?" Suzie said. "Oh, yes, you needn't worry about her."

"I'm only worrying about you. I've been so scared about the consequences for you if she was really in danger. Is she still in hospital?"

"Yes, I expect so," she said indifferently.

"But don't you know?"

"Oh, yes, she is in hospital—but I haven't finished telling you about my bad time in the monkey-house yet. Oh, it was terrible! I told them, 'You let me out! I'm not a bad girl! My boy friend's an Englishman. He's in Japan just now for a big American company, getting more money in one week than your Number One gets in a month, or maybe even a year. Look, he gave me this check book, and I just have to write down on one of those checks how much I want, and the bank will give me any amount. Yes, my boy friend's a big man, and when he comes back he will make trouble. He will see that you policemen get a bad time!' But they kept me all night in that horrible place—oh, I couldn't sleep a wink!"

I said, "Suzie, I wish you'd start at the beginning and tell me what happened."

"I told you, that Canton girl said something bad to me, so I just stuck her with the scissors."

"But *what* did she say?"

"Oh, I don't remember exactly," she said quickly. "I just remember it was something bad, that's all—and I wish I had stuck her harder."

"Thank God you didn't! Anyhow, what were you doing with the scissors?"

"I just had them."

"But what on earth—" I began, but she interrupted impatiently.

"Anyhow, why are you so worried about that Canton girl? She only got what she deserved. Everybody said so. Everybody told me, 'Suzie, you did right. You did a very good thing.' They all congratulated me, you know—all except those stupid police!"

On the bus, and again during the ferry-crossing to Wanchai, I taxed her for more details of the stabbing and of what Betty had said to provoke her, but her answers were vague and evasive; and when we reached the Nam Kok I was still little wiser about what had happened than I had been in Tokyo.

My shirt was wringing wet with perspiration after the brief trip from the airport and I was already breaking out in prickly heat. Suzie, who had put flowers in the room for my reception, helped me to unpeel the sticky garments from my body and laid out replacements. I sponged myself down at the basin, and Suzie sponged my back; and after this I felt quite refreshed and ready to tackle Suzie about her reluctance to impart details of the Betty affair. I made her lie beside me on the bed, and said, "Now let's start at the beginning, Suzie. It was three o'clock in the afternoon, and you were sitting in the bar—were you alone?"

"No, I was sitting with Gwenny."

"All right, and where was Betty?"

"She just came into the bar, and she walked past with that show-off wiggle-waggle walk. I think it's disgusting that way she walks. She only does it to—"

"All right, and who spoke first?"

"She spoke—that Canton girl. She said something bad to me."

"Well, what?"

"I don't remember."

"But you must remember, Suzie. If it was so bad that it made you attack her you couldn't possibly have forgotten."

"I just remember it was the same bad thing that she said the day before."

"And what was that?"

"I don't remember."

"Suzie, look at me. No, look at me properly. All right, are you telling me the truth?"

"No."

"You mean you do remember?"

"Yes."

"Then what was it?"

She averted her eyes. "I can't tell."

"But why on earth not?"

She was silent. It was the first time she had refused me her confidence, and I was puzzled and hurt.

"All right, let's leave that for a minute," I said. "Just tell me what happened when she said whatever-it-was the first time."

"I told her, 'If you ever say that again, I will kill you.'"

"You didn't really, Suzie? Not those very words?"

"Yes, I warned her. I told her 'I will kill you.'"

"Oh, Christ!"

"And she said, 'Pooh to you!'" Suzie went on blithely. "'Pooh,' she said, 'I will say it any time I like—I will say it again tomorrow.' So I went out and bought scissors."

"You *what?*"

"Yes, from that first shop round the corner in Hennessy Road. Big scissors—maybe six, eight inches. I can't show you because those police took them away—yes, stole them!"

"And after you'd bought the scissors?"

"I put them in my handbag to keep ready. Then the next afternoon that Canton girl came past the table like I told you, and she said that same bad thing again, so I took out the scissors, and she was just walking way, so I said, 'You've got a dirty, filthy mind, you dirty Canton girl,' and she turned round and I stuck her with the scissors between her titties. I wouldn't mind if I had hit her titties after what she said, but the scissors went between. Then I pulled them out to hit her again, but Gwenny and somebody stopped me, and that Canton girl just fell on the floor with a lot of blood, making a silly noise—but she wasn't half so bad as she pretended."

"Well, thank God for Gwenny, that's all I can say."

"No, I wanted to kill that girl. I was very sorry that Gwenny pulled me off."

"But you're not still sorry?"

"Yes, of course. I warned her the day before, so she deserved it. She had no excuse. I feel angry when I think that Gwenny pulled me off."

I said, "Listen, Suzie. I don't think you've any idea how serious this is, even though you didn't kill her. Frankly, I'm only surprised they gave you bail."

"I'm not worried. You ask anybody downstairs, they all say, 'Suzie you did a good thing.' I shall just tell them in court what happened. I shall tell them that I warned that Canton girl first, so they will understand."

"They'll understand far too much," I said. "We've got to do some hard thinking, Suzie. And first of all you must tell me what Betty said to you, because I can't help you until I know. Now what was it?"

"I can't tell."

I said, "Suzie, for God's sake! Can't you understand what this means? You're in danger of going to prison."

"They won't send me to the monkey-house when I tell them what happened."

"But they will! That's exactly what they will do! You didn't just attack Betty on the spur of the moment, but threatened to kill her and then tried to carry out the threat. And we've got to work out some damn good story, and before we can do that I've got to know what she said. Now, come on. Tell me."

"No."

And then I lost my temper. I lost it as I would never lose it in the cool weather but only in the damp sticky heat, which causes little knots of rage to grow inside you as it causes fungus to grow on your shoes, and I vituperated at her so furiously that she began to cry; but I still went on swearing at her and chastising her for her stupid idiotic pride—for it could only be from fear of losing face that she refused to repeat what Betty had said. And I told her that so far from saving her face in my eyes she was rapidly destroying the last shreds of my respect for her.

And at last she said in tears, "All right, I will tell you."

"Well, thank God for that. Thank God I've at last knocked some sense into you."

And then she told me, and all my anger promptly went and I felt bitterly ashamed—because it was not her own face that she had been trying to save, but mine.

And it made it no better that it was all so trivial. It appeared that Betty had simply taunted her with the malicious little invention that I was a *blankety-blank* (or whatever was the Chinese word), meaning one of those men who favored an unorthodox manner of sexual union which the girls found repugnant. She had told Suzie that on the occasion of her visit to my room I had invited her co-operation in this matter, and that she had refused; but that I had admitted to practicing it with Suzie, who she understood had been more obliging.

On the following day, in the bar, she had simply tossed the one word "*blankety-blank*" at Suzie *en passant*. And it had been enough to bring Suzie within an ace of a capital charge.

"Because I will kill anybody who tries to make you dirty," she said. "I told her, 'You can make me dirty, but not my boy friend'—because dirt doesn't show on a dirty little yum-yum girl who is dirty already, but it shows on you because you are a good man, and you have got no dirt on you, not inside or outside or anywhere, and I will kill anybody who tells lies about you and throws dirt."

I said, "Suzie, I don't know what to say. Except that I've never felt dirtier than I do now, after all those things I just said."

"I don't mind. Not now you understand that I did a good thing, sticking that Canton girl with the scissors."

"I still wish you hadn't done it, Suzie. I'm terribly worried about it."

"You worry too much."

"What did Haynes say?"

"Oh, he is just a stupid old man. He couldn't understand anything. He said, 'Maybe they will send you to Laichikok'—that is the woman's monkey-house. But I heard that the judge is a very kind, good man, and has a very good heart—so he will understand."

"The trouble is, Suzie, that although the magistrate might be very good-hearted, the law's got no heart at all. And the law doesn't happen to approve of assassination with scissors, even if the victim deserved it."

But I could not make her understand how serious her position was, and presently I went out on the balcony to think it over. I remained there for about twenty minutes, and then returned to the room.

"Suzie, there's one lesson I've learned from you," I said, "and that is that whatever one decides to do, good or bad, one must stick to one's own decision and act on it boldly. Well, we're going to do something bad. We're going to commit a terrible offense called perjury. And that means we're going to work out some lies very carefully, and learn them by heart, and tell them in court, although we'll have sworn by all that's holy to us that we're telling the truth. Because if we don't they're going to send you to Laichikok for six months, or even a year, and I'd perjure myself into hell sooner than let them do that. Now, let's think about those scissors. When did you buy them?"

"I bought them after that Canton girl first said that dirty thing to me."

"No, you didn't. You bought them weeks before. You bought them after your house fell down and you'd lost all your possessions. And you bought them at a street stall, not at that shop in Hennessy Road—because we don't want the police investigating."

"I don't want to tell lies. I will just tell the truth, what really happened."

"Suzie, you've just got to believe me that if you do you'll be sent to gaol.

And if you can't understand yourself why that should be so, you must take it from me on trust."

"All right, if you want."

"Good. Now, when did you buy those scissors?"

"After my house fell down."

"And where?"

"Street market."

"And where do you usually keep them?"

"Top drawer."

"No, you don't. You keep them in your handbag because you're always using them for your sewing or knitting in the bar. And where were they when Betty passed your table and flung that taunt at you?"

"In my bag."

"No, they were in your hand. You were using them for your sewing. And when you lost your temper and threw yourself at Betty you just struck out at her blindly, without even realizing what you were doing."

"No, that lie is no good, because other girls saw. They saw everything."

"How many girls? How many were near enough?"

"There was Gwenny and Little Alice, and Wednesday Lulu, and Doris Woo. Four girls—they all saw."

"Well, go and get them. Go and tell them we've got something very important to discuss and ask them to come up here."

The four girls all proved more amenable than I had dared to hope. I had expected the most difficulty from Wednesday Lulu, thinking that her high principles might well be inexorably opposed to organized perjury in the witness box; however, since one of her foremost principles was loyalty to colleagues in trouble, other scruples were overridden and she entered into the occasion calmly and contributed several good suggestions. Doris had also seemed a likely stumbling block; and for a while she did indeed remain noncommittal and aloof, her schoolmarm mouth set with disapproval and her eyes blinking and withdrawn behind the rimless glasses. Her only comment, when it came at last, was the pointed reminder that by attending court as a witness she would be losing business in the bar; so when the others left I asked her to remain behind and gave her fifty dollars, and promised another fifty when the job was successfully done. For having entered on a course of corruption, I saw no reason to jib at a little bribery.

And that left only Haynes. And so I set off to Hennessy Road and boarded a tram, which clanked and tunneled its way through the heat-stuffed streets, shoveling the heat back through the open windows into the passengers' faces. I arrived at Haynes's office already exhausted by two minutes' walk and a climb up a short flight of stairs. The office was a large old-fashioned room, unsuitably hung with mirrors presented by satisfied Chinese clients. The chair at the desk was empty and there was no sign of life. Then I noticed movement behind the glass door of a kind of plaster-board den built into one corner of the room, like the kitchen of a converted mansion flat. A clerk came out and held open the door, and I stepped through into a chilly air-conditioned atmosphere that turned my damp shirt clammy and made my perspiration run like iced water. It was like walking out of a boiler room straight into a deepfreeze.

"Much cheaper than air-conditioning the whole—ah—office," Haynes said. "And after twenty years out here I still can't stand the infernal heat. How's it outside now?"

"Pretty hot."

"And I've got the afternoon in the court."

He looked miserable. He was a tall anxious man with big hands, and knees that he had difficulty in fitting under the tiny desk, which was not a quarter the size of the big desk in the office outside.

"Well, I can't say that I view our prospects with much ah—enthusiasm," he said gloomily. "I only hope we don't get Freddy Gore."

"Who's that—the magistrate?"

"Yes, decent fellow, Freddy. But always hard on these—ah—girls. We must just cross our fingers and hope we get Charlie Kwok. Though I'm afraid even Charlie will give her a month or two."

"You mean gaol?"

"It's no use my trying to paint you a rosy picture. You see, the way she'd thought it out—gone specially to buy those scissors—"

"Oh, no," I said. "She'd had those scissors for weeks."

He blinked at me.

"Well, I'm afraid that—ah—whenever they were bought she was carrying them in her handbag. And unfortunately the facts suggest a certain deliberate—ah—intention. I mean, to open her bag and take them out—"

"But they were already out. She was in the middle of using them."

"That isn't what the young—ah—lady told me."

"How's your Chinese?" I said.

"My Chinese? I don't speak a word."

"Well, her English is hopeless. It was obviously a misunderstanding."

He gave me a long look, and then dropped his eyes and began to shift his knees about uncomfortably under the tiny desk.

"Yes—ah—of course. Only I'm afraid the police will call witnesses, whose impressions may possibly prove contradictory."

"That's all right," I said. "There were only four people who saw what happened, and I know their impressions were all the same."

"Well—ah—in that case we can form a different view."

"And so what's the worst that can happen to her?"

"Well, let's say it's Charlie Kwok. Then it might be three hundred dollars."

"And if it's Freddy Gore?"

"Five hundred."

"They couldn't send her to gaol?"

"They could. But they—ah—won't."

"And when's the hearing likely to be?"

"I'd say in four or five months."

"Months?"

"They're queuing up for the courts, you know."

"Well, we'd better put five hundred dollars on one side."

He saw me to the door of the air-conditioned compartment but no farther. He said good-by rather awkwardly. Then after a hesitation he added:

"By the way, about that—ah—misunderstanding over the young lady's English. I forgot to say that I used an—ah—interpreter."

I could think of nothing to say.

"Now excuse me if I shut you out. We're—ah—letting the hot air in."

Chapter Four

"Suzie, now that we're doing so well as partners in conspiracy, I think we should extend our partnership to other fields. Such as marriage. Will you marry me, Suzie?"

"What's happened? This heat gone to your head?"

"I thought about getting married long before it got hot. Will you, Suzie?"

"Sorry, my husband."

"Don't be silly, you can't call me 'my husband' and refuse to marry me in the same breath. Anyhow, why not?"

"You're a big man. Maybe one day they will make you a Lord. Mr. Lord Lomax."

"What's that got to do with it?"

"Then I'd be Mrs. Lord. Mrs. Lord Bar Girl. 'How do you do, Mrs. Lord Bar Girl? I hear you had two thousand sailors before you were married.'"

"I don't care how many sailors you had. You've got to marry me so that I'll always have you as a model."

"Sorry, my husband. You go and marry some English girl."

I was painting her lying relaxed on the bed in the heat, one hand idly picking at a saucer of melon seeds. I laid down my palette and sat on the bed beside her. Her small Chinese breasts were very white and smooth, like an immature girl's, but the nipples were mature and wrinkled and proud. Her baby had been a biter.

I laid my hand on her thigh.

"You've got Japanese thighs, Suzie."

"How do you know? You told me you never had a girl in Japan."

"I didn't."

"I think so. I think you had a girl."

"All right, I had a girl."

"Then I will kill you! Pass me some scissors, please, my husband! I want to stick you!"

"Will you marry me, Suzie?"

"No, you go and find some English girl."

II

"You like my new shoes?" old Lily Lou said.

"Sure," Typhoo said. "Now listen while I tell you about this Yankee."

"Forty-two dollars, they cost me, these shoes," Lily Lou said.

"This Yankee asked me 'How much one short-time?'" Typhoo said. "I said 'Fifty dollars.' He said 'Sure.' I thought he must be crazy—fifty dollars for a short-time! Then he gave me some money, and I said, 'Hey, what's that? That's not Hong Kong money.' He said, 'No, American money. You said fifty dollars, didn't you?' And you know how many Hong Kong dollars you get for fifty American dollars?"

"I never paid so much for shoes before," Lily Lou said.

"Two hundred," Typhoo said. "Two hundred Hong Kong dollars!"

The harbor had been packed with American ships for the last four days. The girls had known for a week beforehand that they were coming, because ships were their bread and butter and they knew more about the movement of ships than the Navy Department or the Admiralty. They had said there would be seventeen. Then one morning I had gone out onto the balcony and they had arrived. But there had only been sixteen, and I had teased the girls down in the bar that their information had been faulty and that they were slipping. But the laugh had been on me, for they had blithely pointed out that in my ignorance of naval matters I had left one ship out—the aircraft carrier which never came into the harbor, but anchored round the corner in Joss House Bay.

Typhoo said, "Two hundred dollars—for one short-time!"

"I got an all-night last night," Lily Lou said. "Sixty dollars."

"I get worried with too much money," Typhoo grinned. "When I got no money, I got no worries. Money just makes me worried." She looked across the table at the luscious little Jeannie. "Hey, what you doing?"

Jeannie was too preoccupied to answer. She was putting ticks against a list of numbers written on a paper serviette—the numbers of the seventeen American ships. She hesitated over the last. She pulled at the sleeve of her latest boy friend sitting beside her. He had been drinking and had passed out.

"Hey, Joe, what number you said your ship?"

The American opened bleary eyes. "Come again."

"Your ship—what number?"

"Four-two-six."

Jeannie ticked off the last number on her list and turned to Typhoo with a look of satisfaction.

"You know something? I got one boy friend in every ship in the fleet."

III

"That word you just read—what does it mean?"

"Matador? It's a Spanish bullfighter."

"What's a bullfighter?"

"Well, bullfighting is a very popular sport in Spain. They let a very fierce bull into a ring, and a man has to kill it with his sword, and there are thousands of people watching and they all shout '*Ole!*'"

"Aren't Spanish people Christians?"

"Yes, very much so. And so are English people who hunt foxes and otters with dogs."

"But that book you read last week said that Christians must be kind to animals, because they were made by God just like men."

"I know, Suzie, but the human brain is a wonderful organism. It can believe almost anything that happens to suit it. It can believe that black is white today, and red tomorrow, or even that it is both at the same time. You should never underrate the ingenuity of the human brain."

"Then perhaps one day Christian people will say, 'A man must have twenty wives.'"

"Yes, the Mohammedans already say you can have several, and they believe in the same God."

"All right, go on reading."

"No, let's talk a bit more about wives. Suzie, I'm so ridiculously happy with you. Let's go mad and get married."

"No, you go and find some virgin girl. Christian men are supposed to marry virgin girls."

"Perhaps one day they will say you can only marry a girl who has worked two years at the Nam Kok. Anyhow you are a virgin."

"You think so? Well, you said the brain can believe anything!"

"You're an intellectual virgin. That's what I love about you. It makes me feel like a Pygmalion."

"What's that?"

"Never mind. Will you marry me?"

"No."

"You didn't say 'No,' Suzie?"

"Yes."

IV

The telephone rang and Suzie picked it up.

"No, he's busy. . . . All right." She handed me the receiver. "It's that man."

I thought for a moment, from the disdainful way she said "That man," that Rodney must have turned up again. But it was Haynes.

"Well, we're not going to have to wait so long after all," Haynes said. "There's been some re-shuffling at the court, and the hearing's been fixed for next week. Anyhow, we've got the right magistrate. We've got Charlie Kwok."

"Thank God for that."

"Should have a bit of fun with old Charlie. He's got rather an eye for the—ah—girls."

Suzie was delighted when I told her the news. She was looking forward to the hearing as an opportunity for letting off steam about Betty.

"I am going to tell them that girl is no good," she said. "I am going to tell them everything."

"You're not, Suzie. You're going to tell them only what I told you to tell them."

"I forget what you said."

"Don't worry, I shall remind you."

The hearing was on a Thursday, and on the previous afternoon I spent an hour putting Suzie and the four girls through their paces and firing tricky questions to try and catch them out. The next morning we all set off to the Central District by tram—minus only Little Alice, who had disappeared to another hotel with a boy friend the night before and failed to reappear. We left the tram and climbed up through the steep narrow streets. The magistrate's court was next to a police station and the old city gaol. There were several courtrooms and the entrance hall was crowded with people assembling for the various hearings. Suzie went off cheerfully to surrender to her bail. The three girls, who were all much more nervous than Suzie herself, stood in a silent anxious little group, glancing about sheepishly at the khaki-clad policemen. I led them to the room where witnesses had to report and then went and sat in the empty courtroom. It might have been a London magistrate's court except for the heat and the fans. The hot damp heat was appalling even at half-past nine in the morning, and my shirt and trousers were sticking to my body after the climb up the hill. Presently Haynes arrived, wiping his neck with a handkerchief, and said miserably, "I wish our hearing was in the High Court."

"The High Court?" I said, alarmed. "Why?"

"The High Court's air-conditioned."

I had sat down on one of the public benches, but he told me to move up to the press bench because there would be nobody else there, and I would "feel more one of the family."

Soon the court began to assemble desultorily and the hearing began. And the atmosphere was so friendly and informal that it did indeed seem almost like a family party, and it was all I could do to stop myself butting in: I felt sure that nobody would have minded. Charlie Kwok, who was Cantonese but very westernized, was small, twinkling, and birdlike. He punctuated the proceedings with chatty and humorous asides. And even the police prosecutor, a young Chinese inspector, seemed to bear no ill will, and his manner was so obliging and gentle that I felt quite ashamed to think we were taking advantage of him.

The first witness to be called was Doris. She was the girl in whom I had the least confidence, for I would not have put it past her to turn against us in the witness box and expose our conspiracy. I sat watching anxiously. But I need not have worried, for she gave her answers drily but exactly as she had been drilled, and the nice Chinese inspector asked no awkward questions and made no attempt to trick her.

The proceedings were slow because the language of the court was English and the interrogation of witnesses had to be conducted through an interpreter—a small sleek conceited young Chinese with an impeccable Palm Beach suit and a taste for difficult and technical words. Doris was in the box for about fifteen minutes, and as she left the courtroom Charlie Kwok turned to the inspector and said with a twinkle, "I shouldn't think she gets much business, does she?"

"I don't know, sir."

"I mean, those glasses," Charlie Kwok chuckled. "I shouldn't think she gets much business with those glasses. Still, I remember when I was a student in London—you'd hardly believe it—I mean, some of those girls in the streets! Well, certainly not my cup of tea! I suppose it's still like that in London, isn't it, Mr. Haynes?"

"Well—ah—yes, I suppose so."

"Now, let's get on. What else have you up your sleeve?"

Gwenny and Wednesday Lulu both gave their evidence without a slip. Then Betty Lau herself was called. She had only been out of hospital a few days and I could hardly recognize her, for she wore no make-up, no false eyelashes, and she crossed the courtroom with scarcely a sign of a waggle. She was very subdued in the witness box, and less concerned with making things awkward for Suzie than with whitewashing herself. She maintained that at the Nam Kok she had never gone upstairs with sailors: she had only gone to the bar to talk and drink with them. This pretense, which cast doubts on the truth of her other evidence, made her unwittingly more of a help to Suzie than otherwise. And when Haynes asked her what she had said that had provoked Suzie, she was evasive. She had to be pressed. Finally she yielded, and the natty young interpreter rendered her reply in his technical English:

"'I told her what I had heard about her boy friend—that he was perverse and vicious, and addicted to a certain unnatural practice.'"

Charlie Kwok chuckled and said, "Well, she went into rather more detail than that—but evidently our interpreter doesn't think it fit for your ears, Mr. Haynes. Are you satisfied?"

"Yes, I think the witness has made her attitude sufficiently—ah—clear," Haynes said. "I have nothing more to ask."

Then Suzie was called and came down out of the dock. She was looking very pretty in a blue silk cheongsam and as she crossed the court Charlie Kwok twinkled appreciatively and winked at the prosecutor, "I'd like to wrap her up and take her home." And he spoke to her in the witness box like an uncle talking to a pretty niece with whom he is regretfully aware that on account of family relationship he is obliged to behave.

However, it was Suzie herself who came nearest to ruining her own case. She was still so convinced of the justice of her attack on Betty that soon she had thrown all my warnings to the winds; and thrusting aside the questions of the kindly prosecutor, she tried to address herself directly to the magistrate. She just wanted to tell him what a nasty wicked person Betty Lau really was. She knew he would understand. And Charlie Kwok was obliged to rebuke her for these indignant outbursts and call her to order.

"Well, she's got spirit, I will say that for her," he twinkled.

Then Haynes cross-examined her, and all went well until he asked for her assurance that her attack on Betty had been committed thoughtlessly, in a sudden access of anger, and that she was now sorry for what she had done. This was too bitter a pill to swallow. Sorry? For hurting that Canton girl? For punishing her for saying that spiteful dirty thing? I saw her struggle with herself. My heart stopped beating. And then all at once she burst out in Chinese and I could not understand what she was saying but I knew that it meant she was not sorry at all because Betty had deserved it, and—

And then she stopped. She had caught my eye. She looked defiant for a moment, and I went on holding her eyes and trying to exert my will on her; and then she began to look a bit ashamed, and after another moment she glanced at the interpreter and said something in a tone that meant that she did not believe what she was saying, in fact she could see no earthly sense in it, but that she was saying it nevertheless to please her boy friend who had the silly idea that she could be sent to the monkey-house for committing an act of justice.

"'Yes, I am sorry for what I did,'" translated the sleek complacent young interpreter—and for the first time I positively liked him, for fancying himself as an actor, he had put an expression of sincerity into his voice that in Suzie's had been so notably lacking. "'I am very sorry.'"

It was then time for lunch and there was an informal discussion about whether the hearing should be continued in the afternoon or the next morning. Charlie Kwok said obligingly that he was indifferent, and that it was up to Haynes and the inspector. Haynes mopped his brow, and glanced up at the ceiling for the twentieth time to see if the fans were still working. He said that he had really hoped to spend the afternoon at his office. He did not mention that his office happened to be air-conditioned. However, the inspector had just remembered that tomorrow morning he had a case over in Kowloon. He could only manage this afternoon.

Suzie remained in custody during the break and I took Haynes to lunch at the Parisian Grill. He had chosen the P.G. himself because it was air-conditioned. It was also very expensive, but he had handled the case so well for us that I did not mind, and even suggested a bottle of wine to celebrate.

"Wine?" he said. "Good Lord, no! It makes you too damned hot."

"Well, what's in store for us this afternoon?"

"We'll be through by three o'clock. We've just got to sum up, then after Kwok's found her guilty I'll put in a plea of mitigation. I'll say that she's a decent girl though a bit hot-tempered, and that she's now settled down with a regular boy friend of the highest integrity. Then Charlie will deliver a homily, tell her he's being lenient and hopes she's learnt her lesson, and fine her two hundred dollars."

"You said three hundred before."

"It's gone better than I hoped."

An hour later we were back in court. And it all went as Haynes had predicted except in the last particular—Suzie was not fined two hundred dollars, but was sentenced to gaol.

V

It was not Haynes's fault that he had failed to anticipate this sentence. For he could not have done so without knowing why the hearing had been changed to an earlier date, and this did not become apparent until Charlie Kwok enlightened us in his homily.

"Recently we have been given a lot of trouble by girls who work in dance halls and bars," he said, and he did not say it with a twinkle because he had left the twinkle behind at lunch. In fact it was almost as if Charlie Kwok himself had got left behind at lunch, and only the impersonal magistrate had returned; for he had acquired such an appearance of weighty authority that he seemed twice the size of this morning's twinkling little robin. "In the past we have been very lenient with them, and they appear to have got the mistaken idea that they can take the law into their own hands. And there are now so many cases of this kind waiting to be heard that we have brought some of them forward, to show other girls that such nonsense must stop. Now you, Wong Mee-ling, have inflicted a very serious injury on another girl, with a pair of scissors, and you are very lucky not to be standing in the High Court on a much graver charge. I do not even get the impression that you are sorry for what you have done. I take a very serious view, and since I do not think that a fine will teach you a sufficient lesson, I am going to send you to gaol." He paused and wrote something, and said without looking up, "Three months."

I could not grasp it for a minute. After the magistrate's remarks I had been prepared for a heavier fine, but not for gaol. And there was Suzie standing only a few yards from me in her blue cheongsam and looking so pretty. They could not really be going to take her away and lock her up in Laichikok. It couldn't happen.

The interpreter repeated in Shanghai dialect, "'Three months.'"

Suzie frowned. She could not believe it either. She looked at the magistrate for an explanation but the magistrate was writing. One of the two Chinese policewomen in the dock said something to her. She did not hear. The two policewomen took her arms and marshalled her out of the dock. She looked round desperately for me but had lost her bearings and looked over the wrong shoulder. She stumbled over one of the policewomen's feet and nearly fell. Before she could recover herself and look round again she had been whisked away through the door.

I sat stunned. The magistrate rose from the desk on the rostrum. But he was the magistrate no longer—he had cast off the cloak of authority and reassumed the twinkling bird-like personality of Charlie Kwok, as deftly as one might remove bowler hat and overcoat and don a paper hat and false nose.

"Well, I'm off to the dentist," he told the inspector. "Just for a scaling. Wife refuses to go out with me until I get all this black off. Of course it's smoking."

The inspector said, "You haven't tried these new Red Spot cigarettes, sir? I'm told Red Spot don't stain the teeth at all."

"Red Spot, eh? I'd be scared to touch them—might come out in a rash!"

He chuckled off through the door behind the rostrum. Haynes came over mopping his neck. He looked really shattered.

"Well, I don't know what to say," he said. "I don't know what to say."

"It wasn't your fault," I said.

"I ought to have known there was something up. I ought to have guessed."

"Can I see her before they take her off?"

"No, I'm afraid not. Only her solicitor—I can see her. I can give her a message if you want."

"I might see her when they bring her out."

"You'll only see the van."

"I think I'll wait all the same. Will you tell her I'll be waiting?"

I waited with Gwenny at the gate outside the court. It was two hours before the van came, and then it came across the courtyard quickly and a policeman stood out on the road waving it on so that it did not have to stop. The windows were dark blue glass and we could not see inside, but we waved and blew kisses in case Suzie could see out. It swung out onto the road and disappeared. We walked down the hill into the town and turned along the quay. There was a queue of cars at the vehicle ferry and the police van was at the head, waiting to cross over to Kowloon. The ferry was just coming alongside. The cars from the ferry came up the ramp in quick succession. After the last car had come off, the van went forward down the ramp and disappeared into the covered deck. The other cars followed and a minute later the water began churning again. We stood watching as the boat moved off from the pier. I realized that Gwenny was holding my hand. We watched until the boat went out of sight behind an anchored merchant ship, then turned away in silence and walked up to Queens Road to the trams.

Chapter Five

The only girl at the Nam Kok who had ever been in Laichikok before was the heroin-smoker Big Alice, who had served a month for acting as go-between in supplying drugs to sailors. That night I asked her what it had been like, and she shuddered with disgust and said, "Terrible. It is a terrible place. You have to work all the time. If you stop work for one second they beat you up. Sure! They don't care if you die—they just beat you to death."

"Beat up the women? They don't really, Alice?"

"Sure! Lots of women get beaten every day."

Wednesday Lulu said, "I never heard that. I heard it is not bad in Laichikok, and nobody is beaten."

"I have been there, haven't I?" Big Alice said. "I have been one month in that terrible place, and women died every day, and I came out with lice and crabs."

Fifi grinned. "They're just honest. If you take something in, they give it to you back when you come out."

I asked Alice, "How soon can I visit Suzie?"

"Tomorrow."

"But she only went in today."

"Yes, but you can go and see her tomorrow."

Big Alice was very unreliable, and I was no more inclined to believe this than her stories of daily beatings-up. However, I rang the gaol to make sure and found out that it was true: the early visit was allowed so that women who had just been sentenced could arrange their domestic affairs. And so the next day I took a ferry over to Kowloon, then a bus out to Laichikok. After being kept waiting for a while at the gaol I was led to the visiting room and directed to a booth backed with wire mesh. Beyond the mesh was a narrow corridor patrolled by a wardress, then another thickness of mesh. Behind this stood a sad pale little figure with shorn-off hair and sallow unpainted face, wearing coarse gray smock and trousers several sizes too big.

I said, "Hello, Suzie."

"Hello."

Her mouth was dragged down at the corners. Her eyes welled with tears. In another booth a woman was howling. And I understood why most prisons did not allow visitors while the wound was still fresh.

"The girls all send their love," I said. "They were terribly upset to hear what had happened, and we're all just counting the days until you come out."

She could not speak. She could say nothing at all but stood there quite still with her arms at her sides and her mouth dragged down and the tears coming faster and rolling away down her cheeks. I went on talking but she did not open her mouth for fear of breaking down. I knew she could not bear the strain much longer, and presently I said, "Suzie, I'm going now, but I shall be thinking of you every minute," and I turned and walked out of the booth without looking back. The time allowed for the visit was twenty minutes, but I had not been there more than five.

I was so upset by this visit that for days afterwards I could not work. When I tried to concentrate I would see only the pale round little face with the swimming eyes behind the layers of wire mesh. So after a week I decided to get away for a bit and I packed a sketchbook and a few old clothes in a valise and took the boat over to the island of Lantao, and climbed up to the monastery in the hills. Here the Buddhist monks provided accommodation and simple fare at small cost, and it was very peaceful after the town and cool because of the height. The monastery stood in a little vale with rice paddies in the bottom and a pagoda up on the hill at the end. The monastery courtyard smelt of incense from the temple where joss sticks burned on the altar among the dusty wooden images and offerings of fruit. In a room over the temple a monk squatted on a dais intoning prayers from an old manuscript. At the end of each prayer his voice rose to a climax and he pulled a rope and a beam of wood swung against the temple bell, and the deep voice of the bell went booming out across the paddies. I went up to the room and sat sketching him, but he never lifted his eyes from the manuscript or showed that he knew I was there. I also sketched the monks stooping in the paddies and squatting in the courtyard with rice bowls and chopsticks, and in the temple at their prayers.

At the weekend there was an influx of walkers—three English girls in government service, some Chinese students all anxious to air their English, and a silent middle-aged Englishman in old tropical battle dress and bush hat, with lost eyes, who looked as if he had mislaid his battalion in the last war and had been searching for it ever since. After supper he went off again for a lone walk, searching even in the dark, and the rest of us played Consequences by the light of hurricane lamps, calling each other by our Christian names and being very jolly together in the best youth-hostel way. We were still playing at midnight when the Englishman came back, but he would not join us and went to bed and in the morning was gone before dawn. The others shouldered their rucksacks after lunch and trailed off down the hill to catch the boat back to Hong Kong, and I was once more left alone with the praying monks and the scent of joss sticks and my memory of Suzie behind the wire mesh.

I stayed two weeks on Lantao. I would have stayed longer but I had not brought my paints and now I wanted to try and work again. So I returned on a Friday before the next weekend invasion.

When I got back to the Nam Kok there was a note from Haynes saying that he had been trying to get in touch with me. It was evening so I rang him at his home, and he said, "Well, I've good news for you. At least, it's bad in one way, but I think you'll be glad to hear it. They've put our friend at Laichikok in the prison hospital, where I believe they look after them pretty decently—so she'll be having a much better time of it than she would otherwise."

He had inquired about her when visiting another client at Laichikok. She had been given a routine chest X-ray on entering the prison and been found to have a touch of T.B. She had been in the hospital ever since.

"But it's nothing serious?" I said.

"No, I gather they've caught it early. Well, in one sense it all seems to be turning out for the best, because she'd never have got into a hospital outside. They're all so full up, I believe they're harder to break into than a bank. They say the only way to get into a hospital in Hong Kong is to collapse in the street and get taken in as a casualty."

Tuberculosis was rife in Hong Kong because of the overcrowding and I was not greatly surprised by Haynes's news. I had even wondered at one time if Suzie was infected because of a suspiciously persistent cough, and although she had protested that it was only the lingering effect of the chill that she had caught the night her baby had been killed, I had urged her to go to the government clinic for a free X-ray. Finally we had arranged to go together. But just then the cable had arrived from New York and the intention had been forgotten in the excitement of my departure for Japan. And after my return her cough seemed to have gone.

Now, reassured that it was nothing serious, I was more pleased by the news than otherwise. I preferred to think of Suzie in a hospital ward than in a cell or at work in some grim compound. (For although rationally I had discounted Big Alice's story of beatings-up, I had never rid myself of the ghastly vision it had conjured, in which I saw Suzie being kicked and beaten to the point of mutilation by huge tough black-uniformed wardresses, sisters-in-sadism of the human-skin lampshade-makers of Belsen.) I felt greatly relieved, and thought that probably by the time Suzie left prison she would be altogether cured of her T.B.

However, later that evening I received a nasty shock. For when I passed on the news to Gwenny she showed no surprise, and said, "Yes, I thought they would probably put her in hospital. But I did not like to say anything to you before because Suzie had made me promise."

"Promise? Promise what?"

"Promise not to tell you she had T.B."

"You mean she knew before she went into Laichikok? But how? She didn't have an X-ray?"

"No, she was told by the doctor."

"But what doctor? You mean she'd been to see a doctor?"

"No, the doctor came to see her. She was so ill. It was while you were in Japan—after the business with Betty. We had gone to the cinema together, and when we came out the trams were very crowded, and Suzie said, 'I can't bear to go in a tram. There is no air, and I shall choke.' There were no rickshaws so we walked back and she was very tired. I said, 'Suzie, you need a cool drink,' and we went into the bar, and then she began to cough and I suddenly saw her hands were all red, and her dress down the front, and her lap. It was terrible. She was very weak. Wednesday Lulu and I helped her upstairs. I telephoned to a Chinese doctor and when he came he said, 'You have bad trouble in your lungs. You have got tuberculosis. You should be in hospital. But that is impossible, so you must rest in bed and I shall tell you what medicines to get from the druggists.' Then Suzie told him that you were coming back soon, and that she was frightened you would catch the disease from her, and he said, 'I will also prescribe a medicine to prevent the germs passing out of your mouth into your boy friend's. You must take it in water three times a day.' And after you came back it was often difficult for her to take the medicine without you knowing, so she would tell me, 'Gwenny, you keep him talking on the verandah, while I take my medicine inside.'"

"But why on earth didn't she tell me about it, Gwenny?"

"She was afraid to upset you. You were already upset because she had stabbed Betty with the scissors, so that you could not work properly, and she was afraid that if she upset you any more you would not work at all. She said you were very bad-tempered when you could not work, and did not love her as much as when you worked well. Besides there was nothing you could do."

"I could have tried to get her into some hospital for a start—or at least seen that she got proper treatment instead of taking useless Chinese drugs."

"I don't think they are useless. They cost so much money they must be good. The medicine for making her germs safe cost eleven dollars an ounce and she took one ounce every day."

"Good Lord, how awful!"

"And she was ashamed of being ill. She said that sometimes when you told her she was beautiful she would feel very ashamed and think, 'But inside I am ugly, because I am sick and cough blood.' That is why she would not marry you."

"Gwenny, if only I'd known!"

"Anyhow, I am sure that now she is in hospital she will soon get well."

Two weeks later I paid a second visit to Laichikok and found that

Suzie was indeed looking wonderfully well—better than I had ever seen her look before. The hospital ward was a light airy white-painted room that except for its barred windows and grille instead of a door was a good deal more cheerful than many a public hospital ward outside. Suzie was sitting propped up in bed with a picture magazine. Her hair had that pretty fluffiness and sheen that it always acquired after a shampoo, and she looked pink-cheeked and well-scrubbed, and extremely pleased with herself.

"Suzie, you look marvelous!" I exclaimed, laughing with relief—for until that moment I had been dreading another scene like the last, and fortifying myself against the possibility of more tears. "I wish I was allowed to kiss you."

"Oh, that's all right. I fixed it. I told that woman you were coming." She airily indicated the Chinese wardress as though she was some menial. "I told her you were a big man and would want to kiss me. I told her, 'You just look the other way.'"

I duly embraced her. The wardress looked a bit uncomfortable and pretended that something had caught her attention out of the window.

"Yes, she is very nice, that warder-woman," Suzie said condescendingly.

"And what's the doctor like?"

"Half-caste woman. Very nice."

"It all sounds too good to be true. Is everybody nice?"

"No, one warder-woman is very nasty. Sometimes she works in here. She says, 'I know all about you, Wong Mee-ling. I know you used to go with men. Yes, you were a bad girl—dirty!' And then you know what she does?"

"What?"

"Tries to hold my hand."

"Hold your hand? What for, if she thinks you're dirty?"

She looked very complacent. "She's in love with me."

"Good Lord!" I laughed. "And what do you do about it?"

"I tell her, 'Shoo! Go away! I came in this hospital to get better—and you just make me sick!'"

"Well, there's nothing like putting the wardresses in their places. And what about the Governor? Do you talk to the Governor like that?"

"Oh, yes. Chinese woman governor—very nice."

"Well, I'm sure!"

"She came in here once, so I told her, 'Good morning! You've got a very nice monkey-house!'"

"Suzie, you *are* in a frivolous mood!"

"Yes, I told her, 'I like your monkey-house. I will stay a few days longer if you don't mind?' She said, 'Sure, Wong Mee-ling, you stay as long as you like, and if that warder-woman gives you any trouble just let me know.' I said, 'Thank you, I like your monkey-house very much, and you make a very nice Number One Top Monkey!'" She giggled with childish mischief.

"Suzie, it's marvelous to see you like this again."

"I'm happy today. My boy friend has come. I told that warder-woman, 'He'll come, don't you worry. He won't forget.' But I was scared you might forget. Then I should lose face."

"Well, I've got a bone to pick with you. I'm very angry with you for not telling me you'd been ill while I was in Japan."

"Ill? Who said I was ill?"

"It's no good, Suzie. I know all about it."

She was very reluctant to admit the truth and tried to shrug it all off as unimportant; however, assuming that I knew about it already, she let slip that she had actually had another hemorrhage in prison. It had occurred on her second day, immediately after my visit, and had no doubt been brought on by the emotional ordeal; and it was for this reason that she had been sent into hospital, and not because of the X-ray as Haynes had told me. But now she assured me that she was practically cured, and that by the time she left prison her full health would be restored.

However, later, as I was leaving the hospital building, I met the prison doctor herself. She had just pulled up in a little car and I guessed her identity from her Eurasian features, and the wardress accompanying me confirmed it. I went up to her and said, "May I ask you about Wong Mee-ling?"

"Who are you?" she said. "Do you belong to the prison?" She was in her thirties with handsome clear-cut features and a down-right manner that seemed to say, "Now, tell me what you want with no nonsense. I don't mind if you've committed murder or raped a girl of five, so long as you give it me without any nonsense." She wore a white cotton dress and carried a bottle with a glass stopper filled with yellow liquid. It might have been acid or urine.

"No, I've just been to visit her," I said. "I'm a friend."

"A painter?" She saw me look surprised, and said, "Oh, don't worry, I know more about you than you know about yourself. How that little girl can gossip! Well, she's perfectly all right, she's not going to die or anything. We got her just in time. But how long more's she got here? Six weeks? That's no good at all. She'll need at least another couple of months in hospital after she leaves here, otherwise in a few months she'll be back where she started."

"Could you get her transferred to a civil hospital from here?"

"No." She looked at me with the blunt no-nonsense Chinese-English eyes. "They throw patients out of the civil hospitals when they're no better than that girl in there, to make room for worse cases. No strings you can pull?"

I remembered Kay Fletcher at St. Margaret's; but I had not seen Kay since that night when she had driven me back to the Nam Kok, and I had said, "See you on Thursday," and she had driven off in the rain, and then I had gone upstairs and Suzie had rung to say her baby was dead. And when I had rung her to cancel the meeting on Thursday she had been understandably brusque with me, saying "Well, I'm not surprised," and ringing off. No, I could hardly ask Kay.

I said, "No, I don't know anyone."

"Well, you've plenty of time. If you don't want her lungs to pack up on her again you'd better try and talk some hospital into taking her after she leaves here. Or soon after—a short holiday in between wouldn't do her any harm. That's all I can tell you. Except that she seems to me a very nice girl, and I hope you'll manage something—because I hate to see all our good work wasted." She turned away briskly, but turned back in the hospital entrance and said with a faintly ironical smile, "By the way, I'd tell anybody who's had much to do with her to get a check-up themselves. That Chinese medicine's about as effective against infection as this would be." She shook the bottle in her hand. I still did not know whether it was acid or urine.

"Yes, I'll do that."

And a few days later I went along to the clinic in Wanchai, and stood in the queue of Chinese for a free X-ray. The English doctor looked surprised when he saw me and said, "Hello, what are you doing in these parts?" I told him I lived in Wanchai, and he said grimly that in that case I was very wise to come along. But when I returned the next week for the result he said, "Ah, lucky chap. No spots anywhere—you're passed as sound as a bell."

II

I did not know there were so many hospitals in Hong Kong until I began my search to find Suzie a bed. The biggest T.B. hospital was the Ruttonji, a Parsee foundation, but they could not hold out any hope. They would have no vacancy for months, and even then they could only take in much worse cases than Suzie's. The other hospitals were the same. The sudden vast influx of refugees from China after the revolution had meant not only more people to be ill but a higher rate of illness per head of population, since overcrowding was synonymous with epidemics and a low standard of health. The Hong Kong government had done its best to meet the unexpected situation, and was building new hospitals and convalescent homes as fast as it could. But meanwhile the majority of consumptives received no treatment at all beyond the concoctions of Chinese druggists, but sickened and wasted away in congested rooms, breathed their germs into the fetid air, and died. And those who had been infected by the germs became sick in turn, and breathed more germs to infect others, and died likewise.

And so finally I went to Kay. I had already been once to St. Margaret's to try my luck there on my own, and had drawn the usual blank; but now I went again and sent up a note. I explained briefly why I had come and how ashamed I felt to be asking her help, and I said that if she did not want to see me I would understand; though I had no doubt really that, being Kay, she would come down and be very forgiving and nice. However, ten minutes later, when she appeared, she sailed across the entrance hall with a rather cold impersonal smile, and said in a hard bright voice with an edge, "Robert, you really have a lot of cheek! Ashamed my foot! And obviously you haven't a clue about the hospital situation. There's a queue five miles long for every bed in this place, and even if I could help you, which

I can't, it would mean somebody else losing his turn. But I suppose that never occurred to you?"

I said, "Yes, it did."

"You mean so long as you can get your own friends fixed up you couldn't care less what happens to other people, even if they're dying."

"Yes, I could. But I'm prepared to do it."

She was taken aback for a moment. Then she smiled a bit more warmly and said, "Well, anyhow that's honest. But I'm not."

I said, "Kay, one can't fight for everybody, and I'm going to fight for Suzie. I know it's all wrong, and I ought to let her take her turn and get worse again, and probably die. But I'm not going to, because she means more to me than the people I don't know, and because I want to see her properly cured, and because I'm going to marry her."

Kay looked stunned. "You're not?"

"She hasn't agreed yet. But I think she will when she comes out of gaol."

"I think you're mad."

"I probably am."

"Stark staring mad. Well, I wish you luck."

She held out her hand. I realized that I was being dismissed. However, as she accompanied me across the hall to the entrance I sensed a softening of her mood. We paused rather awkwardly on the top step. Then she said, "Are you really? I mean seriously?"

"Going to marry her? Yes."

"I know it's none of my business, but wouldn't it be better just to live with her? Without tying yourself down?"

"I want to marry her."

"I can't help feeling it's only out of pity—because of what she's been."

"No, I've thought all that out," I said. "It's not pity."

"You wouldn't have married her if she'd just been some shopgirl you'd seduced."

"No, but if she'd been a shopgirl she wouldn't have been Suzie. What she's been is part of her."

"Then why *are* you marrying her?"

"Kay, you wouldn't like to have dinner?"

"Well . . . all right."

We had a Chinese dinner and I tried to explain to her why I wanted to marry Suzie, but I did not convince her and she still shook her head and said, "Well, I may be biased, but I'm sure you're being a fool." I was not surprised because I had not even convinced myself. All the reasons that I had given her had sounded superficial, and I felt sure that I had left out the most important reason of all. Yet I did not know myself what it was. Then after dinner Kay took me along to a party to which she had been invited. It was in somebody's flat on the Peak—a party of gay and pleasant young people most of whom were only recently out from England and not yet imbued with the older residents' stereotyped colonial way of thought. There was a high-fidelity long-playing gramophone with loud-speakers mysteriously hidden about the room, and we danced to the oozing sexy voice of a colored American crooner currently in fashion. A silent impersonal house boy filled our glasses with iced gin drinks. There was intellectual discussion about music, books, and films. It was mostly above my head. Then I was approached by a young man with a beard, a professor of English at the Hong Kong university, who said that he had seen my Malayan paintings and pastels when they had been exhibited in London, and had been sufficiently struck by them to remember my name. He had realized that I had "something to offer." I was very touched and flattered, for he could even remember the work well enough to discuss it in detail and give a sound appreciation of its merits and faults. He went on to discuss critical theories of art and the work of various modern artists; but I knew little of theory and few of the artists' names, and when he asked me about my own work I could say little more than that I had wanted to try and express something, and had done my best to do so. I felt ashamed of my ignorance and incoherence. I was self-consciously aware that each time I opened my mouth I sank lower in his estimation. And the flattery over, I began to grow bored, and to feel a creeping claustrophobia in this beautiful hygienic modern flat, among the high-fidelity loud-speakers and the martinis and the hygienic theories of art. Then the Chinese house boy, who was not a boy at all but an elderly man, came to refill my glass, and while he was doing so I noticed his eyes—small deep withdrawn Chinese eyes that belonged to a world infinitely remote from everything else in this room. And it was as though all at once a window had been thrown open and I had breathed fresh air; for although I had only been afforded the merest glimpse of that remote world, it had been enough to reassure me, "Don't worry, you're not trapped in this room. This is only a tiny unimportant corner of life—and there's the whole universe waiting outside to be explored." And I knew that I had come close to the answer I had been seeking. If I had married Kay or the pretty girl in the cocktail dress who was saying, "Of course it's the theater I miss," I would have been shutting myself in this room and bolting the windows and doors. But marrying Suzie would be like taking a flying leap (suicidal, Kay would say) from the sill.

The party looked all set until the early hours. Kay was ensconced on the sofa with an admiring young man and looked all set for a long time, too. I left and walked home alone, musing about beautiful hygienic conventional rooms and leaping from windows. Then suddenly there came into my head a random memory of Suzie, as I had encountered her one evening in the entrance hall of the Nam Kok on my return from a stroll. She had at that moment been parting from a sailor with whom she had just been upstairs. The sailor was no more than a blurred face in the background, with one hand lifted to tilt his hat, and that expression of false jauntiness with which men leaving brothels are wont to hide their disillusionment after the departure of desire. Suzie was half turned away from him, her face pale and a little tired. She had already forgotten the sailor's existence and had just caught sight of me. Her expression showed fleeting embarrassment, for she wanted me to be in love with her and knew my feelings about her job. She wished that I had come a second or two later after the sailor had gone. But instantly she realized that embarrassment was pointless and only a refusal to face facts; and in a moment the embarrassment had passed and a new expression had taken its place that seemed to say, "There is a whole world behind me, a whole field of experience, that you can never understand. But it is part of me, and I cannot be otherwise, even though it means losing you." And there was hurt in her eyes, and sadness, but there was also pride. And now in memory the expression seemed to me very moving and beautiful, and I knew I must paint it.

And I had no sooner felt this compulsion to start a new painting than I glanced about to see where I was walking, and quickly moved from the center to the side of the road. For at such times I would always go in dread of being knocked over by a car, or of war breaking out, or of some cataclysm occurring; for an unborn painting was like an unborn child and made me responsible for another life besides my own. I began to hurry. I did not usually paint at night because in artificial light the colors changed their values, but the impulse was so strong that I determined to try, and the moment I got back to my room I placed a new canvas on the easel and started.

I painted all through that night. My mind was clear and the memory so vivid that I could have done no better even with Suzie there as a model. I did not feel any need for sleep. And when the dawn came and I saw the colors I was very pleased, because although the tones were not what I had intended, they were oddly effective and heightened the feeling.

I finished at ten o'clock in the morning. I had painted the scene exactly as I remembered it, with the matelot behind Suzie with his hand tilting his hat, and Suzie half turned away from him with the hurt and the sadness and the pride in her eyes. And Ah Tong, bringing tea for the fourth time, stood gazing at it for a long while and I could see he was moved. And then the telephone rang, and it was Kay.

She said, "Well, I've done my best for you, though I can't think why. I've just spent nearly an hour soft-soaping the Registrar, and he's promised a bed in about six weeks."

"Kay, bless you."

"That was the earliest he could manage without seriously upsetting anybody. She'll be able to hang on until then, won't she?"

"Yes, it's perfect. The prison doctor said a holiday would do her good. I think I'll take her to Macao."

"I always wanted to go to Macao."

"You can come with us if you like."

"That *would* be fun for you!"

Ah Tong was still studying the picture when I rang off. He said, "It is very beautiful, sir. She looks so unhappy." And then he said, "She is looking at me, sir. It is very curious. She was looking at me when I stood over there. Then I came over here and she is still looking. Her eyes are speaking to me."

"What are they saying?"

"They are saying, 'My heart is full of so many things. But I do not know how to explain.' Is that what you meant, sir?"

"It's just about what I meant, Ah Tong," I said.

III

There were three weeks left before Suzie came out of Laichikok. The time went slowly and Ah Tong would come in and say, "Only ten days left, sir," and, "Only nine today, sir." He had consulted his Chinese Almanac and noted with satisfaction that the day of Suzie's release, the Fourteenth of the Tenth Moon, was particularly recommended for household removals and the changing of abode, and had solemnly announced, "It is an ideal day for leaving prison."

"I should think that any day's ideal for that, Ah Tong," I said.

"No, sir. If it had been the Thirteenth of the Tenth she might have been very unhappy after she came out. But now she will be happy. It is ideal."

And then, despite all my impatience, when the day of Suzie's release arrived I was not at the prison gate to meet her. I had told her to expect me and had set off from the Nam Kok with plenty of time to spare; but then, by an unhappy stroke of fate, the ferryboat on which I was crossing to Kowloon came into collision with a rusting and dirty old tug, whose opium-dazed pilot had ignored the ferryboat's hooter. There was little damage to either boat but we remained stranded in mid-harbor for nearly an hour while the skippers held their protracted post-mortem. I became so frantic that I could have wept. I even thought of diving over the side and trying to swim for it. But that would have meant abandoning the luggage that I had brought with me so that we could go straight off to Macao. At last the boat began to throb again. It moved. We bumped against the Kowloon pier, the gangplank came down, and I pushed and shoved my way ashore with the two suitcases and the big awkward parcel of canvases. There was no taxi in sight. I staggered up the street with my load. A taxi came and I said, "Laichikok prison," and collapsed in the back. When we reached Laichikok there was no sign of Suzie and they said at the gate that she had waited half an hour and then gone. Then the taxi driver suggested looking at the bus stop, and we drove round the corner and there she was, standing alone and forlorn in the blue silk cheongsam that she had worn in the magistrate's court, and the white high-heel shoes, and the familiar white handbag dangling from her hand.

"Suzie, I'm so dreadfully sorry," I said, and explained what had happened.

"It doesn't matter," she said flatly as if she really did not care; and I knew that after looking forward to coming out of prison for so long the actual event had seemed an anticlimax.

I said, "Suzie, we're going to Macao."

"Macao? What for?"

"I've arranged for you to go into hospital, but I thought you'd like a little holiday first. Away from everybody you know."

"All right."

"You don't sound very enthusiastic."

"I don't care. We will go if you want."

The *Fatshan* was alongside when we arrived at the pier. There was still an hour before it sailed. We sat at a table in the empty dining saloon and Suzie drank a Coca-Cola while I had coffee. Some more passengers came in and took the next table, and Suzie glanced at them but avoided their eyes. She looked sheepish and uncomfortable.

"Don't worry, Suzie," I said. "It doesn't show. Nobody knows where you've been."

She did not say anything. She was silent for several minutes, and then said, "All right, I go now."

"Go? What do you mean?"

"I don't want to go to Macao. You go alone."

"I don't understand, Suzie. What's the matter?"

"I have been thinking in that monkey-house—I had plenty of time to think. You're a big man. You could get any girl you want. You could get some beautiful English girl with plenty of money, or some good-family Chinese girl. Only you have got a good heart, you feel sorry for me. You think, 'I don't want to hurt Suzie—I must be nice to her.' Only that's no good. So I go now. I leave you."

"Suzie, what utter rubbish!"

It was all I could do to keep her from going, and I was thankful when

I heard the gangplank being removed and she could no longer leave the boat. Then, as Hong Kong receded into the distance she began to cheer up and enjoy herself and take an interest in the trip. I told her to go and change out of her silk cheongsam, and she disappeared with the stewardess and came back in her jeans and sandals and with a twinkle in her eye, giggling, "You know what that woman said to me? She said, 'You have such beautiful clothes—you must be so rich!'" And she ran from one rail to the other watching the bare tawny little islands going by, and the great fleets of fishing junks scattered over the horizon like multitudes of toy boats.

"You know, this morning I didn't want to leave that monkey-house," she said. "I thought, 'I have no worries in here. Maybe when I get outside I will just steal something, or stick that Canton girl with scissors again, so they will send me back.' But I feel good now! I feel beautiful!"

She watched happily as we passed close to a great proud junk with eight sails all taut and bulging in the hot damp sticky wind. It carried the red flag of Communist China. A few minutes later the sea abruptly changed from cobalt to the color of milky tea with mud from the Pearl River.

"How long more to Macao?" Suzie said.

"I should think about another hour," I said. "And by the way, I forgot to tell you. We're going to get married in Macao."

"Get married? Who said?"

"It's as good a place as any to get married in. You will marry me, won't you?"

"No."

"Then I'll just have to marry you by force. It's very easy in Macao—it's such a wicked place. I shall bribe the necessary official and have him concealed under the table, and then ask you if you will have some more fried duck's liver; and you will say 'Yes,' and the official will bob up and say, 'Thank you, there is your marriage certificate! Good evening.'"

She giggled. "And next day I will ask you, 'You want some more fried rice, my husband?' And you will say 'Yes,' and this man will poke out his head and say, 'Thank you, you are now divorced.'"

Then she was silent, looking over the rail at the sea. After a while she said, "I dreamed once we were married. I was in a street, and there were crowds of people, and I saw you, only I couldn't get to you because of the crowd. I began to cry. Then you pushed everybody away, and said, 'Go away, you silly people. This is Suzie, my wife.' And they all went away just because you had told them. Then I woke up."

"And found you weren't my wife after all. Were you glad or sorry?"

She did not answer. She was silent for a bit and then she said, "I can't marry you because I am sick. And the medicine I took to stop you getting sick was no good. The doctor at Laichikok told me."

"I still didn't get sick," I said. "Anyhow, you're going to St. Margaret's in two weeks, and then you'll be properly cured."

"I don't think so. I don't think people ever get properly cured."

"Of course they do, Suzie. You're nearly cured now, and with another month or two in hospital you'll be fine."

She was silent again. Then she turned and strolled away up the deck and stood by herself at the rail. After a while she came back.

She said, "Robert, I never knew anybody so good as you. I never knew anybody with such a beautiful heart. I like you very much."

"Bless you, Suzie. Does that mean yes?"

"Yes, if you want. I will do anything you want. I will get married if you want, or jump in the sea, or anything."

"The sea's too muddy to jump in here. I'd much rather we got married."

At Macao we took a trishaw to a hotel. It was bigger than a rickshaw with a seat for two and room for the baggage under our legs. The trishaw driver wore torn khaki shorts and the rim of a straw hat without any crown. It looked like a tattered old halo. The town was very sleepy after Hong Kong and had an air of decadence and decay. We passed a Catholic church that had started as Spanish baroque, but had blended with its surroundings like the face of an old China-hand and begun to look Chinese. We dumped our baggage at the hotel and told the trishaw driver to take us to the office of the British Consul. He grinned and nodded and said he understood. Five minutes later he came to a standstill outside a building guarded by Portuguese East African troops with rifles and bayonets and faces the color of coffee beans.

"Good?" he said.

"No good," I said. "That's the Portuguese government. We want the British Consul."

"All right, I know!"

He pedaled off happily. We eventually found the Consul in an old office with creaking ceiling fans that looked in danger of breaking free and lopping off somebody's head. A beautiful half-caste typist was seated at her machine. She had a pale shy delicate face and masses of loose black hair, and wore a gold crucifix round her neck. The Consul was a fat bald man with perspiring forehead and crescents of perspiration under the arms of his white shirt. He was writing a private letter when we arrived. He listened to our request with irritation, his pen still poised over the letter.

"Now I'll tell you your best plan," he said. "You want to pop over to Hong Kong and get married there."

"But we've just come from Hong Kong," I said. "We wanted to get married in Macao. I thought you were licensed to do it."

"Well, I'm going to be frank with you. This is the first time anybody's ever asked me to marry them, and I don't know the form. So I'm afraid there's nothing more to be said."

"Couldn't we find out the form?" I said. "I mean, surely there are regulations about it?"

"I haven't the time," he snapped. "I'm a busy man." He remembered the letter under his hand. I could read the opening upside down: *My dear old Hughie.* He began to slide the blotter over it, then changed his mind and leaned back in his chair, leaving the letter exposed on the desk as though to say, "There, I'm lying to you and I don't mind your knowing, so that shows you how little I think of you."

I was trying to think of some vitriolic retort when I sensed Suzie's discomfort: she had been nervous enough anyhow about entering the Consul's office, and a scene would only upset her. So I climbed down and tried blandishments instead, telling the Consul that we had only dared to trespass on his valuable time because on the boat we had been told of his great good nature and of his reputation for helping souls in distress—a rather free interpretation of "Not a bad fellow, but bone-headed and bone-idle." The recipe worked wonders, and in a few minutes the thin pale beautiful typist was ransacking shelves and loading his desk with heavy consular tomes, while the Consul was turning pages at random and periodically exclaiming, "Well, I'm blowed! I never knew I could do that!" Finally the idea of marrying us began to tickle him, and he was as disappointed as ourselves when he found that the regulations required us to give notice and he could not marry us for three weeks. And he asked anxiously, "You'll still be here then, I hope? You won't have left?"

"No, I think we'll still be here," I said.

"Good," he said. "Good. That makes it—let me see?—Miss Ruggeroni, you've got my diary? Ah, here! Yes, then that makes it a Wednesday. The morning suit you? Eleven-thirty?" And I fancied that we had furnished him with something really good to tell dear old Hughie, and that as soon as we had gone he would write, "Well, I certainly can't complain there's no variety in my job—now I'm a ruddy parson!"

He conducted us to the door, shook our hands damply, and exhorted us with a humorous wink to see that we behaved ourselves until he had joined us in wedlock. And then we were outside again in the hot sticky street.

Chapter Six

Suzie was very happy for the next few days. She looked radiant. Her favorite game was pretending to be the future Mrs. Lomax, behaving very grandly and snottily and putting people in their places.

"How do you do? I am Mrs. Lord Lomax—my husband is a famous Lord, you know. What, you being rude to me? All right, I will just tell my husband. He will see you get ten years in the monkey-house." She giggled and then suddenly looked anxious, afraid that a telegram would come from Kay before we were married—for as soon as the vacancy occurred at the hospital we should have to return. "Robert, you think that telegram will come today?"

"No, I don't think today."

"No?" She promptly brightened, and returned to her game. "Good afternoon, Mr. Lord Piccadilly. No, I'm sorry, my husband is having tea with the Queen at Westminster Abbey."

"You don't have tea at Westminster Abbey, Suzie."

"So sorry, Mr. Lord Piccadilly—I mean at her house."

Macao was on the tip of a peninsula, and in ten minutes you could walk from the Praya on one side to the beach on the other, and in twenty minutes from the center of the town to the frontier across the peninsula neck, where you could see the Red China flag flying down the road—though of course in that heat you never did walk, but took trishaws everywhere. Macao had flourished for centuries as the gateway to China, but now the gateway was closed and there was no trade any longer, no industry, no business—nothing to keep the town alive except opium and gambling and girls. And at the hotel where we were staying you could get all three—the gambling on either of the two floors devoted to casinos, and the opium and girls in your room by pressing the bell and asking the floor boy. And for that matter the floor boy would also provide a go-between with the casino, so that if you believed in doing things thoroughly you could gamble and smoke opium and have a girl at the same time.

Our floor boy was called Ah Ng and had a walleye. The other eye burnt day and night with an eagerness to do business, and whenever he caught me alone he would sidle against me, fixing me with the good eye while the walleye gazed up innocently at the ceiling, and whisper furtively that he could fix me up with a Portuguese girl of sixteen, who would be far more worthy of my attentions than Suzie. His disparaging tone when speaking of Suzie suggested that even a coolie would think twice before demeaning himself in her embrace. But an hour later, catching Suzie alone, he would whisper to her that she had exceptional qualities which clearly I had failed to perceive, and that she could be making her fortune. And he would offer to introduce her to a Portuguese officer down the corridor for only 30 per cent commission.

During the second week Suzie's high spirits began to desert her and she became depressed. Once I entered her room to find her crying, and the same evening she burst into tears at dinner; but when I asked her what was the matter she only shook her head. Still, I knew without her telling me: the strain of waiting to be married was proving too much for her, and she had begun to think that it was a mistake and to feel shame about her past. Now she would never speak of her past, or even mention the Nam Kok; and when I did so purposely, to try and reassure her that I did not mind, she flushed and pretended she had not heard. And now, instead of dreading the arrival of the telegram, she hoped it would come, for it would be a clear indication that our marriage was not intended by fate, and would conveniently relieve her of decision.

The third week her depression became worse, and she brooded or cried all the time. Her unhappiness made her a stranger to me, so that I began to have doubts about the marriage myself. Then on the day before we were due to be married she finally broke down and said she could not go through with it—she wanted only to go back to Hong Kong, to her girl friends, to the familiar way of life. Because that was all she was fit for. That was all she was: a water-front girl, a sailor's whore, and an ex-gaolbird to boot. Why pretend to be anything else? No, she was going back to the Nam Kok, she had made up her mind.

I said, "If that's what you want, Suzie, I won't try and stop you. But I don't think it is. I think it's just that going back is safe and easy, while going on is difficult because it's unknown, and it scares you."

And I reminded her of an incident that morning, when we had been strolling along the Praya and had run into a nice innocuous young English couple on honeymoon from Hong Kong, whom I had met before in the casino. We had exchanged greetings and then I had turned to introduce Suzie, only to find that she had moved away and was standing along the quay with her back turned. I had gone to her, but she had stubbornly refused to come back and be introduced; and then she had begun to cry, saying that she thought the couple was hateful and she did not know how I could befriend them. But I knew of course that the real cause of her distress was the fear of their contempt—and now I did my best to convince her that such a fear had been quite unfounded.

"Actually they'd told me in the casino that they thought you looked charming," I said. "They weren't contemptuous a bit. But when you're afraid of people's contempt you see your fears reflected everywhere. Every new face is a mirror. But even if they had been contemptuous you shouldn't have turned away. People take you at your own estimate of yourself, and if you're ashamed of yourself they'll point and say 'Yah!' because they're all ashamed of themselves too in different ways, and it makes them feel better to run down somebody else. But if you face up to them, and look them in the eyes, and think 'I may have been a water-front tart, but I'm not ashamed of it—I feel as good as you,' they'll start to respect you. And you know who taught me that? You. You could always look people in the eyes. You always had courage. And you've still got it. Only just lately all your little anxieties have been undermining it, gnawing away at it from underneath like busy mice."

She was silent. She had stopped crying. She asked me to leave her alone for a while, so I went up to the casino on the top floor. An hour later she came in, walking with that careful poise that showed how much tension there was inside her, and how hard she was fighting against her fears and doubts. She looked me straight in the eyes.

"You still want to marry me?" she said.

"Of course, Suzie."

"You're sure? Even after the way I have behaved?"

"Absolutely sure." And now it was true again, because her courage had come back.

"All right, I will marry you."

"Bless you, Suzie. And now let's go and buy you a new dress—you must have a new dress to be married in."

She was very quiet for the rest of the evening. The next morning she wanted to dress alone and I went out for some coffee, and at eleven returned to the hotel to wait for her in the hall. Twenty minutes later she came out of the lift. The new plain primrose-yellow cheongsam was molded smoothly over her figure, and the discreetly split skirt gave a glimpse of nylon.

"I am sorry I kept you waiting," she said.

"Suzie, you look marvelous. I'm so proud of you. I wish we were important and there were crowds of people and newsreel cameras."

"I don't. I don't want anybody."

"I want the whole world to see you. I want everybody to see how beautiful you are, and all the men to want you and to know they can't have you because you're mine."

I had bought her a corsage of three very small delicate orchids, whose subtle smoky blue went beautifully with the primrose dress. I pinned it on for her, then we went outside to the street and took a rickshaw. I could smell Suzie's perfume mixed with the faint clean familiar smell of her hair. I felt the nervous tremor of her hand in mine. She could no longer speak for nerves; and as we entered the Consul's office she withdrew into her protective shell in order to keep her composure, looking aloof and remote as if the occasion left her quite cold, and I thought: now she is really inscrutable. If I saw her for the first time now, I would have no inkling of what she felt.

The Consul was delighted to see us, for he had clearly been afraid that we might not turn up and that he would be denied the novelty of uniting us; but since the Governor of Hong Kong was arriving this afternoon on an official visit, and he was involved in the preparations, he was genuinely pushed for time.

"Right, all set?" he said and stood up behind his desk as if it would have been disrespectful to marry us sitting down, his forehead shiny with sweat and fresh sweat-patches under the arms of his clean white shirt. And we stood facing him, under the dangerous creaking fan, while just behind us stood the two witnesses—Miss Ruggeroni, with her masses of black hair and gold crucifix and white thin beautiful Eurasian face, and Ted Rose, a brokendown English scrounger in tattered khaki shirt and shorts, who had been pestering us daily with hard-luck stories in the streets and whom I had promised twenty dollars for fulfilling this task.

The Consul pronounced the formula of marriage with uneasy solemnity, as if he was afraid he looked silly and was wondering if he might have done better to treat the whole affair as a lark. We murmured our answers, and then I placed a plain gold ring on Suzie's finger. This took her by surprise, for when she had tentatively mentioned the matter of a ring I had said that after living together for so long without one I hardly saw its necessity; and now when she realized what I was doing she could no longer hold back her tears. Then we were required to sign our names, and she wiped her eyes with a knuckle and wrote Wong Mee-ling in Chinese characters, and then Suzie Wong in Roman script.

"I say, the bride must be in a state!" the Consul chuckled, now feeling that he could relax safely into jocularity. "She's written the Z back-to-front!"

"It's her trade-mark," I said. "I'll divorce her if she ever writes it differently."

"Now, I'm afraid I'll have to push you out soon," the Consul said. "But first I'd just like to wish you luck."

He opened a drawer and took out a bottle of Portuguese red wine, and I felt very touched by this kind gesture. He drew the cork while Miss Ruggeroni fetched tumblers, and then poured out the wine and raised his glass for a formal toast, and then added informally, "No, but seriously, I hope you'll be really happy and hit it off, because you're a damn nice couple. And I'm not just saying that. I mean it. Damn nice, both of you." He was growing very emotional about how nice we were. "And I really do mean it. I told Miss Ruggeroni after you first came to see me, I said—well, Miss Ruggeroni will tell you herself. What did I say, Miss Ruggeroni?"

"You said they were very nice," Miss Ruggeroni said in the dreamy yearning voice of a Eurasian who belongs nowhere.

"There you are," the Consul said. "I said you were damn nice the very first time I saw you. Well, here's the best to you again."

Suzie kept stealing glances at her ring. Miss Ruggeroni yearned dreamily. Ted Rose, behind whose ear was the telltale brown callosity caused by the opium smoker's wooden pillow, slyly watched the Consul. He saw his opportunity and sidled up and launched rapidly into one of his self-pitying appeals, almost incoherent in his haste to reach the point before the Consul could stop him.

"Damned interesting, old man," the Consul interrupted coldly. "But you ought to know you're wasting your breath on me. Now, come on, the newlyweds—the other half."

He drained the bottle into our glasses. I finished my glass and Suzie surreptitiously exchanged it for hers because she did not care much for wine. Then the Consul said he must turn us out and warmly wrung our hands at the door, saying with a jocular wink, "By Jove, I hope I got that business right. Damned embarrassing if I made some damn-fool slip-up, and you weren't really married!" He saw Rose hanging back in the office in the hope of catching him after we had gone, and pointedly stood aside for him to leave. Miss Ruggeroni with sudden impetuosity dashed back to her desk, snatched a gold-plated powder compact from her bag, and returned to press it on Suzie, saying, "Oh, it's nothing. It's not new or anything. It's just a silly little present—you can throw it away if it's no use." And then we were outside again, and Rose was muttering resentfully that the Consul had insulted him, and that if we knew all that he knew about the Consul we would understand why despite his consulship he was not fit to lick his, Rose's, boots. I handed him twenty-five dollars, five more than agreed, but he was too preoccupied with his grievance to notice the bonus.

"Thanks for your help," I said, and climbed into the waiting trishaw beside Suzie. The trishaw driver stood up to put his weight on the pedals and give the vehicle momentum and we moved off, and I looked back and saw Rose still muttering on the pavement as if he had not noticed we had gone.

I had ordered lunch at a restaurant in the Beco da Felicidade, which was narrow and cobbled and smelled of incense and was as enchanting as its name, and for a street called the Street of Happiness that was saying a good deal. The restaurant specialized in roast pigeon and you could get good cheap Portuguese wine. We climbed the narrow staircase to the first floor, which was partitioned like most Chinese restaurants into a warren of private rooms, and were given a room hung with a patchwork of decorated mirrors which the Chinese thought lucky. A waiter brought a plate of hot towels smelling of disinfectant. He handed us each a towel with a pair of tongs and we wiped our hands and faces. He poured out cups of pale tea and then collected our towels on a plate and went out, and we sat picking at the saucer of red melon seeds while we waited for lunch. In the mirrors I could see Suzie reflected from all angles, her hand laid casually on the table to facilitate glances at her ring.

"Look at all my new wives," I said. "Not a bad morning's work."

"You gave them all rings—all those wives?" Suzie said.

"Oh, yes, I treat all my wives equally."

"They must have cost a lot of money, so many rings."

"I bought them in a shop with mirrors to make the money go further."

"You know something, Robert? I can't believe we're really married."

"I know, isn't it funny? One expects to feel quite different, but one's just the same."

"Are you really my husband now?"

"Yes, I've got a certificate. I can prove it."

"Maybe if you tell me I will believe it. Say, 'Suzie, I'm your husband.'"

"Suzie, I'm your husband, and you're my very dear and beautiful wife. And I love you in that dress. It gives me indecent ideas. Though I suppose you can't call them indecent any more now we're married."

"Perhaps now we are married you won't want me for going to bed. Just for sewing and cooking—while you go to bed with other girls."

"I think you'll last me for a bit between the lot of you."

"Which one do you want for this afternoon? That one in the big round mirror?"

"No, she looks a bit insubstantial. I think this afternoon I'll start with the one at the table."

That evening there was a telegram from Kay. I had wired her three days earlier for news, and now she replied that she expected a vacancy in about a week, but that anyhow we were not to worry because she hadn't forgotten us. We were both delighted to have another week's reprieve, since Suzie was keeping well and there seemed no urgency about getting her back into hospital. Nevertheless I made her take it easy and rest in the afternoons, and we usually went early to bed. I had brought a good selection of books to Macao, which we had not yet read because she had been too upset for reading before we were married. But now I read to her a great deal, and we would have lengthy discussions afterwards about what I had read, in particular about problems of right and wrong. She was fascinated by ethics, especially in so far as they concerned herself, for she wanted to work out by what standards her own life had been wrong; and with her exact, logical mind she could often pick flaws in my own arguments which I had thought unassailable. And we would keep coming back to the question of her attack on Betty Lau, about which she had left prison unrepentant; and though eventually her logic induced her to admit that she had been in the wrong, she promptly followed the admission with a mischievous twinkle and said, "But I still wish I'd stuck her harder with those scissors—because she deserved it!"

"You're hopeless, Suzie."

"And anyhow, she slept with you. I feel jealous of every girl who ever slept with you."

"It's a good thing I don't feel the same about your boy friends."

"There, you still don't understand about love! Because that was quite different with my boy friends. That was just for money." And once launched on that topic, we were all set for a couple of hours.

I also worked a good deal, and I painted well after we were married. Our room was cramped and poorly lit and I missed my balcony at the Nam Kok, but in my happy frame of mind the material conditions seemed of little account. And indeed it was in that poky little Macao bedroom that I painted my favorite picture of Suzie, which I still think is the best piece of work I have ever done. I began it in the heat of the afternoon, three days after we were married, as she lay on the tumbled bed. She herself looked gloriously tumbled, with her limbs sprawled at absurd angles as if she had been dropped there from a height; and she had no intention of moving, for she was quite obviously deriving profound satisfaction from her own complete wreckage. She radiated a glow of fulfillment that was as womanly as a breast swollen with milk. It was thus that I had intended to paint her; but as I studied her from across the room her expression changed. For no doubt I had been looking too pleased with myself, too smugly satisfied with the scene of destruction and my role of conquering male—and now there came into Suzie's eyes a twinkling half-mocking defiance, which might have been expressed in these words: "All right, you may have conquered me—but only because I wanted to be conquered, and in a minute, when I've savored my destruction a bit longer, I shall become independent again." And so that was how I tried to paint her, showing the reassertion of individuality that must always follow total surrender in love.

We also spent a good deal of time gambling. Sometimes we patronized the hotel casino on the top floor—a big ornate shabby room which in Macao's heyday had been the scene of extravagant splendor—but more often we went to the dim smoky Chinese gaming-house in the Beco da Felicidade, which had the atmosphere of an opium den. It was always packed to the doors, with barefoot coolies and trishaw drivers, and opium smugglers in clogs and battered felt hats, and rich taipans in long gowns, and the stakes varied from twenty cents to thousands of dollars.

We would climb a dark creaking staircase to the first floor where balconies looked down onto the tables below, and lower our stakes in little baskets on strings. Then we would hang over the rail to watch the croupier's pointed stick scooping away the white plastic buttons four at a time from a pile. The winning number, for there were only four possibilities, was the number of buttons that remained for the last scoop. But long before then a great sigh would have passed through the crowd, whose quick eyes had counted the buttons ahead of the croupier's baton.

I was an impetuous gambler and always lost, but Suzie was cautious and played to a system and won on balance every time. But the nervous strain and stale smoky atmosphere were bad for her, and she would leave the tables exhausted; and so after a time I put my foot down and stopped her going to the gaming-house, and we confined our gambling to short spells at the hotel casino.

We often met English people from Hong Kong in the casino, but it still made Suzie nervous to talk to them. And I told her that she must tell herself, "I've nothing to feel ashamed about. I feel proud. I'm as good as you."

"But I do feel ashamed," she said. "It's no good saying I am not ashamed if I feel it."

"Then just imagine what it would feel like if you weren't ashamed. Think, 'I may or may not be ashamed of myself, but this is how someone would feel if they weren't ashamed—if they were proud.'"

And soon she was going about really looking proud; and although at first after we were married she had stopped calling me "my husband," as if it would have been somehow presumptuous, she now began to say it boldly, and to look at strangers with calm level eyes.

"My husband is a painter," I once heard her telling a curious Englishwoman who had been questioning her in a loud patronizing Kensington voice.

"But how fascinating!" the woman exclaimed falsely. "What does he paint?"

"He is painting me just now," Suzie said.

"Not with all those clothes on, I bet," winked the woman's husband. "Oho, I know these artists—I bet he's painting you in the nude, eh?"

"Yes."

And she said this "Yes" so simply and with such dignity, and with her eyes so clear and unashamed as she met the husband's gaze, that, insensitive though he was, he was made to feel a fool. And I felt such pride in her at that moment that I could have cried.

And now that we were married I felt more tender toward her than ever before, and also more possessive. Indeed my possessiveness threatened to become absurd: if she went out to buy me cigarettes and was not back in ten minutes I would grow anxious, and start imagining all the disasters that might have befallen her; and when she eventually returned I would either let fly at her for being away so long, or else burst into joyful relief as if she had returned from the dead. I hated her out of my sight. I was all the more astonished at myself because before the marriage I had half feared that I would regret the tie and think myself a fool; whereas in fact the very opposite had occurred. I had even begun to experience quite unwarranted pangs of jealousy. Previously the floor boy's efforts to conscript Suzie's services had only amused me; but now when I heard that he had spoken to her again I lost my temper, and the next time he came to the room I let him know it, and drove him out with my boot at his backside. And then in the casino I took exception to a man who kept staring at Suzie and undressing her with his eyes, and who in fact was to prove the ruin of our last night in Macao. I had seen him often at the tables, gambling with great wads of hundred-dollar notes and showing ostentatious indifference to both wins and losses. He was a Eurasian, with high cheekbones and narrow black eyes, though in Europe he might quite easily have passed as pure Portuguese. He wore an electric blue jacket with padded shoulders and long American lapels, and a gaudy Waikiki tie. He looked a real slicker. And whenever we were at his table he would fix Suzie with that stare, interrupting it only to place bets or rake in winnings, and indifferent to my presence at her side.

"I can't stand your friend," I told Suzie once as we were leaving the casino. She looked blank and I explained, "That slicker in the blue jacket who can't take his eyes off you."

"Off me? I never noticed."

She obviously hadn't. She was too taken up with the gambling. But the following night, when she was having a run of bad luck, she pointed him out to me across the table, saying that for the last hour he had done nothing but win.

"That's the man I was talking about," I said.

"I never noticed him stare."

"Well, he's staring now."

She glanced across the table without interest. She was interested only in the placing of his stakes. Presently he tossed two five-hundred-dollar notes onto the table, folded into little squares, and with studied carelessness motioned to the blue-smocked woman croupier to put them neatly in place; then he resumed his scrutiny of Suzie, with those narrow black contemptuous eyes that seemed to say, "You'll be easy enough like all the rest." And he went on staring until the pile of white buttons had been reduced to two. He had won again. The croupier added six five-hundred-dollar notes to his stake on the table, and pushed the eight notes across to him with the stick.

"Look!" Suzie gasped. "Look at all that money!" She watched him rake in the money indifferently, his hand protruding from three inches of silk cuff. She caught his eye and smiled across the table. "Next time I shall follow you!"

The man acknowledged her remark with a careless wave of the hand as if her attention meant nothing to him. He did not speak. But his eyes were saying, "She'll be even easier than I thought."

"Suzie, I'm dying for a drink," I said. "Let's go."

"No, I must win back my money. I can't go until I have won it back."

"We'll try again later."

"No, I must follow that man—he's so lucky!"

"Well, I'm going. Aren't you coming?"

"No, I must win back my money first."

I did not really want to leave her but now felt perversely committed, and so I went off through the curtained archway to the big gloomy bar. It was empty except for the barman. I sat down on a bar stool and ordered a double brandy, and when I had drunk it I felt better and thought, "I'm being a fool. As if she'd have any truck with a slicker in a Waikiki tie! I must go back and be nice to her." I paid for the brandy and went back into the casino—but then abruptly stopped. For the slicker had moved round the table and was now seated beside Suzie. They looked very happy together, and Suzie's face was radiant. I turned and went back to the bar.

I had drunk two more double brandies before Suzie appeared. She came in looking flushed and excited.

"I won everything back, and then five hundred dollars! Look! Look at all this money!"

I said, "I'm thrilled."

She stopped being excited and looked at me.

"What's the matter?" she said. "Are you angry?"

"Angry? Why should I be angry?"

"I think you're angry because I stayed to win back my money."

"I'm glad to know that's what you stayed for."

"What do you mean?" she said.

"Nothing. I don't mean anything. I'm just hungry. Come on, let's go and eat."

We left and went to the lift, cut off from each other by my ridiculous mood. But although I knew it was ridiculous I could not change it, and I could not speak without nastiness coming into my tone, so I remained silent. Then as we came out of the lift and crossed the hall the clerk at the reception desk said "Oh, sir!" and held up a telegram, and I knew it must be from Kay, and I went over and tore it open, and it said that there would be a vacancy for Suzie at St. Margaret's tomorrow.

I told Suzie and said, "That means we've got to take the morning boat."

Suzie looked distressed. She did not know how long she would be in hospital and how long we would be parted. She said, "Couldn't we stay one more day?"

"No, they won't hold the bed for you."

"Then it's our last night."

"Yes, our last night in Macao."

And then we were holding hands in the back of a trishaw on the way to the pigeon restaurant in the Beco da Felicidade, and all the jealousy and nastiness inside me was gone, and I was loving her again and trying not to think of being parted; and at dinner I drank a whole bottle of Portuguese wine, which made me rather drunk after the brandies, but not too drunk, and we were both very happy. Then Suzie wanted to pay a last visit to the Chinese gaming-house, and since it was only just across the street from the restaurant, and I wanted to indulge her on her last night, I agreed provided that we only stayed half an hour. However, I forgot the time until I looked at my watch and saw that we had been there an hour, and by then Suzie had lost four hundred dollars and wanted to recoup, and in the end we stayed over two hours and it was after midnight when we left.

There was no trishaw outside so we had to walk back to the hotel. On the way the heel came off Suzie's shoe and she limped along holding my arm. She held my arm across the hotel foyer and into the lift. As we stepped out of the lift on the fourth floor Ah Ng, the floor boy, was standing in the alcove opposite the lift gate. He was talking to somebody seated in an armchair. He broke off and watched us in silence with the smoldering eye. The chair was in shadow and the occupant's face was only a vague white blob, but his arm hung over the chair arm and caught the light from the landing, and I recognized the electric blue sleeve and the white expanse of silk cuff, and the ostentatious cuff link with the big blue vulgar stone. Then as we turned down the landing and passed closer I saw the Waikiki tie with the palm trees and the pink bathing girls in bikinis, and the face with the high Chinese cheekbones and the contemptuous watching eyes. I felt the eyes watching us as we walked on, the eyes of the Eurasian and the smoldering eye of Ah Ng, and I was certain they had been waiting for us to come.

Suzie had also noticed the man in the chair and I had felt her stiffen on my arm, but they had exchanged no sign of recognition, and I thought this strange after they had sat together at the table, and won money together, and looked as intimate as lovers.

I said, "That was your friend."

"What friend?"

"Your friend from the casino."

"Oh, I never noticed," she said vaguely. I only just saw him in the casino across the table."

"I thought he'd sat with you."

"No."

But she had no sooner made the denial than she realized that I must have seen them, and I felt the tension in her arm again, and I knew without looking that the blood had rushed to her cheeks. I opened the door of our room and she detached herself from me with relief, and kept her face turned away in case it should further betray her. She undressed quickly and got into bed, and lay with her back turned and her eyes closed as if utterly exhausted.

"We played fan-tan too long," she said. "We stayed too long in that smoke."

"Yes, it was silly." I glanced at her as I undressed, trying to make out if her exhaustion was genuine or if she was only pretending. There was a knock on the door and Ah Ng entered with a flask, saying with a false seedy grin, "I brought some hot tea, sir." It was the first time he had ever done this without being asked.

"Put it on the dressing table," I said.

"Yes, sir." But he ignored the instruction and went quickly across the room to put it on the pedestal table by the bed, at the same time fixing Suzie with the greedy burning eye and breaking into rapid Cantonese. The walleye gazed upwards with mocking innocence like a gray blob of jelly. I knew the numerals in Cantonese, and I heard him say a number and then repeat it. It was a three-figure number like the number of a room.

I said angrily, "Get out."

"Sir, I only just—"

"Get out!"

He went out grinning. Suzie closed her eyes again with a long weary sigh. I said, "What did he want?"

"I don't know—nothing."

"Now tell me the truth."

"He just talked about the heat. He said Macao was so hot."

"And particularly hot in Room No. 343?"

She opened her eyes and stared at me miserably. "Why do you hate me today?"

"I don't hate you."

"Yes, you hate me. I knew this evening when I came into the bar, and you looked at me, and I thought, 'My husband hates me.'"

"I hate you to tell me lies, that's all."

And then she began to cry, and she admitted that the Eurasian had joined her at the table, and had paid her compliments and tried to arrange a meeting; and she had meant to tell me all about it, but had been too frightened to do so after finding me in such a nasty mood at the bar. And it had also been from fear of upsetting me, and spoiling our last evening, that she had pretended not to recognize the man at the lift. The floor boy, of course, had come on the man's behalf, with an offer of five hundred dollars for the night. He had suggested that for a half-share I might be willing to relinquish her—for such deals to accommodate all parties concerned were commonplace in Macao.

I laughed and forgave her, and said, "My God, what a town! It's a good thing we're getting out before it corrupts us—and before I wring Ah Ng's neck."

"I'm sorry I lied," Suzie said, still crying. "But I am so scared."

"Scared?"

"Scared to lose you. Oh, Robert, I'm always so scared."

I slipped beside her into bed, and she clung to me very tightly, but without passion; and she said that she was ashamed because she was so exhausted and on her last night was failing me.

"It doesn't matter," I said. "I don't think I'd be much good myself tonight."

I turned off the light. I was really feeling worn out and I began to fall off at once. I was vaguely aware of Suzie lying wide awake beside me. I thought she must be worried because she had told lies, and with a last effort of consciousness I whispered that I was so happy with her, and I kissed and caressed her, and then sleep shut down its lid; and then I knew nothing more until a noise in the room penetrated my ears, and I half-woke and felt for Suzie, and I found that she was gone and I was alone in the bed. And then I woke properly and opened my eyes, and in the dim light from the window saw Suzie over by the dressing table, standing rigid with suspense as if afraid that I had been wakened by the noise she had just made. I opened my mouth to ask what she was doing but my tongue froze in my mouth: for at that moment I noticed that she was wearing her cheongsam. She was dressed.

No, I thought. No, she can't be going to him. No, it's impossible.

My body had become petrified by the suspicion. I could not utter a sound. I watched her move again cautiously. I recognized the familiar shape of her silhouette as she stooped, slipping her foot into a shoe.

And then suddenly with great joyous relief, I understood. She was just going to the bathroom. She was using the cheongsam as a dressing gown. She had not been able to lay her hands on the cotton wrap that she usually used for the purpose, and had not wanted to wake me by turning on the light. So she was using the cheongsam.

And now she was softly opening the door. She hesitated as a narrow shaft of light from the corridor penetrated the room. She glanced toward the bed. Then she opened the door quickly and slipped through and closed the door again, pausing outside to release the handle without sound. And I knew that in a moment my mind would be set at rest—that I should hear her take a few steps to the left, enter the bathroom next door.

I strained my ears. I had stopped breathing. Then I heard her footsteps, uneven because of the missing heel. They did not go to the left, but to the right. Not towards the bathroom, but towards the lift and stairs. I heard them fading down the corridor. Then silence.

I lay for a minute without moving, not yet really believing. Then I sat up and turned on the light. The sight of the empty bed beside me gave me a new pang of dismay, as if I had still hoped to find her there. Then I thought: perhaps the bathroom was occupied. Perhaps she tried the door and found it locked and so went upstairs. In that case it must still be occupied, or I would have heard somebody come out. I jumped out of bed and went outside into the corridor to look. But the bathroom door was open, the room in darkness. My heart sank again. I returned to the room and put on my trousers and shirt, and then went down the corridor to the lift. Ah Ng was asleep behind his desk, his head tilted against the keyboard. I leaned over and shook him, and one of his eyelids opened and there was nothing behind it but the gray jelly. The other lid opened in a muzzy slit.

"Where is she?" I said. "Where's my wife?"

"Hah?"

"My wife—where's she gone?"

He began to sit up, eager and interested, thinking for a moment that I was an accomplice. Then he saw that I was hostile and retired again behind the defense of muzziness. "I don't know. I just sleep."

I suddenly thought of her handbag. If she had gone to a man she would have taken it with her. But hadn't it still been in the room? I couldn't remember. I hurried back down the corridor. I went into the room but I could not see the bag. It was not on the dressing table or the chair or the table by the bed. I began to search the room, pulling open drawers and feeling behind the bed and tearing off the bed sheets, and thinking, Oh God, please let me find her bag, please let it be in this room. And then I had turned the room upside down, and it was not there, and I knew that she had gone to the Eurasian slicker, and had taken her bag because she would need her comb and cosmetics afterwards for tidying herself up. She would also need the bag for putting in money as she did with the sailors. And I dropped into the chair, and felt the great ache spreading from my heart, and I laid back my head and groaned.

I do not remember how long I remained in the chair. I remember only the ache, and not thinking of anything but the ache, not even of Suzie, and then finding myself staring at the painting of Suzie on the bed, and the painting coming into focus, and seeing her lying there among the rumpled bedclothes, and saying aloud at the painting all those words that you call women who behave like that, and then thinking that for Suzie you needed something worse, because it was simply like calling an actress an actress, or a shopgirl a shopgirl, and you couldn't revile somebody by calling them what they already admittedly were. I wondered vaguely why she had done it; I supposed it was just reversion to type. You couldn't keep a good whore down. Or at least up. Because at the first sight of a slicker with money and a Waikiki tie down she goes again, whoosh!

And I was still sitting there when the door began to open cautiously, and then stopped—she must have seen that the light was on, and realized with dismay that I had waked. Then it opened wider and she stood there in the doorway, and she looked very white and shaken, because she was afraid of what I was going to do, and she closed her eyes for a moment holding on to the handle. Then she went to the bed and sat down and closed her eyes again and said, "I told you I was no good. I told you I would just give you trouble."

I noticed that under her eyes there were great blue smudges. Well, no wonder, I thought. No wonder. And I got up, and called her all the dirty names that came into my head, and then went out and closed the door.

I walked through the empty streets without caring where I was going. The air was heavy and humid and my trousers stuck to my legs. I noticed the pier where we had landed and the big white silent steamer waiting for tomorrow. Later I noticed the façade of the old cathedral with the gaping windows and nothing behind but the sky. It was all that remained, the lone wall. The rest had been destroyed by fire. Probably self-ignited, I thought. Probably the cathedral had given up in despair and committed suicide, because not even a cathedral could hold its own against the evils of this vicious hole. Then I did not notice anything more until there was somebody barring my way and it was a small African soldier with a rifle and bayonet and behind him was the barrier across the road and behind the barrier was Red China. Red China, where they had closed the brothels and put the girls into factories. Good for Red China. If Suzie was in Red China she would be tightening bolts on tractor wheels instead of selling her body to slickers in Waikiki ties and silk shirts.

I turned and went back down the road, and there was the cathedral again with the gaping windows like the gaping eyes of a skull, the cathedral that had committed hara-kiri because it was no match against sin. It was growing light. I felt tired and sat down under the lone wall of the cathedral and I did not move until the sun was throwing shadows and my watch said half-past eight. Then I got up and went back to the hotel.

I went upstairs in the lift and turned down the corridor to the room. Suzie was lying on the bed. She had been crying and her face was red and ugly and swollen, and her eyes were dull and empty as if life was finished and she wanted to die.

I said, "The boat goes at ten-thirty. Will you be ready?"

She was about to reply but started crying again and the words were lost in her throat. The tears began running down from her eyes as suddenly as if a tap had been turned on, and I remembered a Madonna I had seen in Italy and the priest turning on the hidden tap, and the tears leaking out of the Madonna's eyes and running down the white glazed cheeks, and the priest saying proudly, "The Weeping Virgin!"

The weeping virgin. That was good.

"I'm going to have a shower," I said.

I collected my razor and toilet things and went out, leaving her weeping on the bed. The bathroom next door was engaged so I turned back along the corridor past the floor boy's desk where Ah Ng was quarreling over commission with one of his whores, and went upstairs to the bathroom on the next floor, and locked the door, and undressed, and started the shower over the bath—and it was only as I was about to step over the side of the bath and go under the shower that I noticed the red spattering on the bath, and the pink smears where the spattering had been wiped away, and the water from the shower trickling pink along the bottom of the bath to the outlet, and I wondered grimly if somebody had cut his throat, and I thought, "Well, after all, that's nothing for Macao." And then I caught sight of the yellow enamel spittoon, and the red-soaked woman's handkerchief in the bottom of the spittoon, and my knees went weak, and

I thought, "It's Suzie's," and I picked it out of the spittoon to make sure, and saw the embroidered flower in the corner that I had once said was a rose and Suzie had said was some other flower whose name she had only known in Chinese. It was stiff with congealed blood.

Oh, Christ, I thought. Oh, Christ, oh, Christ.

I stood staring at the red crumpled bit of material in my hand, and now I knew that she had not gone to the Eurasian at all, but had been ill, and had not wanted me to know she was ill, so she had come to this bathroom upstairs where I would not hear; and she had been all alone up here being ill and perhaps nearly dying. And I thought of her coming back into the room, and standing in the doorway with the white ravaged face, and saying, "I told you I would give you trouble," and I thought of the dirty names I had called her and the way I had walked out.

Oh, God. Oh, Christ.

I felt so weak that I had to lean for support against the wall. I closed my eyes with my head against the damp perspiring plaster. I heard the water from the shower drumming in the bath and gurgling away down the waste.

Oh, Suzie, I thought. My poor sweet Suzie. How can you ever forgive me?

And then I opened my eyes again and saw the red little handkerchief in my hand, and I thought, "Perhaps she's going to die," and I noticed that my hand was trembling as though from fever and I felt chilled with fear; and I grabbed my clothes and began to dress, struggling to pull down the wet sticky shirt over my shoulders, and glimpsing my face in the mirror with the perspiration and the night's stubble of beard and the eyes full of fear, and then I pulled on my trousers and fastened them and ran down the stairs.

Chapter Seven

"Suzie, you're so beautiful."

"No, I am ugly. I have cried so much that my cheeks are all swollen. I can see them. They are like big bumps in front of my eyes."

"I don't care, you're beautiful."

We lay clutched together. We had neither of us been able to speak when I had come back into the room, but she had known as soon as she saw me that I had found out what had happened and had begun to cry again, and I had wanted to go to her, but had felt too ashamed. I had felt too ashamed to touch her. And then suddenly I had gone to her and taken her hand, and pressed it to my cheek and kissed it, and then kissed her face, and then she was clinging to me and kissing me and crying at the same time; and then the great joy had swept over us, because the two imperfect halves had come together again, and without speaking or even thinking we had made love, and it had been like the first time we had made love because Suzie had again been shaken by those great cataclysmic sobs; and then the sobs had brought me back to earth, and I had been frightened because of their violence, and because I had been carried away and had forgotten that she was ill.

I kissed her nose, and the red swelling under her eyes. She closed her eyes and I kissed the soft eyelids.

"Suzie, that was awful of us. We shouldn't have done that."

"I'm glad. I feel beautiful."

"I'd get a doctor if there was time—but I think it's better to go if you feel all right."

"Yes, I told you—I feel beautiful now."

"Well, you needn't move yet. Just lie quietly while I pack."

We took a trishaw to the boat. Suzie seemed to have quite recovered, but despite her protests of unnecessary expense I took a bunk for her and made her lie down. The other occupant of the cabin was an English schoolmistress from Hong Kong, who said she always "splurged" on a cabin because she was easily seasick and liked to be sick in private. She already looked green about the gills from apprehension alone. She asked the steward if it was going to be rough and the steward said, "No, it'll be nice today," but after he had gone she said, "Do you think he was telling the truth? You haven't heard anything?"

"I should think it'll be like a millpond," I said.

It was a hot oppressive day with the usual heat haze over Macao and there was no wind in the harbor. However, crossing before the mouth of the Pearl we hit a stiff breeze, and there was a good sea running. The *Fatshan* began to creak and lurch. I went along to the cabin. Suzie did not mind the lurching and was nearly asleep, but the schoolmistress was retching over an enamel spittoon, so I retired again and went into the bar for a brandy. I was still in the bar an hour later when the ship suddenly changed course, and the loud-speaker announced that an overturned sampan had been sighted with survivors clinging to the wreckage. I went out onto the deck. The engines of the *Fatshan* fell to a low throb. A lifeboat was lowered and the passengers hung over the rail to watch the rescue. Next to me a tall powerful bull of a man, with a ginger mustache, exclaimed "Clots!" as the Chinese seamen maneuvered the lifeboat clumsily, and he also called the sampan crew mucking clots for coming so far out in rough weather—the boat people were all the same, it was the third time that this had happened to him on trips to Macao. Then the loud-speaker crackled and a voice urgently requested any doctors among the passengers to go down to "B" deck. "Muck 'em, they won't get me," said the big ginger bull, evidently a doctor himself. "It's the muckers' own fault—let 'em drown." But it was only a token protest and when I looked round a moment later he had gone. I watched the bedraggled figure of an old woman hauled aboard. She looked as tiny and fragile as a featherless bird with her drenched black silk suit clinging to her body. Then a young man was hauled up, nervously tittering and laughing although three-parts drowned, and then somebody touched my arm and I looked round, and it was the schoolmistress. Her face was ghoulish green. "I think you'd better come," she said.

"What's happened?"

Her gray parched mouth moved but no words came, and I did not know whether it was because she was sick or because the answer would have been too distressing. I turned quickly and groped my way along the cakewalk of the deck, and as I entered the cabin my foot skidded and I nearly fell. The floor was smeared with vomit. The cabin smelt of vomit and there was a tinny clatter as the spittoon rolled back and forth on the floor. I went over to Suzie. Her eyes were closed and her face was very white and there was a pink foam at the corner of her mouth dribbling onto the pillow.

"Suzie!"

She opened her eyes and closed them again without speaking.

"I'll get the doctor," I said. "I won't be long."

I clambered down the companionway to the lower deck. Chinese seamen were carrying one of the survivors into a cabin. Others lay on the deck and the big ginger bull of a doctor who had said, "Let the muckers drown," was astraddle a woman on his knees, with his big hands spread over the woman's back. He thrust down on his hands, groaning with exertion, crushing her ribs under his weight. The woman was unconscious but when the doctor lifted his weight the air was sucked through her open mouth with the silver teeth and gurgled down her throat into her lungs.

"Doctor, my wife's ill," I said.

He said without looking up, "Your mucking wife can go to mucking hell. This woman's dying."

"I think my wife's dying."

He did not say anything but went on working on the woman, thrusting down on his big spread hands until the air moaned out of the woman's throat and there was no air left and her throat was silent, and still thrusting, and then lifting his weight so that the air gurgled back, and then thrusting again. And then after a minute he said without taking his eyes off the woman, "Who can take over? Anybody here can take over?"

"Yes, sir, I am a trained lifesaver, sir," a Chinese seaman said smartly. "I have a certificate and a medal, sir."

"Come here."

He went on thrusting but lifted one knee over the woman so that he was kneeling on one side of her, and the seaman kneeled on the other side and placed his hands flat over the doctor's, and they thrust together until the doctor was satisfied that the seaman had got the rhythm, and then he withdrew his own hands, and the seaman lifted one knee over the woman's body and went on thrusting alone. The doctor watched him to make sure he was doing it right and then got up, saying, "Now who wanted me? Who spoke to me just now about his wife?"

"It was me," I said. "I'm sorry, but she's really ill."

He glared at me without belief, as if he suspected that she was only seasick and that I was rating her comfort above a Cantonese fisherwoman's life. "She'd mucking better be," he muttered. He followed me to the upper deck and we went into the cabin. The schoolmistress was standing helplessly by Suzie's bunk, her color-drained mouth dragged down at the corners. There was the sharp sweet smell of vomit. The doctor went over to Suzie and glanced at the pink trickle of foam. He looked up and sniffed and said, "Christ, let's have some bloody air—you two get out."

I followed the schoolmistress out onto the deck. We stood clinging to the rail in the hot sticky wind that left a film on the skin like oil. The last of the sampan family was brought on board, and there was a lot of shouting, and then the lifeboat was hauled up. The engines began to throb again.

"I'm sorry about the cabin," I told the schoolmistress.

"Oh, it doesn't matter," she said. "The cabin doesn't matter. I only wish I could be more help. I'm usually so good at helping at times like this—but I feel so useless when I'm sick."

The doctor came out of the cabin. The ship gave a roll and he lurched across the deck, crashing against the rail and knocking a wooden litter-box askew with his knee. I waited for him to swear but he only winced and nursed the knee with his hand.

That's bad, I thought. If Suzie had been all right he'd have sworn and called me a mucker for wasting his time.

"Well, we're moving again—we'll be in pretty soon," he said. "There's not much we can do until then except keep her cool. Get some ice from the steward and give her a compress. Here, over the lungs."

The schoolmistress said eagerly, "I'll do that. I'll get some ice. I can make a compress from a pillowcase. I've done it before."

"And give her some ice to suck," the doctor said.

I said, "How bad is she really?"

"She'll be all right once she's in hospital," the doctor said. "She's lost a bit of blood, but they'll fix her up all right in hospital. They'll be getting some ambulances for these boat people, so she can go with them to King's."

"She's got a bed waiting for her at St. Margaret's," I said. "They've a special T.B. ward there."

"I can't promise anything." He strained his ear to listen to the loudspeaker as a voice announced that a hat would be passed round for the sampan survivors, whose sampan had not only provided their livelihood but had also been their home. They had lost everything. The doctor looked defiant and said, "Muck 'em—they won't get a mucking penny out of me," and felt for his wallet in readiness to hand out fifty dollars. "Well, I must get down below again—and I'm afraid you may have to settle for King's."

But at Hong Kong, after Suzie had been carried ashore on a stretcher and put in one of the three waiting ambulances, the doctor came up and winked and said, "I've squeezed all the boat people into the others, and told this driver to take you to St. Margaret's."

"You've been awfully kind," I said. "How much do I owe you?"

"Muck all." And he was gone.

I climbed into the back of the ambulance and the orderly began to close the doors. He said carefully, "All right, King's?"

"No, St. Margaret's," I said.

He shook his head. "This ambulance go King's."

"But the doctor said you'd take us to St. Margaret's."

The driver was standing behind the orderly. They watched me in silence as if waiting for something to sink in. I felt in my pocket and took out a five-dollar note. I handed it to the orderly and said, "All right, make it St. Margaret's."

The orderly took the note thoughtfully. He folded it into a square and tucked it into the pocket of his suit. He closed the ambulance doors. I heard the two men climb into the cab and the doors slam but the engine remained silent. The other ambulances had driven off. Suzie lay in silence with her eyes closed. The hemorrhage had stopped with the ice but she was very weak and she had not opened her eyes for the last hour, and I do not think she had even known she was being carried ashore. It was suffocating inside the ambulance. I peered through the window into the cab. The orderly and driver were busy talking. I rapped on the window and made signs to them to hurry. After a minute the orderly got out again and came round to the back. He opened the doors and said, "Sorry, St. Margaret's too far."

"But it's not a mile," I said. "It's nearer than King's."

"Too far."

"You mean you want some more 'squeeze,'" I said. "How much do you want?"

"Give me ten dollars for extra petrol."

I gave him a ten-dollar note. "That'll buy you enough petrol to take you to Pekin."

"Pekin no good now," he grinned. "No fun. No dance girls. No good-time."

"And no 'squeeze,'" I said. "Now for God's sake get moving."

They must have been delighted with the fifteen dollars because the ambulance shot off at once with a great clanging of the bell to clear other traffic off the road. I held Suzie's hand. It was pale and waxen like her cheeks as if she had been drained of blood to the last drop. I tried to remember how many pints of blood there were supposed to be in the human body, and work out how many pints she might have lost. The ambulance stopped outside St. Margaret's. I watched Suzie taken off on the stretcher and then went to the desk in the hall. There was a note from Kay saying that she had gone off duty, but that she had briefed Sister Dunn in the T.B. ward, "who's a poppet, and who I know will do all she can." I found my way upstairs to the T.B. ward and asked a nurse outside for Sister Dunn.

"She'll be out in a minute," she said. "You can't go in, some of the women are doing their ablutions."

I waited in the corridor and presently Sister Dunn came out with a brisk efficient impersonal smile and said, "Don't worry. We'll look after her. Just go home and leave her to us, and I'm sure she'll be delighted to see you tomorrow afternoon."

"Tomorrow afternoon?"

"We only allow visitors in the afternoon—three to four." She smiled, but the smile had been sterilized along with the chromium scissors and scalpels, and picked out with sterilized chromium tongs, and never touched by human hand. Well, she may be Kay's idea of a poppet, I thought, but she isn't mine.

I said, "I'd like to wait until the doctor's seen her."

"I'm afraid you can't wait here. You'll have to wait in the hall."

"You'll let me know when there's any news?"

"Of course. Just wait in the hall."

I waited an hour in the hall and nobody came. I waited another quarter of an hour and then went upstairs to the ward. The ward doors were wedged open and I could see down the long room with the twirling fans and the shining waxed floor down the middle like a bowling alley, and the two long rows of beds and the silent vacant Chinese faces. I spotted Suzie with a bottle strung up over her bed, and a red tube from the bottle bandaged to her arm. I turned back down the corridor to look for Sister Dunn, and just then she came briskly out of a door. She saw me and stopped and said, "Oh, I'm awfully sorry, I forgot all about you." Her manner was less sterilized, almost warm. "I'm afraid I forgot."

"How is she?"

"She's very weak, of course." I had caught her off guard and she looked uneasy. "But we're giving her a blood transfusion, and there's no reason to lose hope."

"I'll try not to lose hope," I said.

But for three weeks I thought she was dying. And now I remember those weeks only as a long blur of pain, in which odd trivial moments stand out like snapshots or like fragments of dreams. Thus I remember walking through Wanchai and glimpsing a wall shrine in a shop, and below it a big white modern Frigidaire, and thinking "How incongruous!" and then thinking how strange it was that I could notice such things when Suzie was dying. And I remember strap-hanging in a crowded tram and imagining God saying, "I will save Suzie, but only at the cost of an accident to this tram after you leave it, with total loss of life—you can take your choice," and wondering what I would do, and then thinking how quickly illness and death scratched through our civilized veneer and found the primitive man—for like the savage I was imagining a God that must be propitiated with human lives. And I remember telling Gwenny and Jeannie for the third time about how Suzie and I had got married in Macao, and both of them crying, and then the comedienne Fifi saying with mock-solemn face that she hoped Suzie had been a virgin as Chinese custom prescribed, and my saying, "I'm afraid we fell to temptation the day before"; and Fifi pretending to look shocked, and Gwenny and Jeannie laughing through their tears. And I remember a woman dying in Suzie's ward when I was visiting, and the loud hollow rattle in the throat that I had never known really happened, and the gaping mouth and the dead staring eyes, and the nervous titter spreading through the ward as if death was funny, and Suzie saying, "That woman is finished. Somebody finishes every day." And I remember leaving the bar because the juke box was playing "Seven Lonely Days" and I could not bear it, and outside on the quay seeing American sailors arriving in rickshaws, and hearing one of the sailors saying, "Jeeze, I hope she's still here, fellers," and thinking I heard him say "Suzie," and hating him, and then joining the sailor at the bar and drinking with him and the sailor saying, "I'm telling you, feller, this kid Suzie can sure put it out," and not hating him any more but loving him, because life was indivisible and we were all part of each other, and hoping that this was true and that I really believed it, and that it wasn't just the whisky.

And I remember the worst day of all, at the end of the three weeks, when Suzie was so ill that when I came to her bedside she did not even open her eyes, but dragged down my hand under the sheets and held it against her breasts, saying, "Robert, I'm scared. I don't want to die. I'm so scared," and beginning to cry. She kept my hand clutched against her for an hour, and I thought that tonight would be the end, and I went up to tell Kay at her hostel where she was playing tennis; and she came off the court to speak to me, her legs brown under the tennis skirt, and looking very radiant and fulfilled because she had started an affair and it was going well. And when I told her about Suzie she looked self-conscious because of the radiance, which she could not suppress.

"I'm on duty tonight," she said. "I'll slip along and see her."

"I wish you would, Kay. I'm afraid nobody will let me know if anything happens."

"Don't worry. I'll see to it."

I stayed in my room until nine waiting for the telephone to ring, and jumping every time a bicycle bell tinkled outside in the street. Then I could not stand waiting alone any longer and told the operator I would be down in the bar. I drank several brandies in the bar and Gwenny came over and asked about Suzie, and then told me that her sister had just got engaged.

"Gwenny, how marvelous," I said. "I hope the man's got lots of money?"

"No, he is not very rich. He has only two cars."

"He sounds fine to me." All the time I was listening with one ear for the phone. "And so you'll be able to give up work?"

"Yes, once my sister is married. I am so happy. We must all have a celebration when Suzie is better."

The telephone on the bar counter began to ring and all my bones turned to jelly. Typhoo picked up the receiver, and then put it down again on the counter and looked round the bar. She saw me and grinned.

"Hey, *Chow-fan*—some girl friend for you. I think she just heard you got married and wants to make trouble."

My knees were so weak as I crossed the bar that I was afraid they would give way. I picked up the receiver and Kay's voice said, "Hullo, Robert? All right, don't get alarmed. I just wanted to let you know I'd seen her, and they're giving her another transfusion."

"But I thought they'd decided against it," I said; for during the first transfusion she had developed some violent and irrational fear of being filled with a stranger's blood, and had tried to tear the tube from her arm; and the psychological effect had been disastrous and had lasted for days. "The doctor told me he couldn't risk another."

"I know, but I think he's decided it's now about the only hope," Kay said. "Anyhow, I'll ring you if there's any news."

I stayed in the bar until midnight and then went back to my room. I sat on the balcony listening for the telephone and watching the neon signs going out along the water front and the last ferries like luminous caterpillars crawling across the harbor, and the sampans tossing in the dark lapping water along the quay and the junk masts swaying. Once a telephone rang in another room and I started so violently that for minutes afterwards my heart was thudding like a hammer. Then I felt suddenly overcome with exhaustion from the strain of waiting and I went inside and fell on the bed. "She is dead," I thought. "She has been dead for hours, and they have forgotten to tell me." I reached out for the telephone to ring the hospital, then thought, "No, that will make it too final." Then dawn came and I lay watching the gray light creep into the room, and the world being reborn in cold dawn gray without joy and without color.

"She is dead," I thought. "And the new day is born without her."

And then there were dull colors appearing among the gray, and then the sun was rising, and I got up and went out onto the balcony, and the town was coming alive and beginning to throb, and the shafts of sunlight were thrusting down like gold bars into the mean little streets, and the harbor was tremulous and glinting, and the first ferry with white dazzling paint was starting out from the pier. And then there were little boats bustling about everywhere, and then all at once a great liner was sliding silently in among them, and all the little boats were blowing their hooters and scurrying out of the way, and the passengers on the liner were crowding at the rails and pointing, and saying, "That's the Hong Kong and Shanghai Bank—and that's the Peak!"

And I thought with a sudden burst of joy, "She's all right—Suzie's all right! She must be all right or I'd have heard." And I quickly washed and shaved, and put on a clean pair of slacks and my best shirt, and stuffed enough money in my pocket to buy flowers and dashed to the door, and then the telephone rang and I stopped.

I stood in the open door and stared at the phone. It gave another long ring and I went over, and stopped again and stood paralyzed with my hand outstretched; and then the bell began to ring in impatient staccato, and then continuously again, and I picked it up, and the ear-piece crackled as the operator went on ringing. And then the crackling stopped and the operator said, "Hullo," and then Kay's voice said, "Hullo? Hullo, is that Robert?"

"Yes, hullo," I said.

"Oh, there you are," she said. "Well, I've good news—the transfusion really did the trick, and this morning she's as bright as a button. . . . Hullo? Hullo, are you there?"

"Yes, I'm here."

There were queues for the tram and I could not find a taxi, so I took a rickshaw to the bottom of the hill and then climbed up the hill to the hospital, and when I arrived the perspiration was pouring down me in rivers and my hair was soaked as if I had just come from under a shower. I dashed up the stairs and into the ward, and a woman balanced on a bedpan looked so startled that I thought she would fall, but I did not see what happened because by then I had gone past and was beside Suzie, and I was laughing and kissing her, and Suzie was saying, "Good morning, I feel beautiful today."

"You look beautiful, Suzie."

"Yes, I didn't mind the blood this time. I think it came from a better person. Oh yes, this time they gave me very nice blood."

Chapter Eight

"Suzie, the doctor says that when you come out of hospital we must live somewhere high up. How would you like to live in Japan? I always wanted to go back there to paint, and there are heaps of wonderful spots in the mountains."

"Yes, that would be nice." She hesitated. "We would go straight to Japan?"

"Yes, we'd go straight from Hong Kong."

She tried not to look disappointed. I knew that she had been hoping that first I might take her on a visit to England: she so much wanted to see London, and Piccadilly Circus, and the big shops, and the Queen. But of course I could never take her, for it would mean lies and deception and pretending she was somebody she was not, and then the truth coming out and everybody sniggering, "Have you heard?" No, it was out of the question.

But it rankled that England should be barred to us. It was a kind of challenge. I had an exhibition coming off in London and Roy Ullman, its sponsor, was pressing us to be there. I could just afford it. And one night I suddenly thought, "If Suzie wants to go, and has the courage to face it—why not?" And the next day at the hospital I told her we would go for six weeks.

And so three months later, when she came out of hospital, we went to England. We went by cargo boat and arrived in the spring, when the tired wintry Londoners' faces were thawing into smiles, and the parks bursting into leaf, and the warm bright sunshine in the streets bade us welcome. We lived in a furnished studio which Roy Ullman had found for us in the Fulham Road, but I did not paint much for the first week or two for we were too busy sight-seeing and riding round on the tops of buses. We went to the Tower and St. Paul's and Westminster Abbey, and down the river in a water-bus to Greenwich, and we got lost in the maze at Hampton Court and fed peanuts to the monkeys at the zoo. But the zoo was not the success with Suzie that I had expected, for she was less interested in watching animals than in watching people; and so we left without completing the full tour and lay on the grass in Regent's Park, where she became so absorbed in watching the passers-by that she would have been quite happy to stay there all day.

We also went many times to the theater, for nothing delighted her more. I first avoided straight plays since I supposed that in the theater, as in the cinema, she would find the English dialogue hard to follow, and I took her to an American musical and then to a popular farce; but her theatrical appetite was now whetted, and so after she had dismissed a light comedy with a rather contemptuous "I never saw anybody behave like that," we graduated to serious contemporary drama. She could understand hardly a word but sat intently, her eyes never leaving the stage; and though I whispered a commentary she would often cut it short with a nod, understanding what was going on from the expressions and actions. And she would remember each play in detail, for she was as impressionable as a child; and days afterwards we would still be discussing whatever human issue had been involved.

And so finally, abandoning all pretension of understanding her taste, I took her off on the top of a bus to Waterloo Road where we queued for the pit at the Old Vic. The play was *Hamlet*, and for Suzie it might just as well have been in Greek; but she enjoyed every moment, and as usual kept interrupting my whispered explanations with the brief nod that meant, "All right, I've got eyes!" And in the interval, her brow puckered with thought, she said:

"You know, that man has got a big worry. I understand very well, because I had a bad uncle like that. And I've been thinking, 'Supposing my father never died in that junk, but really my bad uncle killed him because he loved my mother. And supposing my mother knew what he had done, and they got married. And supposing I found out. Now, I would have so much worry, I might go a bit mad like that man, too.'"

"And what would you do? What do you think's going to happen?"

"I think perhaps he will kill the bad uncle. But not his mother. That is the worry. He thinks, She did something terrible, my mother. But she is still my mother, she gave me her milk. I can't kill her.'"

"Pretty good, Suzie."

"I think this author has a big heart. He understands everything." She looked up at the boxes. "I wonder if he is here?"

I laughed and told her that Shakespeare had been dead for three hundred years. And I was delighted by the discovery that she had not known, for suddenly the drama was no longer an old classic, annotated by scholars and probed by schoolgirls in tunics for their exams, but a new and exciting experience; and seeing it through Suzie's eyes, with her freshness of vision, I could imagine myself an Elizabethan watching its first performance at the Globe.

Suzie's taste for theatergoing was easy enough to satisfy but much more difficult was her desire to see the Queen. She could not leave England without seeing the Queen. One night we stood outside Covent Garden to watch her arrival, but there was already such a dense crowd that we caught not a glimpse of her. I invested fourpence daily in the *Times*, and studied the Queen's official engagements and followed her movements as closely as some anarchist plotting to throw a bomb. Finally one morning, when the Queen was scheduled to attend a function in the City, we went down early to Buckingham Palace to watch her departure. A friendly policeman stationed us near the right gate and we waited two hours, the nucleus for a growing accretion of Swedes, Danes, Swiss-Germans, Arabs, and two American girls whose English made me feel less of an outsider. At last a gleaming limousine crossed the forecourt. Suzie watched calmly. It glided past, the Queen in the back, very pretty and natural and unassumingly spring-clad. A second's glimpse and she was gone, and the polyglot crowd dispersing. Suzie looked satisfied.

"All right," she said. "Now only one more to see."

"One more?"

"Princess Margaret."

I laughed and said we would have a try, but a few days later read in the newspaper that Princess Margaret had left London and would not be returning for a month; and Suzie was very disappointed, though it did not matter so much after seeing the Queen.

Three weeks after our arrival in England the exhibition of my pictures opened at Uliman's Gallery in South Audley Street. The pictures were all of Hong Kong, and 90 per cent of them of the Nam Kok, and since Suzie featured in so many, and often in bar scenes with the sailors, there could be no pretense about her past; and I told Suzie that I did not think she should attend the private view, for it would be too much of an ordeal. However, the evening before the private view she was very thoughtful and preoccupied; and the next morning she came to me with two silk cheongsams over her arm, and said, "Which do you like best?"

"You're not coming, Suzie?"

"Yes."

"Then wear the yellow—the one you were married in."

But then in the taxi on the way to the gallery her nerves gave way and she suddenly announced that she could not go through with it, and that she wanted to go back. I told the driver to pull up, and said that we would just sit there for a minute and talk.

"No, I want to go back," she cried in a sort of panic. "Just let me out and I will go back. I'm sorry, but I'm so scared. I'm so ashamed."

"You needn't be ashamed, Suzie. You're as good as anybody."

"No, I'm ashamed. They will all say, 'She's just a dirty little yum-yum girl.' It's true—I'm no good."

I nodded toward a woman crossing the road. She was tweedy and upper-middle-class and making for Harrods. I said, "You're as good as that woman. You're worth fifty of her."

"No."

"You are, Suzie. I'll tell you about that woman. She's a snob. She's intolerant. She's possessive. She's so overmothered her son that he's turned out a queer. She's bullied and browbeaten her daughter until the poor wretch daren't say boo to a goose. The other daughter's run off with a Jew, so she won't speak to her or have her back in the house. In fact she's a silly old bitch, and you can tell her so from me." Suzie was silent, and I said, "Go on, tell her off properly. Say, 'You're a silly old bitch and I'm worth fifty of you.'"

She shook her head. "No."

"Go on, Suzie. Say it. Give her hell."

"You're a silly old bitch and I'm worth fifty of you."

"'And I've nothing to be ashamed of—I'm proud!"

"No. I'm just a dirty—"

"Say it!"

"I'm proud."

"'I'm the proudest person on God's earth!'"

She said it once and then said it again as if she was beginning to feel it, and then she began to smile, and soon she was sitting up proud and straight in the Chinese way, and then we drove on to the gallery, and she looked so proud and poised as we entered the gallery that you would have thought twice before calling her a whore, and if you'd done so you would have felt that it had made you dirtier than it had made her.

In the gallery she stood close by my side and I held her hand, and I did not let it go all afternoon; and sometimes there was tension in her hand, but her eyes were proud and calm and met other people's eyes with a calm level gaze. The gallery was crowded and all the time Ullman was bringing up people to introduce, and at first you could see them thinking, "I know she was a sailor's whore but I must behave naturally," and so of course they did not behave naturally at all, but were gushing and false, the men trying to be gallant and all but giving her winks, and the women being very patronizing and thinking, "How charming of me to be so nice to her—how broad-minded!" And then they met Suzie's calm level eyes that seemed to be saying, "All right, take a good look, because I've nothing to hide," and they began to feel her presence in a new way; and at this point a few turned hostile, thinking, "Aha, she thinks because I'm nice to her that she's as good as me," and with sudden coolness trying to put her back in her place—but most were pleased and relaxed gratefully, and did whatever they could to show their appreciation and respect, and paid her compliments with real warmth.

"My dear, I envy you," one woman impulsively exclaimed. "I really do—your experience of life! It makes one feel one's lived so narrowly, been so *shut in!*" And she went away in a flurry of frustration as if intending to knock off a policeman's helmet or undress in the street. And another elderly white-haired lady with a silver-topped stick told Suzie that she was beautiful.

"A great beauty, none of the paintings do you justice." And she turned to me and snapped, "You haven't caught it—none of your paintings have caught it." This was true, though not due entirely to my deficiencies as a painter; for all the work on exhibition belonged to my earlier days at the Nam Kok when the prettiness of Suzie's round white little face had been immature, and it was only prison and her long illness that had brought the maturity which alone gives real beauty to a woman's face. But when I tried to explain this to the white-haired lady she just said, "Pah! I'd have liked Humphrey to do her—it's a real Humphrey face. If only Humphrey wasn't in America!" And Humphrey, whoever he was, being in America, she went off and bought two of my pictures, telling me later, "I'm not as wild about your stuff as some of the others appear to be. But one day with a bit of luck you may do something good."

Then it was over and the last viewers had gone, and Roy Ullman was sailing up to us, discreetly wafting scent and beaming all over his white moon face, and saying, "Success! Look at all those delicious, delicious red spots!" He waved a manicured hand round the gallery indicating the number of pictures marked as sold. "I do really, really congratulate you. What a success!"

I said, "It's Suzie who's had the real success today."

"Oh, quite, of course. Everybody thought her quite, quite enchanting. But naturally it's your pictures—"

He was rather a stupid man. He did not understand the ordeal through which Suzie had passed. But all afternoon I had watched people going out through the glass door to the street, because it was then that they would betray themselves, and there had not been a single snigger, and this was a triumph so much greater than my own that I could think of nothing else. And I left the gallery aglow, not because of the red spots but because of Suzie, and because I was so proud of her.

After the opening of the exhibition we became involved in a social whirl. One invitation led to another and our days were filled with engagements; a lunch party with Ullman and an art critic lasting until four o'clock, two cocktail parties between six and eight, dinner with someone in St. John's Wood, then at midnight down to Chelsea where they'd said, "Don't worry what time—our parties usually last three days." And it was at that Chelsea party, as a matter of fact, that Suzie suffered her only real bad moment—when another guest, a cow-eyed woman given to making outrageous remarks with the innocent air of discussing the weather, asked her out of the blue what she would do if in London she ran into some sailor she had known in Hong Kong. There was a ghastly silence. The dozen people round us were paralyzed by the remark. Then Suzie said, "I would say, 'Hello, good morning,'"—and there was a great burst of relieved laughter all on Suzie's side. She had not meant to be funny: her brain had been stupefied with embarrassment and she had said the first thing that had come into her head. But everybody thought her reply wonderful, and it gave her the reputation of a wit.

And it was Suzie who saved me from making a terrible fool of myself. I had begun to enjoy the social life, for the exhibition had had a lot of publicity and I was received everywhere like a lion. Everybody seemed to know me and to admire my work—and if they happened to reveal by some little slip that they had not actually seen it themselves, and were only going on hearsay, I could still flatter myself that they felt ashamed of their omission. In fact we were moving round in a narrow little circle, but it seemed like the whole world, and for the first time in my life I thought, "I'm somebody—I'm really somebody!"

And then suddenly I found I could talk—about art. Gone were the days when I was inarticulate about painting, and could only mutter about myself, "I see something I want to paint, and try to paint it,"—for now all at once I had perceived significance in my own paintings and had begun to spin them round with webs of theory, using high-flown professional words whose meaning I had only just learned. I could be eloquent, I could be amusing; and at dinner parties, where formerly I would have talked only to my nearest neighbors, I was quite ready to take on the whole table. For after all I was an authority now. I was somebody.

One night at Roy Ullman's house I had been holding forth like this at dinner, and after the ladies had retired one of the guests, a producer for television, asked me if I would be prepared to give an illustrated talk.

"In fact we might discuss the idea of a series," he said.

I said I wished that he had asked me a month ago—it was too late now, for we had only three days left in England. We had air passages booked for Japan—with a night stop at Hong Kong en route when we would stay at the Nam Kok.

Roy Ullman examined his manicured nails. "Of course I don't want to influence you—but not even an artist can afford to ignore his public. And taking the long view, I believe the advantages of your staying in England a bit longer might be simply, simply enormous. . . ."

I was soon won over, and when Suzie returned to the room I put the same arguments to her, and eventually she said without much enthusiasm, "All right, I don't mind," and Ullman, who really disliked her, said, "Hurrah, the little lady agrees," and rang up the airline for us and canceled our bookings.

On the way home Suzie was silent and remote and I was a little piqued, for I felt very flattered at being asked to talk on television and I would have liked her also to be pleased. Her mood was a challenge. I had to reconquer her. But when we were in bed and I made the familiar overtures she said she was tired and withdrew from me, and I turned away feeling rebuffed and annoyed.

However, the next morning, as I was trying to get on with a half-finished portrait of her which was the only work I had done in London, I noticed a spark in her eye, accompanied by other invisible but provocative feminine emanations which meant only one thing: that she herself now felt disposed toward what last night she had denied me. I laughed and teased her for a bit, and then went to her; and when later I asked her to explain her unusually capricious behavior she said, "I like you today. I like you when you work, and wear that dirty old coat full of paint."

"And when don't you like me?"

"When you get stuck-up and talk too much, and go boom! boom! boom!"

She gave an imitation of me pompously holding forth. I was very hurt and flew to my own defense, saying that after living so long in the artistic vacuum out East it was wonderful to be among people who talked the same language and who appreciated one's work, and that I was deriving great benefit from mixing with other painters, and with critics and connoisseurs.

"I don't think so," she said. "I think in England you just get hard. Too many people. Too much talk. Too much boom-boom-boom. You get hard inside."

"You know what's the matter with you?" I said. "You're jealous. You're jealous of my success at parties—and of all those pretty girls who come up and tell me I'm wonderful."

She shook her head.

"Of course you are—you're exhibiting all the classic symptoms. Go and look at those green eyes in the mirror!"

I was delighted at the way I had turned the attack, and remained well-satisfied with myself all day. And it was only that night, after I had lain awake for a long time in the dark with a gnawing uneasiness, that all at once I saw the truth of Suzie's caricature of me—saw myself smugly seated at some dinner table, dogmatically holding forth about things of which I had scarcely an inkling, contriving theories to boost my own work and belittle the work of others. Thinking "I'm somebody" because really, deep down, I was afraid of being nobody. Talking instead of doing. Criticizing instead of creating.

Oh, God, it was horrifying—those smart sterile cocktail parties, that aesthetic chitter-chatter, that endless boom-boom-booming that made you feel big but that killed you inside—that killed that little flame that needed so desperately to be nourished. And I was seized by panic, and the wild urge to escape before it was too late, and I woke Suzie and switched on the light and said, "Suzie, I've been a fool—a perfect fool."

"What's happened?" she said. "What's the matter?"

"You were right, Suzie. I'm just destroying myself here. We mustn't stay."

"What about your talks?"

"To hell with the talks."

"But you like talking. You won't be able to talk in Japan."

"I don't want to talk. I want to paint."

And the next morning we went to the airline office and got back our old bookings, and five nights later we were back at the Nam Kok.

II

And I do not think there has been another night like it at the Nam Kok before or since. The girls were far too excited by Suzie's return to think of working, and they ignored the sailors and stood crowded round our table so that we could hardly breathe, and they would not move except to feed a new coin into the juke box; and they played "Seven Lonely Days" in our honor all evening. And each time the record restarted there were ironical catcalls from the sailors, and I could not help sympathizing with them because the girls' neglect was quite sufficient hardship in itself without such musical monotony to drive them mad.

Suzie had brought presents for all the girls, and they opened them with suitable exclamations of surprise and delight. The only girl who remained apart was Doris Woo who sat primly alone in the corner, blinking like a schoolmarm behind the rimless glasses, until at length two rather drunk sailors started a row over her because she was the only girl going. However, as she got up to leave the room with the winner Suzie called to her to come for her present, and the other girls joined in the exhortations and made way for her to approach.

"I don't want anything," she snapped. "Who was it meant for?"

"For you," Suzie said. "It is a present from London for you."

"I don't believe you," Doris said bitterly.

She tore the paper off the little parcel as if she was doing us a favor, saying she knew better than to believe that in London we had ever given her a thought; but her words were cut short as she saw the contents, a little leather note-case with *Doris Woo* in gold letters across the corner. She stared at it in silence, her glasses misting. She could not say anything for a long time, but remained at the table; and when the drunk sailor impatiently summoned her she just shook her head, and the other girls pushed him away. Then Doris asked Suzie how much it cost to go to London, not because she wanted to know but just to show interest, and I told her the cost by sea, saying "That's in pounds," and the comedienne Fifi said, "Well, what does that make in short-times?" And this provoked such an outburst of merriment that nobody noticed "Seven Lonely Days" come to an end, until a sailor had seized his opportunity and some other tune had burst upon the room, whereupon they all turned on the poor matelot with cries of anger and dismay.

Then Typhoo asked if there were many Chinese people in London, and Suzie said we had been to a Chinese restaurant with a Cantonese cook and waiters, but the food had been a travesty of real Chinese food; and then the luscious little Jeannie wanted to know if there were any Chinese bar girls or dance girls in London.

"They do not have any bar girls or dance girls in London," Suzie said. "Only street girls."

"Ugh!" shuddered little Alice, who had a new expensive hair-do of tight little curls, and she shook with giggles.

"And they are all European," Suzie said. "But some of them are very beautiful, and wear beautiful furs."

"How much do they charge?" Jeannie asked. She looked tired and much older and was just beginning to run to seed, so that soon she would no longer be luscious, but just fat; and I had a sudden distressing vision of the old overblown whore, calling from some darkened doorway, that would be Jeannie in ten years.

"I think they charge more than—than us," Suzie said. She had been about to say "more than you," but had been afraid to sound stuck-up.

Old Lily Lou leaned across the table. "What about the Queen?" she whispered huskily. "Did you see the Queen?"

"Yes, as close as you," Suzie said. "Oh, yes, she was very pretty."

"That's right, I've seen her in the cinema," Lily Lou said in a voice like coarse sandpaper. She turned to the others. "Suzie's quite right—she's really pretty, Queen Margaret." There was laughter and somebody corrected her. She looked rattled and said, "All right, I know what I'm talking about. I know, you needn't tell me."

Just then about a dozen sailors with red pom-poms on their hats came in from the quay.

"Sorry, Frenchee-boys," Typhoo said. "No make-lovey tonight."

"So sorry," everybody said happily in chorus. "We're busy. Closed for repairs. You better go somewhere else. So sorry. Good-by."

However, the sailors did not go, and presently the manager limped up to intervene on behalf of the disgruntled clientele. The girls groaned and drifted sulkily back to work, except for Gwenny and Mary Kee who remained. The floor round the table was scattered with paper from the presents. On the table one present remained unopened: a handbag we had bought in Regent Street for Wednesday Lulu. But we had arrived too late, for a week ago Wednesday Lulu had made her decision and gone back to China—back to her mother, and rehabilitation, and work in a factory or the fields.

Suzie noticed a big blue and yellow bruise on the upper right arm of her former protegee, Mary Kee. "What happened?" she asked.

"Nothing, only a sailor who was a bit drunk," Mary said.

"I told you before, you shouldn't go with drunks," Suzie said. "Some girls can manage drunks, but you get too scared."

"It has been such a terrible month, we have not been able to pick and choose," Gwenny said. "There have been no ships at all until yesterday."

"I suppose I ought to go and work," Mary said, and glanced nervously at two matelots at a neighboring table. "But I think they're just drinking—they haven't come to catch girls."

"The fair one wants to catch a girl," Suzie said. "You must learn to tell. He wants a girl but is scared. You must go and be very soft and nice."

"Well, I'll try."

Suzie looked troubled as she watched Mary go off. I turned to Gwenny and said, "Gwenny, what about your sister? Isn't she married yet?"

"No, the parents of the man she was to marry found out where I worked, so they broke it off," Gwenny said. "But now we have arranged another marriage. It will be next month."

"And then you'll be able to give this up?"

She shook her head. "No."

"No? But Gwenny, why not?"

"The man is very poor. I will have to help them. He will only marry on condition I help."

Suzie said, "Gwenny, how awful! How terrible!"

"She's getting married, that's all that really matters." She turned her face away. "Oh, look, there's Mary going upstairs—wasn't she quick? Well, I had better go and try my luck, though I hate leaving you." She went and sat down with a French sailor, but twenty minutes later gave it up and came back, saying, "I couldn't understand a word. He just pinched my arm and held up five fingers. I suppose he meant I was too skinny, and only worth five dollars. But I haven't descended to five yet."

Suzie said, "Gwenny, you know where that Canton girl lives? You know, Betty Lau—the girl I stuck with the scissors?" Gwenny nodded, and Suzie carelessly pushed over Wednesday Lulu's parcel. "She can have this if she wants."

"You mean you've forgiven her?" Gwenny said.

"Of course not," Suzie said quickly. "I'd never forgive her—not for all those dirty things she said. I just don't want that bag, that's all. It's just a nuisance. Isn't it, Robert?"

"An awful nuisance," I said, and gave Gwenny ten dollars to have Wednesday Lulu's initials taken off and Betty's put on.

"Well, I will go home now," Gwenny said. "And I will come in the morning and see you off."

It was after midnight. The juke box was silent. The only girl left was Minnie Ho, who was snuggling in the arms of a Frenchman. They got up and went out through the swing door.

"Poor Gwenny," Suzie said. "I thought this evening, 'Anyhow, Gwenny will be all right when her sister is married. That means two of us are all right.'"

"Come on, Suzie, let's go to bed."

We went out to the hall. Minnie and the French sailor came from the reception desk and followed us into the lift. Minnie took the sailor's hat from his hand and nuzzled the red pom-pom, and then put the hat on her own head and entwined herself around his arm. She rubbed her cheek against his sleeve. "I love you," she giggled, looking up at him. "Love—you understand 'love'?"

The sailor glanced down at her cynically, a Gauloise drooping from his mouth.

"*Bien sûr,*" he said in a tone of "So what?"

"He doesn't understand," Minnie said: "You speak French, Robert? Tell him I love him."

She watched his face as I told him. The sailor said with a bored cynical smile, "I know this innocent virgin sort. They're the ones who always give you a packet."

"What did he say?" Minnie said.

"He said you're just like a little kitten, Minnie," I said.

"To speak frankly, I prefer yours," the sailor said, the Gauloise waggling in his mouth and his eyes narrowed against the smoke. "I like her bottom. I noticed as she entered the lift. She has a real peach of a bottom."

"Among her other qualities," I said.

The lift stopped at the third floor. The sailor watched Suzie as she went out. "Yes, that bottom really says something to me. It is a bottom for a connoisseur. You will exchange girls?"

"Nothing doing."

"Never mind, I will take your girl tomorrow night. You can let me know your opinion of her."

"It's very high," I said. "She's my wife."

"You can stuff that remark up the appropriate aperture," he said.

I joined Suzie in the corridor. We walked along toward my old room. "What was that man saying?" she said.

"He wouldn't believe you were my wife."

"He looked cruel," she said. "He had a cruel mouth."

"He was very taken by you. He's booked you for tomorrow night." She gave me a quick half frightened look, and I laughed and said, "Don't worry, we'll be safely in Japan by then."

She was worn out after the long day and was asleep before I was in bed. I also fell off quickly, but later woke to hear her sobbing and uttering broken incoherent cries. I touched her gently to wake her. She thrust me violently away. "Who's that?" she cried. "Who's that?"

"Robert."

She sobbed with relief and rolled against me. She buried her face in my neck. "I thought you'd left me. I thought you'd gone."

"It's all right, I'm still here."

"My husband," she said. "You've got the tickets?"

"Yes, they're quite safe."

"You're sure? You haven't lost them?"

I laughed and turned on the light. I reached for my wallet and gave her the tickets. She examined each ticket carefully, turning the pages, though she could not read anything except our names. She handed them back to me, but I told her she had better look after them herself, and she smiled and put them under the pillow. She lay hugging the pillow, her face peaceful again, and I kissed her and turned off the light.

CULT CLASSICS FROM PENGUIN

The Best of Everything

Rona Jaffe

ISBN 978-0-14-303529-9

When her superb page-turner was first published in 1958, it changed contemporary fiction forever. Some readers were shocked, but millions more were electrified when they saw themselves reflected in its story of five young employees of a New York publishing company. Almost sixty years later, *The Best of Everything* remains touchingly—and sometimes hilariously—true to the personal and professional struggles women face in the city.